P9-DHH-024

By J. A. Jance

J. P. Beaumont Mysteries

UNTIL PROVEN GUILTY • INJUSTICE FOR ALL
TRIAL BY FURY • TAKING THE FIFTH
IMPROBABLE CAUSE • A MORE PERFECT UNION
DISMISSED WITH PREJUDICE • MINOR IN POSSESSION
PAYMENT IN KIND • WITHOUT DUE PROCESS
FAILURE TO APPEAR • LYING IN WAIT
NAME WITHHELD • BREACH OF DUTY
BIRDS OF PREY • PARTNER IN CRIME
LONG TIME GONE • JUSTICE DENIED
FIRE AND ICE • BETRAYAL OF TRUST

Joanna Brady Mysteries

DESERT HEAT • TOMBSTONE COURAGE
SHOOT/DON'T SHOOT • DEAD TO RIGHTS
SKELETON CANYON • RATTLESNAKE CROSSING
OUTLAW MOUNTAIN • DEVIL'S CLAW
PARADISE LOST • PARTNER IN CRIME
EXIT WOUNDS • DEAD WRONG
DAMAGE CONTROL • FIRE AND ICE

Walker Family Thrillers

HOUR OF THE HUNTER • KISS OF THE BEES
DAY OF THE DEAD • QUEEN OF THE NIGHT

Ali Reynolds Mysteries

EDGE OF EVIL • WEB OF EVIL
HAND OF EVIL • CRUEL INTENT
TRIAL BY FIRE • FATAL ERROR

Coming Soon in Hardcover

JUDGMENT CALL

J.A. JANCE

BREACH OF DUTY

A J.P. BEAUMONT NOVEL

HARPER

An Imprint of HarperCollinsPublishers

HARPER

An Imprint of HarperCollins *Publishers*
10 East 53rd Street
New York, New York 10022-5299

Copyright © 1999 by J.A. Jance
Excerpt from *Judgment Call* copyright © 2012 by J.A. Jance
ISBN 978-0-06-208816-1

First Harper premium printing: July 2012
First Avon Books mass market printing: November 1999
First William Morrow hardcover printing: February 1999

HarperCollins ® and Harper ® are registered trademarks of Harper Collins Publishers.

Printed in the United States of America

Visit Harper paperbacks on the World Wide Web at
www.harpercollins.com

10 9 8 7 6 5 4 3

For the Silent Witnesses
and for Kathy Williams, my guide to Everett

PROLOGUE

"THAT'S IT, THEN, JONAS," BEVERLY PIEDMONT SAID to me, watching as the last of my grandfather's ashes disappeared from view, slipping silently away and into the slate-gray depths of a dead-flat Lake Chelan.

The Lady of the Lake was moving slowly north and west from Chelan to Stehekin at the far end of the lake. Eastern Washington is supposedly the sunny side of the state. That wasn't true though on this mid-April day. The sky overhead was as dim and gray as it no doubt was back home in downtown Seattle.

When my grandmother had called me two days earlier to ask if I could take her to Lake Chelan to dispose of my grandfather's ashes, I had taken a look at the weather report and attempted to dissuade her. There was a storm blowing in off the Pacific. In Seattle proper, it most likely wouldn't be anything more serious than rain, but in the mountain passes that lay between Seattle and Lake Chelan— Snoqualmie and Blewett or Stevens—it might well turn into new snow to make the passes treacherous if not impassable. Initially, I suggested we wait a week or two until the weather improved. After all, what was the rush? In the months since my grandfather died, the box containing his ashes had languished on the floor of my entryway closet. It seemed ironic to me that Jonas Logan Piedmont and I had spent far more time together after he died than we had in all the years he was alive.

My suggestion of a delay, however, fell on deaf ears—both literally and figuratively. "No, Jonas," Beverly had insisted firmly. "Now that Mandy's gone, it's time."

Jonas Piedmont Beaumont is my legal name, but it's not the name I go by. Friends and the people I work with down at the Seattle Police Department call me Beau or else J.P. My mother, long deceased, used to call me Jonas when I was little. Now that I have mended a family rift and reestablished contact with my long-estranged grandparents, my grandmother calls me that as well. It still sounds odd to my ear—both strange and pleasing at the same time.

"Mandy's gone?" I asked. "Why didn't you call me? When did this happen?"

Mandy was my grandfather's silver-haired golden retriever. Pining for the old man, Mandy had slipped into a slow decline once he was gone. I had known she was failing, but I hadn't realized things had deteriorated that far. I had taken the dog to the vet on two separate occasions and had been prepared to take the poor old girl on her final trip there.

"Last week," my grandmother said. "When she stopped being able to get up and down by herself, I didn't want to bother you. After all, you're much too busy to be worrying about an old woman and her sick old dog. I called on the phone and found a mobile vet who came to the house and took care of things here. That way Mandy didn't have to be loaded in and out of a strange car—she didn't much like going for rides, you know. Besides, I was able to be here with her when she went. But that's why I'm calling today, Jonas. The vet stopped by this afternoon and dropped off her ashes. It's what I've been waiting for. Mandy was so devoted to Papa, you see. I wanted to be able to sprinkle their ashes together."

Weather be damned, there was no arguing with that. "What day do you want to go?" I asked.

"Wednesday," she said at once. "I already checked. That's the day *The Lady of the Lake* starts making daily trips up and down the lake from Chelan to Stehekin. I thought we'd drive as far as Chelan on Wednesday, catch the boat and stay overnight at the lodge in Stehekin on Thursday, and then come back Friday. If you can get off work, that is. If not, I suppose we could always go over the weekend."

I'm a homicide detective for Seattle PD. After years of being a growth industry, murder in the Emerald City had taken a sudden sharp and unexpected downturn. Not willing to cut head count, the brass upstairs had us working like hell on cold cases stretching back as far as twenty years. They were also encouraging any and all unpaid leaves of absence.

"Don't worry," I told her. "Getting off work won't be a problem."

"Good," she said. "I'll call and make reservations."

Once off the phone, I studied the weather forecast then called Avis and arranged to rent a four-wheel-drive Explorer. I love my Porsche 928, but not in blizzard conditions, and certainly not with my eighty-something grandmother along for the ride.

"Where did you get this?" she asked when I picked her up bright and early Wednesday morning from the Phinney Ridge-area bungalow she and my grandfather had shared for more than fifty years.

"I rented it," I said.

"For this trip?"

"Yes."

"What's the matter with your cute little red car?" she asked.

"It's not that good on long trips," I said.

"Oh," she said, seeming to accept my little white lie at face value. "I hope this one didn't cost too much money."

"No, Grandmother," I told her. "It's dirt-cheap."

That was hardly true, but four-wheel drive came in handy. We were within ten miles of the summit on Stevens Pass going east when the rain turned to snow—serious snow. If it hadn't been for the Explorer, I would have been out on the ground, rolling around on wet pavement, putting on chains.

Now, a day later, standing side by side in the dreary, overcast afternoon, my grandmother and I remained on the stern of the boat until long after the ashes disappeared. I had thought Beverly would be tearful when it came time to empty the ashes into the lake. Instead, she had performed the task with a quiet dignity that commanded my utmost respect. In the course of the trip I had learned, for the first time, that Chelan was where she and my grandfather had spent their one-night honeymoon years before, and that my grandfather had specifically requested that she strew his ashes there.

Since she said nothing more just then, I can't be sure what she was thinking. For myself, I was glad that at this late date I was finally having the opportunity to get to know more about her and about my grandfather, too. One story at a time, I was piecing together my family's history. I was also wondering how long eighty-six-year-old Beverly Piedmont would be able to remain in her own home. Rationally, I knew that she'd been essentially alone for several years, ever since my grandfather's crippling stroke had silenced him. Nonetheless, with both husband and dog now gone, the problem of Beverly's living alone seemed far more critical.

The issue had come home to me poignantly in the last twenty-four hours since my partner, Sue Danielson, and I had spent most of the previous day investigating the death of a sixty-seven-year-old woman in North Seattle who had burned to death in her home. The likely, but as yet unconfirmed, cause of Agnes Ferman's death was smoking in bed. Beverly Piedmont was a lot older than sixty-seven, but she didn't smoke. There was no cause to worry about her on that score, but still . . .

I wondered briefly about broaching the subject of maybe looking into finding a retirement home for her. I decided, however, that for the moment the best thing for me to do was to keep my mouth shut and mind my own business.

We might have stood there indefinitely, but eventually the bone-numbing chill drove us inside along with three or four other passengers who had been braving the great outdoors. "How about a sandwich and a cup of coffee?" I asked.

"That would be very nice," Beverly said, pulling her old-fashioned wool coat tightly around her. "It is chilly out here." It was also turning choppy. Even with the Dramamine I'd swallowed, I suddenly found myself feeling a bit gray around the gills.

Once Beverly was inside and settled at a small table, I went to fetch food. The coffee was strong and had sat in the pot for far too long. The sandwiches weren't the best, either, but Beverly downed hers with every evidence of enjoyment. She polished off the sandwich then sat back and eyed me in a speculative appraisal that reminded me of my mother. It came to me then that, had my mother survived breast cancer and lived to be her mother's age, this was how she would have looked as an old woman.

"So, Jonas," Beverly said, settling back with her coffee cup. Again there were echoes of my mother in the way she spoke. "What are you going to do with yourself?"

"Me?"

"Yes," she said. "You're not going to be a detective all your life, are you?"

Just because I had decided to mind my own business didn't mean my grandmother would do the same. "What do you mean?"

"Well, you started out as a uniformed patrol officer. Now you've been a detective for some time. Isn't the next step chief or something?"

I almost choked on a sip of my own coffee. "Most cops I know would call becoming chief a misstep rather than a step," I told her with a smile.

"You mean to say you don't want to be chief?" she asked. Words about what must have seemed a shocking lack of ambition weren't spoken aloud, but they lingered in the air nonetheless.

Decades ago the book *The Peter Principle* addressed the idea that people rise to the level of their own incompetence. I've found, however, that doesn't always hold true. In some bureaucracies, there are people who, through a combination of guile and/or political maneuvering manage to rise far above that level. In my humble opinion, the top floor of the Public Safety Building is rife with overreaching folks.

"Sorry," I said. "I'm just not into politics."

"I didn't mean you should run for office, although, now that you mention it, you'd make a fine legislator down in Olympia," Beverly returned, misunderstanding what I meant. "Still, isn't there some path for promotion available to you inside the department?"

As an expression of grandmotherly concern, this was a not-so-unreasonable question with no reasonable answer. Of course there were promotional opportunities available inside Seattle PD—for those who wanted them, that is. For those who were willing to play the game. Unfortunately, climbing that ladder presupposes either *wanting* to or *needing* to, neither of which applies to me. Game playing has never been my strong suit, and I don't really need to work, although I had yet to hit on anything I'd rather do instead.

Ralph Ames, my attorney and financial guru, has been telling me for years that my continuing to work only adds to my tax problem. Grandmother or not, I had no intention of discussing the ins and outs of my financial situation with Beverly Piedmont. Nor did I see any reason to tell her that the main consideration keeping me on the job was the lack of any viable alternative. I've been a cop for more than twenty years, most of that time on the homicide squad. It has crossed my mind on occasion that if I ever stop being a detective—something I think I do relatively well—I might be tempted to return to my other favorite pastime—drinking. Not surprisingly, my history of drinking was another topic that had no place in this little familial heart-to-heart.

Hoping to somehow derail the conversation and send it into less-sensitive territory, I settled for one of those stock replies that fills the void but is notably short on content. "But Grandmother," I objected, "I happen to like what I do."

She sniffed disapprovingly. "You mean to tell me you *like* dealing with all those terrible people?"

When Beverly Piedmont said that, I imagine she was thinking about rapists and serial killers. I thought, instead, about Sue Danielson, my new partner. Sue's a single mother stuck with the daunting assignment of working full time and raising two young boys without, as far as I can tell, the boys' biological father feeling obliged to lift a hand. I thought about Ron Peters, my wheelchair-bound ex-partner and his new wife, Amy. They're raising Ron's two girls from a previous marriage and expecting a boy of their own sometime in the next week or so. Then there's Sergeant Watkins and Capt. Larry Powell. There are the gun guys from the crime lab down in Tacoma who send out group Christmas cards year after year. Then there are the other criminalists in the crime lab and the people who work in the prosecutor's office. They're nice folks, most of them. They come complete with kids and dogs, jobs and mortgages, and slices, however thin, of the American dream.

The same can be said for most of the survivors—the relatives and friends of homicide victims—that we work with in the process of our investigations. These are people whose lives have been impossibly shattered. All their hopes and dreams have been irretrievably wrenched away from them by the unexpected loss of a loved one, but they're mostly nice, too. Heartbroken and hurting, but nice.

"Killers may be the scum of the earth," I told my grandmother. "But they come and go. We have to try to understand them—try to learn what makes them tick—but we don't spend all that much time with any of them. Most of the people I work with on a day-to-day basis aren't all that bad. In fact, I wouldn't call them terrible at all."

Unconvinced, Beverly clicked her tongue and shook her head. "You remind me so much of Kelly," she said. "That's exactly the kind of comment she would have made. She was always so contrary. There was never any reasoning with her."

For a disconcerting moment or two, I thought Beverly was talking about Kelly, my daughter. The unreasoning part certainly sounded familiar.

"You look like her sometimes, too," Beverly added softly as unexpected tears suddenly filled her eyes. "Especially when you smile, Jonas. I still miss her, you know—miss her terribly. And I do so regret all those lost years when we should have been together."

And that's when I understood Beverly was talking about *her* daughter Kelly, not mine. About Carol Ann Piedmont, my mother. When Kelly—that's what they called her, rather than Carol—became an unwed mother at age seventeen, my unbending grandfather had disowned her. He had thrown her out of the house and forbidden any contact between Beverly and her daughter or between Beverly and her grandson—me. It was only in the course of the last two years—long after my mother's death and with my aging grandfather in ill health—that the decades-old rift had finally been healed.

Reaching across the table, I covered my grandmother's small, frail, liver-spotted hand with my own massive mitt. I was glad to know I reminded someone of my mother—thankful that Carol Ann Piedmont wasn't totally forgotten by everyone in the world but me.

My mother had raised me at a time when being a single mother wasn't in vogue. She had struggled to support us by working at home as a seamstress, by sewing fancy dresses for people far above our station in life. Countless times I remember going to bed on the living-room couch while she worked long into the night. On those nights I fell asleep to the steady hum of Mother's treadle-operated Singer. As a boy growing up, I knew our lives were different from those of most of the kids I knew. For one thing, most of them had fathers. For another, their mothers didn't work. It wasn't until much later—until long after I was a father myself—that I realized Carol Ann Piedmont was very much a hero.

"Good," I said, patting my grandmother's hand and trying to make a joke of things in hopes that she wouldn't notice how touched I was. "People have called me contrary for years. I'm glad to hear I'm a chip off the old block."

CHAPTER 1

THERE ARE PEOPLE WHO LIKE CHANGE. THERE ARE even a few who thrive on it. That's not me. If it were, I wouldn't have reupholstered my ten-year-old recliner, and I wouldn't resole my shoes until they're half-a-size smaller than they were to begin with. When I move into a house or, as in the present case, into a high-rise condo, I'd better like the way I arrange the furniture the first time because that's the way it's going to stay until it's time to move someplace else. In fact, my aversion to change probably also accounts for my Porsche 928. George Washington's axe, with two new handles and a new head, probably doesn't have much to do with our first president. And my replacement Porsche doesn't have a lot of connection to Anne Corley, the lady who gave me the original. Still it's easier to hang on to the one I have now out of sentimental reasons than it is to admit that I just don't care to make the switch to a different car.

In other words, I'm a great believer in the status quo. It also explains why, on the Monday morning after Beverly Piedmont and I drove home from Lake Chelan, I came back to work expecting things at Seattle PD to be just the way they had been. And to begin with, there was no outward sign of change. Sue Danielson and I walked into our cubicle to discover a yellow Post-it note attached to the monitor of the desktop computer we share when we're in the office as opposed to the laptops we're supposed to use in the field.

"See me," the note said. "My office. Nine sharp."

There was no signature. On the fifth floor of the Public Safety Building, no signature was necessary. Captain Lawrence Powell has never made any bones about hating electronics in general and computers in particular. His idea of surfing the net is to go around the Homicide Squad slapping Post-it notes on every computer in sight.

Sue sighed. "What have we done now?" she asked, glancing at her watch. At 8:02, there was no reason to hurry to Larry Powell's fishbowl of an office. If we were going to be chewed out for something, I'm of the opinion later is always better than earlier.

"Who knows?" I said. "But remember, whatever it was, I was out of town most of last week, so it can't be my fault."

"You'd be surprised," Sue returned.

Sitting down at the desk I removed the note and turned on the computer. In typical bureaucratic fashion, when the department finally decided to create a local-area network and go on-line, they bought computers from the lowest possible bidder. As a consequence, they take for damned ever to boot up. I tapped my fingers impatiently and stared at the cyberspace egg timer sitting interminably in the middle of an otherwise blank blue screen.

"Probably has something to do with that well-done smoker who set herself on fire last Tuesday," I suggested.

"Oh," Sue said. "That's right. I forgot. You missed it."

I didn't like the sound of that "Oh." My antenna went up. "Missed what?" I asked.

"Marian Rockwell's preliminary report."

Marian Rockwell is one of the Seattle Fire Department's crack arson investigators. "Agnes Ferman's death is no longer being considered accidental," Sue continued. "Marian found residue of an accelerant on Agnes Ferman's bedding."

Smokers die in their beds all the time—in their beds or on their sofas. As far as I was concerned, arson seemed like a real stretch.

"What did she do, dump her lighter fluid while she was refilling her Zippo? Right. The next thing you're going to tell me is that Agnes Ferman is Elvis Presley's long-lost sister."

Sue scowled at me. "Don't pick a fight with me about it, Beau," she said. "I'm just telling you what Marian told me. You can believe it or not. It's no skin off my teeth either way. It's all there in the report I wrote up Friday morning."

Squabbling with my partner in the face of an imminent and possibly undeserved chewing out from the captain more or less took the blush off the morning. Up till then, it had seemed like a fairly decent Monday.

"So what else did you do while I was gone?" I asked.

"On Ferman? Not much. I counted and inventoried all the money and . . ."

"Money? What money?"

"The three hundred some-odd thousand in cash we found hidden in a refrigerator in Agnes Ferman's garage. I had planned on starting the neighborhood canvass and talking to her next of kin, but counting that much cash takes time. Agnes has a sister who lives up around Marysville and a brother and sister-in-law in Everett. That's about all I know so far. I haven't had a chance to track any of them down. The same goes for neighbors. Marian interviewed some of them—the one who reported the fire—but so far nobody's really canvassed the neighborhood."

Cash or no cash, homicides come with a built-in timetable. A murder that isn't solved within forty-eight hours tends to not be solved at all. As with any rule, there are exceptions, but the chances are, the longer a case remains unsolved after that deadline, the worse the odds are that it will ever be cleared. Next-of-kin and neighbor interviews are where investigations usually start. The fact that no interviews had taken place so far wasn't good. Furthermore, since my whole purpose in life is to see that killers *don't* get away with murder, I wasn't the least bit pleased by the seemingly unnecessary delay.

"Great," I fumed. "That's just great. Our case goes stale while all those concerned stand around twiddling their thumbs."

Sue shot me an icy glare. "I don't suppose you watched the news when you were east of the mountains."

Watching television—particularly television news—isn't my idea of a good time. I seldom watch TV on either side of the mountains. "As a matter of fact, I didn't. Should I have?" I asked irritably.

"For your information, all hell broke loose the minute you left town, including two drive-bys on Wednesday, a fatality vehicular accident under the convention center in the middle of Thursday-afternoon rush hour, and a homicide/suicide over in West Seattle on Friday morning. Add in a couple of assault cases and some role-playing ghouls in Seward Park and you can understand how poor old Agnes might have taken a backseat."

"Role-playing ghouls?" I asked. "What's that all about?"

"Funny you should ask," Sue told me. "That case happens to be ours, as well."

"What case?"

"The ghouls. About three o'clock Wednesday morning someone called to report a body in Seward Park. Supposedly the park is closed overnight, but it was hopping that night. When uniforms showed up, they found the place full of Generation X'ers dressed up like vampires and zombies and acting out some kind of role-playing game. Your basic Halloween in April. One of the guests freaked out when they stumbled on some non-make-believe human remains. He went home and called the cops. So since the Haz-Mat guys had the Ferman neighborhood shut down most of Wednesday, I got sent out to crawl around Seward Park looking for more bones instead of starting on the Ferman interviews."

By then I had finished calling up the file and was starting to scan it. The only words that penetrated my consciousness were vampire and Haz-Mat.

"Wait a minute," I said, turning away from the screen. "What does Halloween revisited have to do with the Hazardous Materials Unit?"

Sue nailed me with an exasperated glare. "Either listen or read," she told me. "Obviously you're incapable of doing both at once."

Sue Danielson is not short-tempered. Anything but. Between the two of us, I'm the one who's the grouser. But her tone of voice combined with a chilly stare warned me that I had blundered into risky territory.

"You talk; I'll listen," I said. "Let's start with Haz-Mat."

"I was about to head out to Bitter Lake on Wednesday morning to start interviewing neighbors when Marian Rockwell called and told me not to bother because she was in the process of evacuating the whole neighborhood. It seems she had just taken a peek inside Ferman's detached garage. According to her, it's a miracle the whole place didn't go up in a ball of flame during the fire on Tuesday morning. If it had, it might have taken half the neighborhood with it."

"What was in it, dynamite?"

"Not quite, but close enough. Old oxygen and acetylene tanks and welding equipment along with an old Plymouth van. One whole wall was stacked floor-to-ceiling with deteriorating cans of paint and paint thinner, all of which would have burned like crazy if the garage had happened to catch fire. It was such a mess that it took the Haz-Mat guys almost the whole day to clear the place out. There was an old refrigerator in there, too. Sitting in the back with its face to the wall. That's where they found the money.

"Like I said before, it turns out to be a little over three hundred thou," Sue told me. "Most of it in hundred-dollar bills. I had been sent to work the Seward Park case, but once they located the money, Marian wanted me to come take charge of it. Which is how we get to have both cases—Seward Park and Agnes Ferman. One old and one new."

"So where do you suppose all this money came from? How much was it again?"

"Three hundred eleven thousand to be exact, plus change. Agnes must not have liked banks very much. As I said, it took most of Thursday to inventory it all and record the serial numbers. It's in hundreds mostly. Some of them have been circulated, but the majority haven't. The better part of a quarter of a million came straight from the U.S. Mint sometime after 1973 and before 1990. Since about 1993, incoming cash slowed to a trickle."

"You think that big chunk has been in the refrigerator the whole time?"

"Maybe not in the refrigerator, but the bills have

definitely been out of circulation. A lot of them are still banded with consecutive serial numbers."

"And the earliest serial numbers date from the mid-seventies?"

Sue nodded. "Right. They're old bills, but they look brand new. Meanwhile, knowing there was that much money at stake, Marian Rockwell decided maybe it was premature to declare the fire accidental. And what do you know! As soon as she went looking for an accelerant, she found it."

"With Agnes Ferman dead, who does the money go to?" I asked.

"No idea. So far there's no sign of a will. My guess is we're not going to find one."

"Makes sense," I said. "If Agnes didn't like banks, she probably didn't like lawyers, either."

"Which means we need to talk to both the brother and sister," Sue said.

"ASAP," I agreed. "Now what about Seward Park? Any chance the Generation X'ers did the deed?"

"No," Sue said. "The bones look like they've been out in the elements for a long time—longer than most of those asshole kids have been on earth. All we've found so far are skeletal remains. A femur here and a tibia there. Not enough for even a partial autopsy, and no sign at all of cause of death. Over the weekend some Explorer Scouts were supposed to go over the whole area inch by inch. So far, though, I haven't heard what if anything more they found. It could be some long-dead guy whose bones washed up during last winter's floods, or it could be a previously undiscovered victim of the Green River Killer. Until someone in Doc Baker's office has a chance to tell us otherwise, however, we have orders to treat it as a possible homicide."

"In other words," I added, "it looks like we're back to business as usual with everyone working multiple cases."

"For the time being," Sue said.

For a while I had enjoyed the laid-back, eight-hour-a-day pace of chasing cold cases, but now the novelty had worn off. I was bored. "Good," I said. "It's about time."

While the printer was spitting out a hard copy of Sue's report, I continued to scan the screen. The date of birth listed on Agnes Ferman's driver's license was within one month of my mother's. Had I not spent so much time with my grandmother the previous week, that's a detail that I might have simply glossed over. As it was, however, it struck me as significant somehow. It made me want to know more about the dead woman. And her killer.

Dying of smoking in bed implies a certain amount of self-destruction, a kind of willfulness. It's the sort of death that doesn't evoke a lot of sympathy. Like dying of a drug overdose or booze. People pretty much shrug their shoulders and say "Who cares?"

On the other hand, dying in bed because of an arson-related fire makes the victim doubly victimized. After all, in the Saturday afternoon Westerns I used to watch at the old Baghdad Theater in Ballard, the Indians never attacked until after dawn. Staging a surprise attack in the middle of the night was definitely not okay. Not honorable. Killing a defenseless, sleeping victim wasn't considered fair play in those old movies, and it didn't seem fair in modern-day Seattle, either—no matter how much money the old girl had hidden in her firetrap of a garage.

Lost in the report, I had gone through Marian Rockwell's Haz-Mat part of the story and was just getting to the inventory of Agnes Ferman's stash of money when Sue sliced through my concentration.

"Time to go," she said. "It's almost nine. You know what'll happen if we're late."

Larry Powell's all-glass office allows the captain to keep his finger on the pulse of his troops at all times. Meticulously clean glass makes for an unobstructed view of the status board behind Sergeant Watkins' desk. By reading that the captain can tell at all times which teams of detectives are assigned to which cases. The check-in board next to the status board lets him know who's in, who's out, and when they're expected back. Coming around Watty's cluttered desk, I was surprised to see the Fishbowl crammed wall-to-wall with people—fellow members of the detective division who populate the fifth floor of the Public Safety Building.

"If this is going to be an ass chewing," I whispered in an aside to Sue, "it's a world-class, group-grope event. No one on the floor is exempt."

Sue shot me a stifling glance that effectively silenced me while we wormed our way into the crowd. Surprisingly enough, we weren't the last to arrive. As more people squeezed into too-little space we found ourselves mashed into the far corner of the office with our backs right up against the glass partition. About the time I figured no one else could possibly wedge himself into the room, someone else showed up—Detective Paul Kramer.

Kramer has never been high on my list of favorite people. In January, he had broken his leg and had been off on medical leave for a while. When he came back from disability still on crutches, the brass took him off homicide and dragged him upstairs to work on some kind of special project for the chief. Until he shoehorned his way into Powell's office that morning, I hadn't seen the man in weeks and that's exactly how I like it. A little bit of Kramer goes a very long way.

"All right, folks," the captain said. "It looks like everybody's here, so let's get started. I'd like to keep this brief so all of you can get back to work as soon as possible. Most of you have met my wife, Marcia. Some of you may be aware that in the past few months she's been dealing with a series of health difficulties. At first we thought it was some kind of leg or back injury. It turns out, however, that it's a good deal more serious than that. Last Wednesday, we finally received confirmation of her preliminary diagnosis. Amyotrophic lateral sclerosis—ALS. Marcia has Lou Gehrig's disease."

There was an audible gasp from some of the people in the room, but Captain Powell plunged on without acknowledgment. "From what we've been able to learn so far, this is a neurological disease in which, over time, various limbs and organs lose their ability to function and become paralyzed. From diagnosis on there's a life expectancy of approximately three to seven years. Although there may be some treatments that can slow the progression of the disease, at this time there is no cure.

"Right now, Marcia's symptoms are little more than an inconvenience, but there's no telling how long that will last or how fast the disease will progress. Bearing that in mind and knowing that our time to do things together is severely limited, I'm pulling the pin. As of Friday, I have submitted my letter of resignation to Chief Rankin. This morning, he has accepted it, with regret, as of May fifteenth. With accumulated sick leave and vacation time, today is my last day on the job. That's probably just as well since I'm not very good at long goodbyes or short ones either, for that matter.

"I want you all to know that I'm very proud of you. You're a hell of a team, and I'm going to miss you—each and every one." He paused long enough to glance around the room. There was no mistaking the moisture in his eyes—or in anybody else's, either.

"So, that's how it is. You've given me your unqualified support, and I expect you to do the same for my successor, whoever that may be. Naturally, with so little advance warning, you can understand that there have been no firm decisions yet as to who will be occupying this desk."

I happened to glance at Paul Kramer just as Larry said that. The look on his face was an open book. I've seen the same unqualified yearning on little kids pressing their noses against the glass shields protecting containers of ice cream at Baskin Robbins.

Kramer? I thought. *Captain Paul Kramer? Are you kidding? No frigging way!*

"So, that's all then," Larry was saying. "The people in benefits have assured us that between my insurance and Marcia's we shouldn't have too many worries on that score. For now we're going to be busy doing some of the things we always expected to do in retirement—starting with a Caribbean cruise. We leave for Miami this Thursday afternoon. During the summer we expect to get in our motor home and do some traveling around the States. We're going to go as far and as fast as we can. When we can't go anymore, then we'll stop. So, wish us well." He paused again and then managed a shadow of a grin. "And don't let the door hit your butts on the way out."

People breathed again. Tension in the room—which had been almost palpable—let up a little. A few of the old-timers managed a chuckle at hearing the familiar phrase. Larry Powell never was a believer in long, drawn-out meetings. When it was over, it was over. That was the way he often ended his briefings—by pointing to the door and sending us on our way. This time, though, people didn't leave right away. We dribbled out one at a time, like mourners leaving a church after a funeral, with each man or woman pausing long enough to mumble a few words of comfort and encouragement and to shake Larry's hand.

Because of the way we had been crowded into the far corner of the room, Sue and I were among the last to leave.

"Sorry," she said. "I'm so sorry."

Larry nodded. "Thanks," he said. "I know."

With that, Sue left. Then it was just Captain

Powell and I standing facing one another across the smooth surface of his desk. "I don't know what to say," I began.

The captain sighed. "You don't need to say anything, Beau," he said. "Of all the people in this room, you probably know more about what's coming down the road than anyone here, me included. You've lost two wives instead of one. How do you get through it? How did you?"

Anne Corley was a long time ago, but it was only a few months since my ex-wife, Karen, had died of cancer. I had a pretty good idea of how much Larry was hurting right at that moment, but I also knew what he was feeling now was nothing compared to what he'd feel before long. It would get worse, much, much worse, before it got better.

I reached out and shook his hand. "You do it one day at a time," I told him. "And you make the most of every minute you have."

"Thanks," he said. "We intend to."

On my way back to our cubicle, I noticed there was none of the usual banter drifting from the doors I passed. It was as if Larry Powell's unexpected farewell address had hit all of us where we lived. Knowing about Marcia Powell's illness reminded us, all too disturbingly, of our own mortality.

Being partners is a whole lot like being married—with none of the side benefits. When I stepped into the cubicle, Sue glanced at me over her shoulder and gave me "the look"—one that was unmistakable to any man who's ever been married. *Are you okay?* it said. *Do you want to talk about it?*

Naturally the answer I should have given to both

questions was *No, I'm not okay* and *Yes, I need to talk about it.* But I didn't. Instead, I walked over to the computer and switched it off. "Come on, Sue," I said. "Let's get the hell out of here."

"Where are we going?" Sue asked.

"We're going to do our jobs and try to figure out who the hell turned poor old Agnes Ferman into a shish kebab."

CHAPTER 2

UNTIL SUE AND I HAD DRIVEN THERE THE PREVIOUS Tuesday, I had never heard of Wingard Court North. Number 706 sits right on the banks of beautiful Bitter Lake—some might call it Bitter Pond—in the far north end of Seattle. It was far enough off the beaten path that when we took the call we'd had to haul out our *Thomas Guide* to help with navigation.

Agnes Ferman had lived and died in an unpretentious neighborhood made up of summer cottages that had, over time, been transformed into year-round middle-class housing. The lots were such that, even in the current world of greedy real estate, developers would be hard-pressed to knock one down and put a megahouse/no-lot dwelling in its place. On Wingard Court, developers would need at least two lots to do that. Maybe that's why so many of those original houses were still around.

On the way there, I drove the departmental "bulgemobile," otherwise known as a Caprice. Since Sue and I obviously weren't going to talk about what was going on with Larry and Marcia Powell, she reached into her purse, pulled out her ragged spiral notebook and began reviewing her notes on the Ferman homicide, covering everything that had happened once I left town.

These days we're all supposed to carry around little laptop computers which the city, after great debate, purchased for use by its law enforcement officers. And we do carry them—far more than we use them. Both Sue's and mine were safely stowed in the trunk of the Caprice we were currently driving. That's where they usually ended up—in whatever trunk happened to be available.

Computers are good for lots of things, but not in the world of homicide investigations. For detectives, nothing beats a notebook and pencil. They're portable, cheap, accessible, never have those pesky General Protection Faults, and they take no time at all to boot up. In my opinion, if a cop wants to go really high tech, all he has to do is invest in a ballpoint pen, which is exactly why Sue was reading to me from her trusty notebook.

"According to what I have here, Agnes was sixty-seven years old at the time of her death. She was a widow. Her husband died several years ago—1993. No children, but her survivors include a brother and a sister. The brother—Andrew George—lives in Everett. Hilda Smathers, the sister, lives somewhere up around Marysville. She's the one who provided the ME's office with the name of Agnes Ferman's dentist. His records confirmed identification of the body. At the family's request, no services are scheduled."

"The old guy who reported the fire, the one who was out of bed because his dog needed to take a leak. What's his name again?"

"I have no idea what the dog's name is," Sue responded dryly. "The man's name is Malcolm Lawrence."

"Right. Have you talked to him?"

"Not since you and I did Tuesday afternoon," Sue replied.

"That means nobody's interviewed him since the money was found?"

"Right. Marian Rockwell may have spoken to him. If so, she didn't mention it in her report."

"Let's start with Malcolm," I told her. "After that, we'll talk to some of the other neighbors as well. And if we finish canvassing the neighborhood early enough, we'll head up north to see the brother and sister."

That's how homicide investigations work. We start by talking to the neighbors—to people who live or work near the scene of the crime and who may have seen something out of the ordinary around the time the murder took place. From there we gradually expand the inquiry to include relatives, friends, and as many known associates as possible. Interviewing relatives can often be the tricky part of the deal since, more than occasionally, the person nearest and dearest to the victim also happens to be the murderer.

According to Sue's notes Malcolm Lawrence had spotted the fire and reported it right around 5:30 A.M. By the time responding fire units arrived, the house was fully engulfed. That meant the arsonist had come and gone sometime earlier. In the middle of the night, there's not much hope of a neighbor being up and seeing something, but it does happen. On the other hand, I've had more than one case solved by an alert newspaper-delivery kid who was smart enough to pay attention to what was going on around him—to an unfamiliar vehicle or to unusual activity in an otherwise sleeping neighborhood.

"Let's be sure to check with the newspaper carrier," I said.

"Right," Sue agreed, scribbling a note. "I meant to do that on Friday, but I ended up cataloging serial numbers instead."

We pulled up in front of what was left of Agnes Ferman's house. On Tuesday an old battered Lincoln had been sitting on the parking strip. "Where's the car?" I asked.

"I had it towed into the garage so we could check it for prints."

We had no sooner parked the Caprice where the Lincoln had once been when the front door of the house across the street opened. An elderly man I recognized as Malcolm Lawrence appeared on the porch along with two amazingly fat dachshunds. Barking like mad, the dogs reminded me of a pair of powerful but noisy tugboats. So short that their swollen bellies seemed to drag on the ground, they nonetheless moved fast enough and with enough force that Lewis was swept along in their wake, across the porch, down the steps, and then up the walkway. Ineffectually hauling back on the leashes and ordering the dogs to heel, Lawrence came dragging along behind them like some kind of hapless human dogsled. By then the two ugly mutts and their pointy, sharp little teeth were almost within striking distance of my ankles.

I suppose the idea of an armed homicide cop being worried about a pair of yappy little dogs sounds like some kind of joke, but of all the dogs known to man, dachshunds are my least favorite—with good reason.

In all my life, I've been bitten only once—by an obnoxious little wiener dog named Snooks. The dog nailed me square on the ankle. He sliced right through a new pair of dress socks hard enough to draw blood. Unfortunately, throttling Snooks on the spot wasn't an option since he happened to belong to a cute girl I'd just met at school—a girl named Karen Moffitt. Snooks' unprovoked attack came on the occasion of my stopping by the Moffitt house to take Karen out on our first date.

From that evening on, for the next five years, including the first two years Karen and I were married, Snooks and I were the bane of each other's existence. Eventually he was old and frail, farting and incontinent, but he never stopped barking at me whenever I came into the house. As far as Snooks was concerned, I was the eternal interloper. And I must confess that the animosity was absolutely mutual. I despised him every bit as much as he did me.

All of this flashed through my mind as Malcolm Lawrence came tottering toward us. I don't know if it showed on my face, but I was wondering what the departmental position would be if one of Seattle's finest drop-kicked somebody's beloved pet into the next county. Or maybe even plugged the shin-chewing little rat dog with my regulation 9mm. Not good, I decided. Not good at all.

About the time I was considering beating a hasty retreat back to the car, both dogs veered off in that direction themselves. They made a beeline for the Caprice's rear left tire where they almost tipped themselves ass-over-teakettle in their eagerness to raise their legs high enough to take aim at the city's steel-belted radials.

"Tuffy! Major!" the old man exclaimed, jerking again on the leashes. "You cut that out. Right now. Sit!" he added. "Sit and behave yourselves." Surprisingly enough, both dogs sat. Thankfully, they even shut up.

"You're the two detectives, aren't you," Malcolm Lawrence said, peering up at us through a pair of thick glasses covered with cloudy fingerprints and dotted with flakes of dandruff. The heavy prescription made his rheumy eyes seem enormous. "Aren't you the same ones I talked to the other day?"

I had been so preoccupied with the dogs that I hadn't looked at the man on the other end of the leash. During the intervening days since I had last seen him, I had forgotten how much Malcolm Lawrence resembled George Burns. If he ever entered an *Oh, God!* look-alike contest, Lawrence would undoubtably walk away with first prize. The stooped, wiry octogenarian came complete with a sharp, pointed chin, pursed lips, and the half-smoked stub of an ever-present cigar.

"Right," I said, pulling out my ID. "We did talk to you before. My name's Detective Beaumont. This is my partner, Detective Danielson."

Lawrence barely glanced in Sue's direction. "I forget. Which one are you with?" he asked. "The police or the fire department?"

"We're with the Seattle PD," I told him.

"Good," he said, nodding and puffing on the cigar and then holding it up in the air between two stubby, nicotine-stained fingers. "If you ask me, that girl they sent out here from the fire department last week didn't have much on the ball. Wouldn't tell us nothing about what was going on. We had to read in the paper that the fire weren't no accident. Poor Agnes. Who'd've ever thought somebody'd want to do her like that?"

Behind Lawrence's back, Sue raised one questioning eyebrow. I knew what she was thinking. So was I. If Lt. Marian Rockwell didn't have much on the ball, I'd hate to see someone who did.

"As I recall, you're the one who reported the fire."

"Right," Malcolm said. "I sure was. The flames was just shooting up into the air something awful. Right through the roof. I couldn't hardly believe my eyes. After I called 911, I ran over and pounded on the front door trying to wake Agnes up. She didn't hear me though. At least, she didn't answer. Maybe she was already dead, for all I know. I tried the door, but it was locked. About then the fire truck showed up and they made me get out of the way. I came back over here and stood on the porch. I watched until my legs gave out and I had to go inside to sit down. It's a crying shame getting old. Just wait, Detective. You'll see. It'll happen to you before you know it."

There were times I thought it already had. "How well did you know Agnes Ferman?" I asked.

He shrugged. "Pretty well, I guess. We've been neighbors a long time—twenty years or so. She and her husband—Lyle was his name—bought this place musta been in the early to midseventies, I suppose, when old Mrs. Twitty finally croaked out. They bought this because it was close to where Agnes worked. Lyle was a painter—a house painter, not an artist. He worked out of his van so it didn't much matter to him where he lived, but Agnes was still working for them rich people on the other side of the bluff.

"If you ask me, for somebody being married, it's a funny kind of arrangement. At least it was back then. Agnes lived-in except for her days off, while Lyle was here baching it by himself most of the time—doing his own cooking and laundry. Like I said, he was a house painter. That's what got him, by the way—lead-based paint wrecked his liver. So, up until Agnes retired a few years back, she was only here on her days off."

"How long ago was that?"

"When she retired? Six years, maybe seven," Malcolm said. "She finally quit when Lyle got so bad that he couldn't be left here by himself. He's been gone for a while, now, but I forget exactly how long."

Today not too many people have live-in help anymore, but Wingard Court was within spitting distance of one of Seattle's most high-brow neighborhoods—the Highlands. An exclusive community that lies just north of the Seattle city limits. There, buffered from the rest of the world by the green expanses of the Seattle Golf and Country

Club and protected by a series of manned security gates, people with enough money can do what they want without the lower classes being able to see how the other half lives.

In the old days—when I was growing up in Ballard—having live-in servants in the Highlands was the rule rather than the exception. That's probably reversed now, but since the Ferman residence was physically nearby, that was my first guess.

"She worked for someone in the Highlands?" I asked.

Malcolm shook his head. "Nope. Not *in* the Highlands, but real close by. Below it. Somewhere down the hill from there, although I can't say exactly where."

"Do you happen to know the family's name?"

"No, sir. You got me again. Couldn't tell you that, but I do know she worked for the same people for a long time. They treated her real fine—just like one of the family. Took her on fancy trips with them, and all like that. I believe she gets a retirement check from them real regular. In fact, someone from there—a son, I believe—come around not too long ago to check on Agnes—just to see how she was doing and to make sure she was all right. That's what Agnes told me anyway. Must be real decent folks."

Back across the street, the screen door on the front of Malcolm Lawrence's little house burst open. A woman in a housecoat and curlers appeared on the porch. It had been years since I had seen a woman wearing curlers. I was surprised to discover somebody still made them.

"Malcolm, what on earth is taking you so long?" the woman demanded in a shrill voice. "You told me you were going out to walk the dogs for just a minute. Your coffee's poured and it's getting cold."

Without answering, Malcolm jerked his head in the woman's direction. "That's the wife," he explained. "Becky. Been married to her for over fifty years, but she's still the jealous type. She don't much like it for me to be outside chewing the fat with somebody without her knowing exactly what's going on."

"Well?" Becky Lawrence shouted again when her first attempt to reel in her husband elicited no visible response. "Are you coming in or not?"

"Give me a minute, Bec. Can't you see I'm busy?" Malcolm returned sharply. "I'm talking to this here detective." Becky disappeared behind a slammed door and Malcolm turned back to me. "She can't stand to have me out of her sight for even a minute. Where were we again?"

"You were telling us about Agnes Ferman and the man who came by to check on her."

"Right. Drives one of those fancy new cars. A Lincoln, I think. Town Car maybe? A big one anyway although not as big as the old clunker Agnes used to have."

Sue was busy taking notes, so I didn't. "And he only came by that once?"

"I only saw the car that once," Malcolm said. "The person may have been here more often than that but if he was, I didn't see him."

"Getting back to Monday night. You didn't notice any unusual activity?"

"Well," Malcolm frowned. "Now that you mention it, there was a car here during the evening. Early on. It was brown, I think. Dog-turd brown."

"Any idea what kind?"

Malcolm shook his head. "I'm not sure. It was one of them little foreign jobs and I can't keep 'em straight in my head any more 'cause they all look alike. I'm pretty sure, though, that I've seen this one before. Belonged to one of her relatives, I think."

"When did it leave?"

"Seven-thirty or eight. Fairly early."

"And you didn't see anything else?"

"Nope." He shook his head. "Not that night. Not until morning when I saw the fire."

"What time did you go to bed?"

"Right after the news. Ten o'clock news, that is. Eleven o'clock may be fine for young whippersnappers like you and the lady here, but us oldsters need our rest. Except for Agnes, that is. She was always a night owl herself. Read books all night long, one right after another."

He stopped abruptly. "Is there something wrong?" I asked.

"I was thinking about them books and it really struck me. What Agnes loved most especially was murder mysteries. Read stacks of them. She'd bring 'em home from the library half a dozen at a time. In fact, she told me once that she was thinking about writing one herself someday. But now, of course, she's dead and the same thing's happened to her. Murder, that is."

I glanced at Sue. I hadn't mentioned the word

murder and neither had she. "What makes you think Agnes Ferman was murdered?" Sue asked.

Malcolm attempted a long-but-futile suck on his cigar. Fortunately for all concerned, the foul-smelling thing had gone out. "Maybe that's what it said in the paper," he said, glowering at the dead cigar.

I have a long-running feud with all kinds of members of the media—both print and electronic—but even my old fraternity brother Maxwell Cole wasn't likely to label a death homicide until somebody from the department issued an official statement to that effect.

"What did it say?" I asked.

Malcolm shrugged. "That she died under mysterious circumstances. As far as I'm concerned, a fire by itself ain't mysterious at all. But now, with you two showing up and flashing around badges that say homicide all over them, you don't have to be no rocket scientist to be able to put two and two together. Right?"

"I suppose," I agreed.

Across the street, the screen door to the Lawrences' house opened violently one more time and Becky Lawrence stamped out to the top step. "Are you coming or should I throw it out?" she demanded.

"Maybe we should talk to your wife," Sue Danielson suggested. "She might have seen or heard something that night that you missed."

"You're welcome to," Malcolm said, "although I'm not sure now's the best time. She can be a holy terror, especially when she's in one of her moods like she is today. Besides, I can tell you she didn't see or hear nothing. Old as she is, Becky still sleeps like a baby. She pops one of her pills, takes out her hearing aids, and doesn't hear a thing. That includes sirens. She never woke up that morning until after it was all over. I don't know what would happen if our house ever caught on fire. I'm afraid she'd sleep right through the smoke alarm, even though it's right there in the bedroom with us."

"Malcolm!"

"All the same," Sue said, smiling sweetly. "It's probably still a good idea for us to talk to her."

"When?" Lawrence asked.

"How about now?"

He shrugged. "Suit yourselves, then," he said dubiously, "but if I was you, I'd wait until later in the day. Bee's not much of a morning person. I do need to get going, though," he added. "If I don't hop to it when she tells me, she'll make my life hell for the rest of the day." Yanking on the leashes, he pulled the two waiting dogs to their feet. "Come on, guys," he said. "Off we go."

When we reached the porch of the house across the street, Lawrence stopped with one hand on the screen door. "You'll have to wait out here," he said. "Bec don't hold with having strangers in the house. I'll send her out to talk to you."

Malcolm Lawrence and the two dogs disappeared inside. "Believe me," Sue said, as the door banged shut behind him. "If I had to be married to that old coot, I wouldn't be much of a morning person either."

Moments later, Becky Lawrence opened the door. Her housecoat had disappeared as had the curlers, although the curls themselves hadn't exactly been brushed out. "Whaddya want?" she demanded, glaring up at me.

Sue stepped into the breach. "We're homicide detectives with Seattle PD," she said. "We wanted to know if you could add anything to what your husband told us about Agnes Ferman."

Faced with a woman investigator, Becky Lawrence's features softened a little. "Don't rightly know," Becky said. "Depends on what he already told you," she said, jerking her head toward the front door.

"Mr. Lawrence told us about spotting the fire. That made us wonder if you or anyone else might have seen anything out of the ordinary Monday night or Tuesday morning."

Becky Lawrence paused for a moment, mulling over the question. When she spoke, ill-fitting dentures rattled loosely in her head. "I didn't see nothin' before I went to sleep, and there wasn't nothin' out of line later when I got up along about midnight to drain my radiator. That's the problem with getting older—leastwise it is for me. Have to get up and down time and again overnight to use the bathroom."

"So you say you saw nothing unusual that night?"

"Nope. Not a thing."

"Were you and Agnes friends?" Sue asked.

"Hardly." Becky shrugged. "We was neighbors. Agnes weren't what you'd call friends with nobody from around here. Acted sort of high and mighty, which was kinda funny. I never could understand her bein' snooty, considering she never did nothin' but work as somebody else's fetch and carry. No. Me and her wasn't friends."

"When's the last time you saw her?"

Becky Lawrence's eyes narrowed. "To talk to her, you mean?"

Sue nodded.

"Must've been Sunday a week or so before she died. Came over with a pile of dog shit in a paper bag and dumped it right in the middle of our front yard. Right here beside the front step. I asked her what the hell she thought she was doing? She said Major and Tuffy had left some calling cards in her yard and she was just returning the favor. Made me mad as hell. Our dogs do their jobs right out in our own backyard. The mess she brung over here wasn't even theirs. These are little dogs and that crap was way too big."

That seemed like as good a time as any to put in my two cents' worth. "Mrs. Lawrence," I said. "A sizable sum of money was found hidden in Mrs. Ferman's garage. Did she ever talk to you about money?"

"Are you kidding? The way that woman talked, you'da thought she was one step away from the poor-house, from bein' one of them bag ladies you see all the time downtown. Agnes was forever saying how tight things were and asking to borrow stuff—like tools or lawn mowers—rather than forking over money to buy one of her own. And like as not, if she borrowed a tool, she borrowed the man that went with it as well. After her husband Lyle passed on—and he was a good man, by the way. Far better'n Agnes deserved, if you ask me. After Lyle died, her grass would of growed hip deep if Malcolm and some of the other men in the neighborhood hadn't taken pity on her and mowed it. Agnes may have had all kinds of money in her garage, but she was tight as hell. She never paid nobody nothing for mowing that grass. Not one red cent, not even for gas to put in the mower."

"It sounds as though you didn't like her much," I observed.

Becky Lawrence sniffed. "You could say that. Agnes Ferman's gone. If you ask me, the whole neighborhood's lucky to be shuck of her."

CHAPTER 3

AS DETECTIVE DANIELSON AND I HEADED NORTH TO-
ward Everett on I-5, there wasn't a whole lot of conversation. Sue seemed to be brooding while I started
thinking about something she had said earlier. "No
services," I said. "Doesn't that strike you as odd?"

"What?" Sue asked, sounding as though my question had summoned her back from a million miles
away.

"No services," I repeated. "When my grandfather died, my grandmother chose not to have a
funeral. She said that most of their friends were already gone and, at their ages, there were far too
many funerals. But Jonas Piedmont was in his nine-
ties when he died. My grandmother and I were the
only close relatives in the area. On the other hand,
Agnes Ferman was only in her late sixties. That's
relatively young by comparison, and she has both a
brother and a sister right here in the Seattle area."

"Maybe the whole family has an aversion to

funerals," Sue suggested. "I don't like them very much myself."

With that, Sue turned away and continued to stare out the window. Since she didn't seem interested in talking, I shut up and drove. Traffic moved along smoothly until just north of the I-5/I-405 interchange at Mill Creek. There a combination of express-lane construction and a multivehicle fender bender turned the freeway into a parking lot.

I stopped the Caprice behind a diesel-belching eighteen-wheeler, switched off the engine, leaned back against the headrest and closed my eyes. I was about to doze off when Sue woke me. "Fifty years," she muttered.

"I beg your pardon?"

"Those people back there—the Lawrences. How did they stay married for more than fifty years? I barely made it to six."

In the months Detective Danielson and I have worked together, I've come to appreciate the fact that she's definitely not a Chatty-Kathy type. Until that morning, I didn't ever remember her saying anything about marriage one way or another. I knew she was divorced, but as far as personal life was concerned, she had never mentioned anything beyond talking about her two kids—Jared, a rebellious, obnoxious thirteen-year-old, and Christopher, an easygoing, sweet-tempered eight.

Had I been paying attention, the sharp edge of bitterness in Sue's voice should have warned me to be wary. Judging from past experience, I figured her brooding silence most likely had something to do with Jared. His special form of parental torture seemed to include using weekends to declare open season on his mother.

Sue Danielson and I are partners, but she's also a good ten years younger than I am. There are times when I can't stifle the almost fatherly feelings I have toward her. That's especially true when Jared is giving her hell. Having made my own mother's life plenty miserable when I was a teenager, I have a soft spot in my heart for single mothers. I figured the least I could do was offer Sue an opportunity to vent. She might not want a shoulder to cry on, but I could give her a place where she could let off a little steam.

"What'd he do this time?" I asked.

She swung around and glared at me. "Who?" she demanded.

"Jared," I said. "Isn't he what's bugging you?"

There was a long pause before she answered. "Jared has nothing to do with it," she said finally. "Not directly. Richie's coming home. His plane gets in tomorrow night at six."

"Who's Richie?" I asked.

"My ex," she said.

Until that moment, sitting stuck in northbound traffic on Interstate 5, I had never heard Sue refer to her former husband by name. The only thing I had known about the man prior to that was that he seldom if ever paid child support.

I've been a divorced father. I'm proud to say that I never missed a child-support payment, not even back when I was still drinking. I have a hard time understanding fathers who figure a divorce decree gives them carte blanche to walk out on both their kids and their responsibilities. Admittedly, children can be a real pain in the butt on occasion, but kids—even obnoxious teenagers—are people, too.

"You don't sound too happy about this impending visit," I observed mildly.

Sue shot me a smoldering glance. "Happy?" she snapped. "Why should I be? I'm pissed as hell as a matter of fact. After not being in touch at all for over two years—not even a birthday card or a Christmas present for either one of the boys—now all of a sudden he calls up on the phone, acts as though nothing is amiss, and says he's coming down this week to take the kids to Disneyland. Not next week, mind you, when it's spring break and the kids could go without missing any school. No, it has to be this week or nothing. He wants to take them out of class for three whole days—Wednesday, Thursday, and Friday.

"My first reaction was to take a page from the J. P. Beaumont lexicon and tell him to go piss up a rope—that he can see the kids if and when he sends me some of that back child support. But of course, he didn't leave me that option. The underhanded rat called the boys while I was still at work. The first I heard about it, the kids were already so excited they could barely stand it. Not only about seeing their dad again, but also about going on the trip. Believe me, without any child support, it's all I can do to keep food on the table and a roof over our heads. I sure as hell can't afford to take them on an outing like that. The best I've ever done is a weekend in somebody's borrowed condo over at Ocean Shores."

My own daughter, Kelly, dropped out of school prior to high school graduation, although she's doing fine now. She picked up her GED and she's even started taking classes at Southern Oregon University down in Ashland. My son, Scott, just graduated from Stanford with a degree in electrical engineering. Personally, I've always been a big believer in education.

"Missing school doesn't sound like a good idea to me, either," I told Sue. "It's not good for the kids and the school district isn't going to approve. Did you try asking your ex to reschedule for spring break? Maybe he just didn't realize . . ."

"Of course, I told him. But rules that govern other people don't necessarily apply to Richie Danielson. He says it's this week or nothing. The problem is, if I pull the plug on the trip for whatever reason, it'll hurt the kids that much more."

It was easy to see that Sue was in a bind. If she nixed the trip at this stage, she would be cast as the villain of the piece—at least in the eyes of her two children.

"When did all this trip stuff come about?" I asked.

"Last week," Sue answered. "After you left town for Lake Chelan, I guess."

"Well," I said. "If your ex can afford to take trips to Disneyland, he should be able to afford child-support payments, too. Have you ever thought about taking him back to court?"

"I tried it once. Didn't do any good. On paper, Richie claims he doesn't make a dime."

"How does he support himself then?"

"He's into some kind of bartering business," Sue explained. "Once he stopped being a church . . ."

"A church?" I interrupted. "When was he ever a church?"

"The year we got a divorce. He declared himself a church and didn't pay any income taxes. Two years later the IRS came after me for $2,500 in back taxes on money he earned while we were still married. I asked the lady from the IRS how come she was coming after me instead of him. I'll never forget what she said. 'Honey, *you* have a job.'"

"And you had to pay?"

"Damned straight. Every dime plus interest. It took me two years to pay the whole thing off. That's when I found out he's in the bartering business. No cash ever changes hands. Richie says he put together a mattress deal with some hotel chain. Instead of getting money, he got this prepaid Disneyland package. I'm sure he underreports his income to the IRS. Since he doesn't have a bank account and earns no wages, there's nothing for the court to attach for back child support. Meantime, Chris and Jared think he's the greatest thing going."

With a burst of diesel exhaust, the eighteen-wheeler ahead of us inched forward. I switched on the ignition in our Caprice and put it back in gear. "If you ask me," I told her, "calling the son of a bitch a worm is giving him way too much credit or being far too hard on worms, one or the other."

Sue looked across the seat and gave me a rueful smile. "Thanks, Beau," she said. "I'm glad I'm not the only one who thinks he's a creep."

"Hardly," I said. "Now, the best thing for you to do is to go to work and forget about him. Get out the map and figure out how to get where we're going."

Obligingly, Sue hauled out the *Thomas Guide*. She opened it and leafed through several pages before finally settling on one. "We're looking for Harrison. From this it looks like we turn off the freeway at the Highway 2 exit. The problem is, it's confusing. I can't tell from this map exactly how the freeway exit works there."

"At least these days there is a freeway," I told her. "Back when I was growing up, I-5 was little more than a gleam in the eye of a few far-thinking urban planners. In the fifties Highway 99 was the only way to get from Seattle to Everett—stop and go all the way."

"So what's changed?" she asked. "We're not setting what you'd call land-speed records here."

It was true. The ongoing traffic backup was bad enough that it took another twenty minutes to reach the Highway 2 exit which, it turned out, was the wrong way to go after all. Whoever designed that particular exit is probably the same genius who stuck the city of Seattle with another poor excuse for a freeway exit, a lingering traffic jam-generating jumble that's commonly referred to as the Mercer Mess.

Highway 2 was indeed the closest exit to Harrison Avenue, but you can't get there from there. Instead, we shot out across the Hewitt Avenue Trestle and had to work our way back from somewhere up by Lake Stevens. Our second pass took us back down I-5 with no way to get off until we were well past downtown Everett. The third time was the charm. We went as far north as Marine View Drive and worked our way back south from there.

The residential area east of I-5 in Everett seems isolated from the rest of the city. And it is. Lopped off from town by freeway on one side and river on the other, that isolation shows in some houses far more than in others. The address Sue read off was in the 2400 block of Harrison Avenue in a group of dingy houses situated on long narrow lots with backyards bordering on the freeway right of way.

Mildred and Andrew George's modest little bungalow was covered with puke-green siding that dated from that long-ago time when conventional wisdom still preached that asbestos was our friend. A few of the brittle fireproof, weatherproof shingles had broken off, showing the black layer of tar paper underneath. The asphalt shingles on the roof must not have fared much better since most of the roof was covered by a large blue tarp. On that sunny late-April day having a leaky roof maybe didn't matter so much, but I knew the rains would be back soon—rains and wind, too. When those came, the tarp wouldn't do diddly-squat to keep the water out.

In the unrelenting gloom of that derelict yard, the only antidote was a pair of magnificent rhododendrons standing on either side of the sagging front porch. Their leafy green branches ended in huge magenta blooms the size of dinner plates. Maybe the house and yard had been allowed to languish in neglect, but the rhodies didn't seem to mind.

I had barely stopped the car when an elderly man about the same age as Malcolm Lawrence appeared in the side yard, plodding slowly toward the front fence. Initially, I thought he was coming to the gate to greet us. Instead, he jerked to a sudden stop a few feet beyond a metal clothesline pole. He turned around. Then, without even glancing in our direction, he started back the way he had come.

"Look," Sue murmured. "That poor old man is tethered to a clothesline. I've never seen anything like it."

By the time we were out of the car and standing near the closed gate, he came by for another pass. That's when I saw Sue was right. A leather harness of some kind had been fitted across his chest. The back of it held a leashlike tether the other end of which was, in turn, fastened to the clothesline wire with a padlock.

"Excuse me," Sue called. "We're detectives with the Seattle Police Department. We're looking for Mr. George."

Without raising his head or giving even the slightest acknowledgment, the man reached the end of the leash, jerked to a stop, and reversed course once again, disappearing behind the house. Sue and I exchanged glances.

"Talk about unlawful imprisonment," I said. "What do you think a lawyer from the ACLU would make of that?"

Just then, the front door of the house burst open and a huge black woman flounced outside. "Who are you?" she demanded over the unrelenting roar of traffic that carried up the bluff from the freeway. With that kind of deafening and constant background noise, no wonder Harrison Avenue wasn't considered prime real estate.

"Why are you botherin' Mr. George?" she added.

"We wanted to talk to him," Sue returned, opening the gate and leading the way onto a moldy concrete sidewalk. "It's about his sister, Agnes Ferman."

The man I assumed to be Andrew George himself

appeared again, head still down. He showed no interest whatsoever in the presence of two strangers on his front walk. In fact, he never looked up from the well-worn path—a trench almost—that had been trampled into the unkempt grass under the clothesline. I wondered how many hours a day he paced back and forth like that, never stepping out of the lines of his worn dirt track, never venturing onto the too-long grass of the unmowed lawn.

"Mr. George already knows about his dead sister," the woman replied. "He knows and he don't know, if you get my meaning. He's been told but nothing much registers anymore. It won't do no good for you to try to speak to him about it, either. It might upset him. Besides, he don't talk much."

The woman stood on the porch, hands on her hips, determinedly barring our way. "If you want information," she continued, "I suggest you try talkin' to his missus, to Mildred. But she's not here."

"And where would we find her?" Sue asked. I was more than content to stay in the background and let Sue do the negotiating. If Andrew George's caretaker was less than friendly with my partner, I could well imagine the kind of reception I'd get.

"Work," the woman answered gruffly. "She don't get off until three. She's usually home by three-fifteen or so. Later if she has to stop for groceries."

By then Sue and I had both reached the far end of the sidewalk. As Sue stepped up onto the bottom step, Mr. George reappeared briefly at the side of the house then disappeared again. Seeing him plodding along like that got the better of my short-lived determination to keep quiet.

"How long does he do that?" I asked.

The woman shrugged. "An hour or two usually," the woman answered, "depending on the weather. The man used to love walking. Must've racked up ten miles or so every single day. Problem is, nowadays, he don't remember how to get himself back home, but he still wants to walk. Every day, rain or shine."

Sue held up her ID. "Is Mr. George suffering from Alzheimer's?" she asked.

The woman glanced briefly at the ID and then nodded. "That's what they call it—Alzheimer's. Mind's pretty much gone but he's healthy as a horse."

"And who are you?" Sue asked. "His nurse?"

"Me a nurse?" the woman asked. "Are you kidding?" Suddenly her broad face broke into a wide, toothy grin, then she laughed, a great honking bray of a laugh that shook her whole body. "Not me. Name's Grace Tipton. I'm a neighbor helping out. Live just over there."

She pointed across the street to another asbestos-shingled bungalow that looked like a near relation of the one belonging to the Georges. My guess was that most of the houses on the block had been built by the same builder in the late forties or early fifties. Grace Tipton's house was in somewhat better repair than Andrew and Mildred George's. It was better, but not by much.

"A real nurse do come in most mornings first thing. After the nurse leaves, either his sister looks out for him or I do. We keep an eye on him afternoons until Mildred comes home."

"Agnes Ferman used to come watch him?" Sue asked.

"Her?" Grace Tipton huffed. "Not likely. I'm talking about his other sister. From up in Marysville. If neither one of us can come, my nephew sometimes pitches in. Or somebody from church. We make sure he eats his lunch and then we hook him up to that harness so he can walk. I expect it's good for him."

Once again, Andrew George plodded into view, walked all the way to the end of the leash, then turned and went back the way he had come. I was close enough now so that I could see the harness was fastened with the same kind of padlock that kept the leash affixed to the clothesline wire.

"He doesn't mind being chained up like that?" I heard myself asking. "I mean, it doesn't bother him being treated like some kind of vicious dog?"

"Does he look like he minds it?" Grace Tipton demanded. "He don't seem the least bit unhappy to me. In fact, most of the time he's just like a little kid. Can't wait to finish his lunch and get his harness on so he can go outside. Afterwards he sleeps for an hour or two. What gets to him is *not* walking. That's when he gets cranky. He throws things, kicks at people, even tries to bite 'em sometimes. Most people would've put him in a home long ago, but Mildred's been holding on. It's a matter of money. Them retirement homes is really expensive. Mildred told me the only way she'd be able to afford one was to sell the house, except it didn't work. Asbestos, you know," she added. "The real estate lady told her it wasn't worth nothing. That anybody who bought it would just have to tear it down and the EPA wouldn't even let 'em haul the rubble to the dump. Cost of tearin' it down and hauling it away is more than it's worth. Only thing most of these places is good for is livin' in until they keel over and fall down. It worries Mildred, I can tell you that. All the worry the past year or so since Mr. George got so bad has aged her—aged her something fierce."

I looked at the dilapidated house. To someone living in that kind of poverty and disrepair, the possibility of receiving a sizable inheritance might have been tantalizing. Obviously Andrew George himself wasn't capable of any kind of independent action, but I wondered about his wife. If Mildred George had something to do with Agnes Ferman's death, it certainly wouldn't be the first time that a financially strapped heir had decided to hasten the arrival of a potential cash windfall.

"Has Mildred ever mentioned anything about Mr. George's sister having money?"

"Not Mildred," Grace Tipton said. "But Hilda certainly did."

"Hilda Smathers?" Sue asked. "Mr. George's sister?"

Grace nodded. "That's right, his baby sister. She's all the time hinting around that her sister Agnes has a whole bunch of money stowed away somewhere, but I don't pay no mind. Figure it's just so much idle gossip. After all, from what I understand, the woman worked as a maid all her life. Domestic service ain't usually the kind of career that allows people to lay by a fortune for their old age, if you know what I mean."

I was tempted to tell her that three hundred thou in Agnes Ferman's garage refrigerator was there to prove her wrong, but I didn't. Instead, I glanced over at Andrew George who happened to reappear just then. I wondered if a man who had to be tethered to a clothesline to keep from being lost was capable of handling even the smallest amounts of money.

Grace Tipton must have read my mind. "Mildred got a lawyer to draw up something. I forget what it's called. Means she can handle Mr. George's affairs . . ."

"You mean a power of attorney?" Sue suggested.

Grace brightened. "That's right. Power of attorney. Since Mildred has that, if there is any money, she can spend it however she likes. I for one hope it's true, that there is some. Money, that is. Enough for her to put Mr. George in a home someplace. Maybe even enough beyond that to fix this place up so it'll be nice to live in. Mildred's a practical woman. I wouldn't look for her to go runnin' off on one of them round-the-world cruises, but it sure would be nice if she didn't have to work and worry quite so hard."

"What does she do?"

"Manages a truck-rental office right down the street. Olson's it's called. Mildred never used to have to work outside the home, not until two years ago when things got so bad they had to move in here. As soon as she got Mr. George settled in, she went right out and found herself a job. She's been there ever since."

"They haven't always lived here then?"

Grace shook her head. "Good heavens, no. They started out here, years ago, long before I moved in, as a matter of fact. After their son came along, they moved up to a larger house over near the hospital and kept this one as a rental. It's a good thing, too. When they lost the other house, they still had this one to move into as a back up. It may not look like much, but leaky or not, leastways it's a roof over their heads."

Sue and I exchanged glances. Serious illness aside, it sounded as though the Georges had been through some kind of serious financial wringer. After a life of relative prosperity, those kinds of financial reversals and straitened circumstances might make the possibility of an early inheritance that much more tempting.

"Where did you say we'd find Mildred George?" I asked.

"Olson's Truck Rental," Grace replied. "It's just down at the bottom of the hill here on Summit. It's close enough to be a nice walk in good weather, although, there were times last winter when Mildred had to walk because the Buick didn't start. One day it was so snowy and slippery getting down the hill that I was afraid she was going to break her neck. Think you can find it okay?"

"You say it's on Summit?" Sue asked.

Grace nodded.

"I'm sure we can find it then," Sue told her.

"If you like, I can call ahead," Grace offered. "That way Mildred will know you're coming."

"Don't bother," Sue said.

She made it sound casual enough, but we both knew it wasn't. If there was even the slightest possibility that Mildred George had something to do with her sister-in-law's death, then it would be far better for us to show up unannounced and unexpected. That way there was a better chance of our catching her with her defenses down.

Those preliminary surprise visits with possible suspects—ones with no Miranda warning anywhere within hearing distance—may not hold up in court, but that doesn't mean they're not useful. They don't always point us in the right direction, but often enough, they give us a place to start.

As we headed back down the walkway, Andrew George reappeared around the corner of the house once again.

"Seeing that happen to the person you love must be hell," Sue said to me, nodding in his direction. "Which is worse—losing your mind like Andrew George there or losing the use of your body like Marcia Powell?"

I stopped and stood beside the car long enough to watch the man disappear once more behind the side of his house.

"Excuse me," I told her. "But if I had my druthers, I'd rather not lose either one."

CHAPTER 4

IT TOOK TWO PASSES TO FIND OLSON'S TRUCK RENTAL. Our search was complicated by a maze of one-way streets that wound in and out under a series of raised trestles. The process was made more difficult by the fact that Everett's Summit Avenue was somehow missing from our map book. When we finally arrived at the correct storefront in a mostly industrial area, we found the front door securely locked. A cardboard sign hanging in the window, complete with a clock face, told us they would reopen at one.

I didn't feel particularly hungry right then, but I was more than ready for a break. One of the hazards of working with Detective Danielson has to do with her cast-iron bladder. She's capable of going for hours on end without making a pitstop. In that regard the woman has me totally outclassed.

"Looks like it's time for lunch," I said casually. "There must be someplace to eat around here. I didn't see anything promising while we were driving around, did you?"

"Not right here," Sue agreed, consulting the map once more. "But Alligator Soul isn't far."

"Alligator what?"

"Soul," she replied. "It's a Cajun place. I ate there once before a Preservation Hall concert. Just go straight up Hewitt," she added, pointing. "Now that I finally have my bearings, I know it isn't far from here."

My mother's training kicked in. I did as I was told.

Everett started out over a hundred years ago as a booming sawmill town. The lumber and mills are pretty much gone, leaving an economic gap that's been partially filled in recent years by the arrival of a Navy home port. In the downtown area, low-rise brick construction harkens back to an earlier era. People who live and/or work in Seattle proper assume we exist in a kind of cultural mecca. It disturbed my proud Denny-Regrade neighborhood sensibilities to learn that Everett, a place we regard as little more than a lowly exurb, had constructed something that sounded suspiciously like a concert hall.

"Preservation Hall," I muttered disparagingly. "Never heard of it. Where is it and how did Everett come up with the money to build something like that?"

Sue Danielson sighed. "Preservation Hall, Beau. It's a band, not a building. As in the French Quarter. As in New Orleans-style jazz. They were here for a concert. What kind of a rock have you been living under?"

"I've just never cared for jazz all that much," I

returned. It was the best I could manage with a size-twelve foot stuck firmly in my mouth.

I was still licking my culturally deprived wounds when we pulled up in front of the green awning of the Alligator Soul a few minutes later. We parked in an open space on a street without a single parking meter anywhere in sight—something else that sets Everett apart from downtown Seattle. Inside the restaurant, the young hostess gave us a choice of smoking or nonsmoking. Sue opted for the former. By the time we reached our booth at the back of the long narrow room, she had cigarettes out of her purse and was already lighting up.

Before sliding into the booth, I made a quick dash to the men's room. On the way I noticed that the long, narrow restaurant was clearly an old, rehabbed bar. The major decorating motif—from tablecloths to posters on the wall—was chilies of one kind or another. Bottles of chili sauce lined what was left of a carved oak bar. I couldn't tell from looking at them if they were there for sale or decoration or if they were simply optional condiments to be added to individual servings the way ordinary people might pile on needless salt and pepper.

Back in the booth, Sue and I ordered lunch. While waiting for our food, I wanted to discuss the case, but Sue, staring off into space through an isolating haze of cigarette smoke, still seemed disinclined to talk. I contented myself with watching the goings-on in the kitchen while she puffed through one cigarette and then another. The chef was a butt-sprung disreputable-looking wreck of a guy with a stubbly growth of beard and a silver front tooth. He looked like an old salt to me, a guy likely to have a ship sailing the briny sea tattooed on his chest. I wondered if he hadn't blown into town right along with other folks from the home port.

It soon became apparent why the smoking section was located next to the kitchen. That was where the help—from chef to dishwasher—came on their breaks to grab a smoke right along with the customers.

The food when it arrived at the booth—Sue's red beans and rice and my barbecued ribs—was amazingly good. Hot and spicy, from the jalapeño-laced corn salad to the mouth-and-eye-watering, sauce-slathered ribs themselves. Suddenly famished, I mowed into my lunch without noticing Sue was barely touching hers. I was busily mopping barbecue sauce off my fingers and face when I realized she had pushed her still-full dish to one side and was smoking once again.

"What's the matter with your food?" I asked. "Don't you like it?"

"He kicked me," she said.

Two booths away a little kid in a high chair set up an ear-splitting howl making it almost impossible to hear.

"He who?" I asked, feeling as though I had somehow blundered into a conversation that was already in progress.

"Richie," she answered in a barely audible whisper. Fortunately, someone stifled the noisy kid enough so I could make out what she was saying. "I was pregnant with Chris at the time. Richie kicked me in the stomach so hard that my water broke. I was only seven months along. We almost didn't make it, Chris and I. For years I was petrified that he'd suffered some kind of long-term damage—that he'd be retarded or something. But he isn't. He's fine."

She finished in an offhand kind of way, ducking her head to grind the stub of her latest cigarette into the ashtray. She turned away, but not before I caught a glimpse of tears in her eyes. Detective Danielson is tough. We've done horrendous crime scenes together without her ever turning a hair. Six months into our partnership, tears were something new.

"Chris may be fine," I said. "But you're not. What's going on?"

"I don't know." She shook her head. "It's like living through a flashback. Maybe it's that handy old fall guy, post-traumatic stress syndrome, but just the idea of him being back in town is driving me crazy. I barely slept last night. That's probably what's really wrong with me," she added sheepishly, "lack of sleep."

I suspected the problem went deeper than missing a few zzzs. It also explained why she'd never talked much about either her marriage or divorce. "Is that why you split?" I asked. "Because he beat you up?"

She nodded. "He had threatened me before, but that was the first time he ever turned really violent. I underwent an emergency cesarean and was in the hospital for three days. That gave me plenty of time to think. I wondered if he'd do that to me—if he'd endanger our unborn baby's life like that—what might he do to Jared. Back then I was already working as a dispatcher at the Com Center. When

I was on days, Jared went to day care, but when I pulled night shift, Jared and Richie were home alone. There in the hospital room I knew I couldn't risk doing that any more—I couldn't leave either one of the kids alone with their father. That's when I filed for a divorce. It took two years for it to be final."

Sue paused and seemed to be waiting for me to say something. "I didn't know any of this," I said at last. "You never mentioned it."

She shrugged. "I was embarrassed, I guess. It's just that Richie can be so damned charming when he wants to be—at least with outsiders. He was charming with me, too, in the beginning—just as long as he had his own way. I guess I didn't want anyone to know that I had chosen so . . . well, so badly," she finished lamely. "I thought I was smarter than that."

The waitress came to clear our places. "Was something wrong with the red beans and rice?" she asked, frowning as she picked up Sue's still-heaping plate.

"No," Sue returned. "It was fine, really. I just wasn't as hungry as I thought I was."

"Would you like to take it home?"

"I don't think so . . ."

"What about the boys?" I interrupted. "Wouldn't one of them like it? I've never met a teenaged boy who didn't have at least one hollow leg."

Smiling halfheartedly, Sue nodded at the waitress. "Okay," she said. "You win. I'll take it with me."

The waitress disappeared. I turned back to Sue. "Is that what's worrying you now?" I asked. "Are you afraid that Richie might turn violent with the boys while they're on this trip to California?"

Her face paled. "I've been so pissed at the whole idea that I didn't even think about the possibility— until just now, although God knows I should have. He's a big guy, Beau. Six five. Two hundred and sixty pounds the last I saw him. It's my job to protect the kids. If he were to hurt one of them, I'd never forgive myself."

Why is it people fall for the wrong person? Then, when the inevitable happens, they spend the rest of their lives trying to get over it. That's what happened to me with Anne Corley, and this was much the same. Sue Danielson had never forgiven herself for that long-ago kick to the belly that had catapulted Christopher Danielson into the world some two months prior to his due date.

"What would you do if you were in my shoes, Beau?" Sue was asking earnestly. "Would you let the boys go with him or not?"

Having been a fatherless boy myself, I knew this territory painfully well—from the inside out. I knew how much it would have meant for me to have had the chance to spend some time with my own father just once in my life. A three-day trip to Disneyland would have been a gift beyond compare. Unfortunately, my father died long before I was even born. But I could also see the situation from Sue's point of view. Why should she let the boys go off on a trip with a worthless yahoo who didn't pay child support and who might very well turn violent if things didn't go just right? On the other hand, if she kept the boys home and Richie had somehow come to his senses in the meantime, she might very well be denying her sons their one chance of ever having any kind of workable relationship with their father.

"Did Jared witness that first beating?" I asked. Despite the fact that the truth had to be otherwise, I allowed Sue her pride-saving pretense that there had been only one serious episode of violence in her relationship with her former husband.

Blood rushed back to her pale cheeks. "Yes," she managed.

"Does he remember it?"

"I don't know. I've never asked him."

"He's what—thirteen?"

"Fourteen," Sue answered. "Just turned. His birthday was last week."

"And Chris?"

"Eight. He'll be nine in May."

"And you moved out of the house right after Chris was born?"

Sue nodded. "When we left the hospital, I only went home long enough to pack up and leave. I took the kids and went straight from the hospital right into a temporary shelter."

In the time Sue Danielson and I had worked together, I'd never had any quarrel with her courage under fire. I realized now, however, that nothing the street had required of her could have demanded any more raw courage than leaving a marriage with two children—a six-year-old and a newborn—especially considering Sue's parents and the rest of her family were almost a continent away from Seattle in Ohio.

"That must be about the same time you left the Communications Center," I observed.

Sue nodded. "A representative from the EEOC came through the department and told the brass that they needed more female trainees. A recruiter from Seattle PD came to the Com Center and talked to us about the idea of an upgrade and transfer. I didn't see myself as a women's libber, but I figured if I was going to be raising a family on my own, I needed to be earning a man's wages. I jumped at the chance."

The waitress dropped off our check. It would have been easy for me to pay for lunch each time, but Sue Danielson's pride demanded that she pay her own way. That meant today's meal was on her. I made no objection as she brought a much-folded twenty out of her purse and laid the money on top of the bill.

"You still haven't answered my question," she said, once we were back in the Caprice with the engine running.

"I know," I said. "I'm thinking. Before you let the boys go, talk to Jared. Ask him straight out if he remembers any of what went on between you and Richie before you divorced. He may remember or he may not. Regardless, go ahead and tell him what happened. Don't make a big deal of it. Just be matter of fact. That way he'll be prepared."

"But . . ." Sue objected.

"No, wait. Let me finish. If he does remember, he may have put a little kid spin on it that has absolutely nothing to do with reality. And if he doesn't remember, he needs to be warned. Tell him that time has passed and you're hoping Richie has grown up. But if he hasn't, and the kids do go on the trip, Jared may have to be the one who's a grownup. He'll need to know how to call for help if he needs to."

"But how . . . ?"

"Before the kids leave town, go by one of those cellular telephone places. Get one of those little 'go phones' so he can call you or 911 if there's any kind of a problem. You don't have to say it's because his dad might beat the crap out of him and his brother. Tell him it's for him to use to call you if there's some kind of emergency."

"What if there is no emergency?" Sue asked. "What if Jared uses the phone to run up a big bill talking to one of his buddies?"

"That's simple," I told her. "Tell Jared that if he does that, he won't have to worry about his dad beating him up because you'll kill him."

Sue laughed then, and so did I. "Sounds like good advice," she said. "So how about getting our minds back on the job and going to see Mildred George?"

"How about it," I agreed. "Sounds like a good idea to me."

When we pulled up again at Olson's Truck Rental there were two vehicles parked out front. One was a beat-up old pickup with an inch-thick layer of dried muck on it. The other was a ten-year-old Buick station wagon, one of the old-fashioned woody variety. Years of sitting outside had caused paint to flake and peel, including the paint on the fake-wood panels.

Unlatching the now-unlocked front door, I held it open long enough for Sue to step inside the storefront office. At a chest-high counter just inside the door stood an immense man. He wore a fleece-lined jacket over frayed Levi's and mud-spattered boots. Frowning with concentration, he was painstakingly filling in the blanks on a rental form. On the other side of the linoleum-topped counter stood a woman I assumed to be Mildred George. She was tall and angular with iron-gray hair cut in what we used to call a bob. She wore one of those short, wool jacket/sweaters that would have been more at home in a country-club setting than in that run-down, dingy office.

From what Sue had told me, I knew Andrew George was Agnes Ferman's older brother. Agnes herself had been sixty-seven when she died. The brief glimpses I had caught of Andrew placed his age at anywhere from seventy-five to eighty. The poised, well-manicured woman behind the counter, however, looked to be a good deal younger than that— mid- to late-fifties, tops.

She waved to acknowledge our arrival without losing the beat of her telephone conversation. "We've been over this before, Mr. Tully," she explained patiently. "Your son-in-law is not allowed to drive any of our vehicles—not even in an emergency. He's an unapproved driver, Mr. Tully. If Rob does use one of our trucks and has any kind of accident, the insurance is null and void and you're liable. Period."

There was a pause. The woman held the phone away from her ear while Mr. Tully gave vent to a series of explosive-sounding comments.

"I know it's a busy time of year for your nursery

business, Mr. Tully," she said reasonably, once the tirade was finished. "It's busy for us, too. But Rob already had that one accident. And, as you know, he has two other tickets besides."

There was another pause. "In that case," she said. "I suggest you have one of your other employees do the driving."

Another angry outburst blew through the phone line. It was loud enough for Sue and me to hear Mr. Tully sputtering although neither of us could make out any of the individual words.

"Of course I understand that based on this you may have to take your business elsewhere. If that's the case, we'll certainly be sorry to lose you . . ."

Mildred stopped talking in midsentence. A buzzing dial tone told everyone in the office that Mr. Tully had slammed down the receiver on his end. She put the phone down and calmly collected the paperwork the other customer had pushed across the counter in her direction. Meanwhile she smiled up at the behemoth of a man standing before her. She seemed totally unruffled by his size, his mane of wildly unruly red hair, his tattered red flannel shirt, or his several missing teeth.

"How long do you think you'll be needing the truck, Mr. Parker?" she asked politely.

"A week or so," he said. "Two at the outside, but I'll have to let you know when we get a little closer to the end of the job."

Mildred George and Mr. Parker set about finalizing the deal. Minutes later, Mr. Parker stuffed a wad of rental-agreement paperwork and a set of car keys into his pocket. "I'll be back for the truck in about an hour," he said. "Soon as I get this one home and get my wife to drive me back."

"That'll be fine," Mildred George said with a gracious smile. "You know which truck is yours. You're welcome to come pick it up from the lot whenever it's convenient. As long as you have both the key and the rental agreement, you can do that even if the office is closed."

"Thank you, ma'am," he said. "You've been a big help."

As the door closed on the departing Mr. Parker, a poised and businesslike Mildred George turned to face us. "Good afternoon," she said. "You must be the two detectives Grace Tipton called to tell me about earlier. What can I do for you?"

So much for our making an unannounced visit. "We're sorry about your sister-in-law," I said, pulling out my ID and handing it across the counter. "We're looking for information that might help lead us to the person or persons responsible. Anything you could tell us about her friends, associates, or business dealings would be most helpful."

Mildred George examined my ID carefully before handing it back. "I'm afraid I can't help you there," Mildred said. "When it comes to Agnes, I don't know very much. We were notified of her death, of course, by the medical examiner. And since you're here, I'm assuming that her death is now being treated as a homicide, but beyond that, I don't know anything that would be of use."

"I take it you weren't close?"

Mildred George laughed outright. "You could say that."

"Estranged then?"

Mildred George smiled a sad smile that didn't extend all the way to her eyes. "No," she said. "Estranged presupposes there was some closeness to begin with. In the case of Agnes Ferman and me, there was never any love lost."

"When's the last time you saw her?"

"Christmas," Mildred said. "We had dinner Christmas Eve at Hilda's house up in Marysville. Hilda is Andy's sister—his younger sister. She's also the family's self-appointed peace broker. I think she thought that if she put Andy and Agnes together in the same room, they'd end up burying the hatchet. That didn't happen, though. Hilda waited too long. Andy seems to recognize Hilda, but then he sees her several times a week. Before that Christmas dinner, the last time he saw Agnes was years ago at Lyle Ferman's funeral. Since then, he's slipped so badly that I don't think he had any idea who she was. Since he didn't remember her, he could hardly be expected to remember what it was they had quarreled about all those years ago."

"Maybe your husband doesn't remember what the quarrel was all about," Sue suggested quietly. "But do you?"

Mildred appeared to study Sue for some time before she answered. "They quarreled over me," she said at last.

"Over you?"

"My sister-in-law didn't approve of me," Mildred said quietly. "She was a good friend of Andy's first wife. Agnes and Betty went all through school together. Agnes has always regarded me as a home wrecker, even though Andy and Betty's home was wrecked long before I appeared on the scene."

"When was that?" I asked.

"Thirty-five years ago."

"That's a long time to pack a grudge," I suggested.

Mildred raised one artfully arched eyebrow. "When it came to grudges," she said, "Agnes was an expert."

"I see," I said, wanting to follow that thread all the way to the end. "Can we assume then, if things have been that rocky between you and Agnes all these years, that you're not particularly broken up that she's dead?"

Mildred George shook her head. "No," she agreed. "It would be downright hypocritical to pretend otherwise. I'm not sorry at all."

"So where were you last Monday night?" Sue asked.

"I was home," Mildred said at once. "Home with my husband."

"Will your husband be willing to verify that?"

"Don't be ridiculous," she said. "Grace told me you were at the house this morning. You've seen Andy. His condition makes it so he barely recognizes me from day to day. He has no sense at all for the passage of time."

"There's no one else who would know whether or not you were home all night?" Sue asked.

Mildred George shook her head. "I doubt it," she said. "You'll just have to take my word for it. Andy and I were home alone. After he went to bed, I watched television for a little while, then I read a book."

"What did you watch on TV?"

"Poirot," Mildred answered. "*Law and Order* and Miss Marple."

"So you're interested in mysteries. According to one of Agnes Ferman's neighbors there at Bitter Lake, she liked mysteries, too."

"Is that so?" Mildred replied. "Well, you certainly couldn't prove it by me, but if it *is* true, I'd say that's one of the few things Agnes and I had in common."

CHAPTER 5

Just then a blue Saab pulled up out front. A beefy, middle-aged guy who looked like he belonged on the pro-bowling circuit got out of the vehicle then turned back to retrieve both a hound's-tooth sports jacket and a battered briefcase. He lumbered inside, carrying the jacket and briefcase in one hand while he yanked loose his red-and-blue-striped necktie with the other. Nodding as he passed, he slipped behind the counter. He disappeared momentarily into a small, cluttered office. After depositing the briefcase on the front corner of a desk, he re-emerged.

"So what's happening?" He asked the question of Mildred while his eyes remained trained on Sue and me.

"These are police detectives," Mildred explained. "From Seattle. They're here to talk to me about Andy's sister's death. They wanted to know what I was doing last Monday night."

"What you were doing?" the man repeated. "You

mean they're accusing you of having something to do with that fire business? Call an attorney, Millie. Get hold of Jack Hornsby right away. Tell him I told you to call. Let him know he should get his butt over here ASAP."

"Please, Lonnie," Mildred said. "It's nothing to get so wound up about. And I'm not calling Jack. I don't mind talking with these officers. I've nothing to hide. I already told them I was home with Andy all night long. Unfortunately, there's no way to prove it."

Mildred hadn't bothered to introduce us. However, the proprietary way in which "Lonnie" pushed his wide girth around the place implied ownership—that and a certain amount of arrogant self-importance, as well.

"You're sure?" he demanded of Mildred.

"Yes," she said. "I'm sure."

Lonnie came back over to the counter then, pulling his pants up under the shelf of his generous belly. "It's ridiculous," he said, scowling balefully at Sue and me. "I can't imagine that you're seriously considering the idea that Mildred might have had anything whatsoever to do with what happened."

He looked for the world like a man who was spoiling for a fight. Fortunately for all concerned, Sue defused the situation by stepping up to the counter with her hand extended. "I'm Detective Danielson," she said. "And this is my partner, Detective Beaumont. I don't believe I caught your name."

The man waffled for a moment then took her proffered hand. "I'm Lonnie Olson," he said, losing the scowl. "Glad to meetcha. I'm the owner here. I know you guys are just doing your jobs, but I got to say that thinking Millie could be involved in a murder is about the dumbest thing I've ever heard. She wouldn't hurt a fly. Not only that, she's a valued employee around here. A trusted employee. How you can walk around accusing . . ."

"Mr. Olson," Sue interrupted. "We're not necessarily making accusations, but we are required to ask questions of everyone concerned with the case. And, if at all possible, we're expected to establish readily verifiable alibis from those same people. That's especially true of individuals who may stand to benefit as a result of the victim's death."

"What makes you think Millie stands to benefit from her sister-in-law's death? Millie and Agnes Ferman barely spoke."

It struck me as odd that Lonnie Olson was taking such an interest in every nuance of what was said. He seemed to be displaying far more than a concerned employer's level of interest in what was going on. I was about to tell him our questions addressed to Mildred were none of his business when the telephone did it for me.

"I'll take that call, Millie," he said. "But don't let these cops push you around. If they get out of line, you call Jack, okay?"

Mildred George nodded. "I will," she said. Then she turned back to us. "Tell me, Detective Danielson, how exactly is it that I stand to benefit from my sister-in-law's death?"

"Are you aware that our investigation has turned up a substantial amount of cash on Agnes Ferman's property?" Sue asked.

"Cash?" Mildred repeated. "You mean as in money?"

Sue nodded. "Quite a bit of it, actually. Over three-hundred-thousand dollars' worth. Hidden outside the house. It was concealed in an old refrigerator in her garage."

For the first time, Mildred George looked stunned. "Three hundred thousand dollars," she repeated. "That much?"

"So you knew she had money?" Sue pressed.

"I knew Agnes *claimed* to have money. At least that's what she told Hilda over the years, but I never really believed it. Where would that kind of money have come from? How did she get it?"

"That's what we're trying to find out," Sue explained. "We were hoping you'd be able to help us out."

Mildred shook her head. "I have no idea," she said. "None at all."

"Did your sister-in-law have a personal attorney?"

"A what? You mean a lawyer? I wouldn't know that, either. We weren't exactly on information-sharing terms. Why do you want to know?"

"As I told you, we've located the money," Sue explained, "but so far we haven't been able to find any kind of will. That means we have no idea how she intended to distribute the funds. In addition, the Internal Revenue Service will probably have to ascertain whether or not taxes have been paid before the money can be released to any possible heirs. That being the case, we'll need to locate her accountant, if any, as well."

"Well," Mildred said. "I know nothing about her

accounting situation, but as soon as you do find a will, that will certainly settle things. No matter how much money Agnes Ferman had, I can't imagine that she would have left Andy and me one thin dime."

"She might have done so inadvertently," Sue suggested.

"How's that?"

"In the absence of a properly executed will, the state dictates how property is divided. Generally speaking, that means the estate is divided among the next of kin. Agnes has no living children or grandchildren, correct?"

"That's true. She and Lyle never had any children. Agnes was far too busy taking care of other people's children to be bothered with raising any of her own. That was hard on Lyle. I think he really would have liked having a son."

"As I understand it, her brother—your husband—and his sister—Hilda Smathers—are Agnes Ferman's only surviving relatives?"

Mildred nodded. "That's true. Other than our son and Hilda's two daughters, that's it."

"So," Sue continued, "in view of the fact that you have your husband's power of attorney, you would no doubt benefit as a result of having any of Agnes' money flow to your husband. Unfortunately, Mrs. George, that translates into possible motive. Now is there anyone at all—some neighbor perhaps—who would be able to say that you were home that night? Someone who might have seen your car parked out front all night long?"

Mildred sighed. "No matter what I say, you're still going to think I did it. So I could just as well go ahead and tell you the whole ugly story right from the beginning so you don't have to find out about it on your own. Andy and I met while he happened to be married to someone else. He was a social studies teacher and the head football coach at Everett High School. When I did my student teaching, he was my cooperating teacher, as we used to call them in those days."

Lonnie Olson was still standing at the far end of the counter. All the while Sue had been talking to Mildred George, I had been listening to them with one ear while also attempting to be aware of what was going on with Olson's telephone conversation. As far as I could make out, the negotiations that rumbled back and forth had something to do with someone wanting several trucks to use to haul green peas back and forth to the processing plant when it came time for the harvest in June. When the call finally ended, Lonnie stood at the far end of the counter and stared at Mildred George, hanging on her every word.

Seemingly unaware of her boss's riveted interest, Mildred George continued with her story. "Andy and Betty—his first wife—had been married for fifteen years when I showed up on the scene. If everything had been perfect between them, maybe what happened never would have happened. Betty was a drinker, you see—a closet drinker. Andy would come home from school and find her passed out in bed. For years he did the usual things. He covered for her and made excuses. He was so wildly successful at it—so thorough at keeping a lid on things—that I don't believe anyone here in town ever guessed the truth of it. And that's how things stood when I came along.

"Andy was thirty-five when we met. I was twenty-two. It was love at first sight for both of us. There are a lot of people who don't believe in that kind of thing, but within days of our first meeting, we knew we wanted to spend the rest of our lives together. And we have. Three weeks into the semester, Andy moved out of the house and filed for a divorce. Everything might have been fine, but one night late someone saw me leaving his apartment. Whoever it was—we never found out for sure who it was although I have my suspicions—called Betty, my supervising teacher at the University of Washington, and the president of the Everett school board. Overnight everything blew sky-high. My whole world fell apart, and so did Andy's.

"I never taught a day of school in my life after that. When it comes to being hired, an F in student teaching is a pretty stiff obstacle to overcome. Things weren't easy for Andy, either. Even though he had tenure, he was forced out of the district. He managed to land a job selling athletic equipment. That's what he was doing when we got married. From there he went on to start his own athletic store out on Evergreen Way. He ran that until three years ago when we lost it."

"Lost it?" Sue asked.

Mildred nodded. "Several things hit all at once. For one thing, the margins were getting smaller and smaller all the time. Not only that, the cash flow shrank dramatically. Andy didn't really tell me what was going on. In fact, I see now that he must not have realized what was going on himself. He was already starting to get sick back then, only I didn't know it. He compensated enough that I didn't see what was happening until it was too late. Had Andy been himself, I'm sure things wouldn't have gotten so far out of hand. Little problems would have been handled in a timely fashion and they wouldn't have turned into disasters. As it was, those little problems snowballed into big ones. Then, of course, there was Colin."

"Colin?" I asked. "Who's he?"

Wincing visibly, Mildred paused long enough to wet her lips. "Our son," she said softly. "From the time he was in high school, Colin worked with Andy in the business. We expected to turn it over to him eventually. Four years ago, Andy made Colin comptroller of the company, put him in charge of finances. What no one knew at the time was that Colin had a cocaine problem. Before we caught up with him, he had managed to siphon hundreds of thousands of dollars out of the business and put it up his nose. By the time I realized what was happening, it was too late. Bankruptcy court was our only option. We came out of the proceedings with little more than the clothes on our backs, the house on Harrison, and that eleven-year-old Buick station wagon you see parked right out front."

"What about Colin?" I asked.

Mildred George took a deep breath. "He's in federal prison," she said. "Down in Oregon. Income-tax-evasion charges and drug charges both. That's something else Colin did for us. For the better part of three years he didn't pay any payroll or income taxes. That's why I'm working—to pay off Uncle Sam. Back taxes don't go away in bankruptcy proceedings, by the way. I'm whittling them down a little at a time. If I keep on working, the bill should be paid in full by the end of five years.

"That's why I'm so lucky to have this job," she added with a gesture that encompassed the whole office. "Even though I had never worked outside the home, Mr. Olson here was kind enough to take me on. He gave me both the job and the training to do it. Not only that, the office is close enough to home that I can be there within minutes if something goes wrong with Andy."

"Getting back to Agnes," Sue said. "I still don't understand why she objected so strenuously to your marrying her brother."

"As I told you, Agnes was good friends with Betty. With Andy's first wife. The two of them grew up together. They were friends all through grade school and high school. Agnes was even maid of honor at Betty and Andy's wedding. So it wasn't just the fact that I married Andy and took him away from her friend. It also had a lot to do with what happened to Betty afterward."

"What did happen to her?"

"Two weeks after the divorce was final, two weeks after Andy and I got married, Betty left a bar here in downtown Everett right at closing time. She must have been blind drunk at the time because she walked straight into traffic. An oncoming cab was the first vehicle that hit her. The cab knocked her into the path of a bread delivery truck. She died at the scene. Her blood-alcohol level was something like .35."

"So Agnes was mad at you from then on."

"No," Mildred said. "I think she was mad at me long before that. She disliked me from the moment she knew I existed. It was easier for Agnes to hold Andy and me totally responsible rather than having to accept the idea that Betty, too, was partially at fault for what happened."

I had seen the slight grimace that had crossed Mildred's face earlier when Sue mentioned the fact that the IRS would be wanting to know whether or not taxes had been paid on Agnes Ferman's money. Now I knew why. Agnes wasn't the only one in the family with a federal income tax problem.

"How much money do you and your husband owe in back taxes, Mrs. George?" I asked from the sidelines.

"Really," Lonnie Olson objected, lumbering back down the counter. "That's about enough. I don't see that Mildred's dealings with the IRS are any of your business."

Mildred answered anyway. "Seventy thousand dollars," she said. "Right around that anyway."

"And how much is your new roof going to cost?"

"Don't worry about the roof," Olson interrupted. "You can cross that idea right off your list of possible motivations. I've already taken care of it—the roof, that is. When it started leaking after that big storm last week, I told Millie right then that I'd handle it. One of my friends—someone I've done favors for over the years—is a roofing contractor here in town. I'll pay for the work. Millie can pay me back whenever she's able."

"That's certainly generous of you, Mr. Olson, but if you don't mind, I was addressing my question to Mrs. George."

"It's all right, Lonnie," she said. "I don't mind answering. I assure you, Detective Beaumont, I didn't murder Agnes Ferman in hopes of getting my roof fixed. And I didn't murder her in hopes of paying off my debt to the IRS, either. I didn't murder her at all."

"What about Hilda?" Sue asked quietly.

"What about her?"

"What's her financial situation?"

"She's had her ups and downs," Mildred answered. "Andy and I have helped her from time to time, but then so did Agnes and Lyle. Things were really tough for her and the girls right after the divorce. In fact they lived with Andy and me for a while back then. Of course, that was in our old house where we had lots more room than we have now."

"I believe you called Hilda a peace broker a while ago," Sue said. "Does that mean she managed to stay on friendly terms with both you and Agnes?"

"Hilda is Agnes and Andy's half sister. They all have the same mother, but Hilda had a different father. Hilda was much younger than either Andy or Agnes. In fact, she's a good deal closer to me in age than she is to either of them. Her father died in a logging-truck accident when she was in fifth grade and her mother died a few years after that. Hilda lived with Betty and Andy for a time while she was in high school, so she knew more about Betty's drinking problem and what else went on than anyone other than Andy. So the answer to your question is yes. She stayed on friendly terms with both Agnes and me. And let me tell you, this last year or so, I don't know what I would have done without her. She's been a huge help with Andy. She comes by and looks after him several afternoons a week."

"What about today?"

Mildred shook her head. "Monday's her day off from work and from Andy. She saves that to do laundry and catch up on things around her own house."

"Which is where?"

"Just north of Marysville and east of Highway 99. It's a trailer park called Green Mountain Vista Estates."

The phone rang. Lonnie Olson had no sooner picked up one line than the other one rang. Mildred answered that one. Sue turned to me. "What do you think?"

"I say let's go talk to the sister. With Olson here bird-dogging us, we're not getting very far."

As soon as Mildred was off the phone, Sue asked her for directions to Hilda's house. "And in case we miss her today, where does she work?"

"In the bakery at the Smoky Point Safeway. She starts at five every morning and gets off at one, except for Monday. Tuesdays she usually spends with Andy, so if you don't catch up with her today, she should be at our house most of the day tomorrow."

We left while Lonnie Olson was still talking on the phone. "What do you think?" I asked once we were outside.

Sue rolled her eyes. "I don't believe for a minute

that Lonnie Olson has made arrangements to have Mildred's roof fixed because he likes the way she writes up rental agreements."

"You don't think so?" I asked innocently. I had come to much the same conclusion, but I was curious about Sue's rationale. "Why not?"

"I saw the look she gave him when he first walked into the office. If that was platonic, I'll eat my badge. Not only that, what she said to him about us laid it all out in a nutshell. She wanted to let him know exactly what was going on so he wouldn't say the wrong thing or make some kind of blunder. For all those phone calls, I don't think he missed a word of what we said to her."

I nodded in agreement. "Not only that, I can't imagine that a simple employer/employee relationship would merit Olson's being willing to call his own personal attorney to come riding to the rescue. Based on all that, do you think she's lying about being home all Monday night?"

"Maybe," Sue said. "And if Olson is that eager to leap to Mildred's defense, maybe he's in on it with her."

Without saying anything more, we climbed back into the Caprice. As we backed out of our parking place, the license plate on Lonnie Olson's Saab was fully visible. "How about jotting it down?" I asked. "While you're at it, take down the number on Mildred's Buick, too. Just for argument's sake. Maybe we'll get lucky and someone will have spotted one or the other of those two vehicles in Agnes Ferman's neighborhood Monday night or Tuesday morning."

Sue did as I suggested. "Where to now?" she

asked, closing her notebook and sticking it back in her pocket.

"Green Mountain Vista Estates."

"It sounds very upscale."

"Don't worry," I told her. "Most of the time the more pretentious the name, the less impressive the community."

Following Mildred's directions we drove straight there. People who live in downtown Seattle tend to be a bit parochial in their attitudes toward places beyond the narrow confines of the city limits. Suburbs of any kind are frowned on. In the case of Green Mountain Vista Estates, however, those antisuburban prejudices were right on the money.

Green Mountain Vista—with nary a mountain in sight—was stuck down in a hollow that had probably been a wetland once—a wetland in the middle of someone's farm. This wasn't one of those new affordable-housing modular places where they truck in houses on wheels, put them down on concrete pads, and then drag the wheels away for good. No, these were old-fashioned mobile homes—with rotting tires still attached to wheels—in a development that had been grandfathered into the local planning and zoning codes probably because somebody was related to or a good pal of someone on the Snohomish County zoning commission.

The trailer that belonged to Hilda Smathers was no better or worse than any of its neighbors, but it was a long way from perfect. A few ruined flower beds, rank with weeds, and a scraggly sprinkling of woebegone daffodils, testified to the fact that someone had once cared about the place in a way its current occupant did not. There was no car out front, however, and when we knocked, no one came to the door.

Sue sighed. "So much for her staying home on her day off and catching up on chores. Come on. Tomorrow's another day. What say we give up for the time being and head on back to the city in hopes of beating some of the Boeing traffic."

It didn't work. By three o'clock, southbound rush-hour traffic was in full force. For a while, from Lynnwood south, we were able to do all right in the express lanes, but once we hit Northgate, the diamond lanes petered out and we were stuck creeping along at a snail's pace right along with everyone else. Most of the cars had lone occupants and were very clearly commuters, heading home—wherever that might be.

All the way down the freeway from Everett, Sue and I had discussed the case. My mind remained focused on Mildred George, but somewhere between Northgate and the Montlake Bridge, Sue Danielson started making the gradual transition from detective mode back into motherhood.

"If I ever decide to move to the suburbs 'for my kids' sake,'" she said, "just haul off and shoot me. Where we live now may be a dump, but I can make it home from downtown in just a little over fifteen minutes."

"Your place isn't a dump," I reminded her. "You and the boys have done a great job of fixing it up. But I'll remember you said that. The first time I catch you out looking for places in the burbs, I'll land all over you."

"Thanks," she said.

Sue was quiet then, from there all the way to the downtown exits. We were exiting the freeway when she spoke again. "I've been thinking about what you said earlier."

"What's that?"

"About the kids."

"What about them?"

"You're right. I'm going to put my foot down, Beau. For a change, I'm going to make Richie Danielson play by the rules that govern everyone else. If he wants to take the kids to Disneyland, he'll have to do it next week, during spring break. I'm not letting him pull them out of school this week just because he feels like it. After all, I'm trying to teach the boys to behave responsibly. Shouldn't their father have to do the same?"

"Sounds reasonable to me," I said.

Which only goes to show how little I know.

CHAPTER 6

BY THE TIME WE FINALLY MADE IT BACK TO THE OFFICE and had finished our reports, it was time to head home. I've never been your basic nine-to-five cop, but that day I made an exception. The whole fifth floor could just as well have been draped in black crepe. People were still reeling from Captain Powell's unexpected announcement, but there was little doubt the captain was gone. His fishbowl office was empty. Every personal effect had been removed leaving behind only an empty shell awaiting a new occupant.

When I stopped by Watty Watkins' desk to clock out, he was still there. I caught him staring bleakly at the empty desk a few steps away. The two of them, sergeant and captain, had been constant companions for the better part of a dozen years.

Watty looked up guiltily when I stepped into his line of vision. "Productive day?" he asked.

"Not very," I said. "We're starting to get a handle on it, but I'm afraid my heart's not in it."

"Mine either," Watty returned glumly. "Captain Powell wasn't all that easy to work with at times, but you always knew where you stood with him. No head games. Know what I mean?"

I nodded. "You're right there," I agreed. "Powell wasn't one to yank people around just for the hell of it."

Watty turned to watch as I punched the clock. "What are you and Sue working on again?"

"The Ferman murder," I told him. "The North-End arson. Not your basic high-profile case, just a little old lady with some relatives who maybe liked the idea of having her money a whole lot more than they liked her."

"And who are convinced they'll get away with it," Watty added.

"Not a chance," I told him, and we both smiled.

Leaving the Public Safety Building, I caught a bus up 4th as far as Olive, then I got off and walked the rest of the way home to Belltown Terrace at 2nd and Broad. It was spring. The weather was balmy. After months of dark and wet, the afternoons were growing longer and lighter. The sky overhead was a fragile blue and the street ahead of me was alive with newly leafed trees.

Fifteen or so years ago, hoping to achieve the look of a Parisian boulevard, the city planted trees along the sidewalks throughout the Denny Regrade. For a long time the puny little seedlings seemed like little more than sticks—scrawny branches of nothing reaching up out of a layer of plain gray pavement and even grayer concrete. On this particular day, for some strange reason, it seemed as though they had all matured overnight. Miraculously, they had been transformed from gangly, adolescent twigs into full-fledged trees.

Maybe the reason I noticed had something to do with what was going on with me; with the realization that, in the face of some things ending, it was good to see other things beginning again—to see those trees standing there tall and straight, green and healthy.

Kevin Hotchkiss, Belltown Terrace's latest doorman, greeted me at the building's entrance with a happy grin. "Beautiful spring afternoon, isn't it, Mr. Beaumont."

"Beautiful," I agreed.

I stopped in the mailbox room long enough to extract that day's pound of bills and junk mail. One of the latter was an invitation to, "get in touch with my family roots" by purchasing—for only $39.95, tax and shipping included—a copy of *A Cavalcade of Beaumonts.* Tossing the envelope into the recycling bin on my way past, I wondered how many of the folks who share my surname were, like me, named after a town in Texas rather than after their biological fathers. Unless that was the case, it didn't seem likely that *A Cavalcade of Beaumonts* would lead me to any long-lost relatives.

As I stepped into the apartment, my high-tech security system recognized my signal and turned on both the lights and the CD player. It wasn't exactly like having someone there waiting for me, but it made the place feel less lonely. I had just kicked off my shoes and eased into the recliner when the phone rang.

"Beau," Ralph Ames said. "How did the Viking funeral go?"

I had to be well into middle age before I learned the difference between drinking buddies and friends. Ralph Ames and my ex-partner, Ron Peters, both qualify as the latter. Ralph, who started out as Anne Corley's aide-de-camp, is now mine. His insightful advice guides me through various legal, financial, and investment mazes. He's also someone who knew exactly why my grandmother and I were going over to Lake Chelan.

"The trip went fine," I said.

When I first met Ralph, he was a full-time resident of Paradise Valley down in Arizona. The last year or so, due to the blandishments of his girlfriend—lovely Seattle-area restaurateur, Mary Greengo—he's been spending more and more time in the Pacific Northwest. He used to stay with me whenever he was in town. Now he stays elsewhere.

"So what are you doing this weekend?" he asked.

"Come on, Ralph. It's only Monday. How would I know what I'm doing this weekend?"

Some people hearing that comment might assume that my weekend was so packed with must-do events that I couldn't possibly pencil anything more into the calendar. Ralph, on the other hand, understood full well that my personal calendar was most likely bird-bone bare.

"How would you like to take a little cruise up to Victoria?"

Any mention of boats or boating, whether in little craft or on big ones, brings back painful memories of my ill-fated teenaged attempt at becoming a long-line fisherman. I barfed my guts out as soon as we set sail. An old-time sailor, under the guise of being helpful, offered me a chaw of tobacco. He told me if I chewed that and swallowed the juice, I'd be cured. Needless to say, I never made it as far as the Gulf of Alaska. That whole wretched and retching experience isn't something I need to relive. Boating on Lake Chelan had been stretching my luck.

"I don't do cruises," I said at once.

"Why not?"

"We've gone over this before," I told him. "Because most likely I'll turn pea green the moment we're out of Elliott Bay."

"Come on," Ralph wheedled. "Being seasick doesn't kill you."

"You'd be surprised."

"No, really. There are things you can take for it these days. Patches you can wear. Wrist bands. Besides, it's a perfectly good boat. An old forty-two-foot Chris-Craft. Three cabins. Blond mahogany. And the owner's a blond, too. We thought we'd do just an overnight trip . . ."

"Hold it right there, Ralph. Did you say blond? Is this a blind date?"

"Well, more or less," Ralph admitted.

"End of discussion," I growled. "No cruises and no blind dates."

"It doesn't have to be a blind date," Ralph said. "She's an old friend of Mary's. They've been pals forever, since second grade. How about if you come over for dinner one evening this week and meet her. After that, you can decide whether or not you're interested in the cruise. What about Wednesday?

Mary doesn't have to go into the restaurant that night."

At the prospect of one of Mary's dinners, I could feel my resolve weakening. If Ralph Ames weren't a lawyer, he could have made a fortune in sales. Come to think of it, maybe he *is* in sales.

"What time Wednesday?"

"Six," he said. "If it isn't raining, we'll sit around out in the patio for a while before we eat."

"What's her name?" I asked.

At least Ralph had the good grace not to feign innocence. "Cassandra," he said. "Cassandra Wolcott. Cassie for short."

"Cassandra," I repeated. "Wasn't she the one who caused all the trouble by letting evil out of that box?"

"No, you've got Cassandra mixed up with Pandora," Ralph said. "Cassandra was someone who could predict the future, but no one would believe her. I don't think that's the case here, by the way, because people did listen."

"Why do you say that?"

"Cassie Wolcott is a retired stockbroker," Ralph replied. "She's also thirty-eight years old."

My ideas about the age and appearance of retired stockbrokers did some downward gyrations. "Isn't she awfully young to be retired?"

"She made her money and got the hell out," Ralph said. "I call that smart."

"I see," I said at last. "All right. Wednesday at six, but remember, I'm not making any promises about the weekend."

"Fair enough," Ralph said.

I put down the phone and then headed out to the kitchen to see if there was anything I could scare up for dinner. Without Ralph spending as much time here as he used to, I'm afraid my kitchen stores have fallen on hard times once more. There was still plenty of Seattle's Best Coffee in the fridge, but not much else. At least nothing else edible.

Giving up on the idea of eating at home, I put my shoes back on and headed outside once again.

When I first moved to the Regrade, the neighborhood turned into a deserted village as soon as it got dark. The only people who hung out there at night were the homeless bums and the almost-homeless drunks who beat paths from one sleazy tavern or greasy spoon to another. They're all pretty much gone now—the sleazy taverns and the drunks. For a while during the late eighties, drug dealers moved into the area in a big way. Finally, though, area merchants and residents went on the warpath. They fought back with an aggressive program that included a visible round-the-clock police presence of both beat and bicycle cops augmented by private security guards.

Over time, increased patrols worked their magic. Most of the drug dealers and bums moved on. Businesses that once catered to a lowlife clientele gradually died out themselves, and a whole new set of entrepreneurs came flooding into the void. Within five blocks of Belltown Terrace there are now half a dozen trendy restaurants where Seattle's movers and shakers can go to see and be seen. A beneficial side effect of all the gentrification has been that a number of highly qualified chefs have moved into the Regrade as well. That makes it possible to get a decent meal at any number of places. Not cheap—like in the old Doghouse days—but good.

Drawn by the irresistible magnetism of freshly made bread, I made my way up to Cafe Macrina on 1st and had a bowl of soup and a chunk of crusty, herb-laden bread. They close at six, but lately I've managed to become enough of a fixture around the place so that the staff lets me grab a light supper of soup and bread followed by a leisurely cup of coffee while they work at closing up for the evening.

After dinner, I sat drinking my coffee, enjoying watching people go by outside on the sidewalk, and thinking. One of the things I like about eating in restaurants is the same thing I used to appreciate about bars—they're impersonal. Not entirely. People may know you by name. They may even know something about you, but they don't know you really. They can't push your buttons or tell the world where all the bodies are buried. Unlike friends and families, the people you find in places like that can't nail your hide with all the things you want to keep hidden. That makes them handy for hiding out from feelings, which is something I've been particularly good at all my life.

On the surface, I was thinking about Mary Greengo's friend. What made some young woman want to become a stockbroker of all things? To do that, I supposed she had to be fairly tough and smart. Tough, smart, and aggressive. Even so, however, how had Cassandra Wolcott managed to retire from stock-brokering at the tender age of thirty-eight?

Several possibilities presented themselves. For one Cassie might be a very slick operator. Maybe her exit from the stock-trading business had come about just the way Ralph had said—because she had made so damned much money at it that she could afford to walk away. That was the upside. The downside could have had something to do with corporate mergers or downsizing, or it could have been something altogether different. Maybe hers was an involuntary retirement that had come about as a result of some kind of financial skulduggery. The fact that the woman came with Ralph Ames' personal stamp of approval should have counted for something, but still . . .

"More coffee?" the waiter asked.

"Sure," I said, nodding and pushing my cup in his direction for the promised refill.

Unfortunately, watching the coffee pour into my cup reminded me of a lunchtime conversation I'd shared with Ralph Ames in this very restaurant not three weeks earlier. We were just starting on our second cups of coffee when he had asked the tough question.

"When are you going to get over her, Beau?"

He might very well have been talking about Karen—my first wife—who had died of cancer a few months earlier, but I knew he wasn't. Ralph's "her" could only refer to Anne Corley, my second wife. Even though I hadn't added sugar or cream to my coffee, I picked up my spoon and stirred. It was a delaying tactic—a stall. Ralph wasn't deterred in the least.

"Well?" he insisted.

"Maybe never," I said, only half joking. "Isn't that how fatal attractions are supposed to work?"

But Ralph didn't crack a smile. "You can't spend your whole life living with a legend, Beau. Remember, I knew Anne, too. She was fascinating and exasperating; troubled and troubling; smart and willful; sweet and deadly. She was all those things all at the same time."

"So? What's the point?"

"You've created this spun-glass cocoon around that tiny fragment of time you had together," he said. "And in the process, you've transformed Anne Corley into something she never was—perfection itself. That's it in a nutshell, Beau. Anne's presumed perfection has you stuck. It's keeping you from being able to get on with your life."

"Come off it, Ralph. Lighten up. I haven't exactly been dying on the vine here. What about Alexis?"

"What about her? She's gone, isn't she? You managed to find something wrong with her and with every other woman who's crossed your path since then for one reason and one reason only—she wasn't Anne. Alexis hung around long enough to develop feet of clay. She probably told you to pick up your socks a few times and wanted you to put the toilet seat down. If Anne had hung around long enough to do the same thing—to turn into a flesh-and-blood woman—maybe you'd be over her by now. At least, you'd be over her enough that you could actually look at someone else."

"Thanks for the advice to the lovelorn," I told him brusquely. "If you don't mind, next time I want some, I'll cut out the middleman and go straight to Ann Landers."

My comment put an end to that particular conversation, but I had thought about it for days afterward. When I wasn't able to resolve it on my own, I had discussed it with Lars Jenssen, my AA sponsor. I was hoping, of course, that he would tell me Ralph was way off the beam. He didn't.

"I've noticed that myself," he said. "It's like you meet a woman and before very long, you start building a case—picking out all the things that are wrong with her. Telling yourself why it would never work."

"Maybe I just don't want to be tied down again."

"That's a good one," Lars had said with a laugh.

"What do you mean by that?"

"It's a nice, shiny excuse, picked right off the shelf. Sounds all right first time you hear it. But believe me, if an answer's that easy to come by, it's not the real answer. If I was you, I'd dig deeper."

I hadn't really done much digging, but I could see that I was doing it again. Sitting there in Macrina, I had come up with a whole litany of things that were wrong with Cassandra Wolcott *before* I even met her.

My second cup of coffee was still half full when I pushed it away. "Check please," I said. "I just remembered. I'm due at a meeting in half an hour."

I left Macrina and headed north on 1st. Rather than turning east on Broad to return to Belltown Terrace, I walked two blocks farther and stopped in front of Lars Jenssen's four-story affordable-housing walk-up, the Stillwater Arms. Lars, twice retired—first from the navy and later from Seattle's fishing fleet—is the mainstay of my home AA group—the Regrade Regulars—which meets at a once-thriving restaurant and bar a few blocks back up 2nd. I rang Lars' apartment from the security phone next to the outside door. As usual, it took several rings for him to answer.

"Ja," he said. "Who is it?"

"Beau. You going to the meeting tonight?" I asked.

"Ja, sure," he told me. "Yust getting ready to leave right now. You downstairs?"

"I am, but if you want me to, I can go get the car and come back to pick you up."

"What's wrong with walking?" Lars demanded. "I'm eighty-one. I'm not dead yet, and I'm sure as hell not so stove up that I can't walk that far. I'll be right down."

Lars Jenssen's sole concession to age is a knobby walking stick he's taken to using in the past few months. We strolled the six blocks back uptown, reveling in the balmy spring weather. The meeting's drunkalogue that night was from a guy named Tommy. He had been coming to meetings for some time, principally to have his court-ordered attendance sheet signed. Tommy's lack of enthusiasm had been pretty apparent to all concerned. When it came time for sharing, he'd never said much.

Everybody who goes to AA walks in the door figuring his or her story is unique. Over time, though, all the stories begin to sound strangely alike. The details of each downward spiral may vary slightly, as do the reasons people finally go looking for help, but the broad outlines are much the same. When

Tommy started to talk that night, I wondered what had finally pushed him over the edge.

The particulars weren't long in coming. He told the usual story of early experimentation with hard-core drinking along with the ability to drink prodigious amounts without appearing drunk, but those days were long gone. In the past few years the ability to hold his liquor had disappeared. As a result, in less than two years he had amassed a total of four DUI arrests as well as several domestic-violence run-ins with his wife. A wily defense attorney had helped Tommy beat all the charges except the last one. That judge had called a halt. He had sentenced Tommy to the King County Jail for six months, five of which were suspended on the condition that he seek treatment for anger management, and attend mandatory AA meetings.

Tommy had come to the meetings still steeped in denial and still harboring the unrealistic belief that now that he was sober, he'd be able to talk his wife out of divorce. Not true. Much to his surprise the divorce had become final the previous Friday. His first instinct had been to go out and get roaring drunk. He was in a bar waiting to order when something he had heard at one of the meetings came home to him. "You've got to do it for yourself. Yourself and nobody else." He had left the bar without ordering a drink and had found his way to a meeting instead. For the first time, Tommy was coming to grips with the painful reality that both his wife and kids were gone for good.

I recognized the words. "You've got to do it for

yourself" was one of Lars Jenssen's stock phrases. As Tommy ended his story, I caught Lars' eye and winked. He replied with a discreet thumbs-up. When the meeting was over, I had to wait around while Lars went up to Tommy and talked to him.

"Somebody else in need of a sponsor?" I asked when he finally came away.

Lars nodded. "Poor guy," he added, as we made our way down the stairs. "Why is it we're all so dumb that we never realize we've got ourselves a good woman until after we've lost her?" Seven years earlier, Lars' wife Aggie had finally succumbed to the ravages of Alzheimer's disease.

Up against, the backdrop of what was going on in Larry and Marcia Powell's life as well as what had happened to Sue Danielson and her kids, Tommy's story had hit surprisingly close to home. "I'm sure you're right," I responded. "It's stupidity plain and simple."

Out on the sidewalk, Lars paused and leaned on his stick. "I couldn't have asked for a better woman than Aggie," he said thoughtfully. "It makes me sick, sometimes, to think how I treated that poor woman. Every once in a while, I wish God would give me another chance. I'd like to think I'd do better by her."

Before I could comment one way or the other, the cell phone in my pocket shrilled. "Not that thing again," Lars grumbled. "Whoever invented those confounded cell phones ought to be shot—no, make that tarred and feathered. Phones in houses is one thing, but out on the street, there ought to be a law against 'em."

"Hello?" I said, ignoring him.

"Beau? It's Sue."

"What's going on?"

"Chuck Grayson just called me."

Sergeant Grayson was Watty Watkins' night-shift counterpart on the desk at Seattle Homicide.

"So? What did he want?"

"He says there's someone down at the department demanding to talk to one of the detectives on the Seward Park case."

"At this time of night?"

"That's what I said. The problem is, I can't leave the house right now. I hate to play the mother card, Beau, but with everything that's going on right now, I don't want to leave the boys . . ."

"Don't worry about it, Sue. It's no trouble. I can be there in ten minutes."

"You're not going to mind if I flake out on you this time?"

There was something in the sound of her voice—a worrisome tremor—that bothered me. "Are you okay?" I asked. "What's going on?"

"It's just that I told the boys my decision about not letting them miss school. They're both a little upset with me right now. I don't want to leave them alone."

"They'll be okay eventually. In the meantime, you stay where you are. I'll handle whoever's down at the department."

"Thanks, Beau," she said. "I owe you. Call me when you finish up and let me know what's happening."

"It might be late."

"Don't worry," she replied. "I doubt I'll sleep much tonight anyway. I'll call Grayson back right now and let him know you're on your way."

She attempted to keep her response sounding offhand and upbeat, but the worrisome undertone I had noticed before was still there.

"Sue," I said. "Are you sure you're all right?"

"I'm fine. Really."

Like hell you are, I thought, but I didn't challenge her on it. If she was caught up in some kind of confrontation with her kids, no wonder she couldn't talk.

"Okay, then," I told her. "No matter how late it is, I'll give you a call as soon as I get back. In the meantime, hang in there."

"Thanks," she said with a wary laugh. "I'll do my best."

Lars and I had been walking while I talked on the phone. When I ended the call, we were already in front of Belltown Terrace.

"Sorry about that, Lars," I said. "Duty calls. If you want to come in with me, I can give you a ride back to your place."

"Forget it," he grumbled. "I'd rather walk. When I'm by myself, at least I can walk in peace without the damned phone ringing every step of the way."

CHAPTER 7

"WHAT'S THE SCOOP?" I ASKED CHUCK GRAYSON ONCE I made it to Homicide's home on the fifth floor. "Where's the person I'm supposed to see?"

"Her name's Darla Cunningham," Chuck told me. "I hope you don't mind. I took the liberty of stowing her in your cubicle."

The truth of the matter was, I did mind. I don't like having stray people hanging around my office. "Great," I growled irritably. "Makes perfect sense. Why not leave someone connected to one of my cases alone in my office? That way he or she can paw at will through whatever's out."

My grousing didn't seem to make much of an impression on Sergeant Grayson. "Maybe you should consider not leaving things out," he said pointedly. "In fact, until the desks and cubicles in Homicide become deeded property, you might actually make a practice of putting your stuff away. Besides, when I needed a place to put Ms. Cunningham, both interview rooms happened to be occupied."

Behind me the door to the outside corridor swung open. I turned to see Paul Kramer stagger inside lugging a stack of boxes. "Hey, Beau," he said. "Mind giving me a hand with these before I drop something?"

It took a second or two for me to realize where he was heading—Captain Powell's Fishbowl. Too stunned to object, I took the top box off the pile and then followed him into the office. I stood to one side while Kramer placed the other boxes on top of the desk. After collecting the one I was carrying and placing it with the others, he turned to admire his newly acquired territory.

"What do you think of my new digs?" he said with smug satisfaction oozing from every pore. "Isn't it great?"

"Unbelievable!" I replied.

I had learned that handy response years before in a sales seminar sponsored by Fuller Brush when I was working my way through school. Said with enough fervor, the word "unbelievable" can convey two diametrically opposed opinions. Something can be either unbelievably good or unbelievably bad, depending on your point of view. It's likely Chuck Grayson understood I meant the latter. Paul Kramer was so thrilled with himself at that point he didn't even notice. My one-word piece of sarcasm sailed cleanly over his head, missing the target completely, which is probably just as well.

"So far this is only an interim assignment," he continued with oblivious enthusiasm. "But if I play my cards right, maybe I can make it permanent. Wouldn't that be something?"

"It would be something all right," I agreed, edging toward the door.

"Hey, wait a minute," Kramer added. "There's still one more load in my office upstairs. Would you mind helping me lug it down . . ."

"Sorry, Kramer," I said. "I'm all tied up at the moment. There's someone waiting for me in my office." With that, I bolted out of the Fishbowl and headed down the narrow corridor that leads to the cubicles.

The last thing I wanted to do just then was interview a potential witness. Paul Kramer calling the shots from Captain Powell's desk was an unthinkable joke. The whole idea of having him in charge made me want to gag first and shove my fist through a wall of Sheetrock second. From the first day Kramer had shown up on the fifth floor, everyone in Homicide had pegged him for the brown-nosing, ass-kissing jerk that he was. The problem was, we had all deluded ourselves into thinking that his strategy wouldn't work. We had convinced ourselves that the brass upstairs couldn't possibly be that stupid, but it seemed now that they were. They had fallen for Kramer's snow job. The son of a bitch was going to be my boss. As Bette Davis would have said, we had better fasten our seat belts. "Unbelievable" hardly covered it!

Wanting to regain my composure before entering the cubicle, I paused in the empty corridor and peered in through the open door. A woman was seated on the chair next to Sue Danielson's desk. At first glance, she appeared to be fast asleep. Her eyes were closed. Her head was propped against the wall behind her. Hands with long graceful fingers lay folded loosely in her lap.

"Ms. Cunningham?" I asked.

Almond-shaped, gray-green eyes blinked open and her head came up. With no momentary confusion or sign of transition, she went from being totally relaxed to being totally alert. "You must be Detective Beaumont," she said, rising and holding out her hand. "I'm Darla Cunningham."

Darla Cunningham's light brown hair, parted in the middle and utterly straight, hung almost to her narrow waist. She was dressed in a well-tailored business suit—a charcoal-gray blazer and matching skirt. A muted plaid pattern had been woven into the lightweight wool. The suit combined with a cream-colored silk blouse and low heels were a statement in upward mobility. The only piece that didn't quite fit the businesswoman image was the bone-and-bead choker necklace that encircled her long slender neck. *Upwardly mobile Native American*, I told myself.

Expectantly, she scanned the empty doorway behind me. "Where's Detective Danielson?" she asked with a frown.

"Sue isn't coming," I said. "It'll just be the two of us."

"Oh," Darla Cunningham said, sounding oddly disappointed.

"Won't you have a chair, Ms. Cunningham? Then, if you don't mind, I'd like you to tell me what this is all about."

Frowning still, she resumed the chair. For a moment or two she said nothing.

"Is there some particular reason you were interested in speaking to Detective Danielson, Ms. Cunningham? If you aren't comfortable speaking to a man, I could possibly arrange for another female detective . . ."

"Oh, no," she said quickly. "That's not necessary. I'll be happy to talk to you, but I do have a question, Detective Beaumont. Do you believe in magic?"

Homicide investigations usually call for hard work—not magic. "Let me see," I quipped. "There's 'Puff the Magic Dragon' and . . ."

"I'm not kidding, Detective," she said. The green seemed to disappear from her eyes, leaving them the color of flint. "This is a very serious matter. Lives are at stake."

"Well then, seriously, I'd have to say no, I don't. Not really."

"That's too bad," Darla Cunningham said. "It would be easier for us both if you did. Let me ask you another question. Has the medical examiner's office given you any information regarding the bones that were found in Seward Park?"

"Not so far," I said. "We're a little backed up. Detective Danielson and I are working another case as well, at the moment. Seward Park is pretty much on a back burner while we wait for more information. A troop of Explorer Scouts was supposed to comb the crime scene over the weekend in hopes of finding more remains, as well as some clues that might help with the identification process. As of now, I have yet to hear if they found anything."

"Would you mind calling the medical examiner's office for me?" Darla asked. "I tried, but no one would talk to me or give me any information. I need to know, Detective Beaumont. It's a matter of life and death."

If the ME's office had seen fit not to give her any information, it seemed wise to follow suit. "What kind of information are you looking for, Ms. Cunningham? What exactly is your connection to this case?"

"I may be able to help identify the victim."

"Is it a relative of yours?"

She shook her head. "Not really."

"What then?"

"Before I tell you anything more, I'd like to know one thing. Call the medical examiner's office and find out whether or not the bones belong to one of the People—to an Indian, I mean. If they do . . ."

"Depending on what kind of remains were found, the ME's office may or may not be able to tell . . ."

"Please," Darla interrupted. "Just ask them. See what they say. If they say no, then obviously I'm wrong. If they say yes, I promise I'll tell you everything."

Puzzled and more than a little impatient, I reached for the phone. Years of working homicide have indelibly imprinted any number of telephone numbers in my memory bank. The number for the King County medical examiner is right at the top of the list.

Back in the good old days, the phone rang and somebody answered or else you got a busy signal. Now a disembodied voice read off a menu for me to make a selection. The last choice and several more rings connected me to an actual human being.

"This is Audrey."

Audrey Cummings is Doc Baker's fireplug of an assistant. Middle-aged and utterly no-nonsense, she's someone for whom I have the utmost respect.

"Detective Beaumont here," I told her. "How come you're pulling a night shift? I thought once you got kicked upstairs to second in command that wasn't supposed to happen."

Audrey laughed. "Me, too," she said bleakly. "The problem is, we've got two people out sick tonight. Consequently, I'm filling in. What can I do for you, Beau?"

"I'm working the Seward Park bone case," I said. "Did the Explorers come up with anything more this weekend?"

"Hang on," Audrey said. "Let me check."

Without actually putting me on hold, she left the receiver lying somewhere and was away from it for what seemed like a long time. In the background I could hear a radio or disc player dishing out classical music—a piano concerto of some kind. I've heard it said that Mozart makes you smart. I wondered if that was why Audrey was listening to that kind of music—in hopes of being smarter—or if it was her way to get through whatever it was she was doing just then.

"Here's the file," she announced, coming back on the line. "Dirk Matthews was the investigator assigned to this case. Unfortunately, he's one of the ones who're out sick tonight."

"Had he done any work on it?"

"A little, but not much. All we have so far are two femurs and a tibia. Long bones only. According to this, the Explorers didn't pick up any more than what Detective Danielson brought in last Wednesday. I can tell you that your victim is a male. Five seven or so. A hundred fifty pounds."

"Race?" I asked.

"Native American," she said.

I glanced in Darla Cunningham's direction. "Any idea how old he was or how long he's been dead?" I asked.

"We'd need a skull in order to estimate age," she said. "We estimate age by looking at wear patterns on teeth. As to how long he's been dead, that's hard to tell since we don't know whether the bones were out in the open and exposed to the elements or if they were protected in some way."

"Does that file have a case number?" I asked.

"Good grief, Beau. Your name's right here. What did you do, lose your secret decoder ring?"

She laughed at her own joke. I ignored it. "I was out of town when they assigned this one to me," I told her. "And even though I'm actively working it, so far nobody's bothered to give me the number."

"Don't get sore about it," she said. "Here it is."

After writing it down and thanking Audrey for her help, I put down the phone and turned back to Darla Cunningham. "All right," I said. "The remains are those of a male Native American, but I suspect you already knew that."

Darla nodded.

"Care to tell me how?" I asked.

"That's where the magic comes in. I'm not sure you're the right . . ."

"Try me," I said.

"My father, Henry Leaping Deer, is a shaman," she said.

"A shaman? You mean like a medicine man?"

"Sort of," she said. "Only more so. If you'll pardon a math analogy, a medicine man to the tenth power." She smiled then. Her teeth were perfectly straight and very, very white against a slightly olive complexion. "It's a long story," she added.

I settled back in my chair. "Take your time," I said. "I'm in no hurry."

"My father is a Quinault from Taholah," she said. "When he was little he got sent off to boarding school where he became friends with a classmate from the Port Madison Reservation, a boy named David Half Moon. The two of them were friends all through school. The summer between their freshman and sophomore years, they both went off on separate vision quests. When they came back to school that fall, they both had learned the same thing—that each of them was destined to be a shaman.

"After high school they went their separate ways, never seeing each other again, not until last Sunday night."

"This Sunday?" I asked.

Darla shook her head. "No," she said. "Sunday a week ago. That's when David Half Moon appeared to my father in a dream."

I said nothing, but I must have shifted slightly in my seat. Darla paused. "You don't like all this mystical stuff very much, do you, Detective Beaumont?"

she said. I said nothing. "Neither do I," she continued. "I teach physics at the University of Washington. If some of my colleagues knew I was here telling you this strange story, I'd be laughed off the tenure track so fast it would make my head spin."

"Go on," I urged. "You were saying about your father's dream."

"David Half Moon appeared to my father just as he was long ago when they were both boys. That's how my father recognized him. He said that some Anglo boys had taken him from the tribal burial grounds into the city. He said it was my father's duty, as David's friend and as a fellow shaman—professional courtesy, if you will—to bring his bones back where they belonged."

"Excuse me, but I don't understand what all this . . ."

"Wait," Darla ordered. "Let me finish. On Monday and Tuesday of that next week, my father tried to telephone his old friend. When he couldn't find him, he contacted some of the elders of the Suquamish tribe. That's the same tribe Chief Sealth—the man Seattle was named after—was from, by the way. When my father finally spoke to someone who had known David Half Moon, he learned for the first time that his friend died more than ten years ago of lung cancer.

"David Half Moon's dying wish was that his remains should be accorded all the ancient customs. The People did that for him. As a shaman he, along with his most prized possessions, were loaded into a canoe, then the canoe was raised up into the branches of a tree somewhere out on the Kitsap Peninsula."

For a moment, all I could see was Beverly Piedmont, flinging my grandfather's ashes off the back of *The Lady of the Lake*. "You mean they didn't actually bury him."

"No," Darla Cunningham said quietly, firmly. "We may call it a burial ground, but that's not the way we do it."

We. The word resonated in a strange and powerful way. My rational just-the-facts-ma'am world was thrown topsy-turvy by her use of a "we" that could at the same time encompass both a professor of physics at the U-Dub and an old shaman who had been sent on a dream-inspired search for a long-lost and long-dead friend. This was mystical all right, more so than I was prepared to swallow.

"Did anybody bother to go check his canoe to see if the bones were still where they had left them?" I asked. As soon as the words were out of my mouth they sounded flip and somehow disrespectful, but Darla didn't seem to take offense.

"Tribal burial grounds are strictly off-limits," she explained. "The People don't go there. It's too dangerous."

"Dangerous?" I asked. "Why?"

"Because the spirits of the dead—especially the spirit of a dead shaman—can be very powerful. And unpredictable. People who come in contact with the possessions or the bones of a dead shaman are subsequently at risk themselves. Things happen to them. The white man's world might not see that connection, but it's there all the same."

I thought about Audrey Cummings telling me that the investigator who had been working on the

Seward Park case was out sick. I wondered what was wrong with him. *Probably nothing*, I told myself. Still, it was enough to make me worry.

"So Monday and Tuesday your father attempted to track down his school chum and discovered that he was dead. Then what?"

"Wednesday morning early he had another dream. In this one, there were children, running up and down in a park, playing field hockey. When my father got closer, he realized that the sticks they were using were bones—David Half Moon's bones. His empty skull was the ball. Later, when the game was over, a woman came there—an Anglo woman. She took the bones away from the children and put them in a metal box."

I thought about Sue Danielson retrieving the bones from the role players—if young ghouls could be considered children—and turning the remains over to the guys from the ME's office. The investigators, in turn, would have slipped them into a metal locker—one in a bank of refrigerated body-sized drawers. The hair on the back of my neck seemed to stand on end. Was it possible that Sue Danielson was the Anglo woman Henry Leaping Deer had seen in his dream?

"Did your father say what the woman looked like?" I asked.

Darla shook her head. "By the time he called me about it on Thursday, he could no longer remember exactly what she looked like. He did say he was sure the dream—the game—took place in Seattle. That afternoon, when I read a piece in the paper about the Seward Park incident, I called my father up and told him about it. Even while I was reading it to him, he was sure the two things were connected."

I wasn't entirely convinced, but still, Darla was making a pretty good case of it. "For the moment, let's assume your father is right," I conceded. "Let's say that the remains up in the ME's office really do belong to your father's dead friend. What are you going to do about it? Why are you here? And why did you claim that talking to me was a matter of life and death?"

"Because it is," Darla returned. "I thought I had made that clear. A shaman's power doesn't end with death, Detective Beaumont. Every person who has come in contact with those bones or possessions is now in grave danger as well. My father sent me to sound the alarm. He isn't necessarily concerned about whoever took the bones in the first place—the ones who carted them away from the burial grounds. They'll get whatever they deserve. His concern is that others are now involved, people who are really innocent bystanders. Unfortunately, they, too, came in contact with the bones.

"According to my father one of them is a young man with green hair. The other is the woman I told you about before—the Anglo woman who took the bones away from the kids. I'm here to warn those people in particular, to tell them to be careful and take extra precautions."

"Just them?" I asked. "A woman and a man with green hair?"

"Those are the two my father mentioned, although there may be others, as well. He wanted me to let them know that if they'd like his help, they can come down to see him in Taholah. He'll do whatever he can for them."

"What do you mean?"

"There's a purification process," she said. "A ceremony. If someone wants to avail himself of it, I'm sure my father would do it."

She fell silent then. There were voices outside in the corridor as another pair of detectives walked by. Long after their voices disappeared, Darla and I sat without speaking. I don't know what she was thinking. For my part, I was mulling over her words. She had delivered her father's offer with the same kind of conviction a doctor might have employed when announcing some dire diagnosis, one in which the prognosis for long-term survival isn't good.

"You're convinced the Seward Park bones belong to David Half Moon, aren't you," I said at last.

Darla nodded. "Yes."

"But you weren't sure of that when you first came here."

"No," she agreed. "That's true. My father was convinced, but I wasn't."

"What changed your mind?"

She frowned. "I'm not sure. It happened while you were talking on the telephone."

"With Audrey? The woman from the ME's office?"

Darla nodded. "Before you even said anything, I knew my father was right." She paused. "Believe me, Detective Beaumont. I understand that there's no rational explanation for any of this. I'm a scientist, for god's sake. A mathematician. But I'm also Indian. What's worrying me now is that if my father was right about one thing, he may be right about the others as well. Is Detective Danielson the woman who took the bones away from Seward Park?"

"Yes."

Darla Cunningham stood and held out her hand. "Please tell her from me to be careful."

"I will," I told her. "You can count on that."

Darla started toward the doorway. I made as if to follow, but she stopped me. "Don't bother," she said. "I can find my way back out. That's something we Indians are supposed to be good at—we all have an inborn sense of direction."

She laughed then, a kind of bell-like musical laughter that seemed to bring people together rather than closing them out. Her gentle humor made fun of everyone who pokes fun at another race or culture—Darla Cunningham included.

"How did you go from Leaping Deer to Cunningham?"

Darla laughed again. "I married a Redcoat," she said.

"A redcoat?" I repeated.

She nodded. "Hal's English. He teaches anthropology at the U-Dub."

"That's where I can reach you if I need to—at the university?"

She nodded. "There or at home. We're in the phone book."

Darla left then. I sat for a moment or two thinking, then I switched on the computer. It was still working its way through that interminable boot-up procedure when Paul Kramer poked his head in the door.

"What a looker," he said. "Who was that?"

"A Native American lady," I said.

"Really. So what did Pocahontas want?"

Compared to Darla's gentle good humor, Kramer's lame joke fell flat. "I wouldn't make fun of her if I were you," I told him irritably. "She's a professor of physics at the University of Washington."

"So she's a smart Indian instead of a dumb one," he said. "You still haven't told me what she wanted."

"She came here to give me a tentative ID on the Seward Park bones. It sounds like the dead man is an old Indian guy from the Kitsap Peninsula who died of lung cancer sometime back in the eighties. His name was David Half Moon."

"If he's from the Kitsap Peninsula, how did his bones wind up in Seward Park?" Kramer asked.

The computer was finally booted up and ready to work. I consulted my notes from Audrey Cummings and typed in the case number. "That's what I'm about to find out," I said. "My guess is, if I apply a little pressure to one of our dungeons-and-dragons jerks, I'll find out they also rob graves."

Once the file was called up, I sat there and started scanning. It seemed reasonable that Kramer would take the hint and leave. He didn't. "I hope this checks out," he said finally. "It'll be great if we can clear one case my first day at the helm. What about the other one you and Sue are working—the North-End arson?"

"We're on task," I said. "We interviewed several people today, and we'll do more tomorrow."

"Let's clear that one, too," Kramer said. "We've got the momentum here. Let's keep it going."

He left then—finally, leaving me with the impression that I had been listening to a member of a cheer-leading squad rather than Captain Powell's successor. Staring at the empty doorway he had just vacated, I realized how different we were and why he had been promoted and I hadn't been. For him it was a game—a numbers game with the score rising or falling depending on the cases that ended up in the cleared column. For me it's different— more personal. I bring to this job the firm conviction that no one should be allowed to get away with murder.

That's as true for Agnes Ferman as it is for anyone else, I told the empty doorway. *Clear it my ass!*

CHAPTER 8

THE GUY WHO HAD CALLED IN THE INITIAL SEWARD Park incident was one James Greenjeans. Sue's written report listed his home address as an apartment on Boren on Capitol Hill and his place of work as bartender at the Hurricane Cafe.

Not part of the usual role-playing group, he had been invited along as a last-minute, fill-in replacement for a ticket-paying no-show. Apparently, none of the other participants had been disturbed when one of the so-called directors had emerged from a clump of bushes brandishing what he later bragged was a real human bone. Bowing to peer pressure, Mr. Greenjeans had kept his mouth shut at the time. Later, once he got back home—around 4:30 in the morning—he had called 911 and reported the incident.

According to Sue's report, the two guys who were in charge were a pair of good friends now turned partners. Despite being high school dropouts, Don

Atkins and Barry Newsome had nonetheless turned a youthful interest in video games into lucrative career paths. Now in their late twenties, they worked together as freelance graphic designers, creating blood-and-guts graphics for one of the Eastside's computer-game manufacturers. Their free-time hobby and part-time moneymaker was a company called Bloodlust. That enterprise consisted of creating and directing live-action participatory costume dramas, complete with role-playing ghouls, zombies, and vampires, at various locations all over the Pacific Northwest.

When confronted by Sue Danielson with James Greenjeans' claim, they had reluctantly produced three bones—the ones Sue had later delivered to the medical examiner's office. Under questioning, they both claimed they had stumbled across the bones in a blackberry bramble in Seward Park, but subsequent searches by detectives, uniformed officers, and Explorer Scouts had failed to unearth any additional remains. That would make sense if one bought Darla Cunningham's assertion that the bones had been imported to Seward Park from an Indian burial ground somewhere in the wilds of the Kitsap Peninsula.

When I finished reading Sue's report, it was only nine o'clock. Rather than going straight home, I decided to try calling Mr. Greenjeans' home number to see if he could give me any additional information. A breathless and youthful female voice answered the phone. "Jimmy's not here right now," she told me.

"Do you know where I could find him?"

"At work, I suppose," she said, and slammed the phone down in my ear.

That's one of the problems with young people today. No one has bothered to teach them the rudiments of proper telephone etiquette.

I looked at my watch again. On the way back home to Belltown Terrace, the Hurricane Cafe would be only a block or two out of my way. I was torn, though, between wanting to talk to James Greenjeans and not wanting to set foot inside what I still regard as a Johnny-come-lately restaurant.

The Hurricane Cafe came into existence as a direct result of the demise of one of my favorite longtime haunts—the Doghouse. The new place had been open for years now, but I hadn't ventured inside out of what was probably misplaced customer loyalty. That was about to end. *Don't be a sentimental slob*, I told myself finally, making up my mind. *Just do your job.*

On my way to the elevators, I had to pass Chuck Grayson's desk once more. It didn't surprise me to see the desk sergeant in Kramer's office. Kramer and Grayson were both totally engrossed in some aspect of unpacking. Neither of them noticed me as I slunk by. I figured it was best for all concerned if I didn't let on I was there.

On the way up 4th Avenue in the 928 I was thinking about Mr. Greenjeans' improbable name. I wondered if Henry Leaping Deer's dream landscape had somehow crossed its little psychic wires. Maybe the man's colorful name had translated into a headful of green hair. *After all*, I told myself, *nobody ever said dream interpretation was an exact science.*

It was Monday, a weekday night. Even so, verging on ten o'clock, the parking lot outside the Hurricane was full as were most of the on-street spaces in the near vicinity. I had to park over half a block away and walk. I did so with misgivings only partially attributable to nostalgia.

One of the precepts of AA is accepting things you cannot change. Nonetheless, I sometimes find that ignoring them is my best bet. You really can't go home again. Preserved in a haze of memory and with no current contradictory information, I had managed to keep the spirit of the old Doghouse alive and well exactly as it once was. Approaching the outside door, I knew I wouldn't be able to play that game any longer. The restaurant had changed and so had I. There seemed to be a whole collection of ghosts being summoned by this oddball investigation and those specters didn't all belong to David Half Moon. Some of J. P. Beaumont's demons were in attendance as well.

When I first came to live in downtown Seattle's Regrade neighborhood, I was a newly separated refugee from a marriage that had fallen apart in the distant suburban outpost of Lake Tapps. On my own and disinclined to do my own cooking, I gravitated to nearby round-the-clock joints. Over time I had settled on one in particular. The Doghouse, within easy walking distance of my Royal Crest condo, had become my home-away-from-home. There I had enjoyed the ready availability of food, booze, and camaraderie, not necessarily in that order.

Long before I arrived on the scene, the Doghouse had been an institution in Seattle—a fixture. For sixty years it was a standard-bearer for cheap, mostly fried food, tough, battleaxe-style waitresses, and clouds of undiluted second-hand cigarette smoke. For me, the most important item in the bar had been an unending supply of MacNaughton's. For other Doghouse regulars, though, the bar's real attraction had been the resident electric organ along with a series of talented organists who had reigned over and provided accompaniment for nightly amateur and more or less drunken songfests.

When economics and failing health finally forced the second generation of owners to close the place down, a lot of us old-timers had grieved the restaurant's passing as much as if we had lost a good friend. I had been there along with the TV cameras and other diehard regulars the night they locked the doors for good. Months later, new owners had opened a new restaurant in the same location. I had heard rumors that the new place appealed to a far younger and much hipper clientele. As I walked up to the once-familiar glass front-door entrance, I wondered whether or not any of the other old guys had gone back in the meantime. If so, I was proud that J. P. Beaumont wasn't one of them— until now.

Pushing open the door, my initial impression was that little had changed. There was a new layer of tile on the floor, but the thick pall of cigarette smoke that instantly assailed the nose was familiar. So was the noisy clatter of pinball machines that still lined the lobby area. The partition that had once separated the bar and lounge from the restaurant proper had been removed as had the organ. The orange upholstery in the booths had changed to something newer, but other than that the dimly lit, cavernous interior was much the same.

The old Doghouse had catered to working class folks—neighborhood secretaries and salesmen during the day. At night there had been an unlikely collection of retirees, cabbies, cops, and building security personnel sprinkled with a few assorted drug dealers and crooks. Peace had been maintained by the tough-talking, take-no-prisoners wait-staff.

That same kind of wait-staff was still in evidence—starting with a crew-cut, purple-haired, overalls-and-work-boot-clad hostess sporting black lipstick and a diamond in her left nostril. She met me at the door with a fistful of menus. "Booth or table?" she asked.

Looking down the long dining room, I realized the place was jammed with similarly clad, punk-looking young people. For clothing, unrelieved black seemed to be the order of the day, while hair color had more in common with Easter-egg dye than with Miss Clairol. At first glance, I assumed I was in a roomful of men, but seconds later the sounds of girlish laughter told me I was mistaken, fooled by my curiously old-fashioned notions about gender-based dressing.

"Booth or table?" the hostess asked again, more firmly this time.

Over time and with Ralph Ames' careful guidance, I've gradually updated my wardrobe. The dining room of the Hurricane Cafe wasn't a place where

I could expect a Brooks Brothers sports jacket and Johnston & Murphy shoes to blend in with the regular clientele.

"What say we try the bar?" I asked.

"Do you want a menu then or not?" the hostess asked.

More out of curiosity than hunger, I took one and made my own way to the bar. Hauling myself up onto an empty stool, I was relieved when I glanced down the bar and saw a bartender who, at first glance, appeared to be totally bald.

Quickly, I scanned through the menu. Other than the addition of a shareable twelve-egg omelette and *lattes*, the food wasn't all that different from Doghouse days. No doubt one of the continuing appeals the Hurricane Cafe held for its Generation-X customers had to do with affordability.

"What can I get you?" the bartender asked.

"How about a single tall skinny?" I asked.

One of the old Doghouse bartenders would have been insulted if a customer had ordered a *latte*. In the Hurricane Cafe, this guy, with a name tag that said Jimmy, didn't bat an eye. "Decaf or regular and what flavor?" he asked.

There are more options for ordering coffee in Seattle than some restaurants have for ordering entire meals. I was doing fine, ticking off my specifications until the guy turned away to reach for a coffee cup. That's when I saw his pony tail. The top and sides of his head had been shaved clean. The only hair remaining was a six-inch patch on the back of the head just over his shirt collar. Out of that patch sprouted a ten-inch pony tail. Even in the dim light there was no mistaking the color—emerald green, verging on chartreuse. Damn!

"That'll be two bucks," he said moments later, pushing my *latte* across the bar.

"Mr. Greenjeans, I presume?" I asked, peeling the requested amount and an extra dollar out of my wallet. I laid the money on the counter along with my ID.

"Jeez!" he exclaimed. "A cop!" He didn't sound overjoyed to make my acquaintance.

"Got a minute?"

Jimmy glanced warily toward the back of the restaurant. "Look," he said curtly. "I can't talk right now. I'm already in enough trouble as it is."

"For calling in the report?"

His jaw tightened. "What do you think? Look, those guys don't fuck around. If they see you talking to me or to Tony . . ."

"Tony," I said. "Tony who?"

"Never mind," Jimmy Greenjeans said. Shaking his head, he turned and walked away. Left to my own devices, I spun around on my stool. With my *latte* in hand, I casually surveyed the other people in the restaurant. Since no one had actually been arrested in regard to the Seward Park case, I had no mug shots to go on and no real description. I waited until Jimmy Greenjeans passed my way again.

"You'd better tell me who they are, or I'll have to ask everyone in the place, one customer at a time. That won't be too good for business."

Jimmy glowered at me. "All the way to the back," he said. "The booth next to the wall. Just don't tell them I sent you."

I sat on my perch a little while longer, taking in the details. At the last booth a pair of long-haired, earring sporting young men held a pair of blond teenyboppers in thrall. The report had said that Don Atkins and Barry Newsome were in their late twenties. Neither one of the two girls looked old enough to drive. Seward Park bones aside, the age discrepancy between the two guys and their jail-bait dates predisposed me not to like them.

Leaving my partially consumed *latte* on the bar, I stood up and sauntered through the restaurant. Whether or not Hurricane regulars suspected I was a cop, my out-of-place appearance was enough to stifle conversations at every booth I passed.

When I stopped beside the booth in question, one of the girls with everything pierced *but* her ears, looked up at me, gave an involuntary little cough, quickly stubbed out her cigarette into an ashtray, and then pushed it across the table.

"Which of you is Don Atkins and which is Barry Newsome?" I asked.

The one guy, with flowing blond locks and a string of diamond studs lining both ears, put down his beer and looked up at me. He had the neck and shoulders of a bodybuilder. When he spoke, however, his words emerged with the wispy incongruity of a ninety-pound weakling. "I'm Barry," he lisped. "What do you want?"

I tossed my ID into the middle of the table. "Been visiting any Native American burial grounds lately?" I asked.

Don Atkins, seated on the other side of the table, gave the girl sitting next to him a shove that almost sent her sprawling off the end of the bench seat. "Go on, Jen," he said. "I think I hear your mother calling. Go powder your noses, both of you."

Without a word of objection, the two girls gathered their tiny, wallet-sized purses and beat it for the rest rooms while I slid into the booth next to Barry Newsome.

He leaned over and gazed at my ID without ever touching it. "What do you want?" he asked.

Atkins did reach across the table. He picked up the leather wallet, examined my ID, and then tossed it back. "We haven't done anything," he said. "We're just running our little business, minding our own affairs. I don't see why . . ."

If Henry Leaping Deer had been right about Mr. Greenjeans' emerald green hair, it was entirely possible he was right about some of the other issues as well. The shaman claimed David Half Moon had died of natural causes, of lung cancer. If murder wasn't an issue in the Seward Park case, there didn't seem to be any harm in pulling out a few procedural stops.

"Let's see. I believe you picked up the bones a week ago last Sunday, didn't you?" I said, bluffing and watching for a reaction. I got one, too. Next to me on the bench, Barry Newsome squirmed uncomfortably.

"Did you go out to the reservation looking for them on purpose?" I continued. "Or did you stumble over them by accident?"

Barry's eyes flicked away from my face and settled on his partner's. Don Atkins shot him a single warning glance. It was enough to cause Barry to settle back in his seat. "I don't have any idea what you're talking about when you say reservation," he said. "Like we already told that other detective. We found the bones in Seward Park and . . ."

"It's what you told my partner," I said, cutting in. "But it's not true, and you know it. The bones came from somewhere out on the Kitsap Peninsula, from a sacred Indian burial ground. I want to know how that happened. Did you find them yourselves or did someone else lead you to them, someone who knew where and what they were?"

This time, when Barry Newsome opened his mouth as if to answer, Don Atkins headed him off. "Shut up, Barry," he snarled. Barry stifled.

But Newsome's obvious discomfort was enough to keep me interested. "Look," I continued, trying to strike a reasonable tone. "As you no doubt saw from my ID, I'm with the Seattle PD's Homicide Unit. That puts grave robbing and Kitsap County both outside the range of my official jurisdiction. However, I have it on good authority that the Seward Park bones belong to a powerful medicine man—a shaman—named David Half Moon. According to my Native American sources, anyone coming in contact with Mr. Half Moon's remains is in, pardon the pun, grave danger. Taking that into consideration, wouldn't it be best for all concerned if his bones were returned to their proper resting place as soon as possible? You two could facilitate that by simply coming clean and telling me where they came from. With corroboration from you, I'd be able to make arrangements to have the ME's office release Mr. Half Moon's remains to his people."

Don Atkins reached into his shirt pocket, pulled out a cigarette, and lit up. "Barry and I have nothing more to say to you, Detective Beaumont," he said, feigning casual indifference. "If you have any further questions, you're welcome to take them up with our attorney, Troy Cochran with Owens, Milton and Cochran. In the meantime, I'd . . ."

"Why, J.P., long time no see," a familiar voice interrupted. "What brings you here? Seems just like old times."

A cloud of vermouth, diluted only slightly by the haze of smoke, blew past my face. I looked up to see my old nemesis from the *Seattle Post-Intelligencer*— a bleary-eyed columnist named Maxwell Cole— standing leering over me. Drunk or sober, Max is one of the last people on earth I ever want to see.

"Look, Max. I'm busy right now. Do you mind?"

Disregarding my objection, Max reached across me to drop a load of cigarette ashes into the brimming ashtray the young blond had pushed aside. He looked like hell. His tie was loose and his shirttail hung out of his pants. The wax on his handlebar moustache had given up the ghost leaving the long, wispy ends trailing limply down the front of his shirt. He straightened up and stood swaying, gazing wistfully around the room.

"Not exactly like the old days around here," he mumbled. "But still, it's a good enough place to come tipple a few on occasion."

I guessed he had tippled several more than a few, but I also know from personal experience that there's no point in arguing with a drunk. "Max," I said patiently, "why don't you go wait in the bar. I'll join you in a minute. Matter of fact, tell the bartender that you'll have one of what I'm having—on me."

"Okeydokey," Max responded cheerfully. Taking the hint, he staggered toward the bar while I turned back to Don Atkins.

"You know who that is, don't you?" I asked. Atkins shook his head. "His name is Maxwell Cole," I continued. "You probably recognize the name because he's the crime columnist with the *P.-I.* Max and I go back a long way. We were fraternity brothers at the U-Dub years ago. Now that I think about it, even though grave robbing may be outside the realm of my personal responsibility and jurisdiction, it certainly wouldn't be outside Max's. With a little bit of direction, I wouldn't be surprised if he came up with a wonderful human interest piece on Mr. Half Moon. A story like that would most likely attract the attention and unwanted scrutiny of any number of local Native American activists. They'd rain down around Bloodlust's ears and make your life hell. It's possible they might even follow you on your travels around town or picket your place of business. They might also suggest publicly that people boycott your role-playing dramas. I know that's just a hobby for you guys, but I have a feeling that most of the people who come on those middle-of-the-night adventures pay good money to be there."

"That's blackmail," Atkins said at once.

I smiled back at him. "No, it's not," I said. "It's called getting the job done. You think it over," I added. "Max doesn't seem to be in any condition to write anything at the moment, so I probably won't actually give him the information until tomorrow.

Say around noon. Unless somebody calls before then and gives me a good reason not to."

Pausing long enough to extract a few business cards from my wallet, I dropped them on the table. "My phone numbers," I explained. "If you don't get through to me directly, feel free to leave a message. I'll get right back to you."

With that, I got up from the booth and left them. The two girls, out of the rest room, were hanging around the pinball machines as I headed to the bar. "You can go back now," I told them. "Your friends and I are all done with our little chat."

Back at the bar, Maxwell Cole was looking at his *latte* with all the distaste of a tree-hugger faced with a clear-cut. "You don't expect me to drink this shit, do you J.P.?"

What I had told the two creeps at the booth about my history with Max was true as far as it went. Our acquaintance dated all the way from college days. However, I had left out a few telling details, including the fact that a mutual antagonism dated from those old college/fraternity days, as well. My first wife, Karen, had been dating Max when I stole her away from him. Later on, our career choices—mine as a cop and his as a journalist—kept us on opposite sides of the fence. Our views on truth, justice, and the American way just didn't jibe. They still don't.

In my postdivorce binge-drinking days, Max and I had frequented some of the same watering holes. I found it disconcerting to discover that on occasion we still did.

"A little milk and coffee mixed in with whatever else you're drinking isn't going to kill you," I said.

Max picked up the cup, examined it as though it might be poison, and then set it down without tasting it. "I suppose," he said with just a hint of sarcasm, "that since you're on the wagon now, you expect everyone else to be, too."

That wasn't true. One of the things I had vowed when I first ventured into AA was that I wouldn't turn into one of those proselytizing AA fanatics. I'm neither a hypocrite nor a spoilsport. I actually enjoyed my drinking days. At least I did, up to a point. The only reason I quit was because my doctor gave me a choice between my liver and the booze. End of story. People who knew me back then sometimes assume I've turned into some kind of moralizing prude. That's not true, either. All I really want to do is live long enough to see my granddaughter, Kayla, grow up to be the spitting image of her mother and grandmother.

In feeding Max a *latte*, I was doing the same thing—protecting my butt. Being forced to share the streets of Seattle's Denny Regrade with a driver too drunk to walk straight didn't make sense for long-term survival—his, mine, or anybody else's. I figured pausing long enough for him to consume a nonalcoholic coffee drink would give me a chance to assess the situation. In the process I'd try to determine if Max was actually sober enough to drive home or if he needed to be stuffed in a cab and sent there.

"Shut up, Max, and drink your drink," I told him. "I'm working my own program here, not yours or anybody else's."

I picked up my now-cold cup and tasted the contents. There's hardly anything less appealing than a dead *latte*. "Hey, barkeep," I said to Mr. Greenjeans. "Hit me again, too."

He glowered at me, but he turned to comply. By the time my second one came, Max had lit another cigarette and was hunched over his cup in typical barfly fashion. "Do you know my old buddy here, Mr. Greenjeans?" he asked.

"We've met," I said. "But we're not exactly best pals."

"Know where he got his name?"

"No idea. From his parents, I'd imagine."

Max laughed, slapping his pant leg as he did so. "That's where you'd be wrong, J.P. Wrong, wrong, wrong." He paused and frowned. "Or else maybe you'd be right. I'm not sure which."

The whole issue seemed a no-brainer. I couldn't see how Max could find it so puzzling. He continued. "Jimmy told me once, that Captain Kangaroo . . . You remember him, don't you, good old Captain Kangaroo? You know, the guy with the weird haircut?"

"Yes," I said, "I remember."

"Jimmy said that when he was little watching *Captain Kangaroo* in the morning was the nicest part of his day. That as soon as his old man rolled out of bed, he came looking for the kids with a belt and some excuse or another to beat the crap out of them. Out of Jimmy especially, I guess. Jimmy told me that once he was old enough, he went straight down to the courthouse to have his name changed.

Cost him four-hundred bucks. He said he tried for Kangaroo, but the judge wouldn't go for it. So he settled on Mr. Greenjeans instead. Cute, huh?"

"I'll say."

Jimmy Greenjeans came back down the bar and slammed the change on the counter in front of me. He was obviously unhappy that after going over to tackle Atkins and Newsome I had returned to his bar. Now that I knew those two creeps better, I didn't much blame him. More than anything, though, I felt sorry for the guy—sorry that he had somehow gotten mixed up in a game that put him in danger from a long-dead Indian shaman and sorry, too, that he had grown up in a situation where an hour-long weekday television program was the only thing that had offered his young life any respite from misery. That kind of home situation went a long way toward explaining his green hair, his alternative lifestyle, and his somewhat unfortunate attitude.

On the face of it, I had come to the Hurricane Cafe in hopes of contacting the role-play ringleaders, which I had done. Secondarily, I guess I had wanted to check out Mr. Greenjeans to find out for myself whether or not anything Darla Cunningham had told me was on the level. Now that I had done that—now that I had met the man with the green hair, the one Henry Leaping Deer claimed was in danger—where did my duty lie? Should I pass along Darla's message and try to warn him? Or should I forget it?

I tried to put myself in Jimmy Greenjeans' place. If someone I didn't know came into my place of work—the department, for example—hassled me about something I had done or said and then went totally against my wishes in talking to someone I wanted left alone, I probably wouldn't be feeling especially warm and cuddly toward that individual a few minutes later. And then, if that same person, now in the company of a babbling drunk—which Max Cole inarguably was—tried to tell me that I was in danger of being harmed by the angry spirit of a deceased medicine man, I probably would have thrown the guy ass-first out the door.

Let it go, Beaumont, I told myself. *MYOB.*

CHAPTER 9

EVEN THOUGH I HAD LONG SINCE STOPPED PAYING AT-
tention to him, Max was still at my side and still yak-
king away, too drunk to notice that he was mostly
talking to himself.

"Hey, Maxi, old sport," I told him, interrupting
his sodden monologue. "What say we call it a night.
Let me call you a cab."

That brought him up straight. "Like hell!" he
snorted. "I don't need a goddamned cab! Whaddya
think I am, drunk or something? I'm totally capable of driving myself home."

*And wrapping yourself around a dozen telephone
poles in the process*, I thought. Faced with his angry
reaction, I knew there was no sense arguing. Instead, I led him outside into the cool night air. "If a
cab doesn't suit you, how about a ride home in a
nice Porsche 928?"

He stopped and stood swaying, eyeing me crook-
edly. The movement of the planet must have been
too much for him. As he dipped to one side, I caught

hold of one arm to keep him from pitching off the sidewalk into the street. "Which one?" he asked. "That cute little red Porsche ol' what's-her-name gave you?"

I nodded. "It's not exactly the same one Anne Corley gave me. It's a replacement, but yes, it's close enough."

"How about letting me drive it my own self?"

"Sorry, Max," I said, opening the passenger door and pouring him inside. "Not tonight. Maybe some other time."

As I drove Max to his house on top of Queen Anne Hill, I realized that something I had said earlier really was true. I *was* working my own program—the eighth step. That's the one that involves making a list of the people I had harmed and making amends to them all. Maxwell Cole was one of those people. I'd pulled several stunts on him through the years, the most flagrant of which had been stealing Karen Moffitt right out from under his nose. Giving him a ride home obviously wouldn't make up for that, but it was a start, a step in the right direction.

Max lives on Bigelow Avenue, a winding street lined with lushly leafed chestnut trees. I stopped in front of his place and then left the 928 idling while I went around to the passenger's side to help him out. As I led him up onto the front porch of the Tudor-style house that had once belonged to his parents, Max fell into a fit of maudlin weeping. "I really appreciate this, J.P.," he croaked. "I just don't know how to thank you."

Within minutes he had drifted from one extreme

to the other, from being pissed about being offered a ride home to being absurdly grateful. Mood swings go with the territory.

"It's all right," I told him. "I did it for me as much as I did it for you. What's your phone number, Max?"

"Why?" he asked, after he gave it to me.

"Do you have a machine?"

"Sure. Why do you need to know that?"

"Never mind," I told him.

I watched him fumble a set of keys out of his pockets and then I waited through his interminable struggle of putting the key in the lock. Once the door finally opened, he stumbled inside. Once again, it took several tries before he managed to relock the dead bolt from the far side of the door. Only when I heard the lock hit home did I turn and walk away.

Back in the car, I picked up my cell phone and dialed the number Max had given me. He had turned on the lights in a room which, due to the frosted windows, I assumed to be a bathroom. I wasn't surprised, then, when no one answered and his voice mail switched on.

"This is Maxwell Cole. I can't come to the phone right now. Please leave a message . . ."

"Max," I said. "This is J. P. Beaumont. In case you can't find your car this morning, you might try checking the parking lot at the Hurricane Cafe."

That was all I said. When Max sobered up in the morning, I doubted he would remember where he had left his ugly orange Volvo. I know how those kinds of things can sneak up on you. After all, it happened to me once or twice, too. Maybe even more than once or twice, but then who's counting?

On the way back down Queen Anne, I tried calling Sue's home number. She had told me to call when I finished up. If I reached her on my way home, calling at eleven was marginally better than eleven-fifteen. Because her son Jared seems to spend most of his waking hours with a phone glued to his ear, I was accustomed to having to dodge my way through the teenage phone screen. As soon as Sue's voice mail switched on, I gave up and dialed her pager instead.

She called me back before I even hit the bottom of the hill. "Doesn't your son know there's school tomorrow and he ought to be in bed?"

"Jared is in bed," she told me.

"Oh," I said. "When the voice mail came on, I thought . . ."

"It was me," she said. "After three screaming phone calls from Richie, I finally took the phone off the hook and left it there."

I heard the ragged catch in her voice as she finished the sentence. Now that I was paying attention, I noticed she sounded stuffy. Either she was dealing with a terrible allergy attack or she'd been crying.

"Sue," I said. "Are you all right?"

She took a deep breath. "I'm fine," she said. "It's been a hell of a night, that's all."

I had planned to call her and bring her up to speed, but her voice sounded so bleak that I wondered if a phone call was enough. "What are you doing?" I asked.

"Cleaning house like a madwoman." She laughed without humor. "That's what my mother used to do whenever she and Dad had an argument—she'd clean the place like there was no tomorrow. I just figured out that I'm doing the same thing, but at least when Richie gets here the damned house will be spotless. What about you?"

"I just finished paying a late-night visit to the Hurricane Cafe," I told her. "Ran into some friends of yours, Don Atkins and Barry Newsome. If you're not on your way to bed in the next couple of minutes, maybe I could stop by and tell you what went on. That way I won't be in danger of being called a Lone Ranger tomorrow morning."

"Sure," she said. "Come on by. There's not much sense in going to bed. I've been so upset all evening that I wouldn't be able to sleep anyway."

"Well, since you're not planning on sleeping, let me add one little bit of bad news. When I got down to the department tonight, after you called, Captain Powell's temporary replacement was moving into the Fishbowl. His initials are P.K."

For a moment there was nothing on the air but stunned silence. "You're kidding! Not Kramer."

"I wish I were kidding, but I'm not."

"What the hell is the brass thinking?" she demanded. "How dare they put that officious jackass in charge even for a day."

"I'm sure it was easy. We can talk more when I get there, but we're probably better off discussing it in private rather than on the fifth floor with a dozen little ears to hear."

In the preceding year or so, both Sue and I had

been granted the dubious honor of working with Detective Paul Kramer on a one-to-one basis. Together she and I were privy to more about the man than almost anyone else in Homicide.

When I arrived at Sue's house in the Fremont neighborhood a few minutes later, she was sitting on the front porch. "Where's the vacuum cleaner?" I asked. "I thought you'd still be at it."

"I shut it off," she said. "Now I'm too mad to vacuum. What's the matter with those people? Kramer's not even a good detective. How could they possibly promote him?"

"He's a number cruncher," I explained, sitting down beside her. "And this is the golden era of number crunchers. All we'll have to do to keep Kramer happy and off our backs is to show him cases that get cleared in a timely fashion."

"Cleared and timely and holding up in court aren't necessarily one and the same," Sue responded.

"Right," I said. "But he's going to be looking for percentages. By the time those half-assed cases fall out in court, he'll be long gone. Guys like Kramer are always angling for the next promotion long before they get settled into the desk on their current one."

"Still," Sue said. "If anyone was going to be promoted, I think it should have been you."

Her vote of confidence, while gratifying, made me laugh aloud. She looked up at me, her face serious and frowning in the glow of a corner streetlight. "What's so funny about that?" she asked.

"My grandmother's of the same opinion you are," I told her. "Grandma would like to see me promoted, too. Only she'd like me to skip the captain and major ranks altogether and go directly to chief. Believe me, I know my limitations. It wouldn't be a good fit."

"But doesn't it bother you to be skipped over?" she asked.

I thought about it. "Some," I admitted at last. "It's not the first time I've helped train a fast-tracker who ended up being my superior officer. If I really wanted a promotion, I'd have gone after one, but I think I'm far better suited to being a mentor than I am a boss. Besides, who knows what'll happen when Kramer moves up or out? Maybe it'll be your turn then."

"Mine?" Sue asked.

"Sure," I said. "You're a good detective. It won't be long before you're promotable yourself. Kramer notwithstanding, the brass doesn't always pick jackasses. When you turn captain on me, somebody else will shake his head and say, 'Poor old Detective Beaumont. He taught her everything he knew, and now she's ordering him around.'"

For the first time a ghost of a smile appeared in the corners of Sue Danielson's lips. She seemed genuinely surprised by my praise—surprised and pleased. "Do you really mean that?"

"You bet I do," I assured her. "Now, tell me about Richie and the kids. What's going on?"

The smile disappeared and she sighed. "I spent half the night fighting with the kids and the other half screaming at Richie on the phone."

I tried to imagine Sue screaming at anyone. I had worked with her for months, long enough to appreciate the fact that she seldom raised her voice.

"I take it he took exception to your laying down the law about spring break?"

She nodded. "The last thing he said to me was 'I'll see you in hell first.' That's when I took the phone off the hook and left it off."

A cold chill that had nothing to do with the weather passed over my body. "That sounds like a threat," I said.

Sue nodded. "He thinks he can still boss me around, but it isn't going to happen."

For almost a minute we sat on the steps, thinking and not speaking. The threat of bodily harm may have come over a telephone handset and in Richie Danielson's voice, but it sounded a distinct warning bell. I wondered if the real origin of that threat didn't lie somewhere else—in the set of bones Sue had lugged back from Bellevue and delivered to the ME's office. Darla Cunningham had claimed that whatever happened wouldn't necessarily seem to be related. It struck me now that David Half Moon had somehow drafted Sue's ex-husband, Richie, to be the bearer of the shaman's bad tidings. Those thoughts all crossed my mind, but they sounded so kooky, that I wasn't sure how to go about saying them.

"Maybe you shouldn't see him at all," I suggested. "Sounds to me as though it might be better if you and the boys weren't even here when he shows up."

"I'm not running away," Sue said determinedly. "Not again. Richie Danielson may have chased me out of one house, but he isn't driving me out of this one. And I'm not going to let him get away with playing uproar, either. That's what this whole trip was designed to do—throw our lives into turmoil."

"How did the kids take the news?" I asked.

"Not at all the way I expected," she said. "I explained to them what the two school principals said when I talked to them—that since these wouldn't be excused absences, they wouldn't be allowed to make up the work. I thought Jared would give me the most grief, but it turned out to be Chris. He was heartbroken. He finally cried himself to sleep about an hour ago."

Sighing again, she stood up and rubbed her arms. "Now that I'm not working, it's chilly out here. Come on inside. I'll brew us up a cup of tea."

I followed her into her little rented house. The vacuum cleaner and a basket stocked with cleaning supplies sat in the middle of a seemingly spotless living room. In the kitchen the refrigerator door was covered with a dozen handmade paper Easter eggs. I sat down at the small, cloth-covered kitchen table while Sue set a copper-bottomed teakettle on a burner.

"So tell me," she said, changing the subject. "Who was the woman who came to the department to see us tonight? What was her name again?"

"Cunningham," I supplied. "Darla Cunningham."

"What did she want and why was it so urgent?"

Good luck, I told myself before launching off into it. *Either she'll believe me or she won't.*

"What do you know about Native Americans?" I asked.

"Not much," she admitted, lighting a cigarette. "I've eaten fry bread at the Puyallup fair. And I took an alternative U.S. history course. Naturally, I was properly appalled. The whites screwed the Indians six ways to Sunday."

"Did that course you took happen to mention anything about medicine men or shamans?"

"Are you kidding? It was a history course, all battles and broken peace treaties. Why?"

In the next few minutes, I gave Sue a brief outline of what Darla had told me including the spooky dreams that had led Henry Leaping Deer to investigate whether or not his boyhood chum was still alive and how another dream, one of children playing with David Half Moon's bones and skull, had led Darla to make a connection with the Seward Park role-players.

"That's so weird," Sue said. "Not to mention tenuous. Yes, it's true Jimmy Greenjeans has green hair, but how could this Darla put what her father had said together with that single tiny blurb in the paper? How does that work?"

"I don't know how," I agreed. "It would be real handy if people working Homicide had those kinds of skills. I suppose, though, that it's the same kind of chance occurrence that makes a routine traffic stop lead to the arrest of a serial killer. The point is, the ME's office says the bones really are Native American. I for one am convinced that they belong to David Half Moon and that we should try to get them sent home as soon as possible. I'm also worried that we should take her warning seriously— that anyone who handled those bones might be in danger, you and Jimmy Greenjeans included."

To my dismay, she laughed then. "Come on,

Beau," Sue said. "You're a homicide cop. You may be falling for all this hocus-pocus, but I'm not."

"Right," I said. "You must be from Missouri."

Sue gave me a puzzled frown. "No, I'm not," she declared in all seriousness. "I'm from Ohio. I thought you knew that."

That's one of the hazards of working with younger cops. Sometimes it seems as though we don't even speak the same language. At that moment, this particular age-based breakdown in communications didn't seem worthy of an explanation.

"I did know that," I said. "That you were from Ohio, I mean. It must have slipped my mind. Anyway, after hearing Darla's warning and now listening to you talk about Richie, I'm worried, Sue. What if he tries to pull something? What if this Disneyland thing pushes him over the edge and he does something to you or the kids?"

"He won't," she said.

"He did it before," I countered. "You told me so yourself."

"That was different," she said. "I wasn't armed then, and I wasn't a trained cop, either."

I could have reeled off a few grim statistics about how many police officers a year are shot with their own weapons, but just then the teakettle started whistling. "What do you take in your tea?" she asked, pulling out a box of Celestial Seasonings Sleepytime. "Lemon and sugar?"

"Both," I said.

We didn't say much more until Sue had served the tea and was once again seated at the table. "So did you tell Mr. Greenjeans about all this medicine man . . . this shaman stuff?" she asked.

I shook my head. "No."

"Why not? If I'm in danger from handling those bones, what about him? I might or might not be the 'Anglo woman' Darla Cunningham mentioned, but there can't be much doubt about the guy with green hair."

"I didn't think he'd believe me."

For the first time since I'd arrived at her house, Sue Danielson smiled a genuine smile. "I suspect there's a lot of that going around. You worry too much, Beau. The boys and I will be just fine, and so will Mr. Greenjeans. Now, did you learn anything new when you talked to Newsome and Atkins?"

"The name of their attorney. Troy Cochran of Owens, Milton and Cochran."

She shook her head. "It figures," she said. "Troy Cochran is as big a jerk as his clients are. Speaking of which, you should see Newsome and Atkins' house over in Bellevue. It's one of those *Architectural Digest* numbers that looks like it was put together by a committee playing with Tinker Toys and building blocks. Inside was nothing but chrome and glass and leather. Do you think they're just roommates or are they a couple?"

"I'm sure the two little underage cuties who were with them weren't thinking in terms of gay blades. Who knows? Maybe they're switch-hitters."

"How old?" Sue asked.

"The two girls? Fifteen at the outside."

Sue shook her head. "Makes me wish we could

find a way to lock them both up, but if Darla Cunningham's ID is correct, we just lost our homicide victim, so sending those guys to the slammer isn't going to happen."

"It looks that way," I agreed.

One cup of Sleepytime was more than enough for me. We shot the breeze for a little longer and then I headed back home to Belltown Terrace. It was past midnight when I slipped off my shoes and settled into the recliner to try to gain some perspective on what had been a deceptively tough day. Nothing much had happened and yet so much had changed—and not for the better, either.

Had I been gifted with Henry Leaping Deer's ability to see through the mists, I might have realized that I was a man standing at the bottom of a mountain peak, totally unaware that far above me a chunk of ice and snow had broken free from a cliff and started downward. Silent and deadly, an avalanche was headed my way and I had yet to figure it out.

Lulled by the Sleepytime, I soon fell sound asleep. The next thing I knew, it was four o'clock in the morning, I was still in the recliner, and my back was killing me. That's one of the things I miss most now that I'm not married. There's nobody around to wake me up and tell me it's time to go to bed.

CHAPTER 10

I WOKE UP THE NEXT MORNING DETERMINED TO DO MY job, the job the City of Seattle pays me to do, which is to say, find killers. I went to the office intending to stop off only long enough to collect my partner and a white charger—in this case a Chevy Caprice. After that, my game plan consisted of going straight to Marysville, interviewing Hilda Smathers, and then doing whatever was necessary to track down whoever had killed poor old Agnes Ferman.

As soon as those words crossed my mind, I had to revise them. Agnes may have been relatively old and unfortunate, but she certainly wasn't poor. She was, however, most certainly dead.

Getting into the office worked fine. Getting out again didn't. On the first day of a new assignment, most middle managers are smart enough to let things ride. Maintaining things as is gives the new guy an opportunity to see what works and what doesn't before he sets out to reinvent the wheel. Kramer was the exception that proves the rule.

His briefing that first morning—a meeting that in Powell's day would have taken ten minutes at the outside—lasted an interminable hour and a half. By the time Sue and I headed for the garage, I was fuming, but Sue Danielson was on a tear.

"If I'd had to listen to that arrogant asshole for one more minute, I think I would have puked," she said once we were finally alone in the car. "What does he think we are, a bunch of little kids? And why should we write up our goals and objectives? Our job is to catch killers, what's so mysterious about that? And which is finding Agnes Ferman's killer? Is that a goal or is it an objective?"

"Don't worry," I told her. "This isn't going to last." I said, "I think Kramer was a little nervous. The goals-and-objectives bit is just to let us know it's the start of a new regime."

"New regime, my ass!" Sue returned. "He was just throwing his weight around."

"Forget it," I said. "Now that we're finally out of there, let's get on with the job. Read me back everything we know about Hilda Smathers."

Sue opened the notebook and was reading back some of our interview with Mildred George when she stopped. "Do you know what I just realized? We still don't know the name or address of the family Agnes Ferman worked for all those years. Help me remember to ask Hilda Smathers about them when we see her."

"I'll do my best."

For a change there was no big traffic tie-up along the I-5 corridor. Forty minutes after leaving the Public Safety Building, we stopped that day's bulge-

mobile in front of Hilda Smathers' somewhat derelict mobile home in Green Mountain Vista. An old,
rusted-out Toyota Camry that had once been
bronze was parked under an awning off to the side.
Sue knocked several times, however, before there
was any sign of life from inside the trailer. Eventually, after a series of squeaking floorboards, a woman's voice came from the other side of the door.

"Who are you?" she demanded. "What do you
want?"

"We're police officers," Sue returned. "We're
here to talk to you about Agnes Ferman."

"Just a minute," the woman said. "Let me make
myself presentable."

We waited outside for several minutes before
squeaks approached the door once more. When it
opened, the woman standing there might have been
Mildred George's age, but she looked much older.
Her face was lined with the deep crevices that come
from a lifetime of sucking on burning tobacco. Her
voice, too, had the unmistakable and deep-throated
growl of a long-term smoker. Her hair, dye-job
blond with dark roots showing, had been haphaz-
ardly pulled back into a bun at the nape of her neck.
She wore a loose-fitting pair of sweats. The hur-
riedly applied lipstick took a sudden dip on one
corner of her lower lip. In her estimation, Hilda
Smathers might have been more presentable, but she
was a long way from put-together.

"You must be the two detectives Millie told me
about yesterday."

Sue nodded. "That's right. I'm Detective Danielson and this is Detective Beaumont."

"Come in," Hilda said. "You'll have to forgive me. Things are in a bit of a mess around here."

That was actually a gross understatement. The place was a pit. Hilda Smathers' house reminded me of one or two crack houses I've seen over the years—places where the alleged adults have been so spaced out on drugs and/or booze that whatever children resided there had been left to fend for themselves through spoiled, rotten food and unimaginable filth. Fortunately for the rest of the world, Hilda Smathers appeared to live alone.

While she went to clear a spot on the couch, I tried to remember exactly what it was we knew about Hilda in advance of this interview. The only thing I could remember was that she worked in a bakery or deli somewhere. If her home was any demonstration of her idea of cleanliness, I hoped she wasn't in charge of keeping the bakery clean.

"Here," she said, indicating a spot on the sagging, soiled sofa where she had swept a mound of debris onto the floor. "You can both sit here."

The spot wasn't nearly big enough for both Sue and me. "Go ahead," I said to Sue taking refuge in that old standby—gentlemanly behavior. "I don't mind standing."

Sue gave me a wan smile that I took to mean she, too, would have preferred to stand. Nevertheless, she took the proffered seat. Hilda Smathers reached down to pluck an already burning cigarette from an ashtray on the coffee table, then she plopped down on a worn armchair in the far corner of the room.

"What is it you want?" she asked.

"When's the last time you saw your sister?" Sue asked.

"Agnes was my half sister, not my full sister," Hilda corrected. "But Sunday was the day I saw her—the day before they found her dead. I saw her that evening. It was around six, I think, although it could have been later."

"Why did you go to see her?" Sue asked.

Hilda didn't answer right away. Instead, she took a long, thoughtful drag on her cigarette. "It wasn't social," she said at last. "Not your usual Sunday night visit if that's what you're asking."

"What was it then?" Sue persisted.

"I went to ask her for money—to fix my car."

"Your car wasn't working?"

Hilda's eyes narrowed. "That's what I told her," she said. "But it wasn't true. Agnes could always understand if it was car trouble, but if I had told her the real reason I needed the money, she would have told me to take a hike."

"What was the real reason?" I asked.

"To pay the rent," Hilda responded. "I own the mobile, you see, but I rent the space. I was two months behind. I was afraid the manager was going to start eviction procedures if I didn't give 'em something pretty soon."

"And did Agnes give it to you?" Sue asked. "The money, I mean?"

Hilda shook her head. "No, she said she'd have it for me the next day, but then you know what happened. She died before she ever had a chance to give it to me."

"How much money did you ask for?" Sue asked.

"I told her it was a transmission problem. That it would probably end up costing twelve hundred bucks or so. That way, after I paid the rent, I'd have a little extra—a cushion. What I don't understand is if Agnes had all the money Millie says she did out in her garage, why didn't she just go ahead and give it to me right then? Here she's dead. I'll probably end up with a whole bunch of money eventually, but in the meantime, I still have the landlord breathing down my neck."

There are things about being in the homicide business that still surprise me. Hilda Smathers' aggrieved reply was one of those. Her whole attitude implied that Agnes Ferman had a hell of a lot of nerve to up and die without giving Hilda the money she wanted even though she had lied about her reasons for needing it. This was another one of those cases where that handy term "unbelievable" barely did the situation justice.

"You don't sound particularly sorry that she's dead," I observed.

Blowing a long plume of smoke, Hilda Smathers turned to study me for some time before she replied. "I'm not," she said. "Agnes was mean as they come. To almost everybody—her husband, her brother, Millie. I tried to get along with her. She liked me, you see, but only because I was the baby. Because she thought she could boss me around."

"Did she?" Sue asked, "Boss you around?"

"I let her *think* she did," Hilda replied. "But I still did pretty much what I damn well pleased. That's what you have to do with people like that—humor them, but go around them, too."

In my pants pocket, my silent pager vibrated against my leg. Choosing to ignore it, I continued with the interview. "What can you tell us about Mildred?" I asked.

Hilda blinked. "Millie? What about her? We're sisters-in-law, but friends, too."

"You also knew Andy's first wife, Betty?" I asked.

Hilda nodded. "Once, a long time ago, I lived with Betty and Andy for a few months," she said. "Agnes never believed it, but Betty was a mess. The best thing that ever happened to Andrew was when he dumped Betty in favor of Millie. She's an absolute gem."

"Mildred George seems to have the same high regard for you as you have for her," Sue said. "She told us that you've been a real lifesaver in the past year or two since her husband has been so sick."

Hilda ducked her head at the unexpected compliment. "I try," she said. "Andy and Millie have been good to me and my girls over the years. Helping them out a little now is the least I could do."

I noticed, however, that we'd strayed off the subject a bit. "Tell us about Mildred," I urged again.

"What about her?"

"Is she the kind of woman who might cheat on her husband?"

"Cheat?" Hilda repeated, as her eyes met and held mine. "What's there to cheat on? Half the time Andy doesn't even know who she is. She keeps a roof over his head and sees to it that he eats. She makes sure there's someone there to take care of him twenty-four hours a day. At night she has to keep him tied in his bed to keep him from wandering around loose or burning the house down. When a man's that far gone, who's to say what's cheating and what isn't?"

"I take it you know about her boyfriend, then?" No one had told us for sure that Mildred's boss, Lonnie Olson, was also her boyfriend. Hilda's response, however, went a long way toward confirming it.

Her eyes narrowed. She stubbed out the cigarette and turned to face me with her arms folded stubbornly across her chest. "What I know is this," she said. "After what Millie's been through these past few years, she's entitled to whatever happiness she can find wherever she can find it."

"On the Sunday night in question, she claims she was home all evening long. You wouldn't by any chance be able to confirm that, would you?" I asked.

Hilda glared at me. "If Millie says she was home, she was home, and that's that," Hilda said. "You're not trying to say that she had something to do with what happened to Agnes, are you?"

"It's our job to eliminate all possibilities," I said. "We need to verify her whereabouts at the time in question. Your whereabouts as well, for that matter."

"Mine!" Hilda blurted.

"Yes. After you left Agnes Ferman's house that Sunday night, where did you go?"

Hilda bit her lip. "The reservation." She said the words so softly I could barely make them out.

"The reservation?"

"The Tulalip," she said. "To the casino. I go there

sometimes on my time off. When I'm not helping Millie with Andy, that is."

"Was there anyone there that night who would remember seeing you?"

"I doubt it," she said. "A week ago Sunday is a long time back for people in a place like that. They don't remember who's there from one night to the next. Over a week later, I'm sure no one would remember. I did win a jackpot that night, though. It happened just before closing. I won three hundred and fifty bucks at electronic blackjack. I don't know how those things work, but there might be some record of that."

As Sue jotted the information into her notebook, I considered our next move. In the course of talking to her, Hilda Smathers hadn't made a very good impression on me. And knowing she'd had enough money to go gambling after trying to dupe her sister out of more than a thousand dollars for bogus car repairs, I couldn't help tweaking her ever so slightly.

"So then, after winning that much money, I assume you went ahead and paid off at least one of those months of back rent, right?"

"That wasn't rent money," Hilda replied indignantly. "That was gambling money."

"I see," I said, although I didn't see at all.

Meanwhile, Sue veered off onto another topic. "From what you said, I assume you know all about the fortune in cash hidden in Agnes Ferman's garage."

Hilda nodded.

"Would you have any idea where the money came from?"

Hilda Smathers shook her head. "None at all. Agnes always said she had money. How much was it again?"

"Just over three hundred thousand dollars."

Hilda shook her head. "I never would have dreamed she'd have that much. The Considines were well-off but they weren't that well-off."

"The who?"

"The Considines. The people Agnes worked for all those years. She started out as a nurse to the older son, Lucas. There was something the matter with him, with Lucas, but I never really knew what it was. Freddy came along a few years later. I'm not exactly sure what happened. Something went wrong after that second pregnancy. Regina, the mother, was pretty much an invalid from then on. Agnes took care of the boys as long as they needed her. Later on she was Mrs. Considine's full-time nurse."

"Trained nurse?"

"Well, companion, then. She looked after Mrs. Considine. Did whatever needed to be done."

"Any relation to Forrest Considine?" I asked, thinking of the man who had started one of the local Washington state banks—a bank that had long since been merged into oblivion with one of the large multistate conglomerates.

Hilda Smathers nodded. "Forrest. I'm pretty sure that's the father's name," she said. "I think they started out originally in timber—both his family and Regina's—somewhere up around Stanwood. At any rate, Regina had money in her own right. Rumor had it that during Prohibition Forrest had some involvement in bootlegging. All I know is, by the end of the Depression when everybody else was flat broke, the Considines had plenty of money. That's when Forrest made his move into banking. From what Agnes told me, the two boys never wanted for anything except good sense, maybe."

"And the Considines were the only people Agnes ever worked for?"

"As far as I know," Hilda responded. "They treated her very well, too—almost like family. Still, she might have done work on the side for someone else that I never knew anything about."

"Do you know where the Considines are now?" Sue was asking.

"The mother and one of the boys—Lucas, I believe—are both dead now," Hilda answered. "The last I heard, Forrest was in a nursing home somewhere in Seattle or maybe Shoreline. I don't know anything at all about Freddy."

We stayed a little while longer. When we finally got back in the Caprice, Sue leaned back against the headrest and closed her eyes. "I guess that answers at least one of your questions from yesterday," she said.

"What question is that?"

"About why there weren't any services scheduled in the aftermath of Agnes Ferman's death. Nobody gave a damn about her one way or the other. Where to?"

"Sounds like time to visit the reservation." Sue nodded.

Heading toward the casino, I thought about Sue's

previous statement for some time. "That's not true," I said finally.

"What's not true?"

"By actual count," I said, "we've interviewed a total of four people so far. Three of those definitely fit in the 'don't care' category, but I'm not so sure about number four."

"Who's that?" Sue asked.

"Malcolm Lawrence," I said. "Somehow, I picked up the impression that he actually liked the old bat."

"Really?" Sue said. "It didn't seem that way to me, but then . . ."

Before she could finish that thought, the voice of one of the dispatch operators came over the radio. "Where are you?" he asked, when Sue responded.

"Everett," she said. "We're up here interviewing a next of kin. We're on our way to the Tulalip Casino in an attempt to verify an alibi."

"You'd better put that on the back burner for the time being. Sergeant Watkins has been looking all over for you." Remembering the page, I checked the display. Sure enough, there was the number for Watty's extension.

"Put me through to him then," Sue said impatiently.

"Sergeant Watkins," she said a few seconds later. "This is Detective Danielson. Dispatch said you wanted us. What's up?"

"Is Beaumont with you?"

"Yes. Why?"

"Kramer's looking for him with blood in his eye. Maxwell Cole called 911 about nine o'clock this morning to report his car was missing from the parking lot at the Hurricane Cafe. Somebody located it about an hour ago now sunk off the end of a public boat ramp down in Renton with a body inside it. Max told the detectives that all he knows is that J.P. Beaumont left a message on his machine late last night telling him that his car was in the restaurant parking lot. Do you know anything about this, Detective Beaumont?"

The words "dead body" and "Hurricane Cafe" left a clutch in my gut. Mr. Greenjeans! I had gone there with Darla Cunningham's warning and had left without ever delivering the message. Any warning issued now would be too late.

In true partnerships just as in true marriages, there comes a time when words become unnecessary. I'm sure Sue took one look at my face and knew what I was thinking.

"Do we have a description on that Lake Washington victim?" she asked into the mike.

"Midtwenties. Dark hair. Brown eyes. Hundred and sixty pounds. ID found with the victim gives his name as Anthony Lawson. The people at the Hurricane Cafe have confirmed that they have a busboy by that name, but it's still too early for a positive ID."

Relief washed over me. At least the dead man wasn't Jimmy Greenjeans.

"Now, where are you two again?" Watty continued. "And how soon can you be back here at the department?"

"We're just coming up on the freeway in Marysville," Sue replied. "We'll be back as soon as traffic will allow. Half an hour if we're really lucky." With that, she put the mike back in its holder. "For the time being," she added, "it looks as though that trip to the Tulalip is on hold."

CHAPTER 11

THE REST OF THE WAY BACK IN TO SEATTLE, I TOLD SUE everything I could remember about my visit to the Hurricane Cafe the night before, including my running into Maxwell Cole and the fact that I had threatened to turn him loose on Newsome and Atkins.

"That would have served them right," Sue observed.

It was while we were talking though, that I remembered one almost-forgotten detail, something Jimmy Greenjeans had said when I first got there. "He said he didn't want Newsome and Atkins seeing me talk to him or to Tony. He seemed really worried about it. What was the name of that victim again?"

Sue checked her notebook. "Anthony Lawson. Why?"

"See there?" I said. "Tony/Anthony. It could be the same person Jimmy Greenjeans was talking about. If it is, this may be related to the Seward Park case after all."

"Maybe," she said finally, "but who do you suppose you're going to have to walk that theory by? None other than Paul Kramer. Something tells me he isn't going to have any more faith in medicine men than I do."

"You're right," I agreed, after a moment's reflection. "It could be a pretty hard sell."

"That's okay," Sue said brightly. "You should be used to it. After all, you used to be a Fuller Brush salesman."

"A long time ago," I said.

When we arrived back at the Public Safety Building, Sue headed straight to our cubicle to see what she could do about finding Agnes Ferman's former employers while I went to see Paul Kramer. Despite Sue's warning, I told him pretty much the whole story, including my concern that if Anthony Lawson was actually Jimmy Greenjeans' "Tony," then the dead guy in Lake Washington might very well have some connection to the ghouls of Seward Park. In addition, I tried to convince Kramer that if "Tony" had been in danger from Newsome and Atkins, so might Jimmy Greenjeans. Kramer wasn't buying.

"Let me get this straight," he said, when I finished. Regarding me with a sardonic, superior smile, he was leaning so far back in Larry Powell's old leather chair that he was almost horizontal. I couldn't help wishing he'd fall over and land on his head.

"According to what the Renton detectives are telling me, if the guy in the Volvo hadn't drowned, the only other danger he was in was the possibility of dying of cirrhosis of the liver. There must have been a dozen empty booze bottles floating in the car right along with him."

I thought about the condition Maxwell Cole had been in the night before. I had a strong suspicion as to who owned those empty booze bottles, but Kramer was on a roll and there wasn't any point in interrupting him.

"That's the assumption the Renton police are going on at the moment. Lawson was driving drunk and mistook the boat ramp for a freeway ramp or even a ferry dock ramp. It happens, you know. They'll be checking blood-alcohol and all that jazz."

"They're not treating it as a homicide?"

"Beaumont, would you just can it?" Kramer returned impatiently. "Listen to yourself for a minute. Instead of going for the obvious—the drunk-driving scenario—you want me to call the chief down in Renton and try to convince him, solely on your say-so, that Anthony Lawson died as a result of some kind of mystical medicine-man bullshit? Are you looney or what?"

He paused, but not long enough for me to say anything.

"And all this is based on the fact that some broad whose father is a medicine . . . Wait, excuse me—a shaman—claims that the bones we found in Seward Park last week actually belong to some long-dead pal of his from over on the peninsula? Give me a break. For all we know, the two Indians got in some kind of a brawl, the one guy—Leaping Deer—killed the other one and now he's trying to get the bones back in the ground in a hurry so we won't take the time to investigate. What a deal! He kills somebody and then hides behind the Native American Graves Protection and Repatriation Act."

"The what?"

"NAGPRA for short, Beaumont. I'll bet you didn't think I knew anything about this, but I do. As soon as I heard about the Seward Park bones, I started doing my homework because I was afraid something like this would happen. That we'd have a whole bunch of Indian activists parading up and down the streets and causing trouble. That's why I got this promotion. Because I see things other people miss. But I got to tell you, I didn't expect one of my detectives to be the one raising the issue. That's one I didn't see coming, and I'm disappointed. Really disappointed."

I was no stranger to the Fishbowl's traditional hot seat. Over the years and due mainly to my unfailing knack for being in the wrong place at the wrong time, I'd ended up being grilled there time and again. The only difference between this session and the others was that previous coming-to-God sessions had been administered by Lawrence Powell. Larry had somehow perfected the art of telling his detectives exactly how wrongheaded they were without necessarily making them feel like dog turds. That was one facet of the captain's job I doubted Paul Kramer would ever master.

"So," I concluded, "your position is that no one is to mention to the Renton officers that their case might actually be connected to the other one."

"That's right," Kramer replied. "It's not necessary."

"But . . ."

"No buts!" Kramer bellowed, slamming his fist on the desk. "End of discussion, Beaumont. Do you hear me? I know exactly what the hell you're up to, and by God it's not going to work!"

His explosion of anger came so quickly that it surprised me, but I was packing around a little pent-up anger of my own.

"What *I'm* up to?" I demanded in return. "What the hell are you talking about?"

"You can talk about medicine men and little green-haired men until you're blue in the face, Detective Beaumont, but I'm here to tell you, Paul Kramer wasn't born yesterday." He took a breath and attempted to haul his temper back under control. Templing his fingers under his chin, he continued in a somewhat calmer voice.

"I'm not falling for this, you see. I'm not buying into this phony baloney that you actually believe any of this medicine man bullshit. I can spot a sucker punch a mile away."

"Sucker punch?" I returned. "What do you mean?"

"Can the innocence. I'm not falling for that, either. It's a perfect setup. For one thing, with two jurisdictions involved, it's a surefire way to turn me into an interdepartmental laughingstock. Pulling a stunt like this in the relative privacy of the squad room wouldn't be good enough. You want to spread it around, don't you? First day on the job and you drag me into a mess that sounds like it's straight off the psychic network. And who comes out looking like a bozo? Me."

"You think that's what this is all about? That it's some kind of hazing?"

"That's right, hazing. You and your pal Maxwell Cole probably cut your teeth on this kind of thing back in the old days when you were fraternity rats together. Let me remind you, though, this isn't a college campus, Detective Beaumont. This is the real world where reputations and jobs are on the line. That said, I'm pulling you off the case as of right now."

"You're what?"

"Pulling you off the Seward Park case. Both you and Danielson."

"You can't do that."

"The hell I can't. I've had enough of your fruit-cake notions, Beaumont. I believe I'll turn it over to a couple of real detectives—Wayne Haller and Sam Nguyen, for example. That way you and Sue can concentrate on that North-End arson case that's already a week old and isn't going anywhere at all as far as I can tell."

It would have been easy to blow up at him. God knows I wanted to, but I was concerned that other lives might be at stake in addition to Anthony Lawson's. "We're working on it," I said doggedly. "In fact, we were on our way to interview someone when you called."

"I suggest you get back to it then, ASAP."

I've never been any good at playing the role of sweet reason, but I gave it one more try. "Look,

Kramer," I said, "obviously something isn't getting through here. Let's say, for argument's sake, that Anthony Lawson really was murdered. When I talked to Jimmy Greenjeans at the Hurricane Cafe last night, he was scared to be seen talking to me. If Atkins and Newsome targeted Lawson, what are the chances that Jimmy Greenjeans is also in danger?"

"Zero," Kramer replied. "But speaking of Newsome and Atkins reminds me. We've gone so far afield that I almost forgot the reason I called you in here in the first place. I've had a call from a guy named Troy Cochran. You know him?"

"Not personally. I've heard the name."

"He's an attorney who represents Mr. Atkins and Mr. Newsome. He says his clients are considering filing a police harassment charge against you. He also mentioned that if anything derogatory about them appears in print, they'll be looking into filing a libel suit against you. Which brings me back to your friend, Mr. Cole."

"What about him?"

"Until the dust settles around here, there's to be no further fraternizing between you and the press."

"Fraternizing? With Max? Kramer, you've got to be kidding. All I did was give a poor drunk a ride home. Kept him off the streets. Probably kept him from running down some innocent pedestrian."

"The report I read said you were out barhopping with Maxwell Cole . . ."

"We were in one bar. The Hurricane Cafe."

"Boozing it up."

"Drinking *lattes*."

"If all Cole was drinking was *lattes*, how come he forgot where he left his car?"

I didn't bother answering. Kramer's mind was made up. No amount of factual information was going to change it. Instead, I sat back in my chair and tried to let his diatribe roll off me.

"The point is, Detective Beaumont, regardless of what you personally were drinking, you were drinking it with *him*, with a guy who happens to be a reporter. Furthermore, you know chumminess with members of the media is officially frowned on by the folks upstairs even when no bodies show up in said reporter's parked car. Can't you see how all this is going to play in the *P.-I.* tomorrow morning?"

So much for good intentions. So much for staying calm in the eye of the storm. "I'll tell you what, Mr. Kramer," I snapped back at him. "I, for one, don't give a flying fig how any of this plays in the morning paper. Worrying about what the media will and will not do isn't my job. My responsibility is solving homicides with whatever help happens to be available."

Kramer's no dummy. I'm sure he didn't miss the snide reference to Henry Leaping Deer, but he ignored the jibe. "Like I said earlier, the Ferman homicide, the one you're currently supposed to be solving, isn't going away. Now that you and Danielson will be able to focus totally on that one, maybe you'll actually make some progress."

"Right," I said sarcastically, standing up. "Is that all?"

"For the time being, but remember—when you hand off your Seward Park files to Haller and

Nguyen, there'd better not be a word said about medicine men. You got that?"

"I've got it, all right!"

With that, I stormed out of his office. Watty, seated at his desk just outside the open door, raised a single eyebrow as I flew past. He seemed more amused than sympathetic, and that pissed me off that much more.

Out in the hallway I paused long enough to lower my blood pressure by counting to ten. Once in control, I could have taken a direct route back to the cubicle. Instead, I took a long, thoughtful detour through the rest room on the way. I needed time to get over Kramer's pompous, self-serving reprimand. I also needed time to think out a course of action.

I had no quarrel with Wayne Haller and Sam Nguyen. Without a doubt, they're both good cops. I was certain that, if the links between Anthony Lawson and the ghouls existed, Haller and Nguyen would ferret them out eventually. The only question in my mind was how long would it take, especially if Lawson's death was being handled as a routine traffic death? Kramer assumed that the call from Cochran would warn me off when, in fact, it was more like waving a red flag.

By the time I finished washing my hands, I'd made up my mind. Darla Cunningham had brought me her father's warning in good faith and with some degree of risk to her own reputation as a physics professor at the university. She must have worried about whether or not I would listen or simply laugh her out of my office. The fact that I paid attention had far more to do with the way my mother raised me than it did with a natural proclivity toward things mystical.

To say my mother came from an intolerant background is understating the case. Seventeen years old, pregnant, and unmarried, she might have chosen what must have seemed like the line of least resistance and put me up for adoption. Instead, she had insisted on keeping me and raising me on her own, thereby setting the stage for a lifelong estrangement from her hard-nosed Bible-thumping father.

Even as a child, I remember being puzzled by the fact that she never had anything bad to say about her parents. "They have their beliefs and I have mine," she told me. "I have to respect that." Her tolerance of her parents had translated into tolerance for others as well, for people of other races, customs, and religions. The lessons my mother taught me had served me well once I left behind the de facto segregation of my old white-bread Ballard neighborhood, and I had no doubt they had come into play once more when I found Darla Cunningham asleep in my office.

Kramer was welcome to his opinion. He could call Henry Leaping Deer's warning crap if he wanted to. I, on the other hand, found it impossible to dismiss. Those Native American beliefs might differ from my own, but they came with an obligation of respect and also one of action. I had left the Hurricane Cafe the night before without fulfilling my charge, without passing along the warning that should have gone to Jimmy Greenjeans. If the green-haired bartender was still alive, then I had another chance. I may have been pulled off the case, but Paul Kramer be damned, I wasn't going to blow it a second time.

Having made up my mind to go see Greenjeans after all, it did cross my mind that I wasn't being entirely fair to Sue Danielson. She had been ordered off the case just as much as I had. The only difference was, I knew it and she didn't. I rationalized my way around that one by convincing myself that if she didn't know about it, no one could hold her responsible.

Sitting on hold with the phone stuck to her ear, she looked up questioningly when I came back to the cubicle. "That took long enough," she said.

"Kramer was being Kramer," I told her. "What's happening here?"

She held up a finger to silence me when someone must have come back on the line. "Good," she said. "And what did you say is Mr. Considine's ETA?"

She scratched a hurried note onto a piece of paper and passed it over to me. "King County Airport," the note said. "At 3:00 P.M."

"Okay," she added. "We'll probably meet him there."

"What's up?" I asked when she put down the phone.

"I managed to locate Freddy Considine. Frederick, actually. He evidently made a killing in the stock market and was smart enough to hang on to his money. Now he's joined forces with a David Ambrose who's supposedly a hotshot golf-course developer. Considine is jetting into Boeing Field this afternoon, fresh from some end-of-season skiing in Sun Valley. Like it says in the note, his estimated time of arrival is 3:00 P.M."

"Boeing Field?" I repeated. "You mean as in a private jet?" I asked.

Sue nodded. "That's right. A Citation. The guy must be loaded or else his partner is."

"What about our trip to the casino? I thought . . ."

"Can't that wait until tomorrow?" Sue interrupted, glancing at her watch. "I hate to play the mother card on you again, Beau, but it's already close to two. If we head back up to Marysville now and get stuck in rush-hour traffic on our way back into the city, there's a good chance we won't get back until late. The problem is, Richie's plane is due in at Sea-Tac late this afternoon. I really do want to be at the house before he gets there."

I could see why she did. I also didn't have any great desire to spend any more time stuck in late afternoon I-5 traffic. "Great idea," I said with unfeigned enthusiasm. "How about grabbing some lunch between now and the time to be at Boeing Field? If memory serves, it's my turn to buy."

Once back in the Caprice, I headed straight for the Hurricane Cafe. I probably should have come clean with Sue right away—should have told her everything Kramer had said, but she didn't ask, and I didn't tell.

"You don't mind if we kill two birds with one stone, do you?" I asked casually, pulling into the lot. "I thought we'd try dropping by to see Mr. Greenjeans one more time. I'd like to get this Tony business settled once and for all."

Sue shrugged. "Why should I care?" she asked. "It doesn't matter to me one way or the other."

There are times when ignorance is bliss.

We walked into the restaurant at five of two. If the Hurricane had a regular lunchtime crowd, it had long since disappeared. Plucking a menu off the table near the door, I steered Sue toward the bar.

"Hey," she said, looking around the room and reaching toward her purse and the packet of Marlboros I knew she kept there. "Why didn't you tell me you could smoke in here?" she demanded. "Nose ring or not, I may just turn into a regular."

Unfortunately, Jimmy Greenjeans was not behind the bar. The young woman who was could have given Jimmy a run for his money in the looks department. She came complete with an ankle-length skirt, a buzzcut hairdo, two-inch-long fingernails, painted black, and a trail of tattooed tears that ran down one cheek from the corner of her eye to the edge of her chin. She didn't seem thrilled when we ordered coffee.

"What time does Jimmy come on duty?" I asked.

"He doesn't. Today's his day off. You a cop, too?"

I nodded. I expected my answer to cause her somewhat surly attitude to go from bad to worse. Instead, she seemed to soften a little. "The others were already here—the cops from Renton. You here because of what happened to Tony?" she asked.

Sue and I exchanged glances. Sue started to reach for her ID, but I beat her to it. If Kramer was going to go ballistic over somebody asking unauthorized questions in the Hurricane Cafe, it was only fair that my name and ID should be the ones on the line. The bartender took the ID packet from my hand and studied it nearsightedly for a long moment before handing it back. Her lower lip trembled as she did so.

"He was such a sweet guy," she said. "I just can't believe he's dead."

"We're talking about Anthony Lawson here, right?"

She nodded. "Who else?" she responded. "It was the first time I'd ever worked with somebody like that. I was worried about it to begin with. You know, when they first hired him, because I didn't know what to expect. But he was just as sweet as could be."

"With someone like what?" I asked.

"With someone who was like . . . well, you know . . . retarded."

"Tony Lawson was developmentally disabled?" I asked.

"Yes, but you almost couldn't tell it. Not if you talked to him just a little. After a few minutes, you could figure it out, though. Still, he was a good worker and always willing to help." She sniffed then. The tattooed tears suddenly glistened with a layer of real ones.

"He was such a nice guy. Real sweet. And so proud of his heritage. He was an Indian, you know. Not an India-Indian—American. I think maybe his grandfather was a chief or something."

I felt the hackles rise on the back of my neck. "No kidding," I said.

Ms. Buzzcut nodded seriously. "No kidding. The other cops said he was drunk, but I never saw him take a drink the whole time he worked here. Maybe he just fell off the wagon or something. What a shame."

When Sue put down her menu, the bartender took the hint. "Did you want to order something besides coffee?" she asked.

We ordered burgers. When the bartender went to deliver the order to the kitchen, Sue turned to me. "That's what Kramer told you, that Lawson was drunk?"

I nodded. "Renton is investigating the incident as a drunk-driving fatality."

Sue thought that over. "Well," she said finally, "the Indian part makes me wonder if the case is connected to Seward Park after all, while the drinking part makes me think it isn't. We'll just have to work on it, that's all."

"We can't," I told her.

"Can't what?" she asked.

"Can't work on it. We're off the case, Sue," I said. "Kramer's assigning Haller and Nguyen to Seward Park. That puts us totally out of the loop because the City of Renton is taking responsibility for Anthony Lawson."

For a moment or two, Sue seemed too stunned to speak. "When did all this happen?" she asked finally.

"A little while ago. When I was in Kramer's office. I was going to tell you, but . . ."

"Then what exactly are we doing here?" The smoke flowing from Sue's distended nostrils put me in mind of a dragon, a pissed-off dragon.

"Having lunch?" I asked, feigning innocence but not succeeding.

"Like hell!" Sue was angry now, as angry as I've

ever seen her. "You tricked me, Beau! We're here asking questions about Seward Park and we're doing it against Kramer's direct orders. Right?"

I nodded sheepishly. "I suppose you could say that."

"*Suppose!*" she snorted. "I don't believe it!"

"Sue, I'm sorry. I didn't mean . . ."

"The hell you didn't! I've never been thrown off a case before in my life. How did you manage that, Beau? And why didn't you bother to tell me? Of all the arrogant . . ."

"More coffee?"

Ms. Buzzcut was back with a steaming coffeepot. Grateful for any diversion that would keep Sue off the subject at hand, I accepted some of the potentially lethal stuff.

"Is it too late to make our burgers to go?" Sue demanded, holding a hand over her own coffee cup.

"No," the bartender replied. "Probably not. I'll go check."

She took the pot and walked away while Sue clambered off her stool. "I'll be in the car," she said.

While I waited for the burgers, I had several long, self-castigating minutes to anticipate my impending and pretty much well-deserved execution. At last lunch appeared, loaded into a pair of brown paper bags.

"Will that be all?" Ms. Buzzcut asked.

"There's one more thing," I told her. "You say Jimmy doesn't work again until tomorrow?"

"That's right."

"He and I have a mutual friend. Do you suppose

you could do me a favor and give him a message for me?"

"I guess."

I took out one of my cards. "Have him try to reach me at these numbers," I told her. "If he can't get through to me, have him call Professor Darla Cunningham at the Physics Department at the University of Washington. Have him tell her I told him to call. She'll know what it's all about."

"That's all?" the bartender asked.

I nodded. I put a single bill on the counter and shoved it in her direction. "Keep the change," I said.

"Thanks," she said without actually looking down at the bill. When she did and saw Mr. Franklin's portrait, her eyes widened. "Thanks a lot. I'll be sure Jimmy gets the message."

CHAPTER 12

SOME HOLES ARE JUST TOO DAMN DEEP TO DIG YOUR way out of, and this was one of them. Sue and I ate our hamburgers in the parking lot of the Hurricane Cafe. In utter silence. Sue consumed hers without so much as a word of thanks. My burger was probably fine. I'm sure it wasn't the cook's fault that it tasted like shoe leather in my mouth.

"Sue, I . . ."

"Shut up and eat," she ordered. "I don't want to hear it."

With the burgers gone and still without exchanging any words we headed south toward Boeing Field. Once or twice I glanced in Sue's direction. Grim faced, she sat with her arms folded across her chest, staring straight ahead.

I'm no stranger to the silent treatment. Karen used to dish it out all the time, but then she was my wife. Having to handle the same ploy from a partner at work was an altogether new and unwelcome experience.

"Who are the other dicks?" Sue asked finally.

The word "dick" is acceptable in polite conversation only when used by a fellow detective. In that regard it's similar to use of the "N" word. Street gang kids may toss the word back and forth among themselves with impunity, but let some outsider use it and all hell will break loose. "Dick" works exactly the same way. It also happens to be a word that Sue Danielson seldom uses in casual conversation. As a consequence, when she used it now as the first icebreaker in our war of nonwords, I didn't answer right away. Instead, I took a moment to try to decide whether or not there were any hidden traps lurking beneath the surface of her question.

"The other detectives," she prodded impatiently when I didn't answer fast enough to suit her. "Who did Kramer assign to our case?"

"Lawson wasn't ours to begin with. City of Renton has that one," I told her. "Wayne Haller and Sam Nguyen drew Seward Park."

"Wayne Haller is your basic Irish setter of a detective—good-looking but not too bright," Sue said after a pause. "He's never going to set the world on fire. Sam, on the other hand, is really squared away. I vote we call him."

I had to agree that Sue's assessment of the other two detectives was right on target. Haller is fine in a pleasant but dim sort of way. Sam Nguyen is a bright go-getter. He had been a rookie cop in Saigon and his father a high-level South Vietnamese bureaucrat before the city fell to the North Vietnamese. Through his father's connections, Sam, his mother, and three younger brothers all managed to get out. They had turned up in Seattle months later, all of them virtually penniless.

In an era of newly arrived and mostly impoverished immigrants, the English-speaking Sam had found work as a translator at Seattle PD. Eventually, he had turned that first job as an interpreter into one that came with a uniform. He had been the oldest rookie in his class at the academy. He had also been the first one to make detective.

"Call Sam and tell him what?" I asked.

"About the possibility of a connection," Sue replied. "Maybe we should even have him ask the ME's office to run some DNA comparisons. The bartender told us Lawson claimed his grandfather was some kind of big deal on the reservation. Maybe he was a shaman instead of a chief. Since we're off the case, neither one of us can make that kind of request, but Sam can. And it'll be a damned sight harder for Kramer to claim the two cases aren't connected if the two victims turn out to be relatives."

Whoa. I could buy the idea that the cases were connected, but adding in the theory that the two sets of remains might be from people who were actually related to each other sounded far-fetched— even to me.

"I'm not sure that'll fly," I said dubiously.

New sparks of anger flamed in Sue's eyes. "What are you saying, Beau?" she demanded. "In other words, you can buy all this medicine-men shit but you can't handle a dose of women's intuition?"

She had me cold. "I'll make the call."

"I'm glad you offered," she said, uncrossing her

arms. "After all, if one of us is going to risk getting fired over this mess, it's better you than me. I have kids to support. You don't." She gave me a sideways grin then, and I knew things were going to be okay.

At five after three we pulled into the parking lot at Boeing Field. "Do you have any idea where he'll come in?"

"According to his office, the company hangar is number 441," Sue said. "I suggest we go find it."

When we located the right number, the door to the hangar was rolled wide open. A guy stood just inside, lounging against the door jamb. He wore a pair of greasy overalls long overdue for a trip to the laundry. A frayed toothpick stuck out of one corner of his mouth. Looking at him, it seemed reasonable to peg him as the company's on-site mechanic.

"We're here to meet Mr. Considine's plane," Sue explained. "They're not in yet?"

The mechanic glanced at his watch. "Not so far," he said, "but they should be pretty soon."

Since the guy didn't ask for any kind of identification, Sue didn't bother to give it to him. Instead, she wandered off across the tarmac to the far corner of the building and leaned up against a sunny wall to wait and smoke. She stood there with her eyes closed, soaking up the warm April sunshine. There was nothing about her stance or attitude that invited company, so I stayed where I was and let her be.

"Mr. Considine's a pilot then?" I asked the presumed mechanic.

The man made a noise that I translated as a derisive chuckle. "Not so's you'd notice, although he likes to think of himself as a real hotshot." The man stopped and shrugged his shoulders. "But then again, if Mr. Ambrose is comfortable turning over the controls to him, who am I to complain? If it weren't for Mr. Considine showing up last year with a whole shitload of investment capital, maybe my paycheck wouldn't cash so well. I may not get in as much flight time as I used to, but the good news is, I still get paid."

The downsized pilot/mechanic and I stood in silence for some time while one plane after another came in on the Boeing Field flight path. "That's them now," he said finally, pointing to an aircraft easing down to a landing. "I'd better go get busy."

While he turned back into the hangar, Sue ground out her cigarette butt and came over to me. Together we waited while a slick little Citation taxied down the runway. By the time it came to a stop outside the hangar, the mechanic was back outside pushing a mini luggage cart up beside the slowing plane. As soon as it stopped altogether, the passenger door opened and a woman stepped outside. Tall, blond, and drop-dead gorgeous, she couldn't have been more than twenty-five. Swathed from head to waist in a thick but totally unnecessary fur jacket, she strolled daintily down the metal steps. Behind her lumbered a huge, bearlike man. He was in his mid-to-late thirties and lugged an oversized ski bag in each hand. Sue and I angled toward the bottom of the stairs.

"Mr. and Mrs. Considine?" Sue asked.

"Yes." Frederick Considine answered for both of them. "Who are you?"

"Detectives J. P. Beaumont and Sue Danielson

with the Seattle PD," she advised them, presenting her ID. "Would it be possible to talk to you for a few moments?"

"What about?"

"Agnes Ferman."

There was a slight flicker in Frederick Considine's eyes. It may have been nothing more than a twitch, but it was there. "What about her?" he asked.

"I'm afraid she's dead," Sue returned. "That's what we need to talk to you about."

The young woman frowned, although it came across as more of a sex-pot pout. "Who's Agnes, Freddy?"

"My mother's old nurse. Mine, too, a long time ago," Considine replied, then he turned back to Sue. "What happened to her?"

"She died last week in an arson fire. How long have you and your wife been out of town?"

"We left early Tuesday morning. Around six or so. Why?"

"Mrs. Ferman died the night before that," Sue said. "The clock on the stove in the kitchen stopped at 4:42. Because we didn't have positive ID until much later, the story didn't actually hit the papers until Tuesday afternoon. That would explain why you didn't hear about it before you left."

"Freddy," the woman said with an impatient toss of her long blond mane. "What's this all about and how long is it going to take? I have a hair and nail appointment at 4:00, and we're due to meet the Slaters for dinner at 5:30."

Reaching in his pocket, Fred Considine pulled out a set of car keys. "Here," he said, handing them over. "You take the Town Car and go on home, Katherine. When I finish up here, I'll have a car come get me. Kauffman?"

The overall-clad guy who was in the process of beginning a postflight check, turned away from the guts of the plane. "Yo."

"Would you help Mrs. Considine with the bags? Then, we'll be using the office for a short conference. Please see to it that we're not disturbed."

The pilot/mechanic, now further demoted to the level of baggage handler, left off what he was doing without a word and went to grapple with the luggage, of which there seemed to be a good deal. Under Katherine's watchful eye, he hauled one bag after another off the plane and around the side of the building. Considine waited until after his wife and the luggage were safely under way in a silver-gray Lincoln before he turned back to us.

"This way," he said.

He led us through the hangar and into a spacious but messy back office that reeked of cigar smoke. When Sue and I were both inside the office, he pushed the door shut. "Go ahead and have a seat," he invited, coming around to the far side of the desk. We sat, as did he. "Now then," he said. "What is it you want to know?"

"We understand Agnes Ferman worked for your family for quite some time," I said.

He nodded. "That's correct. For the better part of forty years, from the time my older brother, Lucas, was born until several years ago, until just before we put my mother in a nursing home. Originally, Agnes was hired to take care of my brother when he was a newborn. When I came along several years later, she looked after both of us. She was doing that when my mother became an invalid herself. Agnes Ferman went from taking care of my mother's children to taking care of Mother herself. She stayed on until her husband became ill. That's when she had to quit. She couldn't take care of Mother and look after her husband, as well. Once Agnes stopped working for us, we tried hiring other help, but nothing quite worked out. Eventually, Father and I had no choice but to put Mother in a home—the same one my father is in now, incidentally. It's called Crescent House and it's located up in Shoreline. That's where my mother was when she died a year ago this month."

"It's my understanding that you stayed in touch with Agnes once she stopped working for your parents," I offered. "Is that true?"

Considine gave me a narrow-eyed, appraising look. "What makes you say that?" There was no mistaking the defensiveness in his response.

"One of Agnes Ferman's neighbors told us that someone came by not too long ago, someone from the family she used to work for. According to the neighbor, Agnes claimed that person had come to check on her well-being. Would that person happen to be you, Mr. Considine?"

"Yes. I guess so. What if it was?"

"You must have had a fairly close relationship with Agnes. Or else, your parents did."

"I suppose we all did," Frederick Considine said,

although he didn't sound entirely convincing. And the fact that his young wife wasn't even aware of Agnes Ferman's name made it even less so.

At that point in the interview I found myself a little baffled. Driving to Boeing Field I had assumed, erroneously, that Frederick Considine would be upset by the news of Agnes' death. I had expected him to express surprise and possibly some grief as well. The fact that he did neither set off little warning bells in my head. What was emerging in grief's stead—more through body language than through anything Considine said aloud—was a sense of relief. Gratitude almost. Frederick Considine didn't seem any more grief-stricken about Agnes Ferman's death than did her various greedy relatives. That raised the number of "don't cares." Now the score was five to one.

"Let me ask you this," I continued. "During most of that forty-year period while Agnes worked for your family, was she live-in help?"

Frederick nodded. "There's a carriage house out behind the main house," he said. "Agnes stayed there during the week. She went home to her own place on her days off."

"Is there anything in what you saw of Agnes Ferman that would have led you to believe she was fairly well-off?"

"Well-off?" he repeated. "No. Not at all."

"Would it surprise you, then, to learn that in the aftermath of the fire we found a fair amount of cash hidden on her premises? A large part of it seems to date from some point in the midseventies."

Fred Considine stared past me as though suddenly transfixed by something happening in the stark emptiness of the airplane hangar outside the window-lined walls of the office. For the better part of a minute, he said nothing at all, then he reached across the desk, picked up a phone, and punched in a few numbers.

"Excuse me for a moment, if you will," he said. "Ray, please," he said, speaking into the phone when someone came on the line. "Tell him it's Fred Considine."

"Hi, Ray," he continued moments later. "Yup, we're back. Just got in a few minutes ago. It was great. Late in the season, of course, but still great and not very crowded. Right, next time we should all go. Sure, but that's not why I'm calling you just now. I have a pair of Seattle PD homicide detectives sitting here in the office at the hangar. They're asking all sorts of questions about Agnes Ferman. What should I do?"

There was another pause, a long one, while Ray—an attorney, presumably—issued some kind of marching orders. His side of the conversation was long-winded enough that, by the time it was over, it was verging on lecture proportions. At the end of it, Frederick Considine put down the phone.

"That was Ray Crosse on the phone," he told Sue and me. "He's our family attorney. Has been for years. He's in the process of contacting a criminal attorney and told me not to say anything more until we hear from Mr. Drachman."

At the sound of the name, Sue sent a startled look in my direction as if to say, "What the hell is going on?"

Caleb Winthrop Drachman III—Cal for short—is one of Seattle's most prominent defense attorneys. He's not quite the same caliber as O. J. Simpson's defense team, but I have no doubt that someday he will have that kind of national prominence. In the meantime, when it comes to defending criminal matters that involve the state of Washington's rich and powerful, nobody has more of a sterling reputation than Cal Drachman.

"I'm sorry, Mr. Considine. We came here to ask you about Agnes Ferman's money. Why would you need the services of a defense attorney?"

Considine looked at me across the desk. "I guess Ray feels it's the prudent thing to do," he said.

The phone rang. He grabbed the receiver. "Yes," he said into it. "That's right, Mr. Drachman. Thanks for calling me right back." He paused. "Yes," he added. "They're both still here. Yes, Detectives Beaumont and Danielson. No, I haven't answered any other questions."

There was yet another long pause during which we could periodically hear a man's voice coming through the phone although it was impossible to make out anything that was being said. Finally, Considine pulled the receiver away from his ear. "My attorney wants to talk to you," he said, handing the handset across the desk to me.

"Hello, Mr. Drachman," I said. "Detective J. P. Beaumont. We met a few years ago. That double homicide in the school district office on Queen Anne Hill."

"That's right, Detective Beaumont," Cal Drachman returned at once. "I remember now. The Kelsey case. How's Pete Kelsey doing these days?"

"I have no idea," I said. "I haven't heard from him since."

"That's not too surprising," Drachman said with a chuckle. "As a matter of fact, I haven't heard from him, either. I hope he's getting his life back together. Now what's all this with Mr. Considine? Is he under arrest?"

"No. Not at all. We came to see him in regard to the arson death of one of his family's long-time employees. We found a rather large amount of cash concealed in an old refrigerator at her residence. Detective Danielson and I came to see if Mr. Considine had any idea where all that money might have come from. There was absolutely no hint that he was under arrest or even under suspicion. Instead of answering our questions, however, he called you."

"I'm sure my client will want to cooperate fully with your investigation," Drachman assured me. "But it's always wise to have an attorney present during an interview process. Bearing that in mind, I'd appreciate it if you would refrain from asking any further questions until I have an opportunity to confer with my client."

"Right," I said.

"Where are you now?" he asked.

"We're down here at Boeing Field—hangar 441. I believe Mrs. Considine took his vehicle, so if you'd like, Detective Danielson and I could give him a ride . . ."

Although it sounded like a reasonable enough

offer on my part, all of us—with the possible exception of Fred Considine himself—knew what was at stake. Everybody else understood exactly how an automobile ride with two homicide detectives might play itself out. More than one guilt-ridden suspect has spilled his guts during a purportedly harmless "ride" downtown, regardless of whether or not any official questioning was going on at the time. Unfortunately for Sue and me, Cal Drachman saw right through the ruse.

"That's mighty nice of you, Detective Beaumont," he said. "A kind offer, but no thanks. Don't trouble yourself. I'll have one of my assistants drive straight down there to bring Mr. Considine directly to our office. I'm sorry, what hangar did you say again?"

"Number 441."

"And remember," he added, "any further questioning is to be done in my presence."

"Of course." I put down the phone. "Mr. Drachman is sending someone to pick you up and give you a ride into his office."

Considine nodded. "Good," he said. "Is that all then?"

It was. Since there didn't seem to be any point to hanging around, Sue and I left right after that. "What the hell was that all about?" she demanded once both doors closed on our bulgemobile.

"Beats me," I said.

"He was answering questions right along until we got to the part about the money. That's when he clammed up."

"I noticed that, too," I responded. "What do we know about the Considines?"

"Not much. Just what Hilda Smathers told us," Sue said, flipping back through pages of her note-book. Frowning, she scanned her notes. "Old-time pioneer-type timber money, possible booze smuggling during Prohibition that grew into quite respectable banks during the war years. I remember Hilda saying something about the two boys being terribly spoiled."

I remembered that, too. "Do we have any idea when or how Lucas Considine died?" I asked.

"None at all," Sue returned, "but I should be able to find out." She stopped long enough to scribble a note.

"What do you think about the way Considine took the news?"

"That Agnes was dead?" Sue asked.

I nodded. "Well," Sue said thoughtfully. "If you ask me, he didn't seem very upset about it."

"Upset, nothing," I said. "He looked downright relieved. Happy, almost. Ever since we've known about that money, we knew it couldn't be legitimate. If it was earned income, Agnes would have put it in a bank account. She wouldn't have stashed it in a refrigerator. Let's think about this for a minute. Agnes was a trusted part of one of the city's leading families for nearly forty years. The Considines are wealthy people. Not only do they have money, they also carry a certain stature in the community, as well. If there were any skeletons in the Considine family closet, Agnes Ferman would have known about them."

"You're suggesting blackmail?" Sue asked.

"Why not?"

"It makes sense."

Just then something else came to me. "When you were counting all that money, was there any way to tell how much came in at a time?"

Sue shook her head. "No. There was that one big chunk. After that, it probably came in by dribs and drabs. A thousand at a time? Two maybe? I didn't really pay that much attention, and from here there's no way to tell, especially since some of each payment may have been spent without ever making it as far as the refrigerator."

"Maybe there's a reason Agnes put Hilda off and didn't give her the money immediately. Maybe there was another payment coming due and by waiting until it arrived, it kept Agnes from having to transfer money in and out of the refrigerator."

"I wonder if it isn't more likely that Agnes didn't want to go get the money at the time because Hilda was right there watching. Hilda Smathers doesn't strike me as absolutely trustworthy. If I had been her sister, I wouldn't have wanted her to know that I had a bundle of cash lying around free for the taking."

"Point well taken," I agreed, "but let's say, just for argument's sake, that Agnes was blackmailing Frederick Considine. What would she have had on him that was worth that much money to keep quiet?"

We drove several blocks without speaking. "It would have to be murder," Sue replied at last.

"Murder," I repeated. "Why do you say that?"

"According to my inventory, the money started coming in as early as the midseventies. If it were based on anything besides murder, the statute of limitations would have run out long ago."

"Good thinking," I said.

Sue grinned again, reassuring me that I had somehow managed to worm my way back into her good graces. "Not bad for woman's intuition, right?" she asked.

"Right," I agreed. "Not bad at all."

CHAPTER 13

IT WAS LATE ENOUGH WHEN SUE AND I MADE IT BACK downtown that I drove her straight to her car and dropped her off. Because parking is so much cheaper in the Seattle Center garage than it is around the department, Sue usually leaves her Ford Escort there and then takes the Monorail and free bus back and forth to the Public Safety Building. I pulled over next to the curb on Mercer to let her out of the Caprice.

"If anyone comes around looking for a report," she said, "tell them I'll type it up on the laptop at home and send it in by modem," she said, stepping out onto the sidewalk. "Tomorrow we can go check the casino and start chasing after the Considine stuff, unless you want to start tracking that tonight."

"No, thanks," I told her. "Tomorrow sounds fine to me. If something's been hanging fire since the midseventies, one day more isn't going to make a difference. By the way, good luck tonight."

A cloud seemed to pass briefly over her face. "We'll be fine," she said. "Don't worry."

With that she slammed the door shut. I opened the trunk so she could retrieve her computer then watched her jog up the stairs until she disappeared crossing the skybridge. Alone in the bulgemobile and reluctant as hell, I drove back down to the Public Safety Building.

Because I'd had more than enough of Paul Kramer to last me for one day, I stayed at the department only long enough to turn the car in at the garage and to check both Sue and me out on Watty's attendance board. After that, I headed home. Truth be known, I bugged out early as much to avoid Sam Nguyen as I did to dodge Paul Kramer. Sure, I had agreed to have Sam ask the ME's office about doing the DNA comparisons. And I would do it, too—the first time I happened to run into him.

My Hurricane Cafe hamburger had been late enough in the day that I wasn't particularly hungry. Still, I was tempted to take another run past the restaurant just in case Jimmy Greenjeans had chanced to drop by on his day off. At the very last minute, that's exactly what I did—I turned into the old familiar parking lot outside the Hurricane Cafe.

The after-work crowd wasn't quite what it used to be. A brief survey of the room told me Mr. Greenjeans wasn't there, but at the nearly deserted bar, I caught sight of a familiar figure—Maxwell Cole. Hunkered down on a barstool, he was staring disconsolately into the depths of what appeared to be a half-consumed Manhattan. Even in my drinking prime, Manhattans were something that could leave me puking drunk in no time. I always figured it was because I was allergic to maraschino cherries.

Kramer had given me orders to stay away from both Jimmy Greenjeans *and* Maxwell Cole. One of my lifelong problems has been an automatic, kneejerk reaction to being told anything is *verboten*. Unfortunately, my being older and supposedly wiser hasn't changed things.

I had spotted Max's hulking figure from the back without the columnist seeing me. It would have been simple for me to simply fade back out the front door and into the street, but I didn't do that. Instead, I slipped onto an empty stool beside him and fanned some of the cloud of cigarette smoke out of my eyes.

"Hair of the dog?" I asked.

He glowered at me and knocked a column of ashes into the ashtray. "You shoulda let me drive myself home, J.P.," he grumbled. "If you'da just minded your own damned business, I'd still have a car."

So much for gratitude over my saving him from a possible DUI or worse. "Maybe not," I said cheerfully. "You were drunk enough that you might have wrecked it anyway, even without Anthony Lawson's help. Still, it's probably time you got yourself new wheels. You've had that old hunk of orange sheet metal for as long as I can remember."

"Hell," Cole growled forlornly, fingering the drooping strands of his foot-long handlebar moustache. "The odometer was just coming up on a hundred-fifty thou. With a Volvo that means it's just getting broken-in good."

"It was a junker, Max. Get yourself a new car.

The way you're swilling those down," I nodded at his glass, "you could probably use a set of front-seat air bags."

"What can I get for you?" the bartender interrupted. This one was a delicate little guy with a lisp, not one but three separate nose rings, and a distinctly girlish sway to his hips. I wondered if he was really a bartender or if he had landed in the Hurricane Cafe straight from central casting.

"Coffee," I said. "Black."

"And another one of these for me," Max called after him. "Put it on his tab," he added, jerking his head in my direction. "He owes me big, so he's buying."

I turned around on my stool and surveyed the room again. I had already ascertained that Mr. Greenjeans wasn't there. Now I checked for the neighborhood ghouls, Mr. Atkins and Mr. Newsome. They weren't there, either, but it was early for them—still daylight. Bats and vampires don't usually venture out until well after dark.

"So why'd the poor bastard have to lift my car to do himself in?" Max whined.

"It was probably the only one left in the lot."

Max glared at me. "It wouldn't have been if . . ."

"We've already been over that once, Max. Give it up. So, are you on foot tonight, or what?"

"No. My insurance agent told me that until they get the car cut loose from the impound lot, she won't know whether or not it's totaled. For the time being, she had me rent one of those little toy cars from Enterprise. It's okay, I guess. Little, but with some pep. Still, it's not a Volvo, know what I mean?"

He had put the first cigarette out. Now he paused long enough to light another.

I suppressed a momentary impatience with the man and his mumbled, prattling whine. It may have been just minutes past five, but Maxwell Cole was already on the verge of being three sheets to the wind. The bartender delivered our drinks. I saw his guarded glance as he collected Max's empty Manhattan glass. I've been on the receiving end of looks like that. I knew from experience that would be Maxwell Cole's last drink of the evening—at least at the Hurricane Cafe. Which was a relief to me. No matter what condition Max was in, I had learned my lesson. I wouldn't be offering him another ride home anytime soon.

"So you remember running into me here last night?" I asked.

Max straightened on his stool. "Sure, I do," he replied, sounding offended. "Whaddya think, I was drunk or something?"

"Do you remember anything else about last night?"

"That's the thing. I remember talking to him, to Chief, but I never woulda thought he'd take my car. I thought we were buddies. Pals."

"Chief?"

"Most people called him Tony. But once I knew he was an Indian, I called him Chief. He seemed to like it, too. He'd stand up real tall and straight whenever I called him that. He'd grin at me and say, 'You damn betcha.' That was funny. Here was a guy who looked like he was pure Native American, but he sounded more like one of those old square-headed Swedes or Norwegians from Ballard."

Doctors don't operate on themselves and cops aren't supposed to investigate cases involving themselves, their friends, or any members of their own family. I wondered whether those same kinds of prohibitions applied to journalists.

"Is that where he's from?" I asked innocently. "From Ballard?"

"From a reservation over on the peninsula someplace," Max replied. "Port Madison, maybe. He was adopted out as a baby. His adoptive parents raised him here in Seattle."

"You seem to know a lot about him."

"It's my business to know things, J.P.," Max said defensively. "You of all people should understand that."

I nodded. "So did you see him in here a lot?"

"Sure."

"Did you ever see him copping drinks from the bar?"

"Never."

"Did he ever talk like somebody with a drinking problem?"

"Not really," Max said. "He wasn't all there, know what I mean?" He tapped the side of his head.

"You're saying he was crazy?"

"No, not crazy. Slow. Retarded-like."

"But he was old enough to drink, so if he had wanted to order a drink in front of you, he could have."

Max sipped his own drink. "I suppose he could

have, but he never did. As a matter of fact, I never saw him take a drink of anything but iced tea. Never smelled booze on him or anything. But maybe he'd been through treatment or something and then just fell off the wagon. That happens, they tell me. Happens all the time."

One of the blessings of being drunk is that you don't ever hear yourself when you're in that condition. You think you're making perfect sense. You don't hear the rambling, droning stupidity. The sad thing is, while you may be deaf and dumb to the problem, people around you aren't. And once you sober up, you aren't either. In the old days, while I was waxing eloquent on a booze-fueled soapbox, I wasn't the least bit embarrassed by all the nonsense pouring out of my mouth. I wasn't then, but I am now—in retrospect. I wondered just then if something similar would ever happen to Maxwell Cole.

"So who are Anthony Lawson's parents?" I asked.

Max put down the cigarette, reached in his pocket, and carefully extracted a tattered notebook. It was the same color as the one I use. In fact, the two of them could have passed for twins. It was enough to make me want to become a devoted computer user on the spot.

Bleary-eyed, Max fumbled through a dozen pages before he finally settled on one. "Here it is," he said. "Annie, Annie Engebretson. The father's dead. Annie lives in one of those retirement homes—the high-rise one over on the east side of Greenlake."

"If the mother's name is Engebretson, where did Lawson come from?"

"Beats hell out of me. I wanted to talk to her, but

I haven't so far," he replied. "Tried calling her earlier this afternoon. She was all tied up with the Renton cops when I was available. Then I had to spend the rest of the afternoon messing around with all this car rental stuff. By the time I finished up, I decided to let it go until tomorrow. My heart wasn't in it. Must be awful, losing an only son like that. Even if Tony wasn't right in the head. Even if he was . . . what's the phrase they use nowadays? You know what I mean."

"Developmentally disabled."

Max nodded. "Right, that's the one. But Tony was still a hell of a nice guy. Anybody around here will tell you so. At least he seemed like it. Right up 'til he stole my car. Even that wouldn't've been so bad if he just hadn't wrecked the damned thing!"

Max was rambling again. I tried to steer him back on course. "How long have you known Tony?"

"As long as he's worked here, I guess," Max said with a shrug. "Four months or so. That's what someone said. I don't know exactly, but I'm in here a lot. He's worked the evening shift for the last several months."

"And where did he live?"

"In a group home of some kind. Up off Aurora. Used to catch the bus coming and going."

"The bus. You mean he didn't drive?"

"Nobody *thought* he drove," Cole said bitterly. "Right up until he stole my car."

"You're beginning to sound like a broken record, Max," I said. "What I'm asking is, did he have a license or not?"

"I don't think so. He had some kind of picture

ID from the state so he could cash checks and things, but he didn't drive. I don't think he would have been able to pass the test. Chief told me once that he couldn't read, but that he could watch television and that was all he needed."

"Did he ever talk about his birth mother?" I asked.

"Not per se. He talked about being Indian. That's what he called himself. None of this Native American bullshit. Indian and proud of it. Said his grandfather was somebody important out on the reservation. Must have been a chief."

Or a shaman, I thought.

"As a matter of fact," Max continued, "I didn't find out about any of this adoption stuff until today. For all I knew, he'd been living on the reservation right up until he came to work here. I thought maybe they'd had some program out there that had turned him into a busboy. You know, one of those job training kinds of things."

Max caught the bartender's eye and tapped his empty glass. Wiping the counter as he came, Mr. Nose Ring worked his way down the bar. "What is it, Mr. Cole?"

"Fill'er up."

"Sorry."

"Sorry!" Max exclaimed. "Whaddya do, run out of vermouth or cherries? I can see how this place might be plumb out of cherries." He laughed uproariously. The bartender did not.

"I believe you've had enough, Mr. Cole," Mr. Nose Ring said carefully. "You might want to consider going on over to the restaurant side and having something to eat. I can send your bar bill along over there if you like."

"Do you mean to tell me I'm eighty-sixed?" Max demanded.

Peering past his nose ring, the diminutive bartender didn't blink, and he didn't back off either. "All I'm saying is that cocktails are over. It's time to eat or go home."

"The hell it is!" Max exclaimed. "See there, Beaumont? That's what happens when a guy drinks with cops. Everybody starts getting so nervous about rules that nobody has any fun."

He flung himself off his stool and made for the door. The bartender had picked up the bill and was about to raise an alarm for a manager when I caught his eye.

"Never mind," I said. "I'll take care of it. Mr. Cole seems to be having a run of bad luck today."

"Thanks," the bartender returned, taking the money. "I heard all about his car, and I'm sorry it happened. Still I appreciate your paying the bill. Getting money from somebody after you've cut 'em off is always a pain in the butt." He studied my face. "Is it true what he just said, that you're a cop?"

I nodded.

"Here because of the car or because of Tony?"

"Mostly Tony," I said. "But I was also hoping to run into Jimmy."

"Greenjeans?"

I nodded.

"Good luck," he said.

Over time, cops become masters at decoding nuances of tone. This one sounded bad to me. "What do you mean?"

"Bridget called here a little while ago looking for him. She's really upset, although I don't know why. I mean, Jimmy probably just had a flat tire or something."

"Who's Bridget?" I asked.

"Bridget Hargrave," the bartender answered. "She's Jimmy's girlfriend. She came home expecting to find him there, except he wasn't. He left a note saying he was coming down here and that he'd be back in a little while. As far as I can tell, nobody here's seen him all day. I did my best to calm Bridget down, but she wasn't having any of it. She can be a real handful at times."

Mr. Nose Ring shoved my change across the counter. I left him a decent tip then hurried out into the parking lot where I was relieved to see there was no sign of Maxwell Cole or his Enterprise car.

Walking across the parking lot, I switched on my cell phone and dialed directory assistance. Naturally, Bridget Hargrave's number was unlisted. Jimmy Greenjeans didn't have a listing at all.

Having struck out on that score, I unlocked my trunk and removed my notebook computer. As I mentioned before, that's where the detective division's handy-dandy computers spend most of their time—locked in trunks. After several mix-ups and one or two losses, we all wised up and learned to move them from city-owned vehicles to private ones at the end of our shifts. Had I used my equipment more often, I probably wouldn't have had quite such a struggle hooking up the Ricochet modem.

A Ricochet is a computer attachment that operates like a cell phone. The purpose is to help us keep in touch with the department's main-frame computer even when we're someplace without a hard-wired telephone jack.

It took several tries before I got the thing to work. When I finally tapped into the SPD computer system, I had to consult my faithful little notebook to come up with the proper case number—the one that had originally been given to the Seward Park case. Minutes later, armed with Bridget Hargrave and Jimmy Greenjeans' address, I headed up Denny toward Capitol Hill.

I expected the address on Boren to be something of a dump. It wasn't. Somebody in the Hargrave/Greenjeans twosome had money in his/her pocket. Since his name wasn't part of the telephone listing, I guessed that the person with the dough wasn't Jimmy. Parking around the corner, I walked up to the front door and rang the security phone.

"Who is it?" I recognized the same breathy-voiced young woman I had spoken to one day earlier.

"Miss Hargrave?" I asked, hoping she wouldn't hang up on me.

"Who is it?" she repeated.

"My name's Beaumont, Detective J. P. Beaumont with the Seattle PD."

"Oh, my God!" she gasped. "He's dead, isn't he? Jimmy's dead!"

Over a keening wail of rising hysteria, I attempted

to explain. "Miss Hargrave, really . . ." I heard a buzz as though she had broken the connection. I was still staring at the receiver when the security door clicked open. I let myself into the building, but that didn't do much good. There was no listing of names and apartment numbers inside, nothing to tell me where I might find Bridget Hargrave. I understand why buildings don't list apartment numbers. It's the same reason there are locks and telephones on the outside doors—security. Still, when you're supposed to see someone and haven't a clue as to their unit number, it can be a real pain in the ass.

Sighing, I went back to the door where I had to stand with one foot inside the door and the other out in order to call her once again.

"Miss Hargrave, I . . ."

She understood the problem. "Apartment 804," she barked into the phone before I had a chance to explain.

When I stepped off the elevator, a frantic young woman was already waiting for me in the eighth-floor hallway. Tears streamed down her ashen cheeks. "Where is he?" she sobbed. "What's happened to Jimmy?"

She caught my jacket by the lapels in both hands and physically attempted to shake me with all the good effect of a tail wagging a dog. The poor tiny thing couldn't have been much more than twenty. Barefoot and wearing clothing that could have come straight from Goodwill, she looked more like a street waif than the monied resident of a high-rise luxury condo.

"Please, tell me what's happened," she begged. "Please."

"I don't have any idea," I said.

She stopped. "But you're a detective, aren't you? You said on the phone . . ."

I fumbled my ID out of my pocket and handed it to her. "It's true," I told her. "I am a detective. But I came here hoping to talk to Jimmy."

"He isn't here!"

Letting go of my jacket, Bridget turned abruptly and headed toward an open door just down the hallway. I hurried after her and was halfway inside the unit before she had a chance to slam the door shut in my face. I made it far enough into the room to have a fairly good look at the interior. The matching Stiffel torchère lamps weren't something that had come from Goodwill. Neither had the all-leather sofa and matching chairs. Or the tasteful marble occasional tables that were scattered about here and there.

"Wait a minute, Miss Hargrave . . ."

"You tricked me," she said accusingly and with heartfelt fury. "You're a cop, and I don't talk to cops. If nothing's happened to Jimmy, why . . ."

"I don't know for sure that nothing's happened to Jimmy," I said. "It may have."

She spun back around. "So you *do* know something then."

"Not really," I said. "But I'm worried that he may be in some danger."

"Why do you say that?" she demanded.

"You sound worried yourself. How come?"

She gave a little shudder before she answered. When she did, it was to ask yet another question. "Just tell me one thing. Was it an accident or not?"

"Was what an accident?"

"That guy down in Renton—the one they found dead in Lake Washington this morning."

"You mean Tony Lawson?" She nodded. "What do you think?" I asked.

Bridget Hargrave sighed then. When she looked back up at me, there were tears in her eyes again. "One of the shift supervisors called to let Jimmy know. As soon as he heard about it, he just went wild. I've never seen him like that. He said, 'If they got to Tony, they'll be coming after me next.' I told him he was being silly, but when I came home this afternoon and he wasn't here . . . . I found a note."

She paused and walked over to a marble entry-way table. I felt a sudden void in my gut. It was the same way I had felt earlier in the day when I first heard about the case in Renton—Maxwell Cole's sunken car containing the body of someone from the Hurricane Cafe.

"You're sure that's exactly what Jimmy said?" I asked. "'They'll be coming after me next?'"

Nodding, Bridget Hargrave handed me a scrap of paper.

"Gone to H.C.," it said. "Back by four."

"We were supposed to see my mother for dinner tonight," Bridget continued. "She's coming in from out of town. We were going to meet her and her new boyfriend at the Four Seasons for dinner at 5:30. It's not like Jimmy . . ."

"Have you reported him missing?"

She blinked back tears. "I tried," she said. "But when I called 911, the operator practically laughed me off the phone. She said if Jimmy's still missing, for me to call back tomorrow at the same time."

Which will be exactly twenty-four hours too late, I told myself grimly. Reaching into my pocket, I pulled out a business card and pressed it into Bridget Hargrave's tiny, ice-cold hands. "If you hear from him, have him call me. Right away."

With that, I turned and charged back into the hallway. I had punched the button and was stepping inside the door when Bridget caught up with me.

"Where are you going?" she asked.

"To look for him," I told her.

Her already-ashen face turned a shade paler. "You think something bad has happened to him, too, don't you?"

"I certainly do," I told her. "Just don't ask me why."

CHAPTER 14

ASIDE FROM KRAMER'S EMPHASIS ON ESTABLISHING "goals and objectives," the major thrust of his interminable briefing that morning had been teamwork—the importance of. His entire pep talk/monologue had been delivered with enough rah-rah football analogies to choke even the most ardent Seahawk fan. Teamwork was a problem for me, however. Having been summarily thrown off the team, I found it difficult to summon up any kind of warm and fuzzy attitude toward his particular concept of teamwork.

Consequently and despite my promise to Sue, I didn't even bother trying to get in touch with Detectives Haller or Nguyen. What good would that do? I was sure Kramer would already have given them the word that I was *persona non grata* on the Seward Park investigation. Instead, I picked up my cell phone and gave the medical examiner's office a call.

Once again, Audrey Cummings answered the phone. "So your guy is still out sick?" I asked.

"I suppose you mean Dirk Matthews?" she replied. "That's right. He's not just sick—he's really sick. He's here in Harborview in critical condition. They have him upstairs in the burn unit with a raging case of necrotizing fasciitis—Stevens-Johnson syndrome as we refer to it in the trade. SJ for short."

"SJ," I repeated. "What's that?"

"Your basic flesh-eating disease—a massive bacterial infection. These are your normal, ordinary bacteria, the kind that are around every day. Then, suddenly, for no known reason, they just go wild. I saw Dirk day before yesterday and he was fine, clowning around like usual. Today he's upstairs fighting for his life. SJ is massive, rapid, and very, very serious."

The more she talked, the worse I felt, and the more I remembered Darla Cunningham's warning. That things might not seem connected, but that they would be. My impression was that Dirk Matthews was the person in the ME's office who had actually handled the Seward Park remains.

"You mean as in he may not make it?" I asked.

"That's what I mean." After a pause, Audrey resumed her customary manner of businesslike efficiency. "All right, now, Beau, with Dirk out, we're really shorthanded. Let's not waste any more time jawing. What do you need?"

"Can I buy you a cup of coffee?"

"I don't drink coffee," she said. "It's bad for the

rain forests. I am due for a lunch break, though. You can come on over if you like. We can go to the cafeteria."

"No," I said. "Not there. I'd like to speak to you in private."

"This sounds serious."

"It's either serious or crazy," I told her. "You'll have to decide which."

Audrey sighed. "All right, then," she said. "You have a car, don't you?"

"I'm in it."

"I brought along a sack lunch. Come pick me up outside the building. You drive; I'll eat."

It seemed as though everyone in downtown Seattle must have gone home to dinner. The place was a deserted village. From the far end of the Denny Regrade, I made it to Harborview Hospital in seven minutes flat. Audrey was waiting outside the building when I drove into the back driveway.

"Nice car," she said, climbing into the Porsche. "How is it a homicide cop can afford to drive one of these?"

"It's a long story," I replied.

"That's right," she said, settling in and fastening her seat belt. "I remember. Something about an heiress."

"Something like that," I agreed.

"Oil was it?" Audrey asked.

"Copper, not oil."

Satisfied, Audrey opened her bag and brought out a sandwich. "It's peanut butter and plum jelly," she said. "Want to share?"

"No, thanks."

Audrey took a bite. "So what's going on?" she asked.

"First, tell me about Dirk Matthews," I said.

She shook her head. "I've pretty much told you everything there is to tell. I'm worried about him, of course. But it turns out I'm glad to have him out of my hair, too. His parents are good friends of Doc Baker's, so, although he's a nice enough young man and even a fairly decent investigator, he has a bit of a wild streak. No, make that a goofy streak. When Dirk was a kid, he probably drove his parents and teachers round the bend. He pulls these outrageous stunts sometimes. In fact, the last time I saw him at work, I was chewing him out for that very thing. One day I bawl him out for some kind of stupid class-clown nonsense. The next thing I know, the poor guy's in intensive care and practically on his deathbed."

"What kind of nonsense?"

Audrey didn't answer right away. When she did, it was to sidestep the issue. "It was just some backroom high jinks. No big thing. I don't see what that has to do . . ."

"Humor me, Audrey," I said. "I'm a homicide detective. The kind of black humor that gets bandied around the squad room would be enough to have normal people locked up. I'm sure the same kind of thing goes on in the ME's office, as well."

"But . . ."

"Please," I begged. "Just tell me. Whatever it was, I'm not going to go blabbing it all over town."

Audrey sighed. "Have you ever seen the Flying Karamazov Brothers?"

"The juggling troupe?"

Audrey nodded.

"I think so," I said. "Years ago when my own kids were little, I think Karen and I took them to see that show somewhere. I seem to remember that in one part of their act, they invited people from the audience to bring up items for them to juggle. There were all kinds of things—a vacuum cleaner hose, bowling pins, bowling balls, knives, and car parts. I can't remember what else. And they managed to juggle them all. It was pretty impressive."

"Right," Audrey said. "I wonder if Dirk didn't see that same show. If so, it made a big impression on him. Some people work all day and dream of writing the great American novel at night, on weekends, and during their vacations. Dirk Matthews, on the other hand, is teaching himself to juggle. His greatest ambition in life is to be accepted into the Barnum & Bailey clown college so he can run away and join the circus."

"So?"

"Two nights ago, I walked in on him and caught him practicing his juggling, only he wasn't doing it with bowling pins. He was using bones, Beau, human bones. I gave him hell about it, of course. Told him that our job requires us to show respect for the dead no matter who they are. That we must always behave as though the bodies entrusted to our care are the bodies of our own loved ones. When I finished reaming him out, he was completely contrite, as usual. Promised it would never happen again and all that. At the time, he looked perfectly healthy.

Less than twenty-four hours later, he was up in the burn unit with a raging case of SJ."

Wanting to talk without having to think about driving at the same time, I swung the 928 into the drive-up window of a closed dry-cleaning shop. "Let me guess," I said. "The bones he was juggling would have to be the ones from Seward Park. Right?"

"Right," Audrey said, nodding. "How did you know that?"

I felt like I was walking into verbal quicksand. Paul Kramer hadn't gone for the idea that there might be a possible link between a dead shaman's curse and a very real murder. What made me think that Audrey Cummings, a scientist, would buy a similar connection between that same curse and the unseemly behavior of her desperately ill investigator, Dirk Matthews.

"Just a guess," I said. "How many sets of bones can you have around there at one time?"

Audrey shot me a sidelong glance. "You'd be surprised," she said.

"Anyway," I continued, "Sue and I have stumbled across a possible ID on those bones."

"Really. Who is it?" she asked.

"We think he's a Suquamish shaman named David Half Moon."

"From where?"

"Over on the Kitsap Peninsula," I told her. "According to our source, Half Moon died several years ago from lung cancer."

"A shaman," Audrey said thoughtfully. "That might explain it."

"Explain what?"

"What happened to Dirk," she replied. "Once we started having to deal with Native American repatriation issues on a fairly regular basis, I made it a point to study the belief systems of various Puget Sound tribes. As I recall, among the Suquamish, disturbing the remains of a shaman is considered to be a very serious offense."

"You're saying Dirk somehow caught an infection from handling the bones?"

"Not directly. But Northwest Indians have their own ideas about what goes around comes around. In a way, it's not unlike the Hindu and Buddhist concept of karma."

"And one thing leads to another?" I asked.

Audrey nodded. "The truth is, Dirk shouldn't have treated anybody's bones that way, but juggling with an old shaman's bones is just asking for trouble."

I could hardly believe the words I was hearing come out of her mouth, and it certainly saved me a lot of time, effort, and explanation. "You wouldn't happen to know a lady named Darla Cunningham, would you?" I asked.

"No. Who's she?"

"She teaches physics at the U-Dub."

"Should I know her?" Audrey asked.

"If you did," I said, "I think you two might have a lot in common. She happens to be the daughter of a Quinault shaman, a guy named Henry Leaping Deer from over at Taholah."

"A Quinault who teaches physics? She sounds interesting," Audrey agreed, biting into an apple.

"Now, is that all you came to tell me, the origin of those bones? Why did we have to be away from the office for that?"

"It's actually a little more complicated than that," I admitted. "You know the body the Renton police pulled out of Lake Washington this morning?"

"Anthony Lawson? I believe he's also an Indian. Don't tell me he's a shaman, too."

"No," I said. "But the two cases may be connected, and that's why I needed to talk to you. We'd like you to do a DNA comparison and see whether or not Anthony Lawson is related to the other man, presumably David Half Moon."

"As you well know, those kinds of tests are prohibitively expensive," Audrey objected. "As officers assigned to the two cases, you and Detective Danielson are welcome to request them, but I'm not making any promises . . ."

I decided it was time to be straight with her. "The truth is, Sue and I have been removed from the Seward Park case by our new fearless leader, Paul Kramer, because he thinks I've been bamboozled by all this shaman hocus-pocus, as he calls it. And, since Lawson died down in Renton, we're not even involved in that one. But it turns out Lawson also was born somewhere over on the Kitsap Peninsula. He was adopted out as an infant, but he told some of his fellow workers that his grandfather was a big deal out on the reservation—presumably Port Madison. And if Lawson's grandfather turns out to be David Half Moon, it's true. He really was a big deal."

"You said Half Moon died of cancer. That means

he's not a murder victim at all, so what's the point of running the tests?" Audrey asked.

"It'll prove the connection between the two cases, one Kramer claims I'm just making up. Furthermore, if Half Moon clearly isn't a homicide statistic, maybe we can expedite getting his bones out of the ME's office and shipped back into the woods where they belong."

"You mean, before they cause any more trouble?"

"Right," I said.

Meticulous as usual, Audrey dropped her apple core into her empty sandwich bag. Then she zipped it shut, dropped that bag into the paper bag. After that she folded the paper until the resulting package was no bigger than a small envelope.

"I get the feeling you know more than you're saying," Audrey said thoughtfully.

"You're right," I admitted. "The woman I told you about earlier, Darla Cunningham, showed up in my office last night. She came to pass along a warning from her father, Henry Leaping Deer . . ."

"The Quinault from Taholah," Audrey put in.

"Right . . . who's had a series of disturbing dreams over the last week or so."

"What's his connection to Half Moon?"

"They were friends," I answered. "Boyhood friends. They evidently went to boarding school together. In the first dream, Half Moon's bones had been carted off to the city. In the next one, a group of children were playing field hockey with the same bones, using Half Moon's skull as the ball."

"We never found a skull," Audrey said. "So maybe

Leaping Deer was using his literary license. Still it isn't all that far from what really went on."

"When I saw her, Darla passed along her father's warning that some innocent people were in danger of being affected by Half Moon's bones."

"Anyone specific?" Audrey asked.

I nodded. "A man with green hair and a white woman. The green-haired guy isn't hard to figure out. Jimmy Greenjeans, the guy who reported the Seward Park bones in the first place, happens to have green hair. I just came from talking to his girlfriend. It turns out he's missing at the moment."

"Missing?" Audrey asked. "That doesn't sound good."

"It isn't."

"And the white woman? Who's she?"

"I'm not sure," I told her. "That's a little harder to figure. She could be you or Sue Danielson, either one."

Audrey thought about that for several long seconds. I waited, more than half expecting her to simply burst out laughing. If so, I would lose the one ally who might actually be able to help. When she spoke, however, there was no trace of laughter.

"I can see how come Kramer might be worried," she said. "On the other hand, I can also see why you're so concerned. Don't worry about the DNA tests. I'll handle the requests myself. Those tests take time, though. While I'm working on those, it might be faster for someone to talk to Anthony Lawson's adoptive mother and see if she has any records that would indicate a relationship between him and

Seward Park. Do you have the mother's address? I could probably give it to you if . . ."

"Thanks for the offer. Maxwell Cole already gave me Annie Engebretson's address. She lives in a retirement home over by Greenlake."

Audrey glanced at her watch. "Fun's over," she said. "You'd better take me back so I can get started on my end of this."

Nodding, I eased the idling engine back into gear and nosed out onto Broadway. For several blocks, neither of us spoke. Audrey broke the silence.

"Once we make the connection between Seward Park and David Half Moon, it will only take a matter of days for me to arrange repatriation. This isn't the first time we've found Indian bones in King County, so I know the drill, but only as far as ordinary people are concerned. Dealing with a shaman may be somewhat more complicated. Is there any cure?"

For a few confusing seconds, I thought we had somehow switched back to Dirk Matthews and his flesh-eating infection. "Cure for what?" I asked.

"For the shaman's curse," Audrey replied impatiently.

"Oh, that," I said. "I think so. I remember Darla mentioning some kind of purification ceremony and that her father would be willing to help."

"That's good," Audrey said, as we pulled into the drive that goes around to the newly remodeled back of Harborview Hospital. "I'll keep that in mind. Where is he again?"

"Taholah."

"Where's that?"

"Somewhere out along the coast. The Olympic Peninsula."

"By Ocean Shores?"

"No," I said. "Taholah's quite a way north of there."

"Too bad," Audrey said. "I have a time share in Ocean Shores. If he were closer, maybe I could go there and have him come to the condo to do a house call."

At that point I finally realized she was making fun of me. "I don't think shamans make house calls," I told her.

Up to then, we had been so engrossed in our conversation that I hadn't seen the squall line, a fast moving layer of low, dark clouds, that was rolling in off the water, lowering in under high, overcast skies. In the process, they had obliterated what had promised to be a glorious sunset. Now, as Audrey prepared to exit the car and make a dash for the building, the clouds burst into a drenching downpour. Even though she had to travel a distance of only a few feet, I'm sure she was soaked to the skin by the time she made it inside.

Watch yourself, I told her silently as she disappeared into a corridor. *Take off those wet clothes and stay out of the way of fast-moving bacteria.*

As if to underscore that thought, a powerful lightning strike flashed off one of the downtown high-rises. The brilliant explosion of light was immediately followed by a deafening crack of thunder. I said a little prayer of thanks that Audrey had been safely inside when it hit.

For several minutes, I sat in the drive, watching

the rain and considering my next move. I was off the clock and working a self-assigned case. No one was waiting for me at home, so my dinner certainly wouldn't be getting cold. Taken all together, there didn't seem to be much point in calling it a day and going home. Instead, I drove straight over to Greenlake and parked in a visitors' spot outside the Hearthstone. Naturally a gatekeeper was posted at the reception desk. "May I help you?"

Most of the time my homicide squad ID can ease me past even the most reluctant of receptionists although why they're not called repulsionists, I don't know. This one may have been young, but she certainly lived up to the latter name. And, considering the circumstances, I can't say I blame her.

"Mrs. Engebretson isn't receiving visitors at the moment," the young woman said. "As you can well imagine, she's had a very rough day."

Since I wasn't officially assigned to the case, flashing my Seattle PD badge might have opened the door, but in the long run I was sure it would be more of a handicap than a help. "I'm a friend of Tony's," I said as sincerely as I could manage. "I would really like to see his mother if it's at all possible, just to express my condolences."

The young woman sighed. "What's your name, please."

"Jonas," I said at once.

"One moment, Mr. Jonas," she said curtly. "We'll have to check."

I did nothing to disabuse her of the mistaken impression that Jonas was my last name. It occurred to me that if somebody from Seattle PD—Kramer, for example—came around asking questions, they might not be astute enough to connect a Mr. Jonas with a troublesome detective named J. P. Beaumont. There are very few people in the department who are aware that the J in my name actually stands for Jonas.

The receptionist turned and indulged in a behind-the-desk *sotto voce* conference with one of her coworkers. The coworker gave me a meaningful up-and-down examination before she flounced away from the desk. She returned several minutes later. "All right, Mr. Jonas. Annie's willing to see you, after all. She's in the chapel at the moment. Please follow me."

I was expecting an LOL, a little old lady, as we sometimes call them. Annie Engebretson may have been old, but she was anything but little. The stately and formidable woman who rose to greet me when I entered the tastefully lit chapel was every bit as tall as I am. She came walking toward me, holding out her hand. Her icy blue eyes were red-rimmed while a thin cloud of snow-white hair haloed her face.

"Mr. Jonas," she said cordially, taking my hand and shaking it with a firm, unyielding grip. "I understand you were a friend of my son's."

Feeling like a reprehensible heel, I nodded.

"Won't you sit down. I'm delighted to meet you. I'm glad to know my son had friends, you see. Friends that were normal, that is, and not developmentally disabled. Anthony had his friends at the home, of course, his roommates, but it's nice to know there were others, too."

You incredible jerk, I railed at myself. *What the hell*

do you think you're doing? I said, "We weren't all that close. I only knew him at work."

She nodded. Behind thick bifocals her eyes filled with tears. "That's all right," she said. "He loved that job. It was his first, you see, and he was very proud of it—proud of making a contribution and doing something in the real world. You know?"

I nodded again. "I'm sad about this, but in a way, I'm glad, too," she continued. "That was always one of Einer's and my big worries. Einer was my husband. He died several years ago. We both worried about Anthony outliving us, especially after Einer got so sick. We couldn't imagine what would become of him after both of us were gone. Now I don't have to worry about that anymore. It sounds like such a terribly cold-hearted thing for a mother to say, but still I do feel as though an awful weight, a burden, has been lifted from my shoulders. Does that make any sense, Mr. Jonas?"

Feeling worse by the minute, I nodded. "Of course it does," I said.

"But now, what is it you wanted? They said at the desk that you especially wanted to see me tonight. That it couldn't wait until tomorrow."

"Well," I said, scrambling. "I was wondering if there was anything I could do to help. With regard to arrangements, that is."

"How kind of you," Annie Engebretson said. "I've already spoken with Hearthstone's chaplain, Reverend Walters. He's agreed that we can have a small memorial service right here in the chapel. As for the actual burial, I'm still not sure what to do about that. I suppose you know that Anthony was adopted?"

"Yes."

"Well, it was a private affair, arranged by someone we met at church. Einer and I were both in our sixties then—far too old as far as the state is concerned to have been given a child. Even though we felt we had so much to offer, regular adoption channels were closed to us. So we found another way. Anthony's paternal grandparents were missionaries over on Port Madison. They were also friends of my late husband. Anthony's birth mother was a young Indian, barely fourteen at the time. She was also totally unsuitable. There was never any question of her marrying the boy. She was determined to keep the baby and raise him on her own. Once she discovered he was retarded, however, she was going to turn him over to the state and have him placed in one of those awful homes. That's when Einer stepped in. He just wouldn't stand for it. Anthony was three when he came to us. Einer was sixty-three, and I was sixty."

Listening to her, I couldn't help thinking about what kind of strength of character it must have taken to tackle the job of child rearing at that age, even with a normal child.

"Einer loved that boy beyond life itself," Annie continued, while her eyes clouded with tears. "They told us that he'd never be able to learn anything, but Einer proved them all wrong. He taught Anthony so much, far more than anyone thought possible. Anthony was eighteen when we received word that his birth grandfather had died. Anthony was invited to the funeral, and Einer took him. He said he was old enough to go."

"His grandfather, that would have been David Half Moon?" I ventured tentatively even though my gut already knew the answer.

Annie Engebretson nodded. "Yes," she responded. "Anthony must have told you about it. The whole thing made such a big impression on him. That was all he talked about for months afterward—about seeing the canoe being raised up into the tree branches. I think that part of it must have seemed like magic to him. Sort of like the flying pirate ship in *Peter Pan*. He loved that story, begged Einer to read it to him over and over again. When it came out on video, we got him a copy. He wore it out. One of the reasons he liked the story so much was because it had *Indians* in it—not real Indians, but they seemed real enough to him. And maybe he liked it because, in a way, he knew he, too, was a little lost boy. That he'd never grow up."

With that Annie Engebretson burst into full-fledged tears. She groped blindly in the cuff of her sweater for a handkerchief. "From then on, Anthony begged to go back, but Einer had gotten sick. So he drew him a map. Not that Anthony would ever have been able to go by himself, just so he'd have it."

That map, lovingly made and lovingly given had, in the wrong hands, become Anthony Lawson's death warrant.

Annie Engebretson took a ragged breath. "I'm sorry to be such a wreck, Mr. Jonas," she apologized. "At least Anthony is safe in the Lord's hands now. The world can be such a cruel place for someone who's different. In fact, I wondered earlier today, if that isn't what happened to him—somebody playing some kind of cruel joke. Anthony never drank on his own, you see. And he never drove, either. I'd like to know who helped him get drunk like that. And who started the car for him, too, for that matter."

So would I, I thought.

"But there's no point in agonizing over such things," Annie continued stoically. "What I have to do now is deal with making final arrangements."

She paused again and took a deep breath. Instead of looking at me, her eyes sought counsel from somewhere at the front of the wood-paneled chapel. "Anthony left the reservation when he was only three," she said softly. "Except for that one visit when he was eighteen, he never went back. Still, knowing him the way I do, I think that's really where he'd like to be buried. On the reservation with the other Indians. That's how he thought of himself. As an Indian. But I'm an outsider there, Mr. Jonas. I have no idea how to go about doing such a thing. I asked Reverend Walters about it. He said he'd see what he could do, but he didn't hold out much hope."

Suddenly, I found enough air in my lungs so that I could take a deep breath, too. I had come to see Annie under false pretenses, claiming to be her son's friend. Now fate was letting me be a friend after all.

"I may be able to help you there," I offered tentatively.

"Really?" The hope in Annie Engebretson's quavering voice worried me. What if I couldn't deliver?

"A friend of mine, Darla Cunningham, is a Quinault," I said. "Through a strange set of circumstances, I've learned that her father, Henry Leaping

Deer, went to school with David Half Moon. They were friends all through boarding school."

Annie's eyes widened. "With Anthony's grandfather?"

"That's right. Henry Leaping Deer may be a Quinault, not a Suquamish, but if anyone could help you make those kinds of arrangements, I'm sure he could."

"You think he'd do that?"

"I'm almost sure of it," I said.

"Do you have any idea how I could reach this man, this Leaping Deer?"

"He lives up at Taholah. He may or may not have a phone. But his daughter lives here in Seattle. She teaches in the physics department at the university. As I said, her name is Darla Cunningham. You probably can't reach her tonight, but if you try the university tomorrow . . ."

Annie already had a pen and notebook in hand. "Darla Cunningham and Henry Leaping Deer," she murmured as she wrote. "I'll be in touch with one or both of them first thing in the morning."

I stood up. "I'd best be going," I said. "I'm sure I've taken far too much of your time as it is. But I do have one more question. If your name is Engebretson, why was Anthony's last name Lawson?"

"Lawson was his mother's name, and Anthony was the name she gave him," Annie said. "And that was the only thing she asked of us. That we leave his name the way it was."

Annie stood up, too. Before I could dodge out of the way, she had stepped forward and wrapped me in an all-enveloping hug. "I don't know how to thank you, Mr. Jonas," she said. "You've been such a great help. Your coming here tonight has truly been the answer to a prayer. Now then, is there any way I'll be able to get in touch with you to let you know when the memorial service will be?"

That's not my usual role in life—as the answer to someone's prayer. To my knowledge, no one else had ever called me that, certainly not to my face. And, in view of the fact I had earned that status in Annie Engebretson's eyes through lies and misrepresentation, I was more than slightly embarrassed. I think I was blushing. Fortunately for me, the gloom in the dimly lit chapel kept it from showing.

"Glad to be of service," I mumbled. "And don't worry about notifying me as to the time of the memorial service," I added. "I'm sure someone from down at the Hurricane Cafe will let me know when it is."

"You work there, too?" she asked.

"No," I said. "But I know several people who do."

CHAPTER 15

IT'S DIFFICULT FOR SOMEONE MY SIZE AND BUILD TO feel lighter than air, but that's exactly how I felt as I drove away from the Hearthside—lighter than air. I had pulled it off. I had played Sue's hunch, one everyone else had discounted, and we had come up winners.

I wanted to call Sue and crow, to let her know that in my humble opinion we had kicked butt. When I dialed her number, though, her voice mail came on almost immediately. That usually means both lines are busy, and this wasn't a message I wanted to leave on an answering machine.

Next I tried calling Audrey. At the ME's office, the voice mail message under her name said Audrey was currently out of the office and would return calls as soon as possible. I didn't want to leave a message there, either, since there was a possibility somebody else might pick up Audrey's voice mail. It wouldn't be a good idea to have a recording of Detective J. P. Beaumont's voice brimming over with good news about two cases he wasn't supposed to be anywhere near.

My third attempt at placing a call went to Bridget Hargrave. That one went through. She must have been sitting on top of the phone because she answered midway through the first ring.

"Jimmy?"

"Sorry to disappoint you, Miss Hargrave. This is Detective Beaumont. Any news?"

"No," she answered. "None."

That was too bad. Jimmy Greenjeans's continuing absence definitely constituted a dark cloud on an otherwise rapidly clearing horizon. That bothered me. It was evidently bothering Bridget even more than it did me.

"I'm afraid, Detective Beaumont," she sobbed into the phone. "I'm afraid he's dead."

So was I.

"Did Jimmy ever talk to you about Anthony Lawson?"

"The guy in the lake? Tony you mean, the retard at work. Yes, Jimmy talked about him sometimes. He worried about him—that people were taking advantage. He said that every once in a while someone on the wait staff cheated him out of tips because he didn't know any better. But that was all he ever said. You don't think it was someone from there who killed him, do you? Someone who worked at the Hurricane Cafe?"

I knew exactly who had done it. What was lacking was proof. "No," I said. "I doubt it was anyone who worked there. I'd better . . ."

"Detective Beaumont, please don't hang up,"

Bridget Hargrave interrupted. "I need to ask you something."

"What?"

"My mother came by a little while ago. She's . . . well . . . sort of stuck up, if you know what I mean. She says dating a bartender is beneath me. That's the way she put it—beneath me. She says the reason Jimmy didn't show up is that he was nervous about meeting her. That he took off so he wouldn't have to. She told me I was silly to be so worried about him and that I should have gone to dinner without him. We had a big fight over it. What do you think?"

There are few men who aren't at least slightly cowed at the prospect of meeting future in-laws. On the other hand, as a bartender dealing with the Hurricane Cafe's day-to-day flotsam-and-jetsam clientele, it didn't seem likely that a mere "stuck-up" woman would scare Jimmy into running for cover. I wondered if Bridget's mother wasn't downplaying the disappearance issue for her own purposes, hoping to drive a wedge between her daughter and her less-than-wonderful choice of heartthrobs. On the other hand, it seemed to me that Bridget had every reason to be worried about what had happened to Jimmy. I also thought she deserved a straight answer.

"Bridget," I said carefully, "in my opinion, Jimmy's disappearance has nothing whatever to do with your mother and everything to do with Tony Lawson. I can't say any more right now, and I need to have your word that you won't pass that information along to anyone—anyone at all—until I give you the go-ahead. Understood?"

"I understand," she said.

"Hang onto those phone numbers I gave you. If you hear from Jimmy—if he calls you or shows up at your apartment—promise that you'll call me right away."

"I promise."

"Good," I said. "I have to hang up now. I'm going into my garage. The signal doesn't work very well from underground."

I parked on P–3 and then rode the elevator up. I stopped in the lobby long enough to collect my mail. The doorman was busy chatting with people I'd never seen before, so I didn't have to bother making small talk on my way upstairs. Picking up messages has become such a way of life these days that as soon as I shed my jacket and shoulder holster, I went straight to the phone.

One message was from Ron Peters saying that artichoke-hearts pizza was on the menu that night in case I felt like coming downstairs and joining them. A glance at my watch told me 9:00 was far too late for dinner. The second was from Ralph Ames reminding me not to forget our dinner date for the following night. Taken together, the two messages left me chuckling that my friends go to such lengths to make sure I don't starve to death. The third and last caller, clocking in at 4:45, didn't bother to identify himself.

"Detective Beaumont, I really need to talk . . ."

That was all there was to it. The recording stopped in midsentence and didn't resume. I played it again, thinking that something was amiss with the recorder. After playing it a second time, I played it once more after that. It was on the third time through that I finally recognized the voice. Barry Newsome!

Once I knew who it was, I listened to the recording a fourth time, just to see if I had missed something, and I had. At the very end, just after the word "talk," there was a little burst of sound, but it wasn't anything I could recognize. The beginning of a shout perhaps. Or maybe a door opening or closing. Without a competent sound engineer tweaking the tape, there was no way to tell. What didn't require a sound engineer to unravel was the nervousness in Barry Newsome's voice. He was either upset or scared, maybe both, and looking for me.

I slammed down the phone. There was no point in dialing 911. Whatever had happened was several hours old. My first instinct was to call back, but the Seward Park file, complete with all relevant phone numbers, was in my laptop. As per usual, the computer was down in the garage, safely locked inside the trunk of my 928.

Rather than race all the way down to P–3 in the elevator, I picked up the phone and dialed Bellevue information. The operator could find no listing for Don Atkins, but she did come up with one for Barry Newsome. I dialed it at once, only to run afoul of some of the phone company's most recent devices designed to bedevil the phone-using public—caller ID complete with call blocking.

Instead of ringing at the other end, a recorded message played in my ear. "The number you have reached does not accept blocked calls. In order to reach your party, you will have to unblock your number for this one call only. To do that, press . . ."

I'm a homicide detective and have been for most of my adult working life. Because of the kinds of people cops have to deal with on a regular basis, almost all the police officers I know have unlisted telephone numbers. For a long time, I resisted. When I finally knuckled under, however, what drove me over the edge wasn't receiving threatening phone calls from people I've helped send to the slammer. It was, instead, the unending flood of telemarketing solicitation calls. The ones I found most annoying came from the boiler-room operation of some lame-brained East Coast securities dealer.

These scuzzy guys always call me at 9:00 their time which happens to be 6:00 A.M. Pacific. The concept of time zones seems to be one that never penetrates their dim bulbs. Nor does the word "No." I turn them down for an Initial Public Offering one week, only to have them call back the next week to offer the next hot deal. After about the twentieth call, I asked the phone company to put a trap on my line, but that didn't work either since the East Coast long-distance provider wouldn't play ball. Finally, I had no choice but to change over to an unlisted number.

Now, however, my fancy two-line push-button phone with its unlisted number didn't allow me to get through to Barry Newsome's equally up-to-date phone. Much as I don't want to give up the convenience of modern telecommunications, there are still occasions when I find myself longing for the good old days when you picked up a phone and some nice, living lady gave you a straightforward, "Number, please."

After dialing the appropriate code to unblock my number, I sat down in the recliner and slipped off my shoes while I listened to it ring. It was answered on the third ring.

"Beau?" a male voice said. "Is that you?"

Stunned, I tried to identify the voice. The person sounded like neither Barry Newsome nor Don Atkins, yet he obviously knew me on a personal basis. My unlisted phone is listed under the name of J. P. Beaumont. Only someone who actually knew me would call me Beau.

"Who's this?" I asked.

"Tim Blaine," he said. "Somebody from the department must have told you I'd be here."

Tim Blaine was a Bellevue homicide dick I had met months earlier in the course of unraveling a New Year's Day murder in downtown Seattle. The last I had heard from Tim, he was dating Latty Gibson, a young woman who had been one of several suspects in that case.

"We're a little busy here right now," Tim continued, "but I can tell you you're on the list."

"What list are you talking about?" I asked.

"The wedding invitation list," he replied. "What did you think I meant? Anyway, the wedding's in late June, the next-to-last Saturday. As soon as the invitations get back from the printer, you'll get yours. After all, since you're the person who introduced us, Latty and I both want you to be at the wedding."

"Congratulations," I told him. "I'm delighted to hear about the wedding. But I wasn't trying to reach

you. I was calling Barry Newsome. What are you
doing there, Tim? What's going on?"

The tenor of Tim's voice changed from personal
to professional. "Are you a friend of his?"

"Hardly. He's part of an investigation . . ."

"*Was* part of an investigation," Tim corrected.
"He doesn't exist anymore. Barry Newsome is dead,
Beau. I'm no medical examiner, but it looks to me
like he took at least two bullets to the heart."

I was stunned. "That's why you're there, you're
investigating a homicide?"

"Two," Tim replied.

Two? Just hearing the word made me almost sick to
my stomach. *Barry Newsome and who else?* My mind
flew at once to the missing Jimmy Greenjeans.

"The second victim doesn't happen to have green
hair, does he?" I asked.

Blaine laughed. "What the hell are you smoking these days, Beau? Of course he doesn't have
green hair. Other than a bullet in the back of his
head, he looks like a pretty normal guy in your
basic Men's Wearhouse double-breasted suit. Do
you know something about this?"

It wasn't Jimmy Greenjeans, then. I was relatively certain he'd never be caught dead in a Men's
Wearhouse suit, double-breasted or otherwise.

"Not exactly," I said. "But your cases are no doubt
connected to something we've been working on over
here in Seattle as well as to a dead guy the Renton
police pulled out of Lake Washington earlier today."

Tim Blaine whistled.

"Your other dead guy, is he Don Atkins?"

"Newsome's roommate? No. The ID in the second victim's pocket gives his name as Calvin Owens. His business card says Sands of Time Gallery in Pioneer Square. Do you know him? Is he connected to any of those other cases?"

"Not so far as I know."

"Where are you right now, Beau? And what are you doing?"

"I'm home. I just slipped off my shoes."

"I hate to pull you right back out," Blaine continued, "but it sounds as though we need to talk so you can show us what you guys have been working on. Would you mind coming over to Bellevue?"

"No," I said. "Not at all, but you'll have to give me directions . . ."

Moments after he told me how to get to Newsome's South Bellevue address, I plugged my unwilling feet back into shoes that felt a full size too small. I had my holster on and was reaching for my jacket when there was a tap on my door. I looked out the peek hole to see Ron and Amy Peters' younger daughter, Heather, standing in the hall holding a dinner plate covered with several loose pieces of pizza.

Ron's two towheaded daughters, Heather, nine, and Tracie, ten, are the light of my life. With them around, I have all the advantages of being a parent or grandparent—taking them to ball games, the zoo, the Seattle Children's Theater and occasionally buying them extravagant stuff—with none of the disadvantages of parenthood like having to worry about them wanting driver's licenses or needing to be put through school.

It may not be fair to play favorites, but I confess that bright-eyed little Heather is mine, and it wasn't unlike her to show up at my door for an unannounced visit. "Hi," I said. "Sorry I can't ask you in, Heather. I'm just on my way out. What's up?"

She held out the plate of pizza. "These are for you," she said. "Dad told me to bring this up to you so these pieces don't go to waste."

"Thanks," I said. I took the plate and headed for the kitchen counter, helping myself to a single slice along the way. As soon as I bit into it, I realized how hungry I was. Invited or not, Heather followed me into the kitchen.

"Guess what, Uncle Beau?" she asked.

"I give up," I said between mouthfuls. Eating standing at a kitchen counter was *verboten* in my mother's house, and I felt a little guilty to be observed red-handed, but Heather didn't object.

"Guess where Dad and Amy went?"

"I have no idea."

"The hospital," she crowed happily. "So Amy can have my baby brother. The pizza just got here when all of a sudden Amy got this real funny look on her face and she said 'Ron, I think it's time.' And when Amy stood up, there was a big puddle on the chair. Like she wet her pants or something. So they left. Right away. That's why there's so much leftover pizza."

"If your folks are gone, who's looking after you?" I asked. Because Ron and Amy sometimes draft me for babysitting duties, I was a little surprised they hadn't called.

"Dad tried calling you first. When your machine

came on, he said you probably weren't home, so he called Mrs. Humphreys instead." Heather wrinkled her nose in obvious distaste.

"You don't like Mrs. Humphreys?" I asked.

"Mrs. Humphreys doesn't fix us root beer floats," Heather said.

I smiled. "I'm glad to hear that," I told her. Wrapping the rest of the pizza in foil, I shoved it in my pocket along with Tim Blaine's directions and herded Heather toward the door. "I'd hate to think Mrs. Humphreys had eclipsed my place in your affections."

"She's an old lady," Heather insisted.

Mrs. Leila Humphreys, Ron and Amy's widowed next-door neighbor, is a svelte sixty-year-old who still plays tennis twice a week and who swims laps in Belltown Terrace's indoor pool every day of the week. "She doesn't seem that old to me," I said.

"Well, she is," Heather insisted. "And I don't like her. I'd rather be with you."

"I'd rather be with you, too, but I have to go back to work."

Heather rode with me as far as the garage, promising to call me either in the car or at home the moment word came from the hospital.

As soon as I was out of the garage, I tried Sue's number again. Still no answer. This time I went ahead and punched in the numbers for Sue's pager. Frustrated, I put the phone back in its holder. While I drove, I helped myself to another piece of pizza and waited for Sue to call me back.

As a downtown Seattle resident, what I know

about Bellevue would fit in a very small thimble. Consequently, I was glad to have Tim Blaine's directions, but even they weren't entirely foolproof. My first attempt to get to the Newsome house led me to a dead end rather than through a tunnel under I-90. My second attempt took me through the tunnel fine. Once I was on 168th, the glow of flashing emergency lights led me straight there. Obviously, Detective Blaine had called ahead. The patrol officer manning the roadblock waved me through.

I drove up a narrow, winding street through a neighborhood of modest middle-class ramblers and split-levels most of which looked as though they dated from the sixties and seventies. Along the way I passed several clumps of concerned onlookers—neighbors from those same houses, no doubt—who stood outside in the cool damp of an April evening trying to fathom what horrors had gone on up the street.

Several blocks up 19th, I ran into the next blockade, one made up almost entirely of emergency vehicles, including a gray van from the ME's office. No wonder Audrey Cummings had been out when I had tried calling her earlier. She was probably already on her way here.

Beyond the barricade at the far end of a cul-de-sac stood a house ablaze with lights both inside and out. Stopping to look at it, I remembered Sue saying she thought it had been put together with blocks and Tinker Toys. I had to agree. It looked like a modern-day castle plunked down in among its less ostentatious neighbors. Beyond it was a patch of black that indicated some body of water or other. My rudimentary knowledge of Eastside geography didn't tell me which one.

Tim Blaine appeared on a grassy parking strip and waved me into the end of a neighboring driveway. As soon as I switched off the ignition, he opened the passenger door and climbed in with me. "Hey, Beau," he said cheerfully, reaching across the seat to pump my hand. "We've got to stop meeting like this. Seems like the only time we run into each other is at crime scenes."

"Occupational hazard," I said. "Now tell me, what the hell happened in there?"

"It's a long story, and we're still trying to piece it together," he said. "There are two people dead inside and a set of bloody footprints leading from the crime scene to the front door. We brought in a canine unit. The dog followed the trail out to the driveway and there it stopped. My guess is the perpetrator took off in a car. According to the DMV, there are two vehicles registered to this address. Barry Newsome is the registered owner of a 1996 Mitsubishi Eclipse. His roommate, Don Atkins, owns an '85 Ford Explorer. Both those vehicles are safely stowed in the garage. What isn't here and may be missing is Mr. Owens' Subaru Outback. I've issued an APB on it, but nothing has shown up so far. Now it's your turn, Beau. What's your connection to all this?"

Another vehicle pulled up behind us and a second canine unit took to the street. From inside the house came the occasional flashes of crime-scene photography.

"I've been working on a case in Seattle that led us to Newsome and Atkins," I said. "When I got home at nine tonight, there was a message on my machine from Newsome that came in about a quarter to five. The problem is, the message was interrupted halfway through."

Tim nodded. "That's probably about when it happened. Our com center reported a 911 call from a house two doors away a few minutes later than that, 4:48. A woman named Mrs. Adams from that house over there . . ." He pointed to the house at the far end of the driveway where I had parked. "She reported that someone in the neighborhood—a teenager, she thought—most likely was setting off firecrackers and scaring her dog. Responding officers found nothing. The second firecracker complaint from the same lady came in at seven-thirty. This time when officers showed up, they found the doors here wide open. One body was in the living room downstairs. That one, Calvin Owens, looked like a fresh kill. The other one, Newsome, was upstairs in an office of some kind. He looks like he's been dead for some time, I'd guess a matter of hours."

"Have you talked to the neighbors?"

"Some. Mostly to Mrs. Adams so far. Sounds as though she didn't like Newsome and Atkins much. Her assessment is that the boys were pretty weird to begin with and not so hot on maintenance, either. She says the house actually belongs to Newsome's family, but the guys have lived here rent-free for several years and have let it go to pot. And she's not wrong there. When I first walked inside, I thought somebody had trashed the place in the course of a robbery. The more I look around, though, the more I think it's just a bachelor pad that's deteriorated into a pigsty."

Headlights flashed in the rearview mirror as a second ME van maneuvered past us and parked beside the first one.

Tim Blaine continued. "Mrs. Adams also said something about how Newsome and Atkins used to have big parties here almost every weekend. That people would show up late at night dressed in all kinds of strange costumes—like vampires and witches, for example. She said the parties finally stopped about six months ago after the neighbors made a stink. Personally, I think the parties stopped because the place was such a mess no one wanted to go inside—not even to party."

"What about Owens? Have you found out anything more about him?"

Tim Blaine shook his head. "Not much. His business card says he specializes in Native American artifacts."

"I see," I said. "That makes sense."

"What does?"

"Newsome and Atkins may have stopped partying at home, but they haven't stopped the costume parties. Role-playing parties, they call them. Now, they've started staging them in public parks, and that's where Sue and I come in."

"Role-playing?" Blaine asked. "What does that mean?"

"It means that everybody dresses up as his or her favorite ghoul or vampire and then they go around scaring the shit out of one another. Your basic ongoing Halloween party for people who've never quite grown up. Only it turns out Newsome and Atkins tend to get a little carried away. My partner and I got involved when, in the aftermath of one of those parties, an attendee called in to report that real bones had been used as props. Sue Danielson, my partner, came over here last week and collected a set of bones from Mr. Newsome and delivered them to the ME's office. Since then, our investigation has led us to believe they are the partial remains of a deceased Suquamish shaman named David Half Moon."

"They were using this guy's body for props?" Tim Blaine asked. "What kind of kooks are they?"

"People with no respect for human life," I told him. "Remember I told you earlier about a body being pulled out of Lake Washington earlier today?" Blaine nodded.

"The victim's name is Anthony Lawson," I continued. "It turns out he's Mr. Half Moon's developmentally disabled grandson. After talking to Lawson's adoptive mother, I believe he had in his possession a map that would have shown where his grandfather was buried. Not buried actually. According to tribal customs, Half Moon's remains as well as his worldly goods were placed in a canoe and raised up into a tree. Lawson was a busboy at Newsome and Atkins' favorite downtown hangout."

Frowning, Blaine paused for several seconds before he spoke again. "Grave robbing," he said thoughtfully. "Would there have been anything else in that canoe besides the bones?"

"Maybe."

"So that's where Owens comes in. His card says he specialized in Native American artifacts," Blaine continued. "He probably came here expecting to make a deal, to buy something."

"What makes you think that?"

"He had a bank receipt in his pocket that shows he picked up $20,000 in cash late this afternoon, but there was no money on him when we found him. None.

"According to my count then," he went on, "we're looking at a minimum of three homicides, one set of partial remains, one missing person, and one stolen vehicle. All of those cases are connected but they all come from different jurisdictions."

"That's right as far as it goes," I said. "Actually, the vehicle Anthony Lawson was found in was also stolen, and there's another missing person that you don't know anything about. His name's Jimmy Greenjeans."

"Who's he?" Blaine asked.

"A bartender from the same place where Anthony Lawson worked. He and Tony Lawson may have been friends, and I think he knew something about the connection between Lawson and Newsome and Atkins."

"Is he the one with green hair?" Blaine asked.

"That's the one."

"And that really is his name, Mr. Greenjeans?"

"Yes."

"And what makes you think he might be dead, too?"

"His girlfriend reported him missing."

"Missing doesn't necessarily mean dead."

"It could in this case," I said.

"And you think what may or may not have happened to Greenjeans is all tied up with what's going on here." I nodded.

"In that case, I think we'd better go talk to Captain Davis," Tim said. "With so many jurisdictions involved, this could get tricky. He needs to know what we're up against. You'll probably want to bring your brass in on it, too."

"That's just the problem," I said. "I can't really do that."

"Why not?"

"For one thing, I've been pulled from the Seward Park case. For another, my new squad commander doesn't like some of my sources."

"Nobody likes informants," Tim grinned. "Most of them are creeps. I don't care for them much myself."

"This one is different," I said. "He's a Native American shaman named Henry Leaping Deer."

"You mean like a medicine man," Blaine put in.

"Close enough," I told him. "Most of what Mr. Leaping Deer told me came to him in a dream. The trouble is, everything he told me seems to be coming true, right down the line. For instance. He dreamed that David Half Moon's remains had been stolen from the burial grounds and that children were playing with them in the city. Calling Newsome and Atkins children maybe isn't literally true, but it's close enough. Mr. Leaping Deer told me that there's a curse associated with handling a dead shaman's bones. So far we know that at least three of the people who did so are dead. Not only that, when Leaping Deer sent his daughter to clue us in on all this, she said her father had mentioned a green-haired man as being involved and that he, in particular, was in some danger."

"You're saying the dream isn't just a dream. It's actually more like a vision."

"I suppose. My problem is, not only have I been ordered off the case, the commander doesn't believe in visions."

"Do you?" Tim Blaine asked.

"I didn't before, but I may now," I answered. "I started out thinking the whole deal was some kind of phony joke. Now I'm not so sure and, with bodies stacked like so much cord wood, I don't think we can afford to ignore Leaping Deer's information. What about you?"

"I still think Captain Davis is our best bet," Tim Blaine replied, opening the door and climbing out of the car. "The guy's pretty broad-minded. Who knows?" he added with a laugh. "Maybe he'll be a little more understanding than your guy Kramer."

And that was when I realized that I really was Paul Kramer's worst nightmare. In less than a day, and without even meaning to, I had managed to turn him into what he had called an "interdepartmental laughingstock."

There's going to be hell to pay on this one, I told myself. But that didn't stop me. I pulled my keys out of the ignition, stuffed the phone in my pocket, and then went looking for Tim Blaine's Captain Davis.

CHAPTER 16

I was two steps from the car when the phone in my pocket rang. "Beau," Sue Danielson said. "What's up?"

"Let's see," I said. "One or two things. Jimmy Greenjeans is missing. Barry Newsome is dead along with a Native American artifact dealer named Calvin Owens. And Don Atkins appears to have taken off. Not only that, Tony Lawson turns out to be David Half Moon's grandson, so you called that one on the money. What else do you want to know?"

"Good grief, Beau!" Sue was aghast. "We were only gone long enough to have dinner. What the hell have you been doing while my back is turned? And where are you?"

"In Bellevue," I replied. "At the scene of a double homicide."

"Does Kramer have any idea you're there?"

"Not so far. I haven't told Wayne Haller or Sam Nguyen, either, for that matter."

"Is there anything I can do?" Sue asked. "Do you

want me to come over? Richie just left and the kids are getting ready for bed."

"You don't need to do that. I'm just on my way to talk to Captain Davis of the Bellevue police to bring him up to speed. I'm not sure what his reaction is going to be when I hit him with all the shaman stuff, but with two dead and Greenjeans missing, we don't have a moment to lose."

"Do you want me to call Kramer?"

Notifying the new squad commander was a tough decision. I knew he had to be called. The further things went without Kramer being informed, the worse it would be in the long run. On the other hand, I suspected that as soon as he had even an inkling of what was going on he'd roar across the nearest bridge to Bellevue and begin knocking heads, starting with mine.

"Go ahead and call him," I said. "We might as well get it over with."

With my call to Sue finished, I caught up with Tim Blaine and another man just as a uniformed officer came sprinting out of Barry Newsome's house. "The photographer's finished, Detective Blaine," he said. "The lady from the ME's office is asking if you want to look around one more time before they remove the body."

Tim Blaine turned to me. "I'd better go take a look," he said and then gestured toward his companion. "This is Captain Davis, Beau. I told him you had some information that might prove helpful."

Captain Davis turned out to be a tall, scrawny guy about my size but several years younger. "Detective

Beaumont is it?" he asked holding out his hand. "Now what's all this about medicine men?"

If I had been a betting man, I never in a million years would have figured Capt. Todd Davis for a sympathetic listener, but he heard me out, all the way to the end. When I finished, he was quiet for several thoughtful seconds. "Do you happen to know how to get in touch with Mr. Leaping Deer?" he asked finally.

"Not really. I mean, I don't have his address and phone number right here, but I could probably find him."

"Maybe you should do that," Captain Davis observed. "It sounds to me as though several of his predictions have been disturbingly accurate. With Mr. Greenjeans still in jeopardy, we should do everything in our power—including using every possible resource—to locate the man. What do you think?"

I was blown away. Tim Blaine had said the man was broad-minded, but having him actually give credence to Henry Leaping Deer's visions was far more than I would have thought possible.

"I'll do what I can to track him down," I said.

Davis nodded.

"Good," he said. "Now, about your captain . . ."

"Squad commander," I corrected. "Paul Kramer is only a squad commander."

"I see. What do you think Squad Commander Kramer would think if we called in the guys from the attorney general's Special Homicide Investigation Squad? It seems to me that we've got so many countervailing jurisdictions here that if we don't bring in one entity to oversee the whole deal, we'll all be stepping on toes and getting in one another's way."

The Washington State Special Homicide Investigation Squad, originally dubbed the Special Homicide Investigation Team, had been the brainchild of one Daniel Seward, an ambitious Washington state legislator known for his get-tough stance on crime. He had envisioned an elite group of investigators, under the aegis of the state's attorney general's office, that would be able to crisscross jurisdictional boundaries in a way individual officers could not. Not only would they assist local police departments in the investigation of major crimes, they would also create a computer database of criminal activity to be used on a statewide and regional basis.

It wasn't a bad idea. In fact, I knew several older detectives who had taken retirement from SPD and then had moved their years of combined experience and expertise straight over to the new unit. The only snag in this otherwise ingenious idea was that Seward had done such a poor job of naming his unit. Somehow he had failed to realize what would happen to the Special Homicide Investigation Team once that unfortunate combination of words was reduced—as it inevitably would be—into a typical cop-speak acronym—SHIT. As soon as someone realized the error, the proverbial SHIT hit the fan and the bureaucrats had tried to do damage control. The word "Team" had been replaced by the word "Squad." There had been a flurry of activity in which official directories, stationery, and business cards all had to be reprinted. Unfortunately, no amount of determined effort made any difference. The original name stuck like so much superglue. In law-enforcement circles, that elite group was now and forever known as the attorney general SHITs. Had Captain Davis known me better, he probably would have used that term himself.

Given Paul Kramer's propensity for empire building and his concerns about negative publicity, I could well imagine his likely reaction. Someone would have had to hold a gun to the man's head to get him to knuckle under and ask for outside help. Davis, however, was intent on doing the job without being sidetracked by ego issues or how his performance would be reported in the media. Not only that, Davis was on the scene. Kramer wasn't.

"He'd probably think it was a great idea," I lied.

"Good, then," Davis said. "I'll put those wheels in motion."

As he turned back to his car, the pager went off in my pocket. When I checked the display, the number on the screen was one I didn't immediately recognize, but the prefix indicated the caller lived in West Seattle—the same neighborhood where Kramer lived with his wife and two kids. Flipping the pager to off, I returned it to my pocket without bothering to note the number. That was one call I had no intention of returning.

A little kid sidled up to my elbow. He couldn't have been more than eleven or twelve. "Are you a detective?" he asked. I nodded.

"I heard my dad talking. He said people are dead in there. Is that true?"

"Yes," I said. "It is true. Do your parents know you're out here?"

He shook his head. "They think I'm in bed. There's a tree by my room. I opened the window and climbed out. I do it all the time, especially in the summer. I go down to the lake late at night and look for frogs."

"What's your name?" I asked.

"Jonathan," he said. "Jonathan Carruthers. That's my house over there," he added, pointing to a house next door to Barry Newsome's.

"Well, Jonathan," I said. "It's late. If your parents notice you're gone, they'll be worried sick. If I were you, I'd shimmy back up that tree before they figure it out."

"They don't care what I do," Jonathan said. "They're down in the family room watching TV."

"Well, I care," I told him. "You shouldn't be out here by yourself. And if you're concerned about what happened, you should talk to your parents about it."

Jonathan didn't move. "It's Mr. Newsome who's dead, isn't it?"

There didn't seem any reason to deny it. "Yes," I said. "I believe he is one of the victims."

"And Mr. Atkins, the mean one, is the one who did it?"

"Why do you say that?"

"Because I saw him leave," Jonathan Carruthers said. "I was sitting by the window and wishing I was outside shooting baskets when I saw him come running out of the house. He jumped in a little white car, and drove away. I thought it was kind of strange that he went off and left the front door wide open."

"Wait a minute. What little white car?" I asked, feeling the slight catch of excitement in my throat that comes over me when I know something important has come my way.

"It's a Subaru," Jonathan said confidently. "An Outback, like they have in those neat commercials on TV. Where the guy from Australia is always tricking the bad guys."

"And Mr. Atkins was alone in the car when he left?" I asked.

"No," Jonathan said. "He came out of the house by himself, but there was somebody else in the car with him when he drove away. I couldn't tell who."

There was still one person unaccounted for in all this, a potential victim who might still be alive— Jimmy Greenjeans. I took a breath. Not wanting to spook the kid, I tried to soften my voice before I spoke again. "What time was that?"

"After seven," Jonathan said. "It was after I went upstairs."

"And you know both Newsome and Atkins?" I asked. "You wouldn't be mistaken? You'd be able to recognize them?"

"Sure," Jonathan said. "I'm their paper boy. Whenever I go to collect, I always hope Mr. Newsome answers the door. He gives me nice tips. At least he used to. Mr. Atkins never did."

"Jonathan," I said. "If all this happened over two hours ago, why didn't you come down sooner and tell someone? If the police had known right away . . ."

"I had a fight with my parents at dinner," Jonathan said. "With my stepmom. My dad sent me to my room and told me to stay there."

"But Jonathan, what you saw makes you an important witness. You should have come forward long before this. Surely your parents would have understood if . . ."

"My dad hits me," Jonathan said matter-of-factly. "If I did that—if I came back downstairs to tell them something when Dad told me to stay in my room, he would have hit me some more."

You can never tell with kids. Some of them take the smallest thing and blow it all out of proportion while others accept the most horrific of circumstances with seeming equanimity. Not knowing Jonathan Carruthers, I didn't know what to think.

"What will your father do if he finds out you left the house?"

Jonathan's wordless but somber shrug was answer enough. It didn't seem fair that his willingness to help with the investigation should come with that kind of price.

"Your father wouldn't do anything to you if other people were around, would he?" I asked.

Jonathan shook his head. "I don't think so."

"Well, then I'll tell you what," I said. "We won't let your parents know that you've been out here talking to us. You go on back to your house, climb up the tree, and let yourself back into your room. In a little while, I'll send one of the Bellevue detectives over to your place. When he rings the bell and asks if anyone there has seen anything, you come downstairs and tell your story."

"So they won't know about my tree?" he asked.

"Right," I told him. "The detective who'll be over there is a good friend of mine. His name's Blaine,

Detective Tim Blaine. If your parents give you any trouble about all this, you tell him. Okay?"

"Okay," Jonathan said. "But will it do any good? Will you guys be able to catch him?"

"Atkins? I think so," I said. "Especially if we have your information to help us do it."

"Good," he said. "I hope you do."

"Go on now," I urged. I stood watching while he walked back across the driveway and disappeared through a hedge of photinia. Moments later, I saw a brief flash of white T-shirt against the dark bark of a towering cedar as he made his way back into the house. Only when a light came on in the bedroom did I turn away and go looking for Tim Blaine.

I found him just inside the front door of Barry Newsome's house where a crime-scene technician was dusting the door for prints. "Hey, Tim," I called. "I have some information for you."

"Okay," he said. "I'll be right with you."

"Beau?" I turned around to find Sue Danielson hurrying up the sidewalk behind me. "Is he here yet?"

"Who?"

"Kramer."

"I haven't seen him. Why?"

"He went off the charts when I told him. I thought he was going to have a coronary right there on the phone. I think he's on his way over. I came by to give you some advance warning and to run interference if necessary."

That made me smile. It was a little like me sending Tim Blaine in to keep Jonathan Carruthers' father from beating the crap out of him. "As you can see, he's not here yet. Don't worry. I can probably handle Kramer all right, but thanks all the same. It never hurts to have backup."

She nodded and smiled back. That's when I looked at her—really looked at her. At work Sue usually wears lady-cop clothes—skirts and blazers cut generously enough to fit over and around the bullet-resistant vests we all wear to work these days. I'd seen her in dresses on occasion, but I always managed to forget what a nice figure she kept hidden under her soft body armor. That night she was wearing some kind of shirtwaist dress. Because of the lighting, I wasn't sure about the color, a pastel of some kind, but it did show her figure to good advantage. For work, Sue's hair is mostly pulled back, but that night it was down, curling gently around her face.

I whistled. "Don't you look nice," I said. "Where've you been?"

"Thanks," she said. "Richie took the boys and me downtown for dinner. Planet Hollywood. He spent a ton of money and then sprang for shirts and caps for both the boys. They were absolutely ecstatic."

"So it worked out all right?" I asked.

"Better than all right," she said. "After talking to Richie on the phone last night, I thought he was going to hassle me about this Disneyland thing when he turned up today. But he must have come to his senses. He's working on getting the reservations moved to next week, and he brought each of the boys one of those roll-aboard suitcases to take with them on the trip. They're both on cloud nine. After all that, when he invited me to go along with them to dinner, I couldn't very well say no."

Sometimes women amaze me. You think they've got brains and then some two-timing jackass hands them a load of BS and they fall over him with gratitude.

"That's great, Sue," I told her, with far more enthusiasm than I felt.

Just then, Tim emerged from the house. "What's up, Beau?"

As quickly as possible, I told him about Jonathan Carruthers. "Which house does he live in again?" Tim asked.

"That one," I said, pointing.

"Good work," Tim said. "I'll go straight there. And believe me, if the father looks at the kid sideways, I'll make sure he realizes that raising a hand to Jonathan would be a very bad idea."

As the bull-necked detective rumbled off in the direction of the Carruthers' two-story split-level, another car pulled up beside us and screeched to a stop. I didn't even have to look to know it was Kramer's.

"Detective Beaumont," he thundered. "What the hell do you think you're doing?"

"My job," I responded.

"You've got no business being here, you or Danielson either one."

"I have every right to be here," I countered calmly. "Barry Newsome called me. When I returned his call . . ."

"Barry Newsome!" Kramer cut in. "God damn it, Beaumont. I ordered—*ordered*—you off that case! You should have . . ."

"Newsome called me at home, hours after I

punched out. If I choose to return calls on my own time, that's up to me."

"It's not up to you," Kramer insisted. "When I issue an order, I expect it to be obeyed."

"Then how about issuing orders that make sense?" I shot back.

That stopped him. Cold. Gasping like a fish, Kramer was just opening his mouth to speak again when Capt. Todd Davis came charging up the sidewalk. "Where's Detective Blaine?" he demanded.

"He went next door to interview a witness."

"Go get him," Davis said, "while I go inside and find his partner."

"Why?" I demanded. "What's happened?"

"That Subaru on Blaine's APB. It's just been located down in Pierce County, but it sounds as though there's not much left of it. The driver evidently tried to beat a freight train to a railroad crossing somewhere outside Edgewood. According to information just in from the Pierce County sheriff's department," Davis added, "there's not much left of the car, or him either. I told them I'd send two detectives down. Investigators from the SHIT squad are already on the way."

"The SHITs?" Kramer yelped. "The attorney general SHITs? Who the hell called them in?"

"I did," Davis replied. "Capt. Todd Davis, Bellevue PD. Who are you?"

"Kramer. Seattle Homicide Squad Commander Paul Kramer."

"Oh," Davis said. "Detective Beaumont's supervisor. When we could see there were so many jurisdictions involved, I went ahead and called my chief to have him put the AG's guys in place. Detective Beaumont said you wouldn't mind. They were already on their way here when the Pierce County call came in. To save time, they want to rendezvous with Tim and Dave down at the Pierce County crime scene as soon as possible."

"I wouldn't mind . . ." Kramer sputtered, tuning up. I didn't wait around long enough for him to finish the sentence. Neither did Captain Davis. He sprinted into the house to fetch Tim Blaine's partner while I headed for the Carruthers' split-level.

"Beaumont!" Kramer yelled after me. "Where the hell do you think you're going?"

"I'm a homicide detective," I called back over my shoulder. "I'm going to do my job."

A few minutes later I came back out to the street with Tim Blaine in tow. He jumped into the rider's seat of a waiting Crown Victoria, and then he and his partner took off. Looking around, I realized Captain Davis was nowhere to be seen. Neither was Sue Danielson. The only person still around was Kramer. He was waiting and fuming. It didn't seem like the right time for the two of us to have a meaningful discussion. Instead of going toward him, I deliberately turned aside and headed back in the direction of my waiting Porsche.

He saw me. "Beaumont," he roared. "You come back here. I want to talk to you."

I got as far as the car and had the door opened when he caught up with me. "I don't know who the hell you think you are or where you think you're going . . ."

"I'm going down to Pierce County," I said coldly.

"In case you haven't heard, the sheriff's department down there is currently involved in an accident investigation. I want to know what's going on."

"Beaumont, I forbid . . ."

"Look, Kramer, we already tried doing things your way and at least three more people are dead with another one missing. You can forbid until you're blue in the face, but until I find Jimmy Greenjeans, dead or alive, I'm not going to stop."

"I'll have your badge."

"Fine," I said. "Do your worst."

With that, I climbed into the 928 and slammed the door behind me. The last thing I saw of Kramer was his image in my rearview mirror. With his face distorted by rage he glared after me, shaking his fist.

Halfway down the block, Sue flagged me down. "Want me to go along?" she asked.

"Who's watching the boys?"

"Richie."

"You go on home," I told her. "Atkins is dead, and it sounds like the whole place is crawling with cops."

"You're sure?"

"Absolutely," I said. "Everything is under control."

CHAPTER 17

HEADING SOUTH ON I-405, THERE WAS NO LONGER ANY reason not to let the department know where I was going and why. I called into Dispatch on my cell phone and had them call the Pierce County sheriff's department for exact directions. Then, with hastily scribbled notes in hand, all I had to was drive.

It was late enough that there wasn't much traffic. That gave me plenty of time to think and to beat myself up. I could never remember a time when I'd had so much advance warning that something bad was going to happen—that people were going to die. Henry Leaping Deer had said they would. He had sent word that anyone connected with moving or messing around with David Half Moon's remains would die. So far those predictions of death were coming true, one after another, with me totally powerless to prevent them.

I counted off the toll in my head. The bodies of Anthony Lawson, Barry Newsome, and Calvin Owens were already accounted for. I had no doubt that the next victims, the ones at the Pierce County site, would turn out to be Don Atkins and Jimmy Green-jeans. As far as I knew, Dirk Matthews—the ME's office's resident clown and bone juggler—was still in Harborview Hospital and barely clinging to life. Only time would tell whether or not his mysterious flesh-eating infection would kill him.

The victims who were already dead or dying were beyond help and worry. But the shaman's warning had included one other outstanding victim, one that worried me—a white woman. As far as I could tell there were at least two potential candidates—Sue Danielson and Audrey Cummings.

Driving south, it struck me that if David Half Moon's curse went after either one of those two women, it wasn't very discriminating. As far as I could see, all the male victims, with the possible exception of Jimmy Greenjeans, shared some degree of culpability. They had all played an active part in moving the dead shaman's remains or in attempting to buy and sell them or, like Dirk Matthews, they had treated the bones with casual disrespect.

Audrey and Sue were different. They had come in contact with Half Moon's bones only by happenstance and only in the course of performing their official duties. They hadn't juggled with them, hadn't dragged them to a public park as part of some macabre game. Nor would they have ventured into the business of buying and selling them.

If there's such a thing as a smart gene or a smart bomb, couldn't there be such a thing as a smart curse? I wondered.

That oddball thought gave me a jolt and made me wonder if maybe Kramer wasn't half right and I was in danger of losing it. *Come on*, I urged. *No honor among thieves is what really killed those guys. The women will be just fine!*

And they were. Or at least they had been the last time I saw them. Audrey Cummings had been her usual brusque and businesslike self when, during the course of my conversation with Jonathan Carruthers, I had watched her oversee the removal of two bodies from Barry Newsome's house. And when I had left Sue with Paul Kramer to go in search of Detective Blaine, she, too, had been fine. In fact she had been more than fine—she had been happy. Happier than I ever remembered seeing her.

Sue and I had both suffered misgivings about how Richie Danielson would react to having his plans changed by a former wife who had once been his personal punching bag. Sue seemed to have accepted Richie's change of heart at face value. I wasn't so sure. I remember my old Fuller Brush manager telling me once, "Men change but seldom do they." Maybe Sue was right and I was wrong. Maybe Richie Danielson actually had changed. Maybe he had finally grown up.

As I came through Auburn, I saw the glow of lights reflecting off cloud cover to the southeast. At first I thought the lights indicated an athletic field of some kind, lit for a late-playing adult soccer or softball league. As I exited on 8th Street, though, I saw the smaller pulses of reds and yellows mixed in with the steady glow of floodlights. This was the accident scene, not a playing field.

Driving south on 136th Avenue East I found it to be a narrow and rutted but supposedly paved road. It led through an industrial area punctuated by residences. Some were clearly well built and well maintained while for others the word marginal would have been giving them the benefit of the doubt. At 16th Street I turned left and drove into an area lit to almost daylight proportions.

Most of the lights came compliments of Burlington Northern. When it comes to hauling freight, time is money. If a nighttime accident halts one of their mile-long freight trains, BN investigators don't wait around for morning. They hustle in the necessary generators and wattage and go to work.

Ahead of me on a raised berm, railroad cars loaded with trailers for eighteen-wheelers had been uncoupled and pushed apart to make way for the investigation. The locomotive or locomotives involved were so far down the track as to be totally out of sight. Between the two lines of railroad cars, on a high, gated crossing, several uniformed sheriff's deputies were busy marking and measuring lines on the pavement. Around them lay a scatter of unrecognizable pieces of crushed sheet metal that had once been Calvin Owens' Subaru. Here and there among the metal and fiber wreckage lay bright blue pieces of tarp no doubt covering the equally unrecognizable bits of bloody flesh and bone that had once been Don Atkins or Jimmy Greenjeans.

I've investigated more than one railroad fatality in my time. Railroad folks tell me that the worst thing about an accident like that—the thing they have to live with for the rest of their lives—is the look. They tell me that the final thing that happens before someone drives or walks under a train is eye-to-eye contact with the engineer. It's a look of utter astonishment, astonishment and dismay. A split second later, it's all over for the guy under the train. For the guy looking out from that side of the locomotive, the pain is just beginning.

Given the fact that mixing it up with a train is almost guaranteed to kill you, given the fact that a loaded freight train going sixty miles an hour will still take the better part of a mile to stop, I can't figure out why people do it. But they do. Part of the problem is the fact that, in the dark, a single light doesn't give you much of a perspective on how far away the train is. The other part is plain stupidity.

A convoy of emergency vehicles was strung out along 16th Street stretching almost half a mile from the crossing itself. I pulled into a spot at the very end behind Tim Blaine's Crown Victoria. When I stepped out of the Porsche, I was surprised by the all-pervasive roar of the light-producing generators.

On the other side of the crossing, a crowd of people gathered around one of the vehicles. It took an ID badge and some talking to get me past the deputies marking the accident scene. When I reached the other side, I saw a young woman leaning back against the front fender of a Pierce County sheriff's department patrol car. The woman appeared to be in her mid-to-late twenties. She was clad in jeans and an oversized sweatshirt. Lank brown hair dangled around her face. As I edged my way into the crowd, I noticed that, although her face showed traces of recent tears, she was no longer crying.

Instead, in a surprisingly calm manner, she was fielding a barrage of questions.

Her attentive audience was made up of an entire collection of law-enforcement personnel, all of them taking notes. Several were people I recognized from the Pierce County sheriff's department. Some of the ones I didn't recognize were clearly investigators with the railroad itself. Two of the investigators standing in the front row were ex-SPD detectives who had gone over to the attorney general's team. *Good work, Captain Davis*, I said to myself. From the far side of the group, Tim Blaine gave me a welcoming nod.

"It must have been about eight-thirty when Donnie got to the house," she was saying. "I had never seen him like that. He was in a total panic. He told Mom that something bad had happened and that he needed a place to stay for a while. She told him no, for him to get out, that she didn't want him here. She told him that since he's obviously preferred the Newsomes to his own family all this time, he should go back there and ask them to take him in.

"Maybe that sounds like a cruel thing for a mother to do to her own son," Don Atkins' sister added, "but why shouldn't she? Ever since the divorce, Donnie treated her like shit, but then he treated all of us like shit. Everybody but precious Barry."

"So he and your mother argued?" The main questioner seemed to be one of the BN guys. Since the railroad had the most at stake here, it made sense that they would be keenly involved in all aspects of the incident itself as well as whatever had preceded it.

"Not just argued," the young woman said. "It was a screaming, yelling fit. Finally, Donnie stormed out of the house. I watched him go. He stomped back to his car and wrenched open the door. When he did that, this dog just came flying out. It almost knocked him over."

"Dog? What kind of dog?"

"I don't know. A big one. It looked like a German shepherd, but I'm not positive. It must be around here someplace, but I haven't seen it since the accident. There was so much noise, it probably got scared and took off. The funny thing is, I didn't even know my brother had a dog. He never mentioned it. Anyway, the dog went running across the lawn. I think it needed to pee. It ran over to one of the trees and lifted its leg. Then, when Don started the car, it went racing back over there like it wanted to be back inside, but Don didn't stop to let it in. He went screeching out of the driveway and up the road here with the dog running after him, trying like mad to catch up."

She stopped then, and wiped her eyes. It struck me that she was crying for the dog rather than for Don Atkins. But then, I had to admit I hadn't liked him much, either.

"My brother was a complete jerk," she said when she could talk again, "but at least the dog must have liked him."

It came to me then. Jonathan Carruthers had claimed someone was in the car with Don Atkins. Now Don Atkins' sister was saying that the other passenger was really a dog. A big dog! Was it possible, then, that from his upstairs room Jonathan

Carruthers had mistaken the dog for a person? Did that mean there was a chance that Jimmy Greenjeans was still alive somewhere? I allowed myself to feel the smallest glimmer of hope.

"Did you see anyone else in the car?" I asked. "Anyone other than the dog?"

Several of the other cops looked back in my direction when I asked the question as though trying to figure out who I was and where I had come from. I must have passed inspection because they let the question ride. Their attention, after momentarily shifting to me, returned to the young woman to await her answer.

"No," she said. "There wasn't anybody else."

"You're sure?" I asked.

"Yes, I'm sure."

So maybe Mr. Greenjeans isn't dead after all—at least not here and not right now, I thought gratefully. Meanwhile the BN guy resumed the questioning controls.

"What happened then, Ms. Atkins, after your brother left?"

"Mom had gone into her room, and I went back there to talk to her. I knew she was upset, and she was. She was crying. Donnie always does that to her—he always upsets her. I wanted to make sure she was okay. I was talking to her and telling her things were going to be all right and that she shouldn't worry when I heard the whistle. Trains usually whistle when they cross 8th. We're used to that. This time it was a lot closer. It sounded like it was right there in the living room. Then I heard the crash, the sound of metal on metal. As soon as I heard it, I knew what had happened. I knew the train had hit him and he was dead."

"You came out to look?"

The young woman shook her head. "Mom came out first. I stayed inside to call 911."

"Did your brother give you or your mother any idea about the kind of trouble he was in, about why he needed a place to stay?" That question came from another newcomer to the group, Bellevue homicide detective Tim Blaine.

The young woman took a breath before she answered. "Donnie said he'd killed somebody. That's when the fight really started. Mom told him she wasn't surprised, that she'd been expecting it for years. All he and Barry ever wanted to do was play with those stupid video games. They're nothing but kill, kill, kill. That's when he took off, when she said that about all the killing."

"How long did Barry Newsome and your brother live together, Ms. Atkins?" Again the questioner was Tim Blaine.

"For a long time," she said. "Twelve years at least. From the time Donnie was fourteen. He wanted to play video games and have nice clothes and stuff. The problem was, Mom was newly divorced and working at the AM/PM. She couldn't afford those things, so Donnie ran away. The next thing we knew, he was living in this big, fancy house there by Phantom Lake. When Barry's father, Mr. Newsome, transferred down to California with a new job, Barry's parents let the two of them—Barry and Donnie—stay in their old house rent-free."

"Were your brother and Barry Newsome . . ."

Tim Blaine paused, as if searching for just the right word. ". . . involved?"

"You mean were they gay?" Ms. Atkins shot back at him.

Tim nodded. "No," she said, frowning. "I don't think so. I mean they both had girlfriends at times. At least they *said* they did. But then they *said* they were making money with their video games, too, but I'm not sure that was true, either."

"Where'd they get money to live on then?"

"From Barry's family. Especially from his mother. That's what my mother said. The Newsomes couldn't have another son, so they bought one— Donnie."

The phone in my pocket rang, interrupting the questioning process. The girl looked at me in surprise while my fellow cops glowered in annoyance. It's never a good idea to interrupt the flow—the give and take—of an interview. Shrugging an apology to all concerned, I hurried away from the group to answer. Figuring there was a good chance for it to be Kramer again, I barked my hello.

"Mr. Beaumont?" Against the noisy backdrop of the humming generators, the voice was so thin that it came through as little more than an exaggerated stage whisper. *What is this?* I thought. *A damn obscene call?*

"Who is this?" I demanded. "What do you want?"

"It's Jared Danielson, Mr. Beaumont. You've got to help us. I think he shot her."

My heart stopped. "He what?" I asked, hoping against hope that I had heard him wrong. I hadn't.

"My dad," Jared continued. "He shot Mom. I think he was waiting for her on the porch when she came home. He was yelling at her and telling her she'd spoiled everything. That's when the gun went off."

My heart raced. Jared's shocking news sent needles and pins shooting through my hands. It was all I could do to keep hold of the phone. Not only that, the noise around me made Jared's thin voice almost impossible to hear. I had to strain to understand him.

"Jared, I can barely hear you. You have to speak up."

"I can't. I'm afraid he'll hear me and know I'm awake. Then he'll come after me, too."

I punched the volume control on my phone. That helped some. "Where are you, Jared?"

"In our bedroom, my brother's and mine. I'm on the cell phone Mom gave me."

"Listen, Jared, I'm clear down south of Auburn. I can't get there soon enough to help. You've got to call 911."

"I can't."

"Why not?"

"I heard what he said—that he's going to kill the first cop who walks through the door. Then us. Then him. That's what he told her."

"She's still alive then?"

There was a catch in Jared's throat before he answered. "Maybe," he said. "I'm not sure."

I've felt helpless in my life, but never more so than at that moment. "Where's Christopher?"

"In bed. He fell asleep before any of this happened. I don't want to wake him up." Jared broke then and sobbed into the phone. "I don't know what to do, Mr. Beaumont. I don't want to die. Please help us."

"Hang on a minute, Jared. I've got to talk to someone else. Whatever you do, don't put the phone down, and for God's sake, don't turn it off."

With the cell phone held to my head, I raced back over to the circle and waved at Tim. The group of cops was too compressed for me to push my way through. All I could do was shout over the other officers' heads.

"Tim, come here. I've got to talk to you."

Startled, he looked up at me. "But . . ."

"Now!"

Shaking his head, he pushed his way through the crowd. "Beaumont, I . . ."

"Listen," I said. "Listen and don't say a word. I need your bubble light. Then I'm going to drive hell-bent-for-leather into Seattle. It's Sue, my partner. She and her two kids are caught in a hostage situation in the 3600 block of Dayton Avenue North, just north of Lake Union. I won't have a radio with me and I won't be able to use my cell phone, so I want you and Dave to follow in your car. Radio ahead and have the state patrol try to clear a path for me as far as Mercer anyway. But tell them absolutely no sirens. Do you understand? No sirens, and once we leave Mercer, no lights, either. You and Dave stick with me like glue, but no lights. You two will be my only backup, but when I go in, you stay out. Got it?"

"Beau, this is crazy . . ."

"Got it?"

"Yes."

"Come on then."

Tim Blaine is a big guy, but it seemed to me that he simply high jumped over the people standing between him and his partner, Dave Dawson. I went jogging back toward the Porsche and heard the two of them thundering behind me. By the time I made it to the 928 and unlocked the door, someone was already in the Crown Victoria, gunning the big police pursuit engine. As I put my key in the Porsche's ignition, Tim appeared at my window and slapped a bubble light on top.

"Don't worry," he said, passing me the cord. "On the way past, Dave borrowed one from somebody else so we'll have one, too. Lead the way."

I put the phone to my ear. "Jared, are you still there?"

"Yes."

"Did you get all that so you know help is on the way? That we're coming as fast as we can?"

"Yes."

"Hang on, then. I have to put the phone down to drive."

Laying the phone on the seat, I swung the Porsche into a tight U-turn and then charged back down 16th and 136th toward Highway 167. It was well after eleven o'clock now. I prayed there wouldn't be much traffic on the freeway headed north. I had owned 928s for years without once driving them at the kinds of speed for which they were designed. Now I might, but only if I could be reasonably sure doing so wouldn't end up killing me and/or somebody else.

As the Porsche and the Crown Victoria roared down the entrance ramp onto 167, I tried to picture the layout of Sue's long, narrow duplex. I had never been any farther inside than the cozy kitchen where the two of us had shared our tea-flavored nightcaps the evening before. I knew that the living room came first, opening off the front door, followed by the kitchen. A hallway led off the kitchen, making me think that the bedrooms and bathroom were somewhere at the back of the house. Unfortunately, I suspected there was a basement of some kind underneath that might make the elevation of the house too high for what I had in mind.

Only when I was back on the highway did I pick up the phone once more. "Okay, Jared, now listen, and listen very carefully. Is there a window in your room?"

"Yes."

"Is there a screen on it?"

"No."

"Good. Can you open it? The window, I mean?"

"Yes."

"How high is it above the ground?"

"I don't know. A long way. Six feet maybe."

"Here's what I want you to do. Strip everything off your bed. Blankets, pillows, everything. Wake Chris and strip his bed, too. You might even empty the clothes out of the closet and drawers. Push everything out the window. Don't throw them; drop them. If you toss them, they'll fall too far from the house and they won't do you any good. Once you have as much cushioning as possible on the ground under the window, I want both of you to go out the window. Maybe you can lower Chris first, and then you drop out next. Put the phone in your pocket when you do, but if we get disconnected in the process, punch redial and call me right back. Okay?"

"But what if Chris won't listen to me? He's just a little kid. He doesn't like it when I boss him around."

I racked my brain. "Tell him it's a game," I said at last. "Tell him it's part of the Disneyland trip and you're doing it to surprise your mom. Okay?"

"I'll try," Jared said, but it was a very shaky "I'll try." An unconvincing "I'll try."

"Once you're outside, go around the other side of the house to reach the front. Do not go to any of the neighbors. Do not knock on any doors. Someone might call 911. Do you understand?"

"Yes."

"Go out to Dayton and walk as far as the corner. Stay out of sight in case your dad figures out you're gone and comes looking for you. You know my car, don't you?"

"It's a Porsche, isn't it?"

"Yes, a red 928. When I come around the corner, I want you to stand up and wave at me. I'll stop. There'll be some other detectives with me in another car, Tim and Dave. I want you to get in the car with them. Then I'll go on up to the house and try to get your mother out. Okay?"

"But, Mr. Beaumont," Jared said. "Will it work?"

"I don't know. But start putting stuff out the

window right now. Quickly. In the meantime, I'm going to have to put the phone down to concentrate on driving. If you need me, yell."

"Please hurry, Mr. Beaumont. I don't think I can do this. I feel like I'm going to throw up."

"Hang on, Jared," I told him. "Please, hang on. Believe me, you're doing great."

CHAPTER 18

I STUFFED THE PHONE IN MY SHIRT POCKET, hoping that if something did happen and Jared needed me I'd be able to hear him. Then I drove. Drove like hell. After midnight there was no traffic at all on Highway 167. So I floored it. Between Kent and Renton on the straightaway, the speedometer went as high as 126. At least that's as high as I noticed. The Crown Victoria didn't stay right on my tail, but it was close enough.

Tim Blaine must have been working overtime on his radio. As we approached the Highway 167 and I-405 exchange, I noticed a state patrol car sitting on the shoulder, lights flashing. Slowing as I approached the intersection, I turned on my blinker to go north on 405. As soon as I did so, the patrol car roared up the access ramp ahead of me and into the far left lane. He cleared the way as far as I-90. When we turned off, he continued northbound, but another state patrol car took over from there, leading us into the city.

As soon as there was enough traffic to require slower speeds, I plucked the phone out of my pocket. "Jared?" I asked. "Are you there?"

"Yes."

"Where are you now?"

"On the corner of Dayton and 36th. Behind a Dumpster."

"That may still be too close to the house. Do you know where the troll is, the one under the Aurora Bridge?"

"Yeah."

"Take Chris and go there. We'll come by for you on our way to the house."

The troll is a piece of Seattle's whimsical statuary, built partially as a joke and partially to honor the Scandinavian heritage of many of the people living nearby. Made of poured concrete, it sits tucked into a hillside under the soaring Aurora Bridge. In one knobby hand it clutches the metal remains of a full-size VW Bug. The VW is a long way from that old Norwegian folktale, "The Three Billy Goats Gruff," but in Seattle's off-the-wall Fremont neighborhood, it works. I thought it might work for Jared and Chris as well.

"Are you boys both okay?" I asked.

"Chris got a bloody nose when he landed," Jared said. "He was crying at first, but he's okay now."

"Way to go, Jared. We're coming as fast as we can. I'm already on the I-90 Bridge. It won't be long."

"Thanks, Mr. Beaumont."

I thought of all the other times I had encountered Jared Danielson, both in person and on the telephone. I didn't think the kid had ever learned any manners. Obviously I had been wrong.

"And Jared?"

"Yes."

"Now that you're out of the house, I'm going to hang up for a minute. I need to call for some other backup. Wait for a few seconds and then dial my number. As soon as I'm off the line, it'll ring again and I'll pick up."

Ending that call, I dialed the speed-dial code for Dispatch. "Beaumont here."

"Where are you?" the operator asked.

"Just coming into the city on I-90 and about to turn onto I-5. Sue Danielson's kids are both out of the house."

"Thank God."

"What about Detective Danielson?"

"She's been shot. I don't know if she's dead or alive, but she's still in the house."

"We're in the process of cordoning off that whole Fremont neighborhood, Detective Beaumont. Like you said, no lights, no sirens, but we have cars in place at every intersection. Any idea what kind of car he'd be driving if he made a break for it?"

"Either Sue's old Escort or a rental of some kind. He's threatened to shoot the first cop who comes through the door. I'm in my Porsche. I doubt he'll suspect someone in a 928 of being a cop. I plan to drive up, blatant as hell, pretending to be Sue's boyfriend."

I heard Chuck Grayson's voice in the background.

"He can't do that. It's crazy. We'd be better off tear-gassing the place and then storming it."

Before the dispatcher had a chance to relay anything more, I ended the call. The phone rang again, seconds later. "Jared? Where are you?"

"At the troll. But it's dark under here, dark and cold. I forgot to bring along a jacket. Chris says he's scared. He wants to go back home."

"Tell him we'll be there in a few minutes. We'll bring along blankets and give you a ride."

As I turned off I-5 onto Mercer, the latest state patrol escort waved goodbye with a thumbs-up sign. Returning the signal I hoped what was coming would be as simple as I had made it sound when I talked to Dispatch.

"Here's the deal, Jared," I said. "When we come under the bridge, the car behind me will stop. It's a gray Crown Victoria. If I'm not there and you want to be sure you have the right car, ask the guy who his girlfriend is. Her name's Latty. Tim and Dave are to take care of you and Chris. There are other cars and other officers from SPD who'll be there to help me."

"But Dad said . . ." Jared began.

"I know what your father said, Jared," I interrupted. "Don't repeat it right now in front of Chris. Your father won't know I'm a cop. I'll pretend I'm your Mom's boyfriend. Maybe that way I can get inside the house to help her. Okay? Does that sound to you like it'll work?"

"Maybe," Jared said. "I hope so."

So did I. Talking as I drove had been a device to bolster my own courage as much as to prop up

Jared's. It had also served to give him a timetable, to let him know where we were and that help was almost at hand.

"We're coming up Westlake now. How's Chris' nosebleed?"

"It's stopped. He's still cold."

"Tell him the blankets are coming, blankets and a teddy bear, too."

It wasn't until I crossed the Fremont Bridge that I became conscious of the sweat running down my collar, beading across my forehead and under my nose. My hands were so slick and wet it was all I could do to keep a grip on the steering wheel and the phone. Coming up 34th I saw several unmarked cars scattered along the street and several plain-clothes cops as well, but I was gratified to see they had complied with my wishes. Backup was there in spades, but without the fanfare of lights and sirens. Setting up a full-scale emergency response team operation would have taken hours. My gut told me we didn't have that much time.

As I approached the troll, I strained forward in the seat, hoping to catch sight of the kids. It wasn't until I stopped and got out of the car that they appeared. Chris came running toward me and threw both arms around my waist.

"Jared says Mom's hurt. Is that true?" he demanded.

"Yes," I said. "I think it is. I'm on my way to help her right now."

"I want to go, too," Chris said. "I can help. I learned how to put on bandages in school."

"I'm sure you did," I said. The Crown Victoria

stopped behind the Porsche. Tim Blaine stepped out. "Here's my friend, Tim," I said. "I want you and Jared to stay with him for now while I go help your mom."

"Is she going to be all right?"

"I don't know," I said. "I hope so."

Chris allowed himself to be handed off. Jared came toward me more warily, as if unsure of his welcome. He seemed exactly the same kid he had always been before. Same baggy pants; same over-sized sweatshirt; same Washington State baseball cap perched backward over long flowing locks. But something was different about him. Behind that scraggly, baggy exterior of his, he had unearthed a stockpile of extraordinary courage. In saving his little brother's life, he had exhibited more bravery than many people twice his age.

I held out my hand as he approached. "Good work, Jared," I said.

He pulled his hand out of the pocket of his sagging pants, but before he could return my handshake, he had to switch his cell phone from his right hand to his left. When our palms met, his was almost as sweaty and sticky as my own.

"I think you can shut that thing off now," I told him. "We've probably run up enough of a bill."

It was a lame attempt at a joke, something to lighten both our spirits. But instead of kidding back, Jared simply switched off the phone. "Okay," he said. His lower lip trembled when he spoke. The fact that he was near tears and trying to hold back got me.

"You stay here," I said gruffly, not knowing how else to comfort him.

He looked up at me then, full in the face, while his eyes misted with tears. "What if you're too late?" he asked. "What if she doesn't make it?"

That was my fear, too. "We've done the best we could, Jared," I told him. "You've done your best."

Fighting back tears of my own, I turned away and went back to the 928. I pulled my extra Kevlar vest out of the 928's vestigial boot and put it on. *Show time*, I told myself. Then I knocked wood on the vest and headed for the showdown on Dayton Avenue North.

On the way, I found myself wishing it were farther away to give myself more time to prepare—rehearsal time, if you will. But then again, if there'd been time enough to think it over, to consider what was at stake, I might have backed out. The only thing I knew for certain was that no matter what happened, the kids were safe. Sue Danielson had taken my advice and bought her son a cellular phone. Between the two of us we had managed to save her children's lives. The question was, could we save hers?

I pulled up in front of the duplex. The place looked as innocuous as it had the previous night. The front porch light was on. So was the light in the front window, but the blinds were pulled shut and the lamplight behind them revealed no movement inside.

What's that line of Lady Macbeth's? I asked myself as I switched off the engine. I knew it was something about screwing your courage to the sticking place, but I couldn't remember the exact quote. Right then, though, I was so soaked with perspiration that the "sticking place" could have been almost any place on my whole body. Before exiting the Porsche, I moved my 9mm from my shoulder holster to the pocket of my sports jacket.

Getting out of the car, I wondered whether or not Richie Danielson had already learned that his sons had escaped. If so, his first response to my ringing the doorbell could very well be a hail of bullets. With every step I took up the walk the Kevlar vest seemed to shrink on my body. It grew smaller and smaller while the nakedly exposed parts of me—my head and arms, abdomen and legs—seemed to balloon in size.

Knees quaking beneath me, I stepped onto the wooden porch. It creaked and groaned under my weight, but nothing happened inside the room, not as far as I could see. I rang the doorbell. No response. I rang again.

"Sue?" I called, opening the screen door and tapping gently on the solid-core door behind it. Standing there I wished this were the same kind of front door as the one on my grandmother's house. Beverly Piedmont's old-fashioned mahogany front door came with three small, stair-step panes of glass. Those tiny windows would have afforded me a glimpse inside the house. In Sue's front door there was only a one-way security peephole.

"Sue," I said. "Are you ready? It's time to go. Larry and Marcia are expecting us."

Those were the only names I could think of right then, Captain Powell and his wife. I don't know why those names in particular surfaced in my head, but they did and I used them, trying to make it sound casual and as planned.

"Who is it?"

Richie spoke from directly on the other side of the door, mere inches away. I almost crapped my pants.

"It's none of your business," I said. "Sue and I have a date. Now, where is she and who the hell are you?"

"Sue's not here," Richie said. "She went out."

Jared had told me Richie was drinking. There was enough slurring in his speech that I was sure he was in fact drunk.

"I don't believe you," I said. "Her car's still here."

"She went with friends," he said. "Now go away and leave us alone."

"I think you're lying to me," I said through the closed door. "You just want to keep her to yourself. Let me in."

"I tell you, she's not here."

"Yes, she is."

"Who are you?"

"I already told you. It's none of your business who I am. Now let me in."

There was a pause and then a stumble. The light from the lamp on the table just inside the window wavered as though Richie might have bumped it. I couldn't see him. When he spoke again it was from a distance, close enough for me to hear his voice but no longer directly on the other side of the door.

"You'll be sorry," he said.

It sounded like a little boy's taunt, one that

harkened all the way back to kindergarten or first grade. If Richie Danielson was going to cast himself as the bad little boy in the drama, I would have to be the daddy.

"What do you mean I'll be sorry?" I demanded. "What's going on in there?"

"You can come in if you want to. The door's unlocked."

Standing to the side of the door, protected as much as possible by the door frame and the wall itself, I reached for the doorknob. As soon as it moved, the door was splintered several times over by a deafening blast of gunfire. My ears rang, but it seemed to me he had fired at least three separate shots, probably with Sue's own 9mm.

I remembered then, with the smell of cordite billowing around me, the shapely shirtwaist Sue Danielson had been wearing the last time I saw her. It had been a softly flowing dress, one that showed off her breasts and waist and hips with no room for soft body armor or a concealed weapon.

I remembered how she had looked in that pastel-colored dress. She had come to Bellevue wearing it in order to run interference for me with Paul Kramer. That was why she left her house in the first place, why she had left her children in her ex-husband's charge, and why she had come home to face a bullet.

The whole time I had been on my way from Auburn, the whole time I had been dealing with the crisis and keeping Jared pumped up and on the phone, I had managed to avoid looking at my own culpability. But now it was there in front of me, as plain as the shattered wood of the door. And the anger that took over then had nothing to do with training or brains or dedication. Unreasoning rage, pure and simple, kicked open Sue Danielson's front door.

Only Richie Danielson wasn't there. He had left the living room and disappeared into the kitchen perhaps, or maybe into one of the bedrooms beyond. The person who was there was Sue. She was slumped over against the far wall. At first I thought she was dead, but as I came into the room, crouching low, gun extended, I saw a slight movement—a shudder—as she tried to raise herself up. On the floor beneath her was a pool of blood.

"Be still," I warned. "Don't try to move. You'll make it worse."

"The boys," she whispered desperately. "They're in the bedroom. He's going to kill the boys."

"No, he's not," I told her. "They're safe. They got out. Jared called me. They're down the street in a car."

Hearing the news, a look of supreme relief washed across Sue's desperately pale face. I was torn. I wanted to go after Richie, but I didn't want to leave Sue there alone, wounded, and defenseless. She understood. "Your gun," she managed. "Your backup weapon. Let me have it."

Without a word, I stripped the weapon out of my ankle holster and handed it over. It's a lightweight Glock, but her strength had ebbed so far that even the Glock was almost too much for her. Strength may have deserted her hand and arm, but not her heart.

"Go now," she urged, her voice coming weakly between panting breaths. "If he gets past you, he won't get past me."

"Sue . . ." I began.

She shook her head. "Don't talk," she said. "Go now. Go!"

I went. I made my way to the doorway that led into the kitchen. Dreading another blast of gunfire, I peered around the doorjamb. The spotless kitchen I had sat in the night before was no more. The room had been trashed. Broken dishes, jars and boxes and cans of food had been smashed and mingled together in a heap on the floor. In among the mess I saw glimpses of those handmade Easter eggs.

Where the hell are the neighbors? I wondered savagely. *Why didn't they call?*

Sidestepping as much of the gooey debris and broken glass as possible, I picked my way around the edge of the room to the doorway that opened on the hall. The hallway in turn led to the back of the house.

Here the shambles continued. Heaps of Sue's clothing and bedding had been tossed into the hall along with framed pictures and more artwork. It was as though Richie had systematically set out to destroy everything that belonged to her.

"Where are they?" he demanded now from the far bedroom. "My sons. What have you done with them?"

"They're gone, Richie," I said, ducking into the doorway of Sue's bedroom. "They're someplace safe where you'll never find them."

"You're lying."

"No, I'm not."

"How did you get here?"

It was my turn to taunt. I wanted him to show himself. "Jared called me," I said. "His mom bought him a cell phone to use in emergencies in case you pulled some off-the-wall stunt down in California. She bought it for him and told him to call if he needed help. Which he did."

"She's a bitch, saying that about me."

"What should she say, you shit head?" I demanded. "That you're the good fucking fairy?"

"She didn't have the right to bad-mouth me to the boys. I wanted to do something special with them. I wanted the three of us to have some fun. She wrecked it for us. She wrecked the whole thing."

"You wrecked it yourself, Richie. You and nobody else."

For the space of almost a minute after that, he didn't answer. All I could hear in the stretching silence was the hammering beat of my own pounding heart.

"Who the fuck are you again?" he asked finally. "Her boyfriend?"

There was no longer any reason for pretense. I wanted him to show himself. I wanted to have my shot at him.

"No, you son of a bitch!" I shouted back at the top of my lungs, giving voice to all the rage that was boiling inside me. "I'm her partner, God dammit. I'm Sue Danielson's partner. The first cop to walk in the door . . . the guy you said you were going to shoot. Come on out and do it then, you sorry son of a bitch. Come on out, with your hands up or not, I don't give a shit which it is."

I heard a slight noise, the scuffling sound of movement. I expected Richie to explode out of the bedroom door with his gun blazing but for the longest time nothing at all happened. The bedroom was silent, so was the hallway, so was the house.

Then there was a click. A single click. The sound of a firing pin hitting an empty chamber. My thought—if it could be called that—was that he was out of ammo. I sprinted down the hallway. Except he wasn't out of ammunition at all. One shot had simply misfired. The next one did not.

I reached the doorway at the exact same time he pulled the trigger. I arrived in time to see Richie Danielson blow his brains out all over a bulletin board covered with his sons' schoolwork and pictures.

Without pausing, I turned and raced back down the hall toward Sue. I picked up the wall phone in Sue's kitchen. When I realized the line was dead, I wrested my own overused cell phone out of my pocket and punched in 911 as I ran. Sue was still there. She had somehow managed to raise herself up and was sitting propped against the wall with my Glock balanced on one outsplayed knee in front of her.

"Nine-one-one," the operator said. "What are you reporting?"

"A shooting," I said. "At 3654 Dayton Avenue North."

"An ambulance is already standing by at that location," she said. "If you care to stay on the line, sir, we've . . ."

"I'm a police officer," I interrupted. "The shooter is dead. Tell the medics they're clear to enter."

"If you'll please stay on the line, sir . . ."

But I didn't. I turned off the phone and knelt beside Sue. "Did you get him?" she asked.

"No," I returned. "He did it himself."

"Good," she whispered. "For once in his life . . . Richie Danielson finally did something right."

She slipped into unconsciousness then. I was still kneeling beside her, holding her, when the Medic One guys burst in the front door. I turned her over to them, then I got up and moved out of the way.

I was sobbing, leaning against a wall when one of the medics came up behind me. "Sir," he said. "You're bloody. Are you hurt, too?"

"No," I said. "I'm fine."

But even as I said the words, I knew they weren't true. I wasn't fine. Not even close.

There was a whole flurry of activity after that. I moved through it all like an automaton. Tim and Dave took the two boys and followed the ambulance down to Harborview. I stayed on at the duplex long enough to give a statement to the first officers and investigators at the scene, then I left, too, and drove myself to Harborview, as well.

It wasn't the first time I'd made that awful trip to the Harborview Trauma Center behind some gravely injured partner. It had happened first with Ron Peters, and then with Big Al Lindstrom. After that, people had ribbed me about being a jinx. The black-humored comments were meant as jokes, but especially after Big Al, no one leaped forward to be my new partner. No one, that is, but Sue Danielson. For everyone but her, J. P. Beaumont had been bad news.

When I reached the hospital waiting room, I found Chris sound asleep, stretched out on a couch with his head resting in Tim Blaine's lap. In his hand he clutched the Teddy Bear Patrol stuffed bear all units carry for just such occasions. Jared stood off by himself, a solitary picture of dejection in his baggy, ill-fitting clothing. He seemed to be staring dry-eyed at the front of the Coke machine. I stopped in front of Tim.

"Any word?" I asked.

"Not so far."

I looked at Jared. "Have you told him about his father?"

"He heard."

"Heard? What do you mean, 'he heard'?"

"We had our radio tuned in to SPD's tactical channel," Tim said. "The news came over the air before I could switch it off."

Shaking my head, I got up and walked over to where Jared stood. He still hadn't moved. "Jared?"

"I called my grandmother," he said, looking up at me. "She and Grandpa are flying in tomorrow morning. Their plane will be here around noon. She asked where we'd be staying. I told her I didn't know."

"You can come home with me tonight," I said. "Tomorrow we'll make other arrangements."

He nodded. "Okay," he said.

"I'm sorry about your father."

"I'm not," Jared choked fiercely. "I hate him! I'm glad he's dead."

The boy dissolved into anguished tears then and fell sobbing against my chest. I held him for a long, long time. In fact, I was still holding him some minutes later when Larry Powell walked into the room. Maybe he wasn't our captain anymore, but he was still there. That meant a lot. Paul Kramer, on the other hand, was notable by his absence.

"Beau," Larry began. Then he stopped and shook his head, unable to continue. At last he cleared his throat and tried again. "These are Sue's kids?"

"Yes," I said. "That's Chris over there." I nodded toward the sleeping child. "And this is Jared."

"This is the young man with the cell phone, the one who raised the alarm?" Larry asked.

"Yes."

Larry turned to Jared and offered his hand. "Good work, son," he said. "If it hadn't been for you, no telling how much worse things might have been. You have a place to stay? Someone to look after you?"

Jared seemed to square his shoulders. "Our grandparents are coming from Ohio in the morning," he said. "Our mother's parents. Tonight we're staying with Mr. Beaumont."

"Good," Larry said. "That's good."

At that precise moment, a door swung open behind Larry. A man in green surgical scrubs stepped into the room. He stopped just inside the door. For a moment his eyes met mine over the top of Jared's baseball cap, then he shook his head.

"I'm sorry," he said. "She's gone."

CHAPTER 19

IT WAS AFTER FOUR IN THE MORNING BY THE TIME I had the boys home and in bed. I went to bed myself, but I didn't sleep. At six, I gave up. I got up, made coffee, and called Ralph. He was in my dining room drinking coffee thirty minutes later. Together we made arrangements for a three-room suite at the Four Seasons where Sue's folks and the boys could stay as long as necessary. I had just finished renting a Lincoln Town Car to ferry people around in when there was a knock on the door and Ron Peters rolled into the room, waving at Ralph as he came.

"I heard," he said. "I called down to leave word about the baby at the department. Watty told me what happened. Are you okay?"

"I'm all right," I said. "I'm sorry. I didn't even think to ask . . ."

"Don't worry about it. There's no need to apologize. Amy's fine and so is the baby. Seven pounds, nine ounces. We haven't named him yet, but we're working on that. Now, what can I do to help?"

There wasn't that much. Until the boys woke up, everything was pretty well done. But both Ron and Ralph knew what I needed—to talk. To tell the story. To unburden myself. And they let me do just that. We sat and drank coffee and I talked. Not that talking fixed anything. When all the words had spilled out, nothing was changed. Sue Danielson was still dead; her two sons orphans.

"Jared must be one hell of a kid," Ron Peters commented when I finished.

"You wouldn't think so to look at him," I said. "I always wrote him off as a lamebrained gang wannabe. But when it counted, he came through and showed some real smarts as well. If it hadn't been for him, the whole family would have been wiped out."

At nine Ron left to go to the hospital and visit Amy and the baby. The moment he walked out the door, the phone started ringing. The condolence calls came mostly from the fifth floor, although there were others as well—Janice Morraine from the crime lab, Phil Grimes from Media Relations, Capt. Anthony Freeman, Ron's supervisor from Internal Investigations Section. There was even a call from Seattle's police chief, Kenneth Rankin. After five or six calls, I ran out of steam. I had wanted to talk to Ron and Ralph, but it turned out I wasn't eager to talk to anyone else. After that, Ralph fielded the remaining calls, jotting down names, numbers, and the gist of each message. Once again Paul Kramer's call was notable in its absence.

"By the way," Ralph told me between phone calls, "I canceled our dinner for tonight as well as the Victoria cruise for this weekend. I didn't think you'd be up to either one. Cassie said to tell you she understands."

About ten I lay down for a nap. I asked Ralph to wake me in time to get the boys down to the airport. Ralph offered to make the airport trip for me, but I wanted to do it myself, to hand deliver Jared and Chris into their grandparents' hands. It was the least I could do.

Mary Beth and Hank Hinkle were due in from Cincinnati at twelve. At eleven-fifteen, the boys and I headed for the airport. They were both subdued and quiet. In less than twenty-four hours their entire lives had been blown apart.

At Sea-Tac, we went to the airport's South Satellite only to discover that their grandparents' plane would be twenty minutes late. Chris, too restless to sit still, went to buy himself a soda while Jared and I waited by the gate.

"What do you think will happen to us?" he asked.

"I don't know what kind of arrangements your mother had in mind. Would you like to go back to Ohio with your grandparents?"

"Maybe," he said. "I think I want to be far away from here."

"Talk to them about it then," I said. "See what they think."

Jared was quiet for a while. "You know," he said at last. "I almost wish you *had* been her boyfriend. Mom liked you. She liked you a lot."

"I liked her, too, Jared. She was a smart, brave woman. You take after her."

"Do you think so?" he asked, his voice quivering. "You think I take after her and not my father?"

"Absolutely," I said. "No question."

The plane came in a few minutes later. I stood in the background while the heartbreaking reunion took place. When Jared brought them over and introduced them as Mary Beth and Hank Hinkle, I noted how much Sue had resembled her sad-eyed mother. Mary Beth shook my hand, then she reached up and hugged me. "Thank you," she whispered. "Jared told us everything you did. Thank you so much."

I drove them to the Four Seasons. Ralph had asked me earlier what I planned to do after I dropped them at the hotel. I had told him I didn't know. Now though, there didn't seem to be anywhere else to go but to the department. I dreaded it—dreaded the black tape on badges, the somber nods, and the furtive looks. But still, like an old broken-up bronc rider who has to get back on the horse one more time, I had to go there and face it.

After checking in, I went straight to the cubicle. There was still a hint of Sue's perfume in the air. Her sons' smiling pictures—this school year's current versions—still graced her desk. I went back out to Watty's office, found a suitable box, and returned to the cubicle. I cleaned and packed as ruthlessly as any widow or widower has ever gone through a dead spouse's possessions. As I was doing it, I told myself that I needed to get things stowed so Sue's parents could sort through them while they were here. In reality, I needed to have them out of my sight.

I was just emptying the last drawer when my phone rang. It was tempting not to answer, to simply let the caller go to voice mail, but in the middle of the fourth ring, I picked it up. "Detective Beaumont," I said.

"Caleb Drachman here. Frederick Considine just told me he thought the police officer who died this morning was the same one who was with you at Boeing Field yesterday."

"That's true," I said, working my way around the catch in my throat. "Sue Danielson was my partner."

"I'm so sorry," Drachman said convincingly. "This is probably a bad time then. I'll tell Fred we'll do it some other time."

"Do what?"

"He wanted to talk with you. In my presence, of course. I have some time early this afternoon, but in view of what's happened . . ."

What had happened to Sue had left me adrift. Going to work and actually doing something constructive might make it possible for me to get through the day. If nothing else, it would help fill up the hours.

"I'll be glad to meet with you," I said. "Where and when?"

"I usually prefer to have these kinds of conferences in my office, but in this case the client wishes us to join him at his residence. Do you know where that is?"

"Up near the Highlands?"

"Yes, on the bluff just south of there. It's probably easier if I send you a map. Do you have a fax?"

I gave him the number, then I went down to the communal fax machine and waited until it came in. From where I stood, I could see Kramer in his office, talking animatedly on the phone. I turned away before our eyes made contact. Larry Powell had come to the hospital because of the kind of guy he is. In spite of his own personal crisis. As Sue Danielson's commanding officer—new or not; temporary or permanent—Paul Kramer was the one who *should* have been there.

Harboring a grudge against Kramer and still missing Sue Danielson's presence in the car, I drove north alone. Considering what had happened, it should have been a dreary, rainy, typical Seattle day, but it wasn't. It was one of those glorious April days when every horizon was punctuated by snow-capped mountains and with the azaleas and rhodies in full glorious bloom. It was a day Sue Danielson hadn't lived to see.

Following Caleb Drachman's directions, I steered my rented Town Car west on 145th just south of the Seattle Golf and Country Club and then wandered over to North West Culbertson. The Considine Compound, labeled as such, was behind an electronically operated and monitored gate halfway down the bluff. Like hillside homes everywhere, what was supposedly the front of the house opened on the spectacular view with the parking area and actual entrance located at the back.

My first view of Frederick Considine's backyard led me to believe I had wandered into a Lincoln automotive museum. The jewel of the collection was clearly the 1941 Continental Cabriolet. But the 1956 Mark II wasn't bad, either, nor was the '79 Mark V. Their high-gloss finishes as well as the damp brickwork underneath gave evidence that someone was taking advantage of one of April's few sunny days to polish up the Considines' rolling stock. I pulled in next to an equally freshly washed pair, a Town Car and a Mark VIII, both of them recent editions. My rented Town Car fit right in. The only odd man out was a single, stray BMW 850 IL. That one, however, had a film of dust on it that made me suspect it belonged to Caleb Drachman.

As I stepped out of my car, the young blonde I had last seen at Boeing Field came darting from the house. Dressed in a show-all spandex top and shorts, she carried a workout bag in one hand and a set of car keys in the other. She shot past me without bothering to wave or say hello and bounded into the Mark VIII. Watching her haul ass out of the compound, I wondered if young Mrs. Considine had not been invited to the coming conference, was not interested, or both of the above.

When I rang the bell, Frederick himself answered the door. "I'm sorry about your partner," he said. Those were certainly not the first words I expected from a possible murder suspect who, in the presence of an attorney, was meeting with a homicide detective.

"Thank you," I said.

"Considering what you must have been through

in the last twenty-four hours, I probably should have let this ride for a while—until next week even—but once I'd made up my mind about this, I wanted to get it over with as soon as possible."

"That's all right, Mr. Considine. I went in to work today because working helps."

"This way then," he said. "Since it's such nice weather today, Mr. Drachman and I decided to sit on the front deck."

I followed him through the spectacularly appointed house and out onto an open-air deck overlooking the Puget Sound shipping lanes. I estimated the difference between this view home and Sue's humble rental duplex several miles away would have been a few million dollars, give or take. The contrast was made all the more striking by my still too-vivid remembrance of the needless wreckage, human and otherwise, Richie Danielson had left in his wake.

"I didn't know if you'd eaten or not, so I had the cook make up a platter of sandwiches," Frederick Considine was saying. "And there are sodas, iced tea, lemonade, wine . . ."

I'd eaten nothing all day, not since those few bites of Ron Peters' leftover vegetarian pizza the night before. Nonetheless, at three o'clock the following afternoon I still wasn't hungry. "Nothing for me, thanks."

Caleb Drachman was seated at a graceful wrought-iron table. On it was a platter heaped high with sandwiches as well as a silver tray set with pitchers of beverages, an ice bucket, and a collection of crystal glasses. Dressed in a spiffy bow tie, crisply pressed trousers, and wing-tip shoes, the impeccable Mr. Drachman looked like someone ready for a courtroom appearance rather than a deckside picnic.

Seeing him there, out of place and yet totally at ease, I couldn't help comparing him to Ralph. As long as I've known Ralph Ames, I've never seen him in a bow tie. As long as I've known Caleb Drachman, I've never seen him without one. That small difference aside, however, the two of them could just as well be twins. I wouldn't be surprised to find that they patronize the same brand of upscale clothiers. And, regardless of the circumstances, they both come across as totally together.

While I was feeling tired and worn and frayed around the edges, Drachman was anything but. The jacket of his expensive suit was carefully folded over the back of a nearby Adirondack chair. Despite the warmth of the afternoon sun, the defense attorney's crisp white shirt barely showed a wrinkle. Not even the stiff breeze blowing in off the water succeeded in ruffling his thinning reddish blond hair.

"Good of you to come, Detective Beaumont," he said, polishing off one sandwich and reaching for another. "I hope you'll excuse me for eating. The only way for me to make this work was to skip lunch."

"You made it sound reasonably urgent," I said, easing myself into a chair.

He nodded. "It is. I'm assuming, of course, that despite what happened to Detective Danielson you're still assigned to the Agnes Ferman murder?"

"Yes."

Drachman looked at Considine. "In that case,

my client has some information that could be of assistance. He has some concerns in that regard, however. Because of his family's position in the community, he's worried about unnecessary publicity. He's also worried about prosecution."

"You know I can't make any guarantees . . ."

Drachman held up his hand. "From what he's told me, I believe his worries are groundless, but I'm here to make sure your investigation doesn't end up targeting the wrong individual."

"Does it have something to do with blackmail?" I asked.

Caleb Drachman raised one eyebrow and nodded. Frederick Considine blanched visibly. "You already knew?" he asked.

"We figured it had to be something like that," I said.

"Go ahead and tell him," Drachman urged.

"It's true," Frederick Considine admitted. "Agnes Ferman was a blackmailer. She blackmailed my parents, both of them. And she tried to blackmail me."

"Over what?"

"It's a long story," he said. "I had a brother once, an older brother, named Lucas. I barely remember him, but he must have been something special—a great kid, right up until he took a spill on his bike out on the road. His brand-new two-wheeler skidded and he somersaulted headfirst into an oncoming car. They brought him home finally, but he was severely brain damaged, in a wheelchair. He was fed through a tube and had no idea who any of us were. My father couldn't stand it, couldn't bear the thought of him living out his life that way. So he took care of it."

"What do you mean?"

"One day, Lucas was sitting in a wheelchair out here in the yard. Right over there." Considine pointed to an expanse of sloping lawn far beneath us. "There wasn't a fence here then," he said. "Something happened to the brake on the wheelchair. Lucas went over the edge. His death was ruled an accident. Agnes Ferman said she saw my father fiddling with the brake a few minutes before the chair went over the edge."

"I take it she didn't tell the police that part of the story?"

Considine nodded in answer to my question. "She didn't tell them, but she must have told my mother. I believe she must have threatened to turn him in."

"You're saying your mother was the one who was actually the blackmail target? Why not your father?"

"I'm not sure," Frederick answered. "Mother had money in her own right, and she paid. Growing up I remember that sometimes my father would hint around that we should let Agnes go, but Mother always insisted we keep her on. Mother's health was bad then, too. She developed MS. No matter what else Agnes Ferman may have done, I have to admit she took good care of Mother. She was paid wages, of course, but my mother also provided for Agnes in her will. She inherited my mother's old Continental which wasn't surprising since she was the one who did most of the driving in that car. There was also a sizable bequest left in Agnes Ferman's name with the understanding that the money be used to buy an annuity so Agnes would have an income in retirement.

"I was executor of Mother's estate. I handled all the arrangements, but at the time there was one thing I never quite figured out. Going over the bank records, I could see that my mother had gone through a good deal of unexplained cash. It's only in the last few weeks that I finally figured out the money must have gone to Agnes."

"What made you draw that conclusion?" I asked.

"About a month ago, *Pacific* magazine did a big article on the bankers behind downtown Seattle's well-known developers. The developers are the guys out front. Bankers, on the other hand, are behind-the-scenes kind of guys. They're the ones who put the deal together. If it hadn't been for Forrest Considine, the Seattle skyline would be far different than it is today. Somebody at the *Times* must have figured that out. My dad was prominently featured in the article. Did you happen to see it?"

I shook my head. *Pacific* is a Sunday supplement to the *Seattle Times*, but it's not something I necessarily read. My interest in newspapers still doesn't stretch much beyond glancing at the headlines and doing the crossword puzzle.

"Agnes must have read it, though. A few days later, she sent me two badly typed chapters of a manuscript she claimed to be working on. I was just going to glance at a page or two, but as soon as I started reading, I realized she was writing about us—about our family, about Mother, Father, Lucas, and me. I learned several things from reading that manuscript.

Number one—for several years after Agnes first came to work for my parents, she and my father were lovers. That was how things stood when my brother died."

"That's all in the manuscript?" I asked.

"That and more," he answered grimly. "I went to see her right away. Dad had just had a stroke. I was afraid of what bringing all this up again might do to him in his fragile state, so I went to see her. Father's ninety-three now and in a nursing home with round-the-clock care. I wanted to bring him home here, but he and Katherine don't exactly get along. He's old, bedridden, and virtually helpless. I tried to explain to Agnes that it wouldn't be fair to bring this all up now when he can't even defend himself. He's lost the ability to speak or read. He knows what's going on and there's nothing wrong with his ability to think. But he can't verbalize, can't form a response."

"What happened when you went to see Agnes?"

"She hinted around that she might stop writing—for a price. I told her I'd think it over. And I did—for about two seconds. What I really thought about was turning her in to the cops so you could deal with her. But then, for all the same reasons I didn't want any of the story published, I didn't want to bring the authorities in on it, either. I couldn't see my father being dragged through all this, not when he's practically on his deathbed.

"What I did do was some detective work on my own. My father was always worried about losing records, so early on he had all the business financial records placed on microfiche. While he was at it, he had someone copy the personal ones as well. I went back through and checked. Sure enough, there was an unexplained lump-sum withdrawal that came out of my mother's personal resources within two months of my brother's death. The smaller cash withdrawals started then and continued until my mother was no longer able to handle her own affairs."

"That was about the same time Agnes quit to go home and take care of her own husband?" I asked.

"No," Considine replied. "They went on for a period of time even after that. Agnes used to come over and take Mother out for rides, ostensibly for lunch, every month or so. My guess is they stopped by the bank and my mother made the withdrawals in person."

"When did the payments stop?"

"After we checked my mother into a nursing home."

I glanced around the spacious house. Knowing that the Considines could well have afforded a whole coterie of servants and private nurses, it didn't make sense to me that first Frederick's mother and now his father had been shipped off to nursing homes for their final illnesses.

"I take it your wife didn't like your mother, either?" I asked.

"Katherine isn't much for clucking and caring."

There didn't seem to be any point in debating that issue. "Go ahead," I urged. "What happened next?"

"A week ago Sunday I went to see Agnes again. I called in the afternoon, hoping for an early evening appointment. She said she was having company earlier and wanted me to drop by later, sometime after nine. I ended up getting tied up myself. It was almost eleven when I called from the car to ask if it was too late for me to stop by, or if we should reschedule. She said no, for me to come on over.

"When I finally showed up, I got the impression that she expected me to open my wallet and hand over money which wasn't at all what I had in mind. We ended up getting into a hell of a row over it. It was the principle of the thing, you see. I have no idea how much she thought her keeping quiet was worth. Whatever it was, I have plenty of money. I probably could have paid the fare without even breaking a sweat, but the point is, this woman—this trusted 'insider'—had betrayed my family six ways to Sunday. I wasn't about to give her another damned dime."

With Considine spouting those kinds of self-incriminating admissions, I glanced in Caleb Drachman's direction expecting some kind of reaction. While he was observing the proceedings with interest, he showed no visible concern.

I said, "With more than three hundred thousand stashed in her garage, I'd say money wasn't the issue for Agnes, either. Why do you suppose she did it?"

Considine shrugged. "For the hell of it, maybe? She had gotten away with it for so long, maybe she thought it was her due. Or maybe she just wanted to press the envelope and see how far she could take things."

I suddenly remembered something Hilda Smathers had said about her half sister—that Agnes Ferman was mean. Maybe that's what this was, just plain meanness.

"Unfortunately, Mr. Considine," I said, "what you're telling me makes you more of a suspect rather than . . ."

"Just wait," he said. "Let me finish. Agnes and I had this big argument. Finally, I told her to go ahead and write whatever the hell she wanted, that after all this time people would just take it for the ravings of some crazy old lady. That's when I left, but when I stepped onto the front porch, I almost broke my neck. There was a dog there, lying right in front of the door. It was dark and the dog was one of those stupid little wiener dogs. I never even saw him. It's a wonder I didn't pitch off the porch onto the sidewalk."

"A wiener dog?"

"Not one, but two. And they both started barking at once. I was sure they were going to wake the whole godforsaken neighborhood. And then I saw this old guy. He was sitting off to the side and he looked . . ."

"Just like George Burns," I finished for him.

"Right," Considine said. "How did you know that?"

"His name's Malcolm Lawrence. He lives across the street from Agnes. He's the one who reported the fire."

I had a fairly clear remembrance of what Malcolm Lawrence had said. He had told Sue and me that he had seen only one car at Agnes Ferman's house that night—Hilda Smathers' Camry, early in the evening. He had also claimed that he had gone to bed early without waiting up for the eleven o'clock news. If Considine was telling the truth, that meant Malcolm Lawrence had lied to us. Twice.

"After I caught my balance and untangled my foot from the leash, I took off," Considine continued.

"Did you say anything to Mr. Lawrence?" I asked. "Or did he say anything to you?"

"No. I was shocked to find someone there listening where I didn't expect . . ." Frederick stopped talking because I was already standing up. "Where are you going?" he asked.

"If you'll excuse me," I said. "I believe I need to see a man about a dog."

Caleb Drachman smiled and nodded. "I thought you would," he said.

CHAPTER 20

FOR ME, HINDSIGHT IS ALWAYS TWENTY-TWENTY. As I roared out of Frederick Considine's Lincoln-littered backyard, my thoughts were entirely on Malcolm Lawrence and his two obnoxious dogs. And on what would have prompted him to lie to me.

If I'd still had a partner, I would have wanted that partner along. But I didn't have one. Given my track record, as well as the weight of squad-room superstition, I knew that none of my fellow detectives would be jumping at the chance to team up with me. The word was out on the fifth floor: As far as partners are concerned, J. P. Beaumont is bad news. *Besides*, I told myself, *Malcolm Lawrence is a little old guy whose bones would probably fly apart if anyone gave him a hard shake.* I was pretty sure I could handle anything Lawrence dished out.

Furthermore, and this was the real deciding factor, Wingard Court North was only a matter of blocks away from where I was at that moment. Why fool around?

In actual fact, I didn't even make it all the way to Wingard Court before I ran into Malcolm Lawrence himself, accompanied by the two dogs. The three of them were hobbling along on North 137th when I turned in off Greenwood. I parked the car about a block ahead of them and waited until they caught up.

"Good afternoon, Mr. Lawrence," I said, fighting to be heard over the yapping of the dogs.

He yanked on the two leashes. Eventually the dogs quieted and sat. Lawrence looked at me in seemingly embarrassed befuddlement. "Detective . . ."

"Detective Beaumont," I supplied.

"That's right. What can I do for you?"

I didn't beat around the bush. "You can tell me why you lied to me, Mr. Lawrence."

"I don't know what you're talking about."

"Yes, you do. You told my partner and me that you went to bed before eleven the night Agnes Ferman died. You also said that you didn't see any vehicles at Agnes Ferman's house that Sunday night other than her sister's Camry. The problem is, Mr. Lawrence, I have a witness who places you on the porch of Agnes Ferman's house well after eleven."

"I didn't really lie to you," Lawrence said quickly. "I was actually lying to Becky. You just got caught up in the middle of it."

"You were lying to your wife?"

"I told you," he said. "She's the jealous type. Most men my age probably would be complimented, but Becky goes to bed so dang early. And after she does, there's nobody to talk to or nothin'. It just gets kinda lonesome, is all."

"Lonesome?"

He nodded. "So me and the puppies here took to going over to Aggie's house of an evening, just to visit and have ourselves a little nightcap sometimes. Just one, mind you. Never had two drinks in a row. Just one to sorta relax you, if you know what I mean. And over the months, Aggie and I just got to be . . . well, you know . . . friends."

"Friends?"

"Well, maybe a bit more than friends," he admitted. "She was lonesome, too, and one thing more or less led to another. Believe me, Detective Beaumont, for her age, she was a good-looking woman. Good bones, you know. And sexy as all get out."

"So," I said, "were you the only one?"

"The only one what?" Malcolm asked.

"The only randy neighbor who was messing around with Agnes Ferman?"

"Detective Beaumont," he objected, "I resent your saying any such thing. I'll have you know Aggie Ferman was a real lady. She might have had herself a boyfriend or two, but she was no two-timer."

There were several descriptions that I thought might well have applied to Agnes Ferman. "Lady" wasn't one of them. And two-timing was exactly what she had done when she had her husband at home all the while she was messing around with Forrest Considine at work. If that wasn't two-timing, what was?

"What if there were others?" I insisted. "What if

one of your rivals heard about you and he was the jealous sort?"

"We were very careful," Malcolm said. "I'm sure no one else knew."

"What about your wife?" I asked. "Did she know?"

"Of course not. Becky has no idea . . ." Stopping abruptly, he paled. "You wouldn't tell her, would you?"

"I might," I said.

"Please," he begged. "You don't understand. She really is jealous, and I've been walking on eggshells with that woman for the last month. If she found out about Aggie, she'd blow sky-high. Even with Aggie dead, she'd probably throw me out of the house. What would I do then? End up sleeping down at the Union Gospel Mission? Don't tell her, Detective Beaumont. Please."

"But what if she already knows?"

In asking the question, I posed it to Malcolm Lawrence and to myself at the same time. He looked stunned. "She couldn't!" he exclaimed.

"Are you sure?" I asked. "Just how jealous is she?"

He shook his head. "You're not sayin' that Becky would've . . . No, you can't mean that."

With that, he jerked on the leashes. He and the dogs set off for home at a surprisingly swift pace. I climbed back into the Town Car and followed, passing them eventually, and then parallel-parking in front of the Lawrences' house. Getting out of the Town Car I noticed that Agnes Ferman's yard across the street was still sealed off with crime-scene tape.

By the time Lawrence and the dogs arrived, I was

standing waiting for them at the end of the sidewalk. "Please don't say nothin' to her," Lawrence said again. "If you need me to, I'll be glad to testify that the other guy was here that night, the guy in the Lincoln. I can also tell you about the fight he and Agnes had. It was a doozy. Maybe he's the one who come back later and set fire to the place."

"Maybe," I agreed. "Did you happen to hear what they were arguing about?" I asked.

Malcolm nodded. "Couldn't help but," he said. "The man called her all kinds of ugly names and a blackmailer besides. He was wrong about that, I'm sure. Aggie was a fine person. A lovin', kind person. She wouldn't ever in a million years do someone that way."

You'd be surprised, I thought. I said, "Look, Mr. Lawrence, I've talked to several people in the course of this investigation all of whom knew Agnes Ferman. You happen to be the only one who holds her in high regard. Unless I'm mistaken, your own wife is included in the camp of Agnes Ferman detractors."

"Becky didn't know Aggie the way I did."

"I suppose not."

"You know what I mean. She was nice to me."

"How nice?" I asked. "What if she had threatened to tell your wife everything that was going on between you? What would have happened then?"

"She never did," Malcolm insisted. "And she wouldn't have."

"But what if she had? What would you have done then? Wouldn't you have had to take measures to protect yourself?"

"You mean would I have hurt her? Me? Please,

Detective Beaumont. You've got to believe me. Aggie Ferman meant the world to me. I never would have done the least thing to harm her."

"And your position is that she was fine when you left her home later that night?"

"Absolutely."

"What time was that? Really, now, Mr. Lawrence. No more lies about being too old to stay up for the eleven o'clock news."

"Midnight," he said. "It was midnight when I left."

"What about vehicles?"

"There was a big Lincoln. A silver Lincoln. The one that guy came and left in."

"And after he stumbled over your dog . . ."

"Dogs," he corrected. "He got tangled with both dogs, but Tuffy's the one he stepped on."

"After he stepped on Tuffy and left, did he come back?"

"No," Malcolm said. "Not that I noticed."

"And when you got back home to your own house, was your wife asleep?"

"I don't know."

"What do you mean, you don't know? Wasn't she in bed when you got there?"

"We don't sleep in the same bedroom," Malcolm admitted in a small voice. "We haven't for years. When I retired, she told me she was retirin', too. Said she'd still cook and clean for me, but there were some things she wasn't doing anymore. Ever. That's when she moved into the other bedroom."

"Was that the difference between your wife and

Agnes Ferman?" I asked. "Aggie would put out and Becky wouldn't?"

Surprisingly enough, Malcolm Lawrence burst into tears then. Dragging his two dogs with him, he walked over to my rented Town Car and stood leaning against the door, sobbing into his arms. There was nothing for me to do but stand and wait.

"Just because you get old don't mean you dry up," he said eventually. "Everybody acts like sex is somethin' that just goes away with time, but it don't. Leastwise, it didn't for me. I still wanted it. I begged Becky to see her doctor and find out if there wasn't somethin' she could take, some of them hormones or somethin', that would give her back her sex drive. She told me the only thing wrong with her sex drive was me. Like it was all my fault hers was gone. I did without for a long time, Detective Beaumont. Until just a year or so ago. That's when I hooked up with Aggie.

"I knew it could never be more than what it was, just a quick little squeeze and such after dark when everyone else was asleep. But I have to tell you, Aggie Ferman made me feel like a man again. She made me feel like I counted for somethin' more than just my pension and my social security check."

"What about Becky?" I asked.

"Yeah," a voice from behind me said. "What about me?"

Malcolm and I both turned. A few feet away, Becky Lawrence, her hair once again in curlers, stood on the Lawrences' front porch. She was a fairly small woman holding a very large gun—a shotgun.

"Becky," Lawrence croaked. "What are you doing with that thing? Somebody might get hurt."

"Somebody's already been hurt," she said furiously. "And it's me. All I asked of you was a little self-control."

"But twenty years," Malcolm argued. "Isn't that asking a lot?"

"You promised to love, honor, and obey," she said. "I don't remember hearing anything that said you could go running around dropping your dipstick into the nearest honey pot just because you weren't getting any at home. So I fixed it," Becky added. "Fixed her, anyway. But it seems to me I should have fixed you, too. Put you out of your misery. Ever since Agnes Ferman died you've been moping around here like your best friend was gone and your whole life was over. I aim to see to it that it is."

As she raised the gun to fire, I had only a split second in which to react. I grabbed Malcolm Lawrence by the arm and pulled him down with me, slamming him facefirst into the gravel. "Crawl!" I commanded. "Go."

Dragging the dogs along with him, he scrambled under the car. With my nose and face scraping the dirt, I did the same. The explosion came a mere fraction of a second after we both hit the ground.

I know a little about guns and recoil. I expected that first shot to go wild—both high and wide—but it didn't. I heard the potentially lethal spray of buckshot spatter into the side of the car. Heard the windows shatter. With terrified yips, the two dogs scrambled forward, passing Malcolm in the process, until they were pulling him by the leash, rather than the other way around.

Emerging on the far side of the car, I saw Malcolm sitting with his back against the car, holding one hand against his chest and gasping for breath. He had let go of the leashes, and the two dogs were long gone.

"What's the matter?" I asked.

"My heart . . ." he managed. His face had gone gray. He could barely talk. "Pills . . ." he added. ". . . in my pocket." He patted his shirt.

I fumbled the little prescription bottle out of his shirt pocket, fought my way past the childproof lid, and passed him one of the tiny, lifesaving nitro pills. He put it in his mouth and then closed both eyes.

"Malcolm," I said. "Listen to me. Is that your gun she has?"

He nodded.

"Do you think she fired both barrels at once?"

"No," he said. "Just one."

Damn!

For the second time in as many days, I used my cell phone to dial 911. "Nine-one-one," the operator said. "What are you reporting?"

I raised my head far enough to peer through the driver's-side back window. Becky Lawrence was no longer standing on the front porch. She had taken the shotgun and disappeared into the interior of the house.

"We've got an armed woman barricaded in a house on Wingard Court North," I told her. "The six-hundred block of Wingard Court North."

"Sir, that incident has already been reported. Units are on their way . . ."

"Tell them to send an ambulance as well as patrol cars," I barked. "I've got a man here suffering chest pains and shortness of breath."

"And you are?"

I told her who I was.

"And what is your position?" the operator asked.

"We're behind a car that's parked in front of the house," I told her. "We're pinned down behind a blue Lincoln Town Car with rental plates."

Just as I said those words, I had a clear vision of the rental agreement. I remembered the line I had initialed, refusing the Loss Damage Waiver. I remembered thinking, *I'm a safe driver. Why would I need that?* Why would I need that indeed! A rental car thoroughly sprayed with shotgun pellets was going to be damned difficult to explain when it came time to return it.

"And the shooter's position?" the operator asked.

"She's gone into the house," I said. "We can't see her now. She could be anywhere inside."

By then I could hear sirens. Medic One arrived first but the aid car stopped out on 137th. They waited there for assistance without ever venturing onto Wingard. Behind the aid car came a pair of blue-and-whites. The patrol cars pulled up close behind us and a pair of uniformed officers scrambled out.

"Is anyone hurt?" one of the uniforms asked as he reached us.

"Mr. Lawrence here is having chest pains," I told the patrolman. "If you can, help him over to the ambulance. Then, when you come back, if you happen to have an extra Kevlar vest just lying around, I'd really appreciate being able to borrow it."

The two cops exchanged disparaging looks. "Detectives," one of them muttered with a shake of his head. "I'll radio back to the lieutenant and see what we can do."

As they headed away, hustling Lawrence into the patrol car, I was dismayed to see the Lawrences' front door come open. I don't remember taking my 9mm out of its holster, but by the time the screen door burst open, the weapon was in my hand. I raised the gun, expecting that I'd have to lay down a fusillade of protective fire to cover the retreat of the uniformed officers who were moving Malcolm Lawrence to safety. To my surprise, when Becky Lawrence appeared on the porch, the shotgun was nowhere in sight. One hand was empty. The other held something that looked like an ordinary overnight bag.

"Drop it, Mrs. Lawrence," I ordered. "Put your hands up in the air so I can see them!"

Becky complied at once. She dropped the bag. It landed on the clasp, breaking it open, and sending a cascade of metal hair curlers rolling across the porch, down the steps, and onto the sidewalk. While Malcolm and I had been huddled behind the Town Car fumbling for his nitroglycerin pill, his wife had been inside the house, calmly taking the curlers out of her hair. She had combed out the curls and even put on some lipstick.

Holding my gun in one hand and fumbling out flexicuffs with the other, I went forward to meet her. "As soon as I saw you drive up," she said. "I knew it was over. As long as you and that lady detective didn't come back, I figured I was all right."

Becky and I rode into the department in one of the patrol cars, with me in front and with her locked behind the screen in the backseat. Once in the Public Safety Building, I took her into an interview room. Because she waived her right to an attorney, we went at it right away. She was more than happy, proud almost, to confess to Agnes Ferman's murder.

"Why?" I asked her when she admitted she had set fire to the couch. "Why did you do it?"

"I may not have wanted Malcolm anymore," she told me, "but I sure as hell didn't want anyone else to have him."

Kramer, showing his face for the first time since the Bellevue crime scene, took it upon himself to observe the entire questioning process although he did have brains enough to keep quiet most of the time.

"A real nut case," he said to me, once a pair of officers were dispatched to take Becky Lawrence down to the King County Jail and book her on an open charge of murder. "Sounds to me as though she was more upset about Agnes Ferman borrowing the lawn mower than she was about the woman screwing her husband."

"Becky's not nearly as crazy as she'd like you to believe," I said. "I think if we do a little digging, we'll be able to show premeditation. You heard what she said. She knew about Malcolm's affair with Agnes for at least six months before she did anything about it. The thing that put her over the edge was hearing Frederick Considine's argument with Agnes Ferman. The only reason she did the murder then was because she expected we'd blame the whole thing on him."

"Well," Kramer said grudgingly. "You didn't. Good job. I'm glad to have that case cleared, but this Lone Rangering stuff has to cease."

Lone Rangering is something I had been accused of before on occasion, but considering all the mitigating circumstances this time it made me see red, even if the man did have a point.

There comes a time in every man's life when he realizes that his childhood dreams are never going to come true. No matter what, he's never going to be president; never going to play second base for the Yankees; never going to walk on the moon. And if you're reasonably squared away when that realization hits you, you're all right with it. Your life is your life and that's okay.

That day on Lake Chelan, I had tried to explain all that to my grandmother. Now, listening to Kramer, I tried explaining it to myself. It wasn't working. My one ambition in life had always been to be a good cop. There were several underlying and accompanying assumptions. One was that being a good cop matters. That police officers save people's lives and make this country a better place.

Maybe those assumptions sound stupidly idealistic, but they were mine nonetheless. I had done my best for twenty-odd years with the expectation that when it came time to leave, I'd do it under exemplary circumstances, with a boring retirement dinner complete with typically boring law-enforcement high jinks, with rubber chicken, plenty of rotten jokes, and even worse speeches. I had never once expected to be run out on a rail by a supposed superior who was less of a police officer than I was in every way.

"You've got to stop running all over the place acting like you're a one-man crime fighting unit, Beaumont." Kramer continued. "We've got procedures for that. And partners. You're not supposed to be out on your own like you have been the past two days. If it doesn't stop, I'll have you up before a board of inquiry on breach-of-duty charges."

"Like hell you will!"

"Detective Beaumont, I—"

"You'll do nothing of the kind, Kramer, you jackass! I'm not going up before a board of inquiry for anything. I'm pulling the pin," I told him. "I quit!"

The words were out of my mouth before I knew it and before I realized how much I meant them. "In the last twenty-four hours, my Lone Rangering, as you call it, has saved the lives of at least three people. So you can stick your bloody procedures where the sun don't shine, buster, and leave me the hell alone!"

With that, I turned and stalked away. I didn't stop to check out that one last time. I didn't have to. Sergeant Chuck Grayson, the night-shift desk sergeant, had heard every word.

It was almost nine as I headed up 3rd Avenue. I walked as far as University. Then, on a whim, I turned up the hill. Sue's folks and kids were still at the Four Seasons. If I was no longer going to be answering my own phone at the department, I needed to stop by and tell them what was going on in person.

Hank Hinkle came downstairs as soon as I rang their room. The two of us sat in the Garden Court and talked. "I hope your quitting doesn't have anything to do with what happened to Sue," he said. "She wouldn't have wanted that."

"No," I said, "the two aren't related." But even as I said it, I could see that wasn't the case. It had everything to do with Sue and almost nothing at all to do with Paul Kramer. I didn't need some half-baked squad commander to point out my failures. I could do an admirable job of that on my own. Sue Danielson was dead. My partner was dead and for one reason only—because I hadn't saved her.

CHAPTER 21

WHILE I WAS TALKING WITH HANK HINKLE, I REALized I'd had nothing to eat all day and stopped long enough for a bowl of soup. After I left the Four Seasons, I considered tracking down an AA meeting on my way home, not because I needed a drink, but because I needed a place to talk. In the end, I decided I was too tired and went straight on home. It's a good thing, too. If I hadn't, I would have missed the impromptu meeting that was going on at my condo.

I'm not sure who called everyone together, but when I walked up to the door in the hallway, I could tell by the murmur of voices coming from inside, that there were several people waiting for me. Ralph's girlfriend, Mary Greengo, heard my key in the lock and met me at the door. She's a lithe blonde with a perpetual upbeat way about her. She drew me inside with a hug. "Thank heaven you're here," she said. "Did you have something to eat?"

I nodded. "Well, come on in then," she added, "I think almost everyone is here."

And they were. Ron's girls, Heather and Tracie, were sacked out on the floor in the den, sound asleep in front of a silenced television set. Ron's chair was parked at the far end of the room where he and Ralph Ames appeared to be deep in conversation. On the long upholstered benches of the window seat sat both my grandmother, Beverly Piedmont, and Lars Jenssen, my AA sponsor.

Even if all the people involved are friends, it's still a bit disconcerting to walk into your own living room and find it seems to have developed a life of its own by declaring a party in your absence. I was too tired to be gracious about it. "Don't let me stand in your way," I groused, "but if you folks don't mind, I believe I'll go straight to bed."

"Don't do that, Jonas," my grandmother said. "We've all been worried about you. Ron told us you had left the department earlier. When you didn't come right home, we didn't know what to think."

"Left the department as in coming home for the night?" I asked. "Or as in I quit?"

"Both," Ron admitted. "Chuck Grayson called and told me what was up. I'm the one who called everybody else. You didn't mean it, did you?"

"Yes, I meant it," I said.

That pronouncement was met with a period of silence. "Well, good for you," Lars said finally, hobbling across the room and giving me a spine-cracking whack on the back. "Congradulations," he told me. "Been sayin' for years that you work too dad-gummed hard for your own good. It's 'bout time you stopped to smell them roses."

"You had a phone call a few minutes ago," Ralph interjected, handing me a note. "You may want to return this as soon as possible."

The name on the note was Bridget Hargrave along with a telephone number. The moment I saw it, I felt sick. I had been so tied up with everything else I had completely forgotten about Jimmy Greenjeans. Seeing his girlfriend's name in Ralph's neat printing gave me a nudge of awful premonition. "If you'll excuse me," I said. "I believe I'll return this from the phone in the bedroom."

Dialing the number I tried to prepare myself for news that would be, in its own way, just as awful as the doctor saying Sue was dead. No doubt Jimmy Greenjeans was dead, too. There had simply been some kind of delay in finding his body.

"Bridget?" I said when she answered. "Detective Beaumont here." Old habits do die hard.

"Thanks for calling. I had to talk to you."

"Why? What's going on?"

"Jimmy called me about an hour ago from somewhere out on the coast . . ."

I closed my eyes and said a silent prayer of thanksgiving. Jimmy wasn't dead after all. Somehow he had managed to outwit David Half Moon's curse.

"That's great," I said. "I'm delighted to hear it."

"You may be, but I'm not," Bridget said. "He gave me some bullshit story about having to go out there with some woman—Carla Something. Jimmy had some lame excuse about having to meet with Carla's father."

"Her name's Darla," I corrected. "Darla Cunningham."

"That's right. So you *do* know her then," Bridget said.

"Yes."

"And is it true that Jimmy had to go see this man, or is it just a way of avoiding meeting my mother?"

"What did Jimmy say?"

"He says he had to go, that it was a matter of life and death, but that he made a promise—a sacred promise—never to tell anyone what went on. I don't know what to think. Should I believe him or not? What if he and Carla . . . Darla . . . have something going and Jimmy just doesn't have guts enough to tell me?"

I could see now what had happened. Jimmy had called Darla and she had immediately packed him off to Taholah for a purification ceremony. And, since Jimmy was still alive, I had to believe that Henry Leaping Deer's promised cure had worked.

"Here's my advice," I told Bridget. "If I were you, I'd take Jimmy's word that he had to go out to the coast to see this man. And I'd also take his promise about not telling very seriously. If he swore not to divulge what went on, you're better off not knowing."

"I shouldn't ask him ever?"

If nothing else, I had learned that a shaman's curse could be tricky. And long-lasting. "Not ever," I said.

"And you don't think I have a right to be mad at him for standing me up and making us worry so much?"

"Whatever you do," I counseled, "don't be mad. As far as I can see, you're lucky that Jimmy Greenjeans is still alive."

"Really?"

"Really."

I put down the phone. *One for our side*, I told Sue Danielson silently. *You and I saved Jimmy Greenjeans' life as surely as I lost yours.*

Swallowing hard, I made my way back out to the living room where the others were still waiting.

"Any word on services?" Beverly Piedmont asked.

"Hank says they're going to have only a memorial service here in Seattle the day after tomorrow, at a funeral home up in Lake City. It'll be at two o'clock in the afternoon. The funeral and actual burial won't happen until they take the body back home to Ohio."

"What about a place to gather after the memorial service?" Mary Greengo asked. "If you wanted to invite people over here to the Regrade Room for a reception, I'd be glad to handle refreshments."

"I don't know. That's very kind of you. I can check with Sue's parents in the morning," I said, trying to waffle. "And the common room may already be booked."

"It isn't," Ron said. "I checked with the manager a little while ago before the girls and I came upstairs. Dick Mathers said that as far as he knew, the room was free for the next three days in a row. I asked him to put a tentative reserve on it until I tell him otherwise."

"All right," I said. I was thinking about the last funeral I had attended for a fallen police officer.

That one, held at the enormous Mount Zion Baptist Church on Capitol Hill, had been standing room only. "The only problem is, I don't know if the Regrade Room will be big enough."

"It's spring," Ron said. "Any spillover can end up outside on the recreation deck."

"How many do you think?" Mary Greengo asked.

I shrugged my shoulders. "I have no idea," I said.

"Probably a bunch," Ron told her.

"We were watching the news a few minutes ago," Ralph said. "I just can't get over the thing about the drugs."

"Drugs?" I asked. "What drugs?"

"Haven't you heard? The crime-scene investigators were going through Sue's house today and they came upon two brand-new roll-aboard suitcases. They were gifts, evidently, and still had tags on them with both Chris and Jared's names on them. The problem is, as soon as one of Janice Morraine's investigators picked one up, he knew there was something wrong with it. The cases were way too heavy to be empty. So the investigator slit open the bottom. Guess what he found inside?"

"I give up."

"Coke," Ralph said. "Pure cocaine."

"Are you kidding?"

Ron looked at me and frowned. "If that news is already on TV, how come you didn't know about it?"

"I'm out of the loop," I said. "That's one of the reasons I quit. You mean you've heard about it, too?"

Ron nodded. "I thought everybody had. The way the boys from the DEA have it pegged, Richie Danielson was on a delivery trip with a set schedule and a set itinerary. He was planning on using the boys for cover. As soon as Sue altered the plan ever so slightly, things fell apart. Richie must have realized that if he couldn't make his connections at the appointed times, he'd lose big-time. No wonder he went off the deep end. The amount of coke involved would have brought a significant amount of change. It must have driven him crazy to have Sue screwing up the whole program for the simple and not-very-complicated reason that she didn't want her sons having unexcused absences from school."

I was still trying to come to grips with the reality of it. "That's why he shot her, over drugs?"

"That's the way it looks," Ron said.

"And he was going to use the boys for mules?"

Ron nodded.

"That rotten son of a bitch!" I muttered. "Dying's way too good for scum like that."

"I agree," Ron said. He had rolled his chair toward the den, most likely intent on waking the girls and taking them back downstairs. In the doorway, though, he stopped and turned back to me.

"By the way," he added, "I thought you'd like to know that Amy and I finally managed to agree on a name. We wanted to name the baby after you, but Amy balked at Jonas. She said it would probably open the poor kid up to a lifetime of Jonas-and-the-whale jokes."

"She's not wrong there," I told him. "That's one of the reasons I switched to plain initials. What did you decide?"

"Jared," Ron answered. "Jared Piedmont Peters.

That way, we can call him J.P., too, for short. What do you think?"

I thought it was wonderful, but a simple "Thank-you," was all I could manage.

"Speaking of Jared," Ralph interjected, sensing that I was out on an emotional limb and in need of rescue. "What's going to become of those boys?" he asked. "Is there anything I can do to help?"

That was vintage Ralph Ames. Give him a problem involving kids, and he'll take the bit in his teeth to get it solved. His diversion gave me an opportunity to get my voice back under control.

"It sounds to me as though it's all pretty well set," I told the roomful of people. "Chris and Jared will go back home to Ohio with Sue's folks. Hank Hinkle told me they had been thinking about selling the family home and moving into a condo. Now, he says, they'll just stay put."

"Good," Ralph said. "Glad to hear it."

Ron and the girls left about then, and everyone else followed suit a few minutes later. Ralph and Mary took my grandmother home. Lars Jenssen walked. And I went to bed. I slept for twelve hours straight. When I finally clambered out of bed at eleven the next morning, I had some coffee and toast. Someone—most likely Ralph—had restocked the larder. After breakfast, I went in to the department to close up shop.

Watty Watkins looked up and smiled when I showed up at his desk. "Hey, Beau," he said. "Hope you've changed your mind about pulling the pin."

"No," I told him, handing over my departmental

laptop. "I came to check this in and then I'm going to pack. You wouldn't happen to have any more of those empty boxes, would you?"

He nodded and went to get me some from the supply room. Minutes later, I was in Sue's and my cubicle packing up more than twenty years' worth of accumulated junk. The phone rang several times while I was going through my desk. One caller was an agent for the IRS who had read about Agnes Ferman's money in the paper and was hoping to get a shot at some of it.

"Good luck," I said. "It looks to me as though the bulk of the cash came from well beyond the seven-year statute of limitations. And I'll bet that what she's been receiving in the annuity since 1993 has all been properly documented."

The IRS agent was not so easily dissuaded. "How do I go about gaining access to your official records?" she asked.

"As of today, there should be another detective assigned to the case. You'll have to check with him—or her."

Audrey Cummings called. I told her about Jimmy Greenjeans, and she promised to be in touch with Darla Cunningham and with Henry Leaping Deer. "Don't let it go," I warned.

"I won't," she said. "I had already made plans to go down to the coast this weekend. And I'm still going. I was actually going to leave tonight, but now I won't leave until tomorrow afternoon. After Sue's services."

"And what about that investigator?" I asked. "The one in Harborview. What's his name again?"

"You mean Dirk, Dirk Matthews. It looks now as though he's going to make it. But he's lost several fingers and part of one hand. I suspect his juggling days are over. Maybe his investigator days as well."

"Talk to him," I said. "He may want to make his own pilgrimage down to Taholah."

Eventually, all the boxes were pretty much packed and labeled. Mine sat in one corner of the cubicle and Sue's in another. That done, I turned on the desktop computer one last time to finish up the necessary reports and to sign off on my cases. When those were done, I called up Sue's case file. I had given a statement to both the officers on the scene and later to detectives. Now that I'd had a decent night's rest, I wanted to check the reports to see if they were reasonably accurate.

They weren't. I printed a hard copy of Sue's file and then stormed down the hall to Kramer's Fishbowl. "What the hell do you mean classifying Sue's death as a DV? It should have been line of duty."

"Richard Danielson was her ex-husband," Kramer replied. "Of course it was domestic violence."

"It may have been one, but it was also the other," I insisted. "Richie Danielson was a drug dealer. Sue was doing her job when she kept him from making those deliveries, when she kept him from using his own children to transport drugs. Sue may have been off duty at the time of her death, but the real reason Richie killed her was because she had fouled up his chance to make a big score."

"She didn't know about that," Kramer argued. "The drugs weren't found until much later. I'm calling it a domestic and that's how it's going to stay."

"No," I said, "it isn't. Detective Danielson was my partner. By the time I reached her, she was hurt so bad she could barely hold my Glock, but the last thing she did is what partners are supposed to do for one another. When I went down the hall after Richie, Sue was my backup, Kramer, off duty or not. She told me that if Richie made it past me, she'd make sure he didn't make it past her."

"Beaumont," Kramer said, "you're way too emotional about all this . . . If you'll just calm down . . ."

"Emotional?" I demanded, hearing my voice rising. "You damn well better bet I'm emotional. In fact, I'm more than emotional. Sue was my partner and a hero. So help me God, she and her kids are going to get every honor she deserves or I'm going to know the reason why. Either you change this DV label, Kramer, or I'll go up and down the chain of command until I find someone who will. And when I'm finished, if you're still squad commander, I'll eat my fucking shoe."

With that. I sailed the paper across the desk at him and I left. Sergeant Watkins was sitting at his desk when I stormed out.

"Way to go, Beau," he muttered after me under his breath. "Way to go!"

CHAPTER 22

FUNERALS AND MEMORIAL SERVICES ARE SOMETHING that have to be gotten through. They honor the dead, but they're *for* the living. On Friday, we all did the best we could. The funeral home was packed, wall to wall. As expected, police officers came from all over the region to honor Detective Sue Daniel-son. The picture of her, on an easel at the front of the room, was the official portrait taken when she graduated from the academy. All I could think of as I sat there looking at it was how very young she was and what a waste it was that she was dead.

The reception in the Regrade Room at Belltown Terrace was also jammed with people spilling out onto the Pickleball court and running track. Mary and her staff did an excellent job, but still when they ran out of dishes and glasses, they had to ask for help. I wasn't surprised to find my grandmother in the party room kitchen busily washing plates, glasses, and silverware. What did surprise me was seeing Lars Jenssen in there with her, armed with a dish towel and playing wiper to my grandmother's capable washer. At the time I noticed that her face was beet red, but I chalked it up to having her hands in warm dishwater.

I had heard that Richie Danielson's remains were being shipped back to Alaska for burial. I asked both Jared and Chris if they wanted to go. If they had wanted to, and if Sue's parents hadn't been able to spring for the airfare, I would have, but neither one of them said yes. I didn't blame them.

I'm not entirely sure how I made it through the next two weeks. I was at loose ends and in a funk. Not working for the first time in my adult life, I had no idea what to do with myself or with my life. Ralph suggested I go with him to a driving range and try my hand at hitting golf balls, but that didn't grab me. Once we did go out for an evening cruise on Cassandra Wolcott's forty-two-foot Chris-Craft, but I'm afraid I was pretty much a wet blanket. Cassie Wolcott may be great, but she's not for me. I mostly did crossword puzzles, went to a lot of AA meetings and tried to stay out of bars.

A week after the funeral my phone rang early on a Monday morning. "Beaumont?" a voice asked.

I was still trying to get used to that missing "Detective." "Yes," I said.

"Chief Rankin here. How are you doing?"

"All right," I said.

"Good. Glad to hear it. The reason I'm calling is, we're getting ready for the Police Officers Memorial Service at Police Plaza. Sue's name is going on the wall. We asked her parents if either one or both of the boys could come back out for the service, but Mr. Hinkle said they just couldn't swing it. So I was wondering if you'd be willing to come to the service in their stead."

Years ago, a fraternal organization called International Footprinters—made up of retired and active police officers as well as interested citizens—started sponsoring nationwide memorial services in honor of fallen police officers. In recent years the City of Seattle has assumed sponsorship of the local service.

"I'll be there," I said.

As soon as I got off the phone with Rankin, I called Cincinnati and talked to Mary Beth Hinkle. I offered to send tickets so the boys could attend as well.

"You shouldn't do that," Mary Beth said. "You've already done so much, what with the hotel rooms, and the reception, and all."

"It's only money," I told her. "Your daughter was a hero, Mary Beth. Those boys have every right to be proud of her. This is an honor for her and for them, too. I'd like them to be part of it."

"All right, then," she agreed. "I'll ask them as soon as they get home from school. If they want to come, we'll let them."

And so, on a glorious May evening exactly two weeks after Sue's funeral, we all assembled in the Police Plaza at 4th and James. The Hinkles were there along with Jared and Chris and me, as well as any number of local dignitaries, from the mayor and police chief right on down. There were other relatives on hand as well—surviving family members of police officers who had died in previous years, including a gangly but poised African American teenager named Benjamin Weston whose father, Officer Benjamin Harrison Weston, had died two years earlier.

The keynote speaker was a sixty-three-year-old man whose father had died when he was only eight. When he spoke of missing his father—of never having had a chance to get to know him—I knew once again that those kinds of hurts never go away, no matter how old you get.

When the ceremony was over, a suddenly grownup Jared Danielson turned to me and shook my hand. "I've been thinking about what you said, about me being like my mother. And I think that's what I want to do," he added. "Be a cop. Like her and like you."

I can't help it. I'm a sentimental slob. I teared right up.

"Good for you, Jared," I said.

A little later, someone came up behind me and tapped me on the shoulder. "Mr. Beaumont?"

"Yes." I turned around. The guy looked familiar, but I had no idea who he was.

"I don't think we've ever been introduced," he said. "My name is Ross Connors."

As soon as I heard the name, I realized I was speaking to the attorney general of the state of Washington. He held out his hand. "Glad to meet you, Mr. Connors," I told him.

"Likewise," he said, "but please, call me Ross. I've been hearing lots of good things about you from some of my folks. Now that you're retired from SPD, several of the boys on my homicide investigation team . . . squad . . . have been asking about you, wanting to know if we could recruit you. Have you ever considered working for us on our statewide hit squad?"

"No," I said. "Not really."

"We always have a spot for really experienced investigators. If you're at all interested, I'd be happy to have the department head give you the sales pitch. What do you think?"

We were still standing on the plaza, but the crowd had thinned enough so that I had a clear view of the spot on the wall where Suzanne Michelle Danielson's name had been chiseled into the gray granite.

"I'll think about it, but let me ask you a question," I said. "Do your people work partners?"

"Sometimes," Connors answered, "but not necessarily. Why?"

"Because," I said, "J. P. Beaumont doesn't work partners anymore."

Here's a sneak preview of
J. A. Jance's new novel

JUDGMENT CALL

Coming soon in hardcover from
William Morrow
An Imprint of HarperCollins*Publsihers*

LATE ON A THURSDAY AFTERNOON, SHERIFF JOANNA Brady sat at her desk in the Cochise County Justice Center outside Bisbee, Arizona, and studied the duty roster her chief deputy, Tom Hadlock, had dropped off an hour earlier.

Her former chief deputy, Frank Montoya, had been lured away from her department with the offer of a new job—chief of police in nearby Sierra Vista. Looking for a replacement, Joanna had tapped her jail commander to step into the job. Tom was well qualified on paper, but he had found Frank's tenure as chief deputy to be a tough act to follow.

When Frank had been Joanna's second-in-command, he had handily juggled several sets of seemingly unrelated responsibilities—media relations, routine administrative chores, and information technology issues—with unflappable ease. Now, after more than a year in the position, Tom was finally growing into the job and had a far better handle on what needed to be done than he had in the beginning. Unfortunately, he still wasn't quite up to Frank Montoya standards.

After months of struggle, Tom had finally tamed the duty roster monster, handing Joanna a flawlessly executed copy of the upcoming month's schedule two days before she absolutely had to have it in hand. At this point, he was hard at work preparing a first go-down of the next year's budget. Joanna knew that he had placed several calls to Frank asking for pointers on both the budget and IT concerns, and she was grateful Frank had been willing to help.

The one place where Tom was still sadly lacking was in media relations. Faced with a camera or a reporter, the former jail commander morphed from your basic macho tough-guy into a spluttering, tongue-tied neophyte. Six months of participation in a Toastmasters group in Sierra Vista had helped some, but it would take lots more time and effort before Tom Hadlock would be fully at ease in front of a bank of microphones and cameras.

When the phone on Joanna's desk rang, she glanced at her watch to check the time before picking it up. At home her husband, Butch Dixon, was battling a tough copyediting deadline on his latest crime novel. As a consequence, Joanna was on tap to pick up the kids. Her nearly sixteen-year-old daughter, Jenny, worked three hours a day after school as an aide in a local veterinarian's office. With equal parts anticipation and dread, Joanna was looking forward to the day, coming all too soon, when Jenny would have a driver's license of her own. Once that happened, driving her back and forth to work and school activities would no longer be a necessity.

Joanna and Butch's two-year-old, Dennis, spent five hours each afternoon at a preschool that operated in conjunction with their church in Old Bisbee. Dennis was a gregarious kid. When the older members of what Joanna termed the "gang of four"—Jenny and the housekeeper's two grandsons—had gone off to school in the fall, Dennis had been lost on his own. When a spot had opened up in the preschool program at Tombstone Canyon United Methodist, they had signed him up for a half-day program four days a week.

Joanna's first thought was that the phone call would involve some hitch in picking up the kids. Or maybe Butch needed her to stop by the store to pick up some last-minute item for dinner before she went home to High Lonesome Ranch. When she answered, however, it turned out that the call had nothing to do with the home front and everything to do with work.

"Jury's back," Kristin Gregovich said.

Kristin was Joanna's secretary, and the returning jury in question was only a few steps away from Joanna's office at the Cochise County Justice Center, a joint facility that not only housed the sheriff's department and the jail, but also the Cochise County superior court offices and courtrooms. The case currently being tried there was one in which Joanna Brady had played a pivotal role.

More than a year earlier, an elderly woman named Philippa Brinson had gone AWOL from what was supposedly a state-of-the-art Alzheimer's group home near the Cochise County town of Palominas. Sheriff Brady had been one of several officers who had responded to the original Missing Persons call on Philippa Brinson.

But Caring Friends had turned out to be a far worse can of worms than anyone expected. For one thing, arriving officers had been dumbfounded by the appallingly unsanitary conditions in what was supposed to be a health facility. The kitchen had been a food handler's nightmare, and they had found evidence that helpless residents had been routinely strapped to beds and chairs and left, trapped in their own bodily filth, for hours on end. A subsequent investigation had brought evidence to light that several Caring Friends patients had died as a result of serious infections that started out as bedsores.

It was while Joanna and her deputies were at the crime scene that they had been confronted by Alma DeLong, the owner of Caring Friends as well as several other Alzheimer's treatment facilities. Outraged to find police officers on the premises, she had launched a physical attack against them and had been hauled off to jail in a Cochise County patrol car.

Hours later, Philippa Brinson had been found safe. Confined to a chair in her room, she had managed to use nail clippers to cut away her restraints. Out on the highway, she had hitched a ride into Bisbee and had made her way to the old high school building. According to her thinking, she had been on her way to work in her old office, a place from which she had retired some thirty-five years earlier. After that misadventure, she was placed in the care of a niece and had gone off to a different facility—hopefully a better one—in Phoenix, while Joanna's department had been left to clean up the mess revealed by Philippa's brief disappearance.

Alma DeLong, arrogant and utterly unrepentant, had brought in high-powered attorneys to fight the charges lodged against her. For years, Joanna had held a fairly low opinion of Arlee Jones, the local "good old boy" county attorney, and that antipathy went both ways. The county attorney didn't approve of Joanna any more than she approved of him. Arlee was a political animal—well connected, smart, and lazy. Everyone knew that whenever possible, he preferred plea bargains to the work of actually going to trial.

When Arlee had offered Alma a plea bargain of a single count of negligent homicide that would have resulted in less than four years of jail time, Joanna hadn't been happy; but Alma had turned that option down cold, choosing instead to take her chances with a judge and jury. Annoyed and galvanized, Arlee Jones had gone after Alma DeLong with a vengeance, charging the woman with three counts of second-degree homicide, which in terms of seriousness, was two whole steps up the felony ladder from negligent homicide. DeLong was also charged with assaulting a police officer and resisting arrest.

After more than a year of legal maneuvering and stalling on the defense's part, the case had finally come to trial. Because Joanna had been a part of that initial investigation, she had been called to testify. She had spent a day and a half on the stand being grilled first by Arlee and later by Alma's defense attorney. Now, a full day after beginning their deliberations, the jury was finally back.

Because Alma was a well-known Tucson-area businesswoman, the trial had attracted a good deal of media attention. Rather than throw Tom Hadlock up against what was likely to be a mob of reporters, Joanna ducked into the restroom long enough to check her hair and lipstick before leaving the office and walking across the breezeway to Judge Cameron Moore's courtroom.

Once inside, Joanna slipped into an empty seat next to Bobby Fletcher. His mother, Inez, was one of the Caring Friends patients who had died. Bobby's sister, Candace, had been more interested in winning a financial settlement than anything else. She had been notably absent throughout the criminal trial. Bobby, on the other hand, had been in the courtroom every day, observing the testimony with avid interest. Bobby was a man with plenty of deficits in terms of social skills and education and some criminal convictions of his own. When he had finally straightened up, Inez had taken him in and had been his unwavering refuge. A guilty verdict wouldn't bring his mother back from the grave, but it would go a long way toward giving her grieving son a measure of justice.

As the jury filed into the courtroom, Bobby said nothing. Looking for reassurance, he reached out and took Joanna's hand.

"Madame Forewoman," Judge Moore intoned. "Have you reached a verdict?"

"We have, Your Honor."

The piece of paper was passed to the judge. While the judge perused it, the defendant, flanked by her attorneys, rose to her feet.

"How do you find?"

"On the first count of manslaughter in the first degree, we find the defendant guilty."

Bobby Fletcher shuddered and covered his face with his hands, sobbing silently as the jury forewoman continued: "On the second count of manslaughter in the first degree, we find the defendant guilty. On the third count of manslaughter in the first degree, we find the defendant guilty. On the charge of assaulting an officer of the law, we find the defendant innocent. On the charge of resisting arrest, we find the defendant guilty."

The last two struck Joanna as incomprehensible hairsplitting. How could someone be innocent of physically assaulting an officer—something Joanna had witnessed with her own eyes—while, at the same time, be guilty of resisting arrest? But Bobby Fletcher had heard the single word he needed to hear. Alma DeLong was guilty of killing his mother. She had been free on bail. Once the judge granted the prosecutor's request to rescind her bail, a deputy stepped forward to lead her across the parking lot to the county jail where she would be held while awaiting sentencing.

Walking side by side, Joanna and Bobby Fletcher moved toward the courtroom door, where Bobby came to a sudden stop. "I want to wait here and talk to Mr. Jones," Bobby said. "I want to thank him."

Not eager to face the media throng that was no doubt assembled outside, Joanna waited, too, but she was also amazed. Bobby had spent huge chunks of his adult life as a prison inmate. The idea of him having a cordial conversation with any prosecutor on the planet was pretty much unthinkable. But then, to Joanna's astonishment, when Arlee Jones appeared, she found herself in for an even bigger shock. The county attorney approached Bobby Fletcher with his hand outstretched and a broad smile on his face.

"We got her," the county attorney gloated, pumping Bobby's hand with congratulatory enthusiasm. "We still have the sentencing process to get through, but one way or another, Alma DeLong is going to jail, starting today. Her bail may yet be reinstated, pending an appeal, but for now she's a guest in your establishment, Sheriff Brady. Unfortunately, the accommodations there will be somewhat better than her victims experienced at Caring Friends."

"Thank you, sir," Bobby Fletcher said.

"You're welcome, Mr. Fletcher," Arlee replied. "I'm not sure I ever mentioned this, but back when I was a kid, I used to deliver newspapers to your folks' place over on Black Knob. Even when times were tough, your mom always made sure I got a tip when I came around collecting. Depending on whether it was winter or summer, she also offered me either hot chocolate or iced tea. Inez Fletcher was a good woman. Sending her killer to jail is the least I can do."

The unguarded sincerity in that statement caused Arlee Jones to move up several notches in Joanna's estimation. She usually dismissed Jones as being a pompous ass in a mostly empty suit. Now she momentarily reconsidered that opinion. And that was the thing that Alma DeLong hadn't realized, either. Bisbee was a small town. The invisible spiderweb of connections running from one person and one family to the next was another reason Arlee Jones had tackled this case with unaccustomed zeal.

"So are you ready to talk to some reporters?" Jones asked.

"Who, me?" Bobby asked. A look of dismay spread across his face. "Are you kidding?"

"Yes, you," Arlee said, placing a guiding hand on Bobby's shoulder. "And I'm not kidding. As far as people following this trial are concerned, you're the living face of the victims. You're the stand-in for every family that ever made the mistake of placing a loved one in a Caring Friends facility. You and the other families did so expecting that their father or mother or grandmother would be well cared for, even though we know now that wasn't the case.

"Having you speak to reporters tonight serves two purposes. It shows families that they can't just drop their loved ones off at one of these places and then not monitor what goes on once the doors slam shut. They have to be vigilant. And it also serves to show people like Alma DeLong that if they deliver inadequate care, there will be consequences. Can you do that?"

"All right," Bobby said uncertainly. "I guess."

Witnessing this, Joanna's approval needle on Arlee Jones dipped back down a bit. No doubt the man would make plenty of political hay from this incident. Having Bobby standing beside him during the press conference would provide a compelling segment on the evening news, and it would probably allow him to bank any number of sound bites that would work well the next time Arlee had to stand for election.

Joanna followed the two men out onto the covered outdoor breezeway. Content to be on the sidelines for a change, she stood next to Arlee Jones and listened in while a number of reporters piled on with a bombardment of questions. To Joanna's surprise, Bobby Fletcher answered all of them in the unassuming but straightforward manner that had made him an effective prosecution witness during the trial. He hadn't just dropped his mother off at the facility. He had seen the quality of care going down the tubes, and his attempts to rectify the situation had come to nothing.

All Joanna had to do was listen and smile and nod. The press conference ended without her having been asked a single question. That was exactly how she liked it, but her makeup had been on straight and her hair had been combed properly. Things didn't get any better than that.

Once the press conference was over, however, a glance at her watch told Joanna she was running late. When the day care facility closed at six, she had exactly five minutes of grace time to pick Dennis up. After that, she would begin accumulating late fines to the tune of twenty-six dollars for every additional five-minute period. Being late was not an option.

Joanna raced out through the back door of her office, jumped into her Yukon, and headed for Dr. Millicent Ross's veterinary office in Bisbee's Saginaw neighborhood, calling Jenny's cell as she went.

"I'm on my way," she told her daughter. "Meet me outside. Then I'll drop you off at the church so you can go in and sign Dennis out. If I have to mess around with finding a parking place there, we're not going to make it on time."

As directed, Jenny stood by the entrance to the clinic's driveway, leaning against a gatepost with one strap of her backpack flung over her shoulder. A stiff breeze blew in from the north, and Jenny's long ponytail fluttered like a blond flag in the turbulent air. Back in high school, Joanna had been a tiny redhead who had often been referred to as "cute." Jenny, on the other hand, was beautiful in a tall, slender, blue-eyed way that would never be considered "cute."

It came as no surprise to Joanna that Jenny, an accomplished horsewoman, would be a natural choice for the title of Bisbee High School's Rodeo Queen at some point in the course of her four years there. The surprise had been in the timing. Joanna had expected it to happen later on. Being rodeo queen as a senior would have been just about right, but Jenny had won the crown as a mere sophomore, leaving Joanna as the mother of a rodeo queen earlier than she'd ever thought possible.

Once she had made the mistake of mentioning all of that to her own mother. Eleanor Lathrop Winfield had responded with a singular lack of sympathy.

"It's one of those surprises that comes with being a parent, and you don't even have time enough to dodge out of the way," Eleanor had told her. "Besides, you're better off as the youngish mother of a rodeo queen than being an underage grandmother."

The implications in her mother's statement were quite clear: As in, your daughter's a sixteen-year-old rodeo queen. Mine was an unmarried, pregnant seventeen-year-old. Which do you prefer?

Guilty as charged, that was pretty much the end of Joanna's taking issue with the rodeo queen situation.

"Hey," Joanna said as Jenny dropped her backpack on the floorboard, scrambled into the passenger seat, and fastened her seatbelt. "How are things?"

"Good," Jenny said.

"And work?"

"Okay."

The older Jenny got, the harder it became to get her to reply to any given question with something other than a single word.

"School?" Joanna ventured.

"School was weird."

That was more than a one-word answer. It was long on worrisome implications but short on meaning. "What do you mean weird?"

"When the buses were leaving this afternoon, the parking lot was full of cops."

"Really?" Joanna asked. "How come? Did something happen? Was the school on lockdown?"

And if it was, she asked herself, why didn't I know about it?

"Mrs. Highsmith is missing or something."

Debra Highsmith, the high school principal, was someone with whom Joanna had crossed swords several times, most notably when Joanna had been invited to speak at Career Day and was notified that, due to the school's strict "zero tolerance of weapons" policy, she would need to leave both her Glock and her Taser at home. Joanna had gone to the school board and had succeeded in obtaining a waiver of that policy for trained police officers.

"Mrs. Highsmith is missing?" Joanna asked.

Jenny shrugged and nodded. "She wasn't at school this morning. When I took the homeroom attendance sheets down to the office, I heard Mrs. Holder talking to Mr. Howard about it—that Mrs. Highsmith hadn't come in and that it was odd that she hadn't called in to let anyone know. After that, I didn't hear anything else until we were going out to the buses. That's when all the cop cars showed up."

Wondering what had happened but not wanting to grill her daughter, Joanna changed the subject. "How was Driver's Ed?"

"Mr. Forte is having a hard time finding a stick shift vehicle for me to practice on."

Jenny had won her local rodeo crown, but there were other titles to conquer. If she intended to run for or win any of those, both Jenny and her horse needed to attend the far-flung competitions, a reality which had underscored the fact that they needed suitable horse-hauling transportation.

With that in mind, Butch had gone on Craigslist and found a bargain basement, used dual cab Toyota Tundra pickup, complete with a heavy-duty towing package. It was a good enough deal that he had snapped it up on the spot. The only sticking point was that the Tundra came with manual transmission, and all the vehicles used for Bisbee High School Driver's Ed classes were automatics.

"If Butch finishes his copyediting, maybe he can take you out for a spin tomorrow since you don't have school."

"I'm working tomorrow," Jenny said. "We're planning to do the driving thing on Saturday."

Faced with severe budget shortfalls, the school district had switched to four-day weeks, leaving the schools shuttered on Fridays and weekends. It cut down on utilities and transportation costs, but it left working parents scrambling for something to do with their kids each Friday when school was out and the parents still had to work. Joanna was fortunate. On those days when extra kids had to be accommodated at the church-run preschool and day care, Dennis was usually able to be at home with Butch. When Butch wasn't available, they could call on Carol Sunderson, their part-time housekeeper, and her two grandsons.

Joanna pulled over to the curb, and Jenny dashed inside to get her brother. While she was gone, Joanna called Alvin Bernard, Bisbee's chief of police. She was still on hold when Jenny came out with Dennis in tow. As Jenny strapped her little brother into the car seat that was a permanent fixture in Joanna's patrol car, Alvin finally came on the line.

"Sorry to make you wait so long," Alvin said. "I'm busier than a one-legged man at a butt-kicking contest."

Like Arlee Jones, Alvin Bernard was a good old boy of a certain vintage. When Joanna was first elected sheriff, Alvin hadn't exactly welcomed her to the local law enforcement community with open arms. Over time, however, they had buried the hatchet and learned to work together.

"What's the deal with Debra Highsmith?" Joanna asked.

"Sorry, I suppose I should have given you a call about this," Alvin said, "but it's been crazy. When she didn't show up at school this morning and didn't call in, we sent out officers to do a welfare check. They found nothing—zip. Her purse and cell phone were there, but her car keys and car are missing. And there's a pair of shoes on the floor beside the door, as though she kicked them off as soon as she came inside. There was no sign of forced entry. No sign of a struggle. It's as though she went home after school yesterday afternoon and then both she and her vehicle simply vanished into thin air. We've checked with all the neighbors. No one admits to having seen or heard anything out of the ordinary with her or with her dog."

"She's got a dog?" Joanna asked.

"A big Doberman," Alvin replied. "The neighbors tell us she's only had him a couple of months, but he's gone, too. Dog dishes and doggy doo-doo are everywhere. No dog, but with the car and keys gone, it's unlikely that she's on foot, and chances are the dog is with her. All the same we're searching the neighborhood in case she went out for a walk with the dog. It could be she suffered some kind of medical emergency and ended up in a ditch where no one can see her. Or else she's in a hospital. I've got someone calling hospitals in the area just in case."

"Where does she live?"

"Out in San Jose Estates, so there's some distance between the houses. I've had uniforms out canvassing up and down the street. No one remembers seeing her out and about on foot or otherwise. However, we did find something pretty interesting."

By then Joanna had put the Yukon in gear and

was driving down Tombstone Canyon with Dennis jabbering happily in the backseat. His brand of non-stop talk was pretty much lost on everyone but his sister, who seemed to understand his every word. Neither of them appeared to be paying the slightest attention to Joanna's side of the conversation.

"What's that?"

"Remember when she gave you all that crap over her zero tolerance of weapons at school?"

"Yes," Joanna said. "I remember it well. Why?"

"I knew she had applied for and received a con-cealed weapons permit. After her giving you so much grief about bringing a weapon to school, I guess I never thought she'd go the distance, but she did. Guess what we found in her purse? One of those two-inch Judge Public Defenders loaded with five four-ten shotgun shells."

A Public Defender loaded with shotgun shells certainly wouldn't have been Joanna's first choice of weapon. It was designed to do serious damage, and it wasn't something that lent itself to harmless practice shooting on a firing range.

"You've got to be kidding. She had one of those in her purse?"

"Yes, ma'am," Alvin said. "Big as life. Considering her very public attitude toward firearms, I thought you'd get a kick out of that."

As far as Joanna was concerned "kick" wasn't exactly the word that came to mind.

"Sounds like she was worried about something," Joanna said. "You don't go around with a handgun in your purse, especially one loaded with shotgun shells, if you haven't a care in the world."

"Who has a gun in her purse?" Jenny asked.

If Jenny was tuning in, that meant that Joanna's part of the conversation was over. "Keep me posted if you learn anything more," she said. "I need to get my kids home to dinner."

Alvin took the hint. "Okay," he said. "Talk to you later."

"You still didn't say whose gun," Jenny objected.

"Police business," Joanna said.

In her family those two words carried a lot of weight, just as they had years earlier when her father had used them with Joanna. It was a conversational DO NOT CROSS line that was every bit as effective as a strip of yellow crime-scene tape. It meant the subject was off-limits and any further discussion forbidden.

"I'm not a baby, you know," Jenny complained.

"No, you're not," Joanna agreed. "Which means that you understand I'm not allowed to discuss an ongoing investigation with anyone."

"I'll bet you'll discuss it with Dad," Jenny said.

Joanna's heart did a tiny flip. She and Butch Dixon had been married for years, but this was the first time she ever remembered hearing Jenny refer to him as "Dad" rather than "Butch." Although the whole idea gladdened her heart, she didn't want to screw it up by overreacting. Besides, there was always a chance that, in this case, Jenny was deliberately zinging her mother.

"What do you want to bet?" Joanna asked.

"Never mind," Jenny said. "I didn't want to know anyway."

With that Jenny lapsed into a brooding silence that lasted the rest of the way home. Joanna tried not to take any of it too seriously. When it came to parenting teenagers, bouts of surly silence were par for the course. When they got to the house, Jenny grabbed her backpack, darted out of the car, and slammed her way into her bedroom before Joanna managed to drag Dennis and all his toddler gear into the house.

"What's up with Jenny?" Butch asked.

From the complex aroma in the kitchen, Joanna could tell that dinner was all but cooked. Butch was busy setting the table.

"Nothing five years won't fix," Joanna said with a laugh.

"Oh, that," Butch said, giving first her and then Dennis quick pecks on the cheek as they walked by. "Wash hands, Little Man," Butch added to Dennis. "Dinner's almost ready."